ADVANCE PRAISE FOR NORMAN ZOLLINGER'S
PASSAGE TO QUIVIRA

"It is seldom that a sequel to a prize-winning book is as powerful as the original. *Passage to Quivira* is an exception. Those of us who loved the boy Ian MacAndrews in *Riders to Cibola* welcome him back into our lives in his middle age via this rich and moving novel by a master storyteller."

—Lois Duncan,
author of *Stranger with My Face*

"Rich in history, local color, and sense of place, *Passage to Quivira* is a strong sequel to the award-winning *Riders to Cibola*. Good writing and human insight characterize Norman Zollinger's work, and this book is vivid with the pigments of life."

—Roger Zelazny,
author of the *Amber* series.

"Though grounded with great authority in the fabulously beautiful *cordillera* that bisects New Mexico, the novel escapes any diminishing judgment as a 'regional' novel precisely because of Zollinger's lucid, muscular prose and his scrupulous presentation of believable people with achingly real problems."

—R. D. Brown,
author of *Hazzard*

"Norm Zollinger's *Passage to Quivira* is a ground-felt, sky-tearing, Southwestern journey with haunting overtones. It will stick to your insides like good venison jerky."

—Max Evans,
author of *The Rounders*

ADVANCE PRAISE FOR NORMAN ZOLLINGER'S
PASSAGE TO QUIVIRA

"Since reading *Riders to Cibola* I've been a dedicated fan of Norman Zollinger's. . . . Now, in *Passage to Quivira*, this master of the western saga gives us a heartwarming story about the latest generation of the MacAndrews clan, while at the same time permitting us to visit both the graves and the guiding spirits of old friends from *Cibola*. *Quivira* is a marvelous achievement."

—William J. Buchanan,
author of *A Shining Season*

"Few write as knowledgeably and as well about the Southwest as Norman Zollinger, and in this suspenseful and evocative story of a man's search into his own past, as in his earlier classic *Riders to Cíbola*, Zollinger immerses you in the atmosphere and mores of a land little known but already well settled before the Pilgrims landed at Plymouth Rock."

—Richard Martin Stern,
author of *The Tower*

"Zollinger, in writing as clean and elemental as sun and wind on slickrock, does in words for this unforgiving, magnificent region, desert, malpais, and incandescent mountains, what Peter Hurd achieved in paintings."

—Jeanne Williams,
author of *Lady of No Man's Land*

PASSAGE
TO
QUIVIRA

Norman Zollinger

BANTAM BOOKS
TORONTO · NEW YORK · LONDON · SYDNEY · AUCKLAND

PASSAGE TO QUIVIRA
A Bantam Book / May 1989

ISBN 0-553-27636-0

Published simultaneously in the United States and Canada

Bantam Books are published by Bantam Books, a division of
Bantam Doubleday Dell Publishing Group, Inc. Its trademark,
consisting of the words "Bantam Books" and the portrayal of a
rooster, is Registered in U.S. Patent and Trademark Office and
in other countries. Marca Registrada. Bantam Books, 666 Fifth
Avenue, New York, New York 10103.

PRINTED IN THE UNITED STATES OF AMERICA

O   0 9 8 7 6 5 4 3 2 1

For Wendy

"And there was nothing else in the country of Quivira?"

"...As for riches and fine living—when you got off your horse at the end of a hard day and had to get some supper to satisfy your hunger, you cooked whatever you had, and you cooked it on a fire made of the only thing to be found, which was cow droppings. That was Quivira."

—PAUL HORGAN
Great River

I leave Sisyphus at the foot of the mountain! One always finds one's burden again. But Sisyphus teaches the higher fidelity that negates the gods and raises rocks. He too concludes that all is well...The struggle itself toward the heights is enough to fill a man's heart! One must imagine Sisyphus happy.

—ALBERT CAMUS
The Myth of Sisyphus

Chapter I

Ian Jennings MacAndrews reached the eastern end of Mescalero Gap—the high mountain pass into the Ojos Negros Basin whose summit marks the Chupadera County line—at sunrise on a day that would reach a hundred in the shade, but when the early-morning ground fog still cowered in the arroyos.

Up where the piñon surrenders to the ponderosas he found himself in the exhaust fumes of a laboring eighteen-wheeler, a tar-spattered old flatbed hauling pumps and generator-housings over the pass and out to Holloman or the missile range. He slowed his MGB-GT and dropped back, then remembered it was still three miles to the summit. He made up his mind to pass on the next straight grade.

When it came, it was a narrow cut in the rocks without a passing lane. He pushed the gas pedal to the floorboards and pulled out to the left, cheating by more than fifty feet on the yellow no-passing stripe.

A big, dusty sedan was bearing down the gunsight notch of the road.

The sedan's horn was blasting. MacAndrews slipped down into third for an extra kick and wrenched the little car back into the right-hand lane just as the sedan blurred past him. The driver of the semi hammered at him with *his* horn, too, as the MG pulled away.

He couldn't blame either driver. Why *had* he done it? If someone didn't know better, they would think him eager to get back to Chupadera County.

His stomach turned sour, but only in part from the scare he had gotten. He hadn't eaten since he began this all-night drive, back in that little cow town this side of Lubbock. What

1

was the name of the place? It didn't matter. The towns had all looked and smelled alike for two days now—dust, feeble neon, and the heavy corn and chili odor of Tex-Mex cooking.

At the top of the pass an overlook had been built since he had been here last, with a stone fence separating it from the canyon on the Chupadera County side. Oil drippings spotted the crushed gravel in the parking apron, and beer cans caught the first beams of the rising sun. He eased the MG into the overlook, braked to a stop, climbed out, and stretched.

MESCALERO GAP, a sign read, ELEVATION 9220 FEET. Chupadera County's Ojos Negros Basin lay almost four thousand feet beneath him.

A fog like the one back at the foot of the pass covered the basin, and from here it seemed as if the Precambrian sea that had once covered it had flooded it again. Thirty miles away, the tops of the Sierra Oscuras broke this sea of fog like the high-riding backs of whales, and south of the Oscuras the sharper peaks of the San Andres cut through the level gray like shark fins.

The hot new sun was getting hotter. In fifteen minutes the fog would burn away. It was already pulling back from the dry reaches of the Jornada del Muerto. Soon the malpais, the lava-flow badlands, would appear, and their volcanic claws would shred the fog as it shrank. Then the town of Black Springs would show him its ragged streets and alleys.

He heard the semi he had passed as the heavy rig lumbered through the last few hairpin turns before the summit. His first impulse was to get on the road again and stay ahead of it, but before he could, the cab bulled its way around the shoulder of the mountain, its smokestack belching.

Air brakes hissed. Tires screeched on asphalt. When the big truck stopped rolling, he heard a country-western song coming from a radio in the cab. The rig, braked down across the road from the overlook, was still running, giving off powerful shudders as it idled.

The window of the cab framed a red, bearded face scowling under a billed cap with the logo of some oil company on the crown.

"You dumb son of a bitch!" The trucker's voice was a tobacco-plug-loaded squawk. "I ought to belt you for that bonehead play back there."

Great. Some macho redneck trucker spoiling for a scrap. It was all MacAndrews needed.

"Maybe you'd like to try, friend, but if I were you—" he snapped. He got a slippery hold on his temper. "Sorry. I guess I had that coming."

The door of the cab opened and the trucker climbed down to the blacktop. He was a head shorter than MacAndrews and sixty-five if a day, and when his boots struck the roadway his legs buckled, not much, but enough to signal he must be half-crippled with arthritis. This old man wasn't looking for a fight, though he might have once.

The trucker limped around the front of the cab and disappeared on the far side, then came in sight again under the bottom of the trailer. He must be going into the ditch to relieve himself. MacAndrews turned away, fished in his shirt pocket for his cigarettes, lit one, and looked down toward the basin.

Black Springs still hid beneath the fog, but the rangeland to the north was clear now, stretching without a wrinkle to the foot of Negrito Peak. The grasslands were green, bright green, all the way to the slickrock. There must have been good spring rains this year. Nine years out of ten, at the start of the rainy season, things were dry and brown here.

The trucker's boots scraped the gravel of the ditch as he left it. MacAndrews turned and found him with one foot on the step of the cab.

"Look, buddy," MacAndrews said, "I really am sorry. It's twenty years since I crossed this pass. Guess I've forgotten how to drive a mountain road."

The trucker pulled his foot from the step, looked up and down the road, and then across at MacAndrews.

"No sweat, amigo," he said, "I ain't exactly bright-eyed and bushy-tailed myself this early."

The trucker started across the road. It hurt to watch him.

"Where you headed?" he asked when he reached the overlook.

"Black Springs."

"Where from?"

"New York City."

The trucker stared at the MG. "In that little jagoff rigging?" he said. "I'd be bent like a horseshoe if I was cramped up in that Tinker Toy for more than a mile! And you've got half a foot on me."

MacAndrews looked over the man's shoulder and read the crude hand-lettering on the door of the cab: NIKE CARTAGE COMPANY—ALAMOGORDO, NEW MEXICO—B. J. HOWLAND, OWNER. "You Howland?" he said, pointing at the sign.

"Yep. That there's my rig." The trucker's eyes gleamed. "B.J.'s enough to get my attention, though. It's my CB handle, too. You ain't got a CB? Damn well ought to get one. The smokeys are something fierce around these parts."

"On your way to the barn with that load?" MacAndrews asked.

"Yes and no. I go right by my truckyard and house on the way to Holloman. What with that Air Force red tape, it'll take more than an hour to drop this trailer instead of the ten minutes it should—and all that time I'll be stewing in my sweat, thinking of breakfast and the sack." He walked to the stone fence and launched his chew of tobacco over it. "That's what makes me such a grouch."

"How have things been going down there in the basin?" MacAndrews asked.

"Got no complaints myself. The military keeps me humping pretty steady. But it ain't been easy pickings for the stockmen hereabouts—not for one hell of a long time."

"The grass looks good."

The trucker shot him a sharp glance. "How does an easterner know about grass?" He didn't wait for an answer. "Yep, the grass is fine, but the price of beef dropped to less than nothing this past three years."

"Do you *haul* cattle?"

"Some. Used to be a regular thing. Ain't much of it nowadays, and what there is don't pay enough to keep a man in beans."

"Ever do any business with the Cuchillo Livestock Company?"

"Rings a bell. Where's it at?"

"Twenty miles north of Black Springs. Family named MacAndrews."

"D Cross A?"

MacAndrews nodded.

"Oh, sure. I remember now," the trucker said. "They went belly-up a few years back. Some dude from California bought the place. Don't think he's running cattle on it, though."

Another gleam lit the trucker's eyes, and they had opened a little wider. "How come you're asking, mister? Far as I know, there ain't anybody named MacAndrews even living in the basin anymore. By the way, what's *your* handle?"

"Jennings, Ian Jennings." It was easier this way—and he wasn't really lying, not in any way that would ever matter. He wouldn't be seeing this old coot again. He had been Ian Jennings ever since he left Chicago for New York, had even gotten used to answering to it.

The trucker stuck out his hand. "B. J. Howland. But hell—you already read that on my cab." MacAndrews took the hand. It must have made a crushing fist at one time. B. J. Howland was smiling now. "You look beat, Jennings," he said. "I got me a pint of Wild Turkey in the rig. How about an eye-opener?"

MacAndrews stepped to the stone fence and crushed his cigarette. Below, on the road winding up to the overlook, he made out a pickup truck climbing out of the basin. He watched it career through the Chupadera-side switchbacks, using the last inch of every turn, and he bet himself its driver would turn out to be an Indian, one of the Mescalero Apaches for whom the pass was named.

"You hear me?" B. J. Howland said. "Would you like a snort?"

The pickup disappeared in the steep rock walls of the nearest turns. If MacAndrews was right about the driver, his ancestors had galloped stolen horses through those same rocks a hundred years ago. He lit another cigarette.

He turned back to the trucker. "No thanks, B.J., I don't drink." Should he go on with this? With a stranger? If he followed his own rules, he had to.

"I'm an alcoholic," he said.

The trucker looked away. He scratched his beard, then looked down at his boots. When he looked up, he smiled again, but this time without meeting MacAndrews's eyes. MacAndrews had seen this reaction before.

"Suit yourself, Jennings. I don't twist nobody's arm," B. J. Howland said. "Actually, I don't drink on the road more than once in a blue moon myself." The last sounded a little lame. It sounded familiar, too.

The pickup shot out of the rocks a quarter of a mile down

the road, and the trucker turned to stare at it. "Well," he said then, "this ain't exactly getting the job done. I'd best get rolling." He put out his hand again. "Stay awake, Jennings, hear?"

"I'll try, B.J. Again . . . I'm sure sorry about that stupid move back there."

B. J. Howland coughed, turned, and started across the road. Every step cost him something. He reached the rig and turned to face MacAndrews.

"Forget it, amigo," he said. "We're both alive, ain't we?" He winked.

He was barely in the cab and behind the wheel when the pickup sped between them. MacAndrews won his bet with himself. An Indian was driving, all right, with an Indian woman in the passenger's seat. The woman was in gingham with a tattered scarf banded around her dark hair, and the man wore a black felt, broad-brimmed, ridiculously high-crowned hat that looked set in place with the help of a carpenter's level. They both stared straight ahead, their faces blank as copy paper, as if the trucker and MacAndrews, the throbbing semi, and MacAndrews's little car, were all invisible.

B.J.'s big rig was moving now, inching forward. The trucker stuck his head through the open window of the cab. A fresh chew lumped his jaw.

"You know, don't you," he said, "there was a time when I sure as hell would have decked you for what you done?"

MacAndrews saluted him with his cigarette. He hoped B.J. saw him.

The rig was moving a little faster. B.J. waved and kept on waving until he needed two hands to wrestle the semi around the first turn. MacAndrews watched the eighteen-wheeler duck in and out of sight in the rocks a couple of times before he looked down again into the Ojos Negros Basin.

"Black Springs, New Mexico," his 1971 Mobil Travel Guide had read when he looked at it last night in the restaurant. "Population 1,580 (1970 census). Elevation 5,490 feet. Government seat of Chupadera County. Founded 1862. Railroad section point. Livestock shipping center."

The town was still the same size as when he left, give or take a few dozen souls. It looked smaller, but then most places do when you come back to them. Black Springs had begun to shrink when he went to military school at Roswell, had shrunk more during his two years of college in Albuquerque, and even more while he was away at war. Now, after twenty years . . .

He opened the door of the MG and got behind the wheel.

Sudden rage gripped him and shook him. How had he gotten himself into a fix like this? Black Springs, New Mexico, was the absolute end of the world—for him, at least.

He gave the ignition key a vicious twist, let the clutch snap out, and tore onto the blacktop. He ripped through the gears with savage, jolting punches of his right hand, and skidded through the first two turns before he realized how insanely he was driving again.

He eased the MG into third, and let the car slow against the drag of the engine. Except for two tight, blind corners where he had to drop it into second, he kept it in third and under fifty until the highway bottomed out in the alkali flats east of Black Springs.

MacAndrews wasn't surprised when the boy at the desk of the Yucca Motel said sure he could rent him a room for a week, but he would have to check with his "old man" about a rate, and no, he wouldn't need a deposit. The corrugated board taped over the NO on the NO VACANCY sign pretty well said it all.

The youngster looked about fourteen, open-faced, sunburned, ingenuous, but making a man-sized try to be all business.

He picked up the registration card and read it, first to himself and then aloud, "Ian Jennings, New York, *New York!*" He pursed his lips in a soundless whistle, and with his eyes on MacAndrews's face again, he reached behind him and pulled a room key from a rack. "I'll put you in number twenty-four, Mr. Jennings," he said. "It's way at the end, where it's a little more privatelike."

"Thanks, son. What's your name?"

"Jody Kimbrough, sir." He looked at the card again. "New York . . . gee." He looked up, beaming. "Can I unload your stuff, Mr. Jennings?"

"Actually, Jody, I'd rather do it myself." The boy's face fell. "Oh, hell, sure. Why not?"

The boy scooted around the desk, grabbed a western hat

from a halltree, and led the way outside. MacAndrews hadn't
worn a hat since he lived in the basin, and seldom then.
Once, in a resort cabin up in Ruidoso, a woman he had
known only half a day had said to him, "You can't be a real
cowboy, Ian. When a real cowboy goes to bed with a woman,
the last thing he takes off and the first thing he puts back on
is that precious hat." MacAndrews wondered why he was
smiling at the memory. That night had turned out to be one
of the worst of his life—but not because of the woman. She
had been fine. It was what happened afterward, when the
man who was paying the woman's rent walked in and surprised the two of them: MacAndrews's father.

Jody was already at the MG by the time the screen door
banged behind MacAndrews. As he stepped down into the
dirt and gravel of the driveway, MacAndrews decided that hat
or no hat, he would have to get a pair of boots. His loafers
were taking on a load of caliche dust with every step, and
their thin soles would let him know about every pebble in the
rough country he had to go to.

Jody stood beside the MG with his mouth open. "Neat
car, Mr. Jennings. Far out!"

That was another thing. For all Jody's delight in the little
car, MacAndrews would have to rent a jeep or a truck,
something with four-wheel drive. He could remember no
real road running through the slickrock to two of the graves
he had to visit.

Jody was struggling awkwardly with his duffel bag, while
his eyes were taking in the MG's dashboard. "I ain't never
seen a car with a tachometer before."

"Put the bag down, Jody," MacAndrews said. "No sense
in hauling it a country mile. I'll drive down. You can unload
right outside the room." The boy's face sagged as he replaced
the bag and stepped away. He looked back at the dash and
sighed.

"Tell you what," MacAndrews said, "you drive it down,
Jody. Mind? I've been behind the wheel all night, and my
legs need stretching."

"Yes, *sir!*" He was behind the wheel before the "sir" left
his mouth.

MacAndrews smiled. There wasn't much the kid wouldn't
do for him now.

The MG showered gravel clear to the end of the block of

units, and MacAndrews winced . . . until he remembered his own lunatic exit from the top of Mescalero Gap.

He started walking. The motel block was a long one. Jody's "old man" or whoever had built the Yucca had once held lofty hopes for it. No cars were parked in front of any of the twenty-four rooms this morning, if he didn't count his own.

Across from the row of units a concrete curb circled what had once been a lawn. Sprinkler heads still jutted above the curbing, but the enclosure ran wild with goathead weeds. The Kimbroughs weren't the only people in Black Springs who had given up on lawns. As he drove into town, he hadn't seen much in the way of greenery, only a few scraggly vegetable plots and the cottonwoods, dust-covered; tomato plants and trees alike more gray than green, unlike the rangeland north of town.

The motel swimming pool gaped bone-dry behind a chain-link fence bellied in where some sun-dazzled tourist had backed into it. More weeds poked up through cracks in the pool's bottom, and the paint that could have been robin's-egg blue once had powdered to gray chalk where it still clung at all.

Jody had number 24 open and most of the gear out of the car and inside the room by the time MacAndrews reached it.

"If this room don't suit you, just say so, Mr. Jennings, and I'll open up another one. It ain't like we ain't got more'n enough of them." He shook his head.

"It will do just fine, Jody. Thanks."

"Anything you need—holler. There's ice and a Coke machine in the office, and instant coffee. We get the Albuquerque and El Paso papers." Jody hesitated, then swallowed hard. "I could drive to the office and bring them down here, if you want."

MacAndrews laughed. "Not right now, Jody."

The boy wasn't licked yet. "We usually have sweet rolls," he said, "but we ain't had a guest in near three days, and I didn't pick any up this morning. I could go over to the Piggy-Wiggly and get you some." He eyes the MG. "It ain't but a fifteen-minute walk there and back."

"All right, Jody," MacAndrews said, "take the car."

"Yes, *sir!*"

Jody had stacked the few bags between the door and the

bed. MacAndrews moved around them and looked through the side window. The highway he had taken down from Mescalero Gap ran on westward toward the malpais, and then on and upward through a break in the foothills of the Oscuras. He couldn't see anything of the town from here. Most of it still lay south of its one crossroads, the intersection of the road he was looking at and the one east of the motel that split the town on its way up from El Paso and Alamogordo and then ran side by side with the railroad for forty miles north of Black Springs. Only a few trailer homes, fenced in by rusted cars and broken-down farm machinery, had managed to make it north of the crossroads in twenty years.

It wasn't yet nine-thirty, but the heat was already peeling the asphalt on the highway. The road and the dim, low hills were the only things he could see through the streaked window. It didn't look as though anything lived out there. He couldn't even spot a buzzard. Pretty bad if the buzzards had given up.

He got the wastebasket from under a desk holding some Black Springs Chamber of Commerce promotion pamphlets and the Gideon Bible, and he carried it to the bed. He slipped out of his loafers, poured the caliche dust from them, and dropped them on the frayed carpet. Lord, he was tired, too tired to think straight. It would be better not to think at all now, but . . .

Why had he registered as Jennings instead of MacAndrews? Habit, sure, since the move to Manhattan, but was there something else? Was he still hiding? And why had he told Jody he would take the room for a week? What could possibly keep him here more than a couple of days, three at most? There were only three things he had to do, and he could probably do two of them today. Once he had taken care of his little bit of business with the lawyer Ernesto Gomez, he would only have to visit the two graves in the badlands and the four up in Las Sombras, around the flank of Cuchillo Peak. Then, everything he wanted to do here would be done, finished . . . over with.

He took the phone book from the night table. He could start with Gomez today, maybe, and with luck have plenty of time to drive up the mountain to Las Sombras. Tomorrow he could get out to the slickrock and still start back over Mescalero Gap before the day was out. Even as exhausted as he was now, he could make it well into Texas tomorrow before the sun went down.

Gomez first then. When the lawyer reached him in New York ten days ago, he had told MacAndrews all the papers were ready for his signature.

The phone book listed the numbers of a dozen small towns in Chupadera, Lincoln, and Otero counties. He flipped to the G's in Black Springs and found the number.

The lawyer sounded glad MacAndrews was in town, but glad only in a polite, professional way. Yes, MacAndrews could see him at eleven. Gomez had a lunch date, but he said he and MacAndrews should be able to get everything done this morning, or by twelve-thirty at the latest.

"I'm surprised you came," Gomez said. "You didn't have to. We could have settled everything by mail."

"I know," MacAndrews said. He had started to say he had *wanted* to come, but there seemed little point in lying to a man he didn't even know.

"Eleven then," Gomez said.

Jody knocked at his door as he hung up on Ernesto Gomez, and when he opened it, the boy handed him a paper sack. "Something with pecans in it, Mr. Jennings," he said. "All they had . . . and here are your car keys, sir." The keys seemed to stick in his hand.

MacAndrews stood in the doorway and watched Jody trudge toward the office. He kept turning back to look at the MG.

A blue Ford pickup, ten years old or more, whined along the blacktop from the west. The pickup must have been doing seventy as it came even with the motel, then it slowed abruptly, its tires wailing.

He thought he could feel the driver looking pretty hard as the pickup rolled on by. A guest at the Yucca must be a rare bird indeed. An easterner in his stocking feet, dressed like a dude and holding a paper bag, must be an even rarer one.

Don't fret, neighbor, he muttered to himself, *I'll be gone soon enough.*

Chapter II

"I think it's best if you read the letter before we take up the will, Mr. MacAndrews." Ernesto Gomez leaned forward and pushed aside some loose papers on his desk. "I haven't read it, of course, but Sarah—" He looked up at MacAndrews. "Forgive me. I mean your aunt . . . Mrs. Balutan. At any rate, she said her letter should come first. Incidentally, Mrs. Balutan looked after your interests here in Chupadera County as well as you could have done yourself."

"Look, Mr. Gomez," MacAndrews said, "if you called her Sarah in your dealings with her, I know she would want you to call her Sarah now. She didn't hold much with ceremony."

"No, she didn't." Gomez leaned back in his chair. "I don't ordinarily call older persons by their first names, but Sarah made it an order."

MacAndrews smiled. "I can hear her." The letter weighed heavy in his hand. He thought of putting it down somewhere, decided to hold it. "Fill me in on where things stand before I start reading."

"All right then. The MacAndrews estate is in perfect order to go to probate. Sarah worked like a trooper that last year, tying up the loose ends with me, with the full knowledge all the while, I'm sure, that she was dying. It was hard for her, and I couldn't make it easy. It seemed we would solve one legal problem only to create another. First there was the sale of various parcels of the D Cross A rangeland and the few assets of the livestock company. As you probably know, your mother sold the house a few months before *her* death. Nothing left from that transaction, I'm afraid. Sarah instructed me to use the proceeds to pay the debts the sale of the cattle company didn't satisfy. As you might expect, we had to fight any number of counterfeit claims as well as pay legitimate ones. There was virtually nothing left in the way of cash. Sarah would never have admitted it, much less have claimed it, but I'm sure she supported your parents until they died."

The lawyer looked straight at MacAndrews as he talked, but he hadn't liked saying that last part. Still, his voice hadn't weakened. It was a good voice, without a trace of the Rio Grande accent MacAndrews had grown up listening to.

After Gomez's secretary—surprisingly not a Hispanic in this otherwise solidly Hispanic firm—had shown MacAndrews into the small office, MacAndrews had shaken hands with the attorney, and Gomez had started right to work even as they were getting seated. He handed MacAndrews the letter from Sarah and remained motionless, his hands folded on his desktop, while MacAndrews looked at the envelope. A less secure man might have tried to impress a new client by shuffling papers or using the telephone.

MacAndrews had been surprised when the lawyer reached him on the phone in Manhattan two weeks earlier, surprised that Black Springs now had a firm of attorneys whose shingle read GOMEZ, GOMEZ, & TRUJILLO. When he left the Ojos Negros Basin twenty years ago, he couldn't have unearthed three Hispanic attorneys-at-law in the whole county—never mind in the same suite of offices. He wondered if Gomez considered himself a "Chicano." With his close-cropped hair and button-down collar he wouldn't look it to most anglos, but MacAndrews's personal demon, strangely quiet since he quit drinking, was now urging him to hope the lawyer wasn't just another Tío Tomas. Knowing Sarah and *her* demon, which *never* checked its tongue, it seemed probable she had bypassed the established Anglo law firms in Chupadera County in favor of young Gomez and his partners intentionally.

The letter seemed to be getting heavier. MacAndrews opened it and read it, and suddenly it was like hearing Sarah's voice. Her letters, when he was still getting them in Chicago, had always come to life like that.

Galeria Rincon
Sarah MacAndrews Balutan, Owner
Taos, New Mexico 97571

Ian—
    Don't let the old stationery fool you. I've already sold the gallery, but I'm too much of a skin-

flint to lay out good money for new letterheads or anything else I can't use up before they plant me.

Yup, as us true-blue western types would say, the same crud that got old Max is getting me. Now don't start pissing and moaning on my account. It's been a long ride and a good one and I was getting a little saddle-sore, anyway.

Since you're reading this, Ernesto must have found you. I never knew you left Chicago, and the people at your company there were so tight-lipped I thought you had joined the CIA or the Foreign Legion. From what my private spies in the Windy City told me, I suspect somebody *ran* you out of town. I'm sure as hell not criticizing. The drinking, fighting, and total hell-raising they told me about struck me as an improvement over the cowlike life you were living when I saw you there—what was it?—ten years ago?

I was more than a little pissed with you that you reneged on your promise to Nash to return to the Ojos Negros, but maybe you had better reasons than I knew.

So much for that. Ernesto will spell out the terms of my will, including the little chore you'll have to do to get any of my hard-earned loot—*and* the easy money I picked up as Max Balutan's widow. If you come across for me, there's a lagniappe in it for you, too. Remember that little bust of Nash that Max did in 1932? You were just a kid, but it was in the studio in Taos for years. Max wouldn't sell it and I won't, either. It's yours if you come through. There's one other thing I want, a favor—nothing to do with the inheritance. If you do come back, check and see how Jacky Begley is making out. If you don't know him, I think you should.

One thing before I close. A friend brought me an article on you from *Advertising Age*. Didn't read it. Knew it would make me puke to hear how well you've done as one of Madison Avenue's pet whores. But the *picture* of you! You're pushing fifty, and you don't look a day past thirty. How do you do it, particularly considering your abiding habits of physical neglect? Have you got a Dorian Gray painting of

yourself hidden away somewhere? I'm not sure it's
good not to age naturally, although there sure have
been times I wished I knew the secret. Which
brings me to something else. For God's sake, don't
come to see me until I'm in the ground next to old
Max. I mean it! I've got my pride, and I know I look
like the steer hides we used to drape across the
cattle guards—saggy and baggy everywhere except
my head, which is as slick as Huevo Knob from the
chemotherapy. And poor, sweet Max used to say I
was "a nifty-looking bimbo."

I'd tell you that if you're still smoking, stop, but
what the hell. Anybody can stop smoking, it takes
guts to face cancer.

                                                        Sarah

P.S. I didn't fool you, did I? Actually, I'm scared
as hell.

                                                        S.

That was Sarah: as tough as an old pair of shit-kicker
boots, and as comfortable. In some ways he would miss her
more than any of the others, more even than his mother and
the vaquero he had called *Tío* Nash when he was a child, and
Nash later on. His mother and his grandfather had called the
rider Ignacio. It was one of his regrets—in a life filled with
them—that he hadn't called him Ignacio, too. That strong,
gentle man's name had meant a lot to him, and it wasn't that
Ian MacAndrews had lacked perception back then. The Ian of
those days had only concerned himself with his goddamned
art, that and his surging, self-destroying rage. No, he wouldn't
miss the vaquero, his mother, or his grandfather. Even dead
and buried they would still be here when everything else
about this country had faded for him, something that couldn't
happen soon enough. Yes, they would still be here, their
memory as searing as the Chupadera sun had been when he
walked from the MG to Ernesto Gomez's office.

Sarah, like Max, was gone. She had died at St. Vincent's
in Santa Fe while Ian MacAndrews had raged through that
last disastrous drunk.

What did she really want of him? The two things in the
letter were only hints. Did she want him to resurrect the
MacAndrews fortunes in the Ojos Negros? No dice. Some

penance? Sure. Contrition had come frequently if not easily
since he'd sobered up.

"You were a hard man to find, Mr. MacAndrews," Gomez
was saying.

"Sorry, but maybe it was just as well. I was pretty much
out of things when you started looking for me."

That's right. As she mentioned in her letter, he had
never told Sarah he had left Chicago, nor why, and Gene
Weaver, who at last had known everything, wouldn't have let
slip a word to an unknown lawyer named Gomez—not under
the sordid circumstances.

"How *did* you find me?" MacAndrews asked.

Gomez smiled. "I got a weird hunch in the middle of a
sleepless night that you might be using the name Jennings.
Don't ask me why. While we're on the subject, how will you
want things recorded—under Jennings or MacAndrews?"

"MacAndrews—Ian Jennings MacAndrews. It's still my
legal name. I only used Jennings as a last name in business,
and then only since I resettled in New York. But look, Mr.
Gomez, unless I'm one of your 'older people,' call me Ian."
He waited. A glint of expectancy showed in the dark eyes that
hadn't left Ian MacAndrews's face. All right, he would give
the man something to chew on. "When I left Chicago for
Manhattan, I was a little paranoid. I didn't want anybody
finding me. *Anybody.*" It wasn't quite the truth, but it wasn't
far away from it. He hadn't been anything like paranoid. What
he had been hiding from had been real enough, but right
now he would draw the line at telling Gomez what it was.
From his look, the lawyer wasn't going to press him, anyway.
He was still smiling.

"Then please call *me* Ernie . . . Ian." Had the smile turned
a degree or two warmer? The "Ian" sounded good. Perhaps
he ought to start thinking of himself as "Ian" instead of the
impersonal two last names he had more or less forced on
everyone in Chicago and New York, everyone but Laura.
Maybe he still was Ian to that unlucky lady, but he had better
forget all that now.

"Do you have to go through the actual reading of the
will, Ernie?"

"Not if you'll swear I did, Ian."

"You've got my word on it."

"Okay. Here's the essence of it. I'm the attorney of
record, but Sarah named my brother Tony administrator. I'd

like you to meet him, but he's fishing, up on the Chama. He'll be back in Black Springs next Wednesday morning."

"Too bad," MacAndrews said. "I'll be gone by then."

"Oh? Sarah had one of her gut feelings that you would come back to Chupadera County for good. I thought you might myself—until we talked."

"Sarah would think that, but it was only wishful thinking. I'm grateful she won't find out how wrong she was. But go on."

"Well, as you may know, Sarah sold her gallery a few months before she died, and for a healthy amount of money, which fortunately we could treat as a capital gain, so it wasn't all eaten up by taxes. The same was true of her late husband's sculpture, which she kept in a warehouse she rented in Santa Fe. I guess I don't have to tell you what happened to the value of Max Balutan's work in the past ten years. Living in New York, you must remember that auction at Christie's. It got a lot of attention even here in the boonies. Well, Sarah still had a dozen large pieces left from his early period, the welded metal, as well as twenty-two of the marbles he devoted himself to in the years before he died. She donated a few things to the Huntington, made bequests to her two employees at the gallery, and she established three scholarships in Max's name.

"At any rate, even after the IRS takes its bite, I estimate that you stand to inherit the better part of a million dollars."

"That much?"

"Yes—and I believe I'm being conservative."

Gomez spelled out the terms of Sarah's will in more detail in a second go-around, naming the gallery workers and the amounts they would receive, the art schools that would get the scholarships, and telling of a separate bequest to the Cancer Fund. Max's sculptures that hadn't gone to New York were identified by title and number, but the small bust of Ignacio Ortiz wasn't listed, or at least Gomez didn't mention it. MacAndrews didn't ask about it, but as if Gomez had read his thoughts, the name of the vaquero came up immediately.

"And of course, Ian, you know, don't you, that you have an inheritance you've never claimed—from Ignacio Ortiz?"

"Yes. It can't amount to much." Gomez must think him uncaring, perhaps cynical, that he had never even checked on it. MacAndrews went on, "I thought Nash's—Ignacio's—will was in Jonathan Hardy's office."

Gomez smiled again, a satisfied smile this time. "This *is* Mr. Hardy's office, Ian. He brought Joe Trujillo and my brother and me into his firm two years before he died. Made us promise we would take his name off the door the moment he was buried. He *said* he didn't want people blaming him for our mistakes, but what he really wanted was to give us our heads without his shadow hanging over us. Great man, Mr. Hardy."

MacAndrews got the feeling Ernesto Gomez had never called Jonathan Hardy by *his* first name.

It made one thing plain. Gomez knew everything there was to know about every MacAndrews dug into the caliche of Chupadera County, not just Sarah and her deathbed business. What the attorney hadn't learned from her, he would have learned from Hardy. It wasn't that the courtly old lawyer had been a talker—far from it—but he had been the family's counsel since the early twenties, and his father Ben had been the MacAndrews banker clear back into the last century. Good Lord, the files Jonathan Hardy must have left.

"Mr. Ortiz's will wasn't complicated," Gomez was saying, "but he left more than you might think. He left his books—a really fine collection—to the Black Springs Public Library. A savings account with over seven thousand dollars in it went to an elderly lady in Los Angeles by the name of Concepción Martinez. John H. Begley, a local man, received a valuable Mexican saddle and a pair of antique Spanish spurs of real worth. There was an oil painting, too. Mr. Ortiz bequeathed it to your mother, but it never appeared in the inventory of her estate, nor among the few possessions your father passed along after he died six months later."

MacAndrews remembered the painting, all right. It was the only one of his canvases to survive the bunkhouse fire. He could guess why it was gone. His father had finally gotten rid of all of them. It was just as well.

And Connie Martinez was still alive, or had been when the vaquero passed away; Nash would have known. Oh, *yes*, he would have known.

"Sarah talked about a Begley in her letter. I don't know him. She wanted me to look him up."

"You haven't asked what Mr. Ortiz left *you*, Ian." It seemed a mild rebuke.

"Sorry, Ernie."

"Remember the sixty sections of slickrock to the north of the D Cross A? Where your great-uncle Mr. Angus MacAndrews and Mr. Ortiz are buried? Your grandfather, as you may recall, left it to Mr. Ortiz. It's yours now. Sarah insisted— against my advice, I'll admit—on paying the taxes on it. I don't think it's worth much. There's no grazing possible on it, certainly no minerals anyone knows about."

Gomez turned away for the first time since they sat down. He appeared to be studying a wood carving of Don Quixote and Sancho Panza on top of a shelf of lawbooks across the office, and he was silent for several seconds before he turned back to MacAndrews.

"All right, Ian. I ducked your question about Jacky Begley, and I ducked it rather peevishly.

"Jacky came into the Ojos Negros right out of high school in Silver City. He cowboyed some near Tularosa for a while, but he never seemed able to hold a job—or didn't want to. Every foreman in the basin gave up on him before he wound up working for Ignacio Ortiz. He was the last hand to ride for the D Cross A, except for Mr. Ortiz himself. He stayed on the MacAndrews payroll until he was drafted." Gomez seemed to be bending over backward to be dispassionate about this man Begley and was not finding it easy.

"Ignacio Ortiz was hard to please where the D Cross A was concerned," MacAndrews said. "He must have had at least *some* regard for Begley. That saddle was the old vaquero's particular pride—that and the spurs. The spurs were a gift to him from my grandfather. Where can I find Begley?"

Gomez looked at the wood carving again. "At the Buckhorn, across the road from your motel, or at the Outpost Lounge on Frontera Street—maybe at the Cantina Luna across the tracks, or any gin mill in the county. I don't know where he lives, and I don't know anyone who does."

"I take it he drinks?"

"Yes, he drinks—a lot," Gomez said with unmistakable reluctance.

Suddenly MacAndrews realized that something more than the simple desire to be fair had shaded Gomez's earlier remarks. Twenty years dropped away. Things hadn't changed nearly as much in Black Springs as finding this confident young man seemed to indicate. Sure, three Spanish-surnamed attorneys were apparently doing well here—pictures taken with U.S. Senator "Little Joe" Montoya and New Mexico Governor Bruce King hung on the wall alongside plaques from the Black Springs Chamber of Commerce, hedged about by university and law school diplomas—but even with all this it was clear the town hadn't completely loosened the ethnic constraints MacAndrews remembered all too well. To half the population of the county Ernesto Gomez was probably still just a jumped-up young greaser, and the lawyer knew it. He was going to be damned careful before he spoke critically of any Anglo, even some hard-drinking drifter who couldn't hold a job.

He was also, it was suddenly apparent from his straightforward, open look, damned well going to have his honest say.

"Yes, Ian," the attorney said, his voice firm, "Jacky Begley drinks . . . and in my opinion, pathologically. He drank pretty heavily before he went to Vietnam. Now it's worse. Before Nam, even if he couldn't hold a job, he was at least easygoing and likeable. He's turned mean. Bad with women, worse with men. He's a brawler and a chaser. Some people think it's more than booze. I don't set too much store by that. We aren't exactly experts on drugs here in Black Springs. I have no personal knowledge that he's smoking dope or shooting up, but I can testify to the drinking and the viciousness."

"Sounds as if you know him pretty well, Ernie."

"You might say so. He broke my jaw a few months back, but that's another story, one I don't think it would serve any purpose to tell you now, maybe ever."

So Gomez, too, had something *he* preferred not to tell. Good. It made the two of them even, and MacAndrews liked that. "If you do look him up, be careful. He's a big, powerful man, in spite of that bad leg."

"Bad leg?"

"He was wounded in Nam. Took a wrong turn in a Cong minefield. The medics managed to save the leg, but he'll sure never run any sprints."

"Does he work?"

"No. He gets a sizable VA disability allowance, I hear. He ought to be able to work from the back of a cow pony, but as far as I know, he hasn't been near a horse since he came back. I think I know why. Before he was drafted, he had some idea he wanted to try the rodeo circuit. He had some success in the small, local arenas around the state, and by all accounts he had a future. He's had to forget that." Gomez spread his hands. His face softened. By God, the young lawyer was letting slip something like real sympathy, and for a man who had done him violence.

Beyond Gomez's warning MacAndrews found himself in another, tougher, predicament. Jacky Begley, the man Sarah wanted him to check on, was a man he would probably have to meet in a saloon. He hadn't entered a bar or a cocktail lounge alone since he had downed that last drink. He would be breaking the first of the rules he had set for himself.

He remembered there was something else Sarah wanted him to do.

"Wasn't there some kind of proviso in Sarah's will, something I had to do in order to inherit?"

"Yes," Gomez said. "There's a codicil, written right after Mr. Ortiz died. Until then, you were her principal heir without qualification, but something must have happened about then, or occurred to her. After she and your mother went through all that red tape to get the old rider buried next to Mr. Angus MacAndrews—instead of in a regular cemetery— she stormed into the office and told me what she wanted."

"It figures. She was bitterly disappointed that I didn't return to Chupadera County then."

Gomez started to say something, but caught himself.

"Let's have it, Ernie."

"You're an artist, a painter, aren't you, Ian?"

Like the rumble of a far-off thunder getting closer, a storm coming in, something was heading his way that MacAndrews knew he wouldn't like.

"I was," he said. "I haven't painted in twenty years. I'm the art director—and only the *director*—at the advertising agency in Manhattan where you found me. *I don't paint.*" It sounded a lot like the way he had told B. J. Howland he didn't drink.

A shadow crossed the lawyer's face. "Well . . . ," he said, "that might present a problem." He spoke with the same deliberate care as when he had talked about Jacky Begley. "Just before she died, Sarah sent her publisher the manuscript of the last book she did on her husband. It's the one the art historians have been begging for. She spent the last five years of her life getting photographs made, and securing the releases for them, of almost every piece Mr. Balutan ever did, material no one but his widow had a prayer of getting. Hampton House in New York is going to start production on the book next year. Sarah knew she wouldn't live to see it, and she had the people at Hampton make up the title pages—front matter I guess they call it—in advance of publication, in order that she might autograph the numbered copies."

As he had when he had discussed the will originally, Gomez kept his eyes on MacAndrews as he spoke. He went on, "In the codicil, Sarah MacAndrews Balutan sets forth that you, Ian Jennings MacAndrews, her nephew, in order to inherit her estate, must deliver to Hampton House, Limited, of New York City, a portrait you have painted of the sculptor Max Balutan, to be used as the art for the dust jacket of her book and as a frontispiece. There are certain specifications as to the size of the canvas, but none on the style of the painting or your treatment of the subject. None of the estate can be made over to you until you deliver the painting to a Miss Lee Berman, Mrs. Balutan's editor at Hampton House, or to her successor." There was something almost liturgical in the way Gomez said all this. He was a pro, all right. He knew how to weight a subject.

He was saying something more, something about a deadline, but MacAndrews hardly heard him through the drumming of the blood in his temples. The lawyer mentioned the lagniappe Sarah had written about in her letter—the bust of Ignacio Ortiz. Apparently Lee Berman had it in her office in New York. The editor was to destroy it if MacAndrews failed to meet the terms of Sarah's will.

All through their meeting he had felt as if the world had been shut away from the two of them. Now, the muffled voice of Gomez's Anglo secretary answering the telephone drifted in from the reception room, and the sound of a truck with a trash-compactor working over a load of refuse echoed from the alley in back of the lawyer's office. There was only one more thing to say before they were finished here, and that had to be said only that Ernie wouldn't think him an utter fool.

"Supposing I were to contest the codicil?"

Gomez shrugged. "You might well win, Ian. *Will* you contest it?"

Now MacAndrews even heard the click of the phone as the secretary hung it up.

"No, I won't contest it. But I will not fill the requirement."

Through Ernesto Gomez's dark eyes something made an even darker passage. It wasn't disbelief, it wasn't shock, and it certainly wasn't scorn.

"It's a lot of money to say no to, Ian," Ernesto Gomez said.

Sarah had trusted this young man. So could he—with part of the truth at least.

"Ernie, the only way I could ever get even a stain of color on canvas again—would be to open up an artery."

Chapter III

No stretch of land in the world appears more open than does the Ojos Negros Basin, but it is so immense there is only one place in the mountains that cradle it where a man can stand and see all of it at once.

This place is high on the side of Cuchillo Peak in the Sierra Sombras, the shadow mountains, but well below the pinnacle itself. The summit ridge of Cuchillo sits far back from its lower flanks, and at the top the view to the south is blocked by the outrunners of the Sacramentos, far beyond Mescalero Gap.

From any of a hundred different points on the high rimrock circling it, more of the Ojos Negros shows itself than can be taken in by any pair of eyes, but there are always a few who insist on seeing every last inch of this vast Laramide depression.

For these stubborn few, the place to go is far up on the rock-littered slope, the talus, that breaks down and away from the vertical granite wall that forms the upper rampart of the mountain, and the best way to reach this slope is on foot, starting from the old, weed-choked graveyard in Las Sombras.

Las Sombras is called a ghost town, but not even spirits lurk there anymore. Whispers come from the shattered old buildings now and then, but they come from the rustling of creatures of flesh and blood. Bats, which once hung in blind sleep in the worked-out mineshafts, have moved in and claimed the deserted town since the shafts filled with water.

From the graveyard, held fast with Las Sombras in a ring

of rocky, jack-pine-spiked hills, nothing at all of the Ojos
Negros can be seen, but above the town a break in the pines
shows the way. There is no marked trail, but none is needed.
Any general south-by-southwest course will eventually lead
to the talus, and crossing the bulge of the middle mountain
takes little more than an hour. After a gradual ascent of about
three miles, most of the basin has come in sight, enough of it
to hint at how much more can be seen from two thousand
feet higher up. To this point it has been easy, pleasant going.

Climbing the slope itself is another matter.

To begin with, it is pitched as steeply as the hunting
stoop of a red-shouldered hawk. Three steps upward on the
restless scree brings a slide of two paces back. Legs cramp.
Tendons in the arches ache from guarding against the wrenching
of an ankle. Breath comes short and hot, and chest muscles
tug at ribs until they almost snap. Sweat fogs the eyes.
Mountain sickness sneaks up on unfit climbers, and dizziness
and nausea can weaken even the strongest of them.

The sun beats down with all its force every hour of the
day, and its heat provokes a thirst that cannot be slaked.
Swallows from canteen or water bottle mix badly with surges
of bile headed the other way. It is head-down work, step by
painful step, and nothing appears underfoot but the jagged
rock.

There is little in the way of comfort, and no encouragement at all, for the struggler on the talus—and no one has
ever said whether the view from the top of it is worth the
effort.

Ian MacAndrews knew this as well as did anyone who
ever lived in the Ojos Negros, but his mind was fixed hard on
other things as he stood in the graveyard at Las Sombras.
Actually he wasn't sure where his mind had been since he
had left the office of Ernesto Gomez.

The sky heaved gray with late-afternoon thunderheads,
but they seemed to be rolling eastward at far too brisk a pace
to spill more than the briefest showers. Good thing, too; the
unpaved road that wound up to the old mining camp had
proved no better than he remembered it. An Ojos Negros
gullywasher would turn it into a quagmire, and he had
already bottomed the MG twice on the drive through the
rutted switchbacks.

The sun, with the racing clouds covering and then

uncovering it, had become a slow-motion strobe light, its beams touching, lifting, and touching again the four head-stones in front of him.

He read them left to right: DOUGLAS GRANT MacANDREWS —1855–1930; AGNES HALL MacANDREWS—1870–1918; ANN JENNINGS MacANDREWS—1891–1969; JAMES HALL MacANDREWS—1890–1969. The arrangement seemed correct enough, with the mounds and markers of the two MacAndrews men flanking those of the MacAndrews women, and the four marble stones would have appeared made on an assembly line had they been quarried, shaped, and set in place at the same time.

There were now slight differences in the massive blocks, but the wind and rain and sun and heat of the Ojos Negros would make them alike again in another fifty or sixty seasons. It was already hard to detect any difference at all in the stones that held Agnes and Douglas MacAndrews fast—even though they had been sunk into the rocky ground almost a dozen years apart.

A straightedge long enough to cover the tops of the four slabs would run tight and true across three of them, without a gap anywhere along its line, but when it rested on the fourth, that of James Hall MacAndrews, Ian's father, this last of the markers would be seen to be skewed from left to right a full quarter of an inch, as if it were trying to break away from its companions. Frost heave, wasn't it?

The tilted gravestone bothered him. Its collapse would be no great loss, except that if it ever rocked back the other way, it could collide with the third, and then topple it and the other two like dominoes.

If he had more time left to him in Chupadera County, perhaps he could find someone to drive up here and straight-en it. But he *didn't* have more time.

Well, he had finished here. Bareheaded, he hadn't even had to remove a hat.

He left the graveyard and walked a footpath toward the center of the empty town, a city block away. His footfalls stilled whatever sounds might have come from the bats, or from any other creatures that might be scurrying through the decaying brick and stone, but they didn't silence the ravens rasping at him from the skyline hills. The breeze picked up as he reached the wreckage of the opera house. Somewhere at the back of it something groaned, an old door probably, swinging on hinges that only now had begun to rust in this superdesiccated air. Seventy years and more had passed since the last of the living, with their oil cans as well as their picks and shovels, had left Las Sombras to the snakeweed and the bats.

He sat down on the flagged steps of the opera house, alerting a lizard that broke the pattern of its camouflage and shot across the steps into the brushy weeds curling over the rough edges of the stairway, vanishing so fast he wondered if he had really seen it. Were things going to come skittering out of his psyche like that as he sat here trying by turns to remember and *not* remember things?

At least one memory he was sure he was safe with was of the first time he had come to Las Sombras, for Grandfather Douglas MacAndrews's funeral in 1930.

It had been what Ignacio called a "serious" day, but not a bad one. No memory of his grandfather, alive, dying, or even in his grave, had ever caused him pain or truly unbearable sadness. Robbed of speech and helpless as the old man had been before the last stroke took him, he had somehow prepared everyone around him for his passing—even a boy who had yet to reach his ninth birthday, a birthday that turned out as all the others had, unnoticed by the one man he wanted most to notice, the man beneath the tilted headstone.

When was the last time he had come to Las Sombras? He wasn't sure, but it must have been some time in the late 1930s. He did remember that he and the vaquero had come up on horseback, racing the wind and their own laughter to the edge of town, and then slowing without words or signals into a silent processional as they neared the graveyard.

Strange. He had never felt any urge to paint Las Sombras.

It was too late now. It had been too late even in the good days, when he was turning out four and five canvases a week in that frenzied six months of twenty-one years ago, right after Max Balutan died of cancer. It had been too late even before that, too late by far after the war and Italy. If he had tried getting Las Sombras fixed in oil—or even on a sketchpad—when he had first come back from combat, he would have gotten it all mixed up with the bombed-out cities of Apulia, such as Foggia and Bari, places he wanted to leave behind and forget. Las Sombras's devastation differed from that of wartime Europe's "cities of the plain" in kind—not only in degree. Its fallen bricks and stones, and weathered, splintered, jackstraw timbers, mute as they were supposed to be, spoke of a *natural* happening, as innocent as that seen in an old forest after a ground fire has raced across it, scorching and blackening the trees, but doing no lasting damage, only clearing away the unwanted, choking undergrowth. Forest fires, and even towns such as this, made sense.

His best work back then, landscapes and portraits alike, had pictured rage, derangement maybe—not all of it, of course—so if there had ever been a time for Las Sombras, it would have been *before* the war and Italy—and in those early days, if he faced the issue squarely, he simply hadn't been good enough.

He shuddered. It wasn't a sound, but something, perhaps a vestigial wilderness sense he had thought atrophied during his long city years, told him he was no longer alone in Las Sombras with his memories.

He stood up and looked back toward the graveyard.

A battered, blue, half-ton pickup had stopped alongside the MG. Unless there were two exactly alike in Chupadera County, it was the same old truck whose driver had seemed to look him over with such care this morning. A big man stood beside Ian's MG with his hands resting on the top. He was peering inside as if he was taking inventory. At this distance it was as impossible to make out his features, as it had been this morning, but he seemed young as well as big.

Ian felt a bristly rub of irritation, not that the man was looking inside his car, but that he was there at all. Then he took himself to task. He had no right to stake out a purely personal claim to Las Sombras and its sun-bleached stones. He started walking.

With his eyes hard on the man at the MG, he didn't take particular care where he placed his feet, and when he hit his toe against a loose stone, the stone rolled off the path and through the tinder-dry weeds that lined it. The noise might as well have been a string of firecrackers exploding. For only a brief moment he flicked his gaze away from the man at his car, but when he looked again, the man was gone. Somehow he had managed to get back in his truck in that fraction of a second.

In an instant the pickup was burning through a U-turn, scattering rocks, and then bouncing toward the first of the switchbacks leading down to the blacktopped highway five twisting miles away.

The half-ton truck needed a muffler; its exhaust rattled and popped like an automatic weapon, bringing sharp echoes from the hills above the town and shocking the ravens and scrub jays into silence. It puzzled him that he hadn't heard the pickup when it arrived. He must have been drifting farther and deeper into the fog of his memories than he knew, almost to the point of no return.

He broke into a run, and when he reached the MG, he checked it over. Nothing seemed amiss. The tires still looked fully inflated, and the chino pants and the denim shirt he had bought at Stafford's after leaving Ernie's office still rested on the seat. The new boots lay where he had crammed them under the dash on the passenger's side, and his good sunglasses still dangled from a spoke of the steering wheel.

What the hell. The man in the pickup was probably just another Chupadera County layabout, as nosy as all of them were about any stranger, for all that they pretended indifference when face-to-face with one. Maybe, like Jody, he was just curious about the little car.

A crack of close-by thunder snapped his eyes toward the sky. Counter to his certainty about no chance of rain when he arrived, he now realized a storm could hit the mountain in a matter of minutes, maybe seconds. Right above his head a white Georgia O'Keeffe cloud was showing reluctance to put on the speed needed to join the dark brutes massing over the Capitans, and it was girding itself for some big, boastful display of flash and fury. Deep shadows were moving into the graveyard and a wind was rising.

As he opened the MG's door, he saw the imprint of a pair of hands in the dust on its top. He placed his own hand on top of one of the prints. It didn't begin to fill it. A raindrop splattered the back of his hand, and in quick succession three, five, a dozen more, splashed on the car's top and steamed away from the sun-heated metal. He climbed into the driver's seat.

By the time he reached the first switchback the torrent was on him, and the ruts of the mountain road were running full, as were the ditches on either side. Without even looking in the rearview mirror he could tell that lightning was lashing Cuchillo Peak behind and to the left of him. Through the slate-blue rain ahead the Ojos Negros Basin itself was still bathed in full, brilliant sun, but some dimly remembered weather-wisdom (was it any more reliable than his offhand forecast earlier?) told him the storm would backfill above the rangeland in a minute or less.

Sure enough, as if the sun had been turned off with a switch, everything in the distance disappeared.

How long would his windshield wipers be able to handle the water streaming down the glass and breaking in waves across the MG's hood? He couldn't see past the nearest switchback, but he certainly couldn't stop. If the downpour lasted, even a more powerful car than the MG would bog down in the low spots, and he could be stranded here for hours.

He kept a light foot on the accelerator, pressing it just hard enough to keep the engine running. He had to fishtail on the straights between the turns so the wheels wouldn't dig in too deeply to keep on turning. The switchbacks fought him hard. He tried to stay in the ruts; if the wheels jumped out of them, he could slide right off into the undergrowth, or worse, plunge into one of the arroyos he could no longer see. It took guts to feed the little car more gas just after the halfway point of each turn; if he didn't, the light engine might not supply the torque to pull him into the next straightaway.

He hadn't counted the switchbacks on the way up, but he knew there must be twelve or fifteen of them before the road turned tame on the long slope above the north-south highway. There was one he recalled in particular, about halfway down. It made a hairpin turn around a rock as big as a unit at the Yucca, and if he remembered rightly, the roadbed there sloped the wrong way, too. He would have to snake through that one turn, at least, with a delicacy he never had to use in New York's or Chicago's heaviest traffic.

He was almost into the turn before he saw it. It was probably better he hadn't had too much time to think about it; he went around the huge rock without a bit of trouble.

But on the far, lower, side, he almost ran straight down the canyon wall.

Not actually blocking the roadway, but sticking out just far enough to make his foot jab at the brake in a reflex he couldn't check, was the dented grill and hood of the old blue pickup. The MG swerved, skidded, and he lost all control for a sickening instant. Both left wheels spun off the side of the road for twenty or thirty feet, and only luck, not skill, brought them back. He was a hundred yards below the rock and almost into the next switchback before the little car settled down again.

The short hairs on the back of his neck buzzed. Goddamn it! Idle curiosity on the part of the man in the pickup was one thing; purposeful spying quite another.

It was too late to stop and investigate. Until the storm had worn itself out, there wasn't a chance in a thousand he could make it back up the slick road except on foot. The rain, if anything, had gotten heavier. He might as well coast on down to the highway, where he could find a pull-off or a side road, and wait for this man as the man had waited for him, confront him then, if it seemed the thing to do—and right now, by God, he wanted a piece of this prying, inconsiderate bastard badly enough to taste it.

By the time he rolled up out of the railroad right-of-way, crossed the tracks, and reached the blacktop, the rain had stopped and the highway leading into Black Springs was steaming like a swamp. There was room to park where the Las Sombras road met the blacktop, but if he stopped and waited here, the driver of the pickup could see him from far up on the mountainside. It could turn into a monotonous, futile waiting game if his watcher decided to lie low until Ian tired of it. Besides, there could have been a half dozen side roads that he hadn't paid attention to on the way up, and of course hadn't seen through the driving rain on the way down, secret ways off the mountain a native would know all about.

He turned on the highway and headed south toward town.

He checked his watch. He had only done two of the three things he had to do. The meeting with Ernesto Gomez had been the easiest one.

"Across the road at the Buckhorn, steaks and stuff. Or if you can take it hot, Big Anita's, the Comida. It's on the plaza," Jody said in answer to Ian's question about a place for supper.

He decided on Mexican food. He had long ago given up on finding the real thing in New York. It probably could be found, but it had presented a dismal prospect, trying every taco joint in the city just to find one that filled the bill, and the people at the agency hadn't been of any help. Their tongues and mouths were scorched by lukewarm imitations.

He started out on foot and was sure he detected a slight

but incredulous shake of the head from Jody. The kid was doubtless wondering why anyone in his right mind would walk to the plaza when they could drive that neat car that was so far-out.

The Comida de Anita was just a diner, a counter and stools and two small tables on either side of the door, tiny but spotless, redolent of the genuine green chilis of the lower Rio Grande. Rich and satisfying as the aroma was, he had a momentary feeling of misgiving when he entered the little eatery, a sense of distrust, not of the food, but of himself. It would be too easy to enjoy himself in this quiet place.

Well, hell! He couldn't spend all of his time here in the basin wearing a hair shirt. He filled himself with tostadas and salsa, guacamole, chili rellenos, and refried beans, while Big Anita, waitress, cook, cashier, and hostess, beamed at him from behind the counter—a dark, pillow-bosomed Juno whose portrait he could have once done in impassioned oil without the fixative of rage.

"*Bueno*, no?" Anita said as he finally pushed his empty plate away from him. She glanced down the short counter at the only other diners, two elderly Spanish men with hair like cottonwood gone to seed, her black eyes seeming to implore— no, command—that they, too, listen for his answer. They looked at Ian with sad, rheumy eyes.

"*Sí, bueno,*" he said. "*Muy bueno. Estupendo!*" It had been twenty years since he had used even that much Spanish. There wasn't much more than that left.

"*Gracias,*" Anita said. She was eyeing him with something more than professional interest. Perhaps it was just his replies in Spanish. Then she went on, "Have I not seen you somewhere before, señor?"

"I don't think so, señora." But maybe she had. He tried to strip her of twenty years and thirty or forty pounds, and to forget the voice she was using, with its almost comic Mexican intonations, deliberate he was sure, designed to enchant, sometimes outrage, *turista* ears. There was no recollection. Perhaps he had once been another MacAndrews such as his father, after all, one who was looked at by people such as Anita here, but who never looked at them.

He stood up and reached for his billfold.

The four of them parted with nods and smiles, his now a trifle forced, and with Anita, for all her considerable size, making a surprisingly dainty Latin curtsy.

He hurried out.

So much for the seduction he had feared.

He looked across the plaza to the small, sumpstone shopping center that housed the offices of Gomez, Gomez, & Trujillo. Good. It would get his mind back on track.

In the morning he would call the people at whatever had taken the place of the old D Cross A and get on with the last things he had to do.

The sun was slanting across the plaza. It was probably turning Cuchillo that watermelon pink that had once given him such swelling pleasure.

He wouldn't even look.

Chapter IV

"Come on out," the woman said over the phone, "but stop at the house before you go up to the north line. I want a look at anybody who's going to be cutting through our fence." Her voice sounded odd, with flutters of static at the end of each word, as if he were hearing someone on an overseas line, not from only twenty miles away.

"Believe me, Mrs. Edwards," Ian said, "if there were any other way—"

"Call me Sam," she cut in.

"I wouldn't trouble you, but my property is blocked from any road except the one out to the D Cross A—excuse me, *your* place."

"Can you fix a fence you've cut?"

"It wouldn't be the first time."

"See you in about an hour. I'll be waiting."

Even with the bad connection, he knew her accent hadn't shaped itself in Chupadera County. Hadn't B. J. Howland said the new owners of the D Cross A had moved here from California? She could have come from Fort Wayne or Fargo.

He could ask Jody about her, but he hadn't seen him

since breakfast, when the boy brought him rolls again only to
turn away with his lower lip quivering when Ian told him he
was checking out sometime in the afternoon. It would be
better if he didn't see Jody again before he left.

Harry Kimbrough, Jody's father, had been at the desk
when Ian walked down to change the registration card to
MacAndrews instead of Jennings. It had seemed important
that he do this, a matter of somehow squaring things before
he left, even if Black Springs and the Kimbroughs didn't care,
and not just because messages might now come in from Ernie
Gomez for Ian MacAndrews.

Harry Kimbrough looked a little hostile until Ian explained
and not entirely mollified afterward.

The motel owner was lean, almost gaunt, and small
wonder; it would wear down any man to run a loser such as
the Yucca. There were probably young Kimbroughs besides
Jody to feed, clothe, and get through school. Harry finally
softened when Ian asked where he could rent a Jeep.

"Use mine," Harry said, eagered by the prospect of
some extra money. "You can have it for ten bucks a day—and
your own gas."

"I'll only need it for the rest of the morning and the early
part of the afternoon. But I'll also need wire cutters, fencing
tools, and a coil of barbed wire. Where can I get them?
Stafford's?"

"I'll get them for you myself. Have it all in twenty
minutes."

His face told Ian the motel owner was going to tack
something on the price of the tools and wire. It wasn't greed,
but need.

"Make it twenty on the jeep, Mr. Kimbrough. The
country I'll be taking it over could be the backyard of hell."

"What ain't in Chupadera County? But thanks, thanks a
heap!" Won now, at least by the thought of the money, he
grinned. He needed a trip to the dentist. Ian would have
raised the rent for the Jeep even more, but there was a point
at which even Harry Kimbrough would smell pity.

In twenty minutes as promised Harry had him loaded up
and on his way, but the needle in the fuel gauge wavered
near empty. He wheeled the Jeep into the Texaco station and
found himself at the pumps behind a two-door Datsun. Anita
from the Comida was filling a car that didn't look big enough
by half to hold her. She was yelling something toward some-

one inside the garage section, and sure enough, the Mex burlesque she had treated him to the night before was gone. She sounded like a redneck truckstop waitress on the interstate.

But when she turned and saw him, the dusky, beaming Latin Juno of the night before returned in an instant, and the nozzle of the gas hose became a scepter.

"*Buenos dias*, Señor MacAndrews." So, she already knew his name. Perhaps she had also decided where she had seen him before, too—if she had. There was no apology in her look at having been caught out for her innocent deception in the diner. He would like Anita very much if he were staying on. He put the thought away from him while she finished and left.

The first surprise of the day was that the old road out to the D Cross A was paved, with broad, graveled shoulders and a well-graded ditch on either side—an expensive road.

The second surprise was slower in coming. He was four miles in from the highway and the sign that read EL RECOBRO—HADLEY & SAMANTHA EDWARDS before he realized he hadn't seen a cow. Then he remembered B.J.'s saying the new owners weren't running stock. Fine with him, it was their ranch now. All the same, he shook his head over the seeming waste. Those rolling pastures of bright, stiff, sweet grama grass: he couldn't recall many years when the range had looked so promising. It didn't seem right, not seeing a single Hereford. Of course, there were cattle people by the dozen who would exult at the sight of grass growing like this and no stock to ruin it this season. Money in the bank.

Something else didn't seem right. The ranch road didn't run quite where it ran twenty years ago. It must have made a big, unnoticed new curve somewhere in back of him. He should have passed the foundation of the house his father had started for his mother, and then abandoned, the scene of his one canvas that Ignacio Ortiz had rescued from the bunkhouse fire.

Ahead, the butte that hid the ranch compound bulked above the swales dotted with yucca and ocotillo. Another two miles and he would make the turn around it and then drop down to the plank bridge spanning the arroyo. The plank bridge? It wasn't likely it was there any longer. These new owners, the kind of people who would feel the need for a fancy road such as this, wouldn't stand for a sagging bridge.

When he rounded the butte, he stopped the Jeep and took a long hard look across the arroyo.

Ignacio's shack was gone. So was the windmill and the tank. This was no surprise, particularly when he saw the other changes in the compound, all made, as the new road had led him to expect, by the spendthrift scattering of money, big money, money with no apparent end to it, money that felt it had a God-given right to the best of everything.

Ignacio's shack—and the tank and the old wooden windmill— hadn't been the best of *anything*.

He scarcely recognized the house. It must have been rebuilt almost from the ground up—in modern Spanish mission style this time, rather than the Territorial New Mexican adobe-and-timber he remembered. In place of the stone wall around the original house, a colonnaded, roofed walkway stretched the length of the two sides he could see. The red tile roof alone must have cost more than Grandfather Douglas had laid out for the whole bill of materials for the house and all the outbuildings back in the 1880s. A new outer wall had been laid up with cut-and-fitted stone unlike any he remembered seeing in Chupadera County. It enclosed a lawn edged by shrubbery and flower beds, landscaping that would soak up a lake of precious water.

A parking apron ran along the new wall. Next to a wrought-iron, ornamental gate, Toyota's ungainly version of the Land-Rover was parked beside a four-door Cadillac.

To the west, where the bunkhouse and the tack room had once blocked the sight of the roundup holding pens, a Butler aircraft hangar now did the same job more effectively, or would have, had the pens still been there.

There must have been a lot of talk among the old-timers in the Ojos Negros when the hangar was hauled out here in sections. No rancher had flown airplanes—much less owned them—back when he lived in the basin. On the other hand, so much else had changed it might be common now.

He shifted the Jeep into first and started down into the arroyo.

Wonder of wonders, the plank bridge was still in place.

Wait. It wasn't exactly *still* in place. An effort had been made to span the arroyo with something more substantial. Both banks held broken concrete bridgeheads that looked as if they had been repaired more than once out of pure stubbornness, and fragments of concrete with torn and twisted reinforcing rods jutting from them littered the arroyo bed for a hundred yards down the otherwise clean-swept wash. When he narrowed his vision to just the bridge, he saw that the planks still stretched over the high-walled cut in the caliche exactly as they had, but they certainly weren't the same timbers Ignacio and he wrestled to higher ground before countless storms, or hauled back, working from horseback with *riata* draglines, whenever a downpour came without warning.

Somehow it seemed right that these nonranching ranchers named Edwards hadn't been able to thwart *every* will of the Ojos Negros. There were forces in the basin that damned well shouldn't be gentled.

When he crossed the bridge, he took a sudden, almost childish, pleasure in the familiar shakiness of it, and then came the remembered, reassuring feel of the far bank when he reached it and began the climb to the compound.

On top, he could look into the aircraft hangar. It seemed large enough to hold a couple of good-sized planes, but only a small, high-winged monoplane, pushed well back and tied down and chocked, was in residence. It looked like some late-model Cessna roughly the size and shape of the Aeronca Chief in which he had gotten his own private pilot's license back in 1941.

Beyond the hangar, the new owners had built bluegrass-country stables where the pumphouse and its generator had once stood. The pumphouse was where Ignacio Ortiz had died, according to the clipping from the *Chupadera County News* that Sarah had sent him. Four good-looking riding horses gazed at him over fences of whitewashed board. It didn't look much like the old piñon-post corral, but the horses didn't resemble cow ponies, either.

From the near side of the hangar, a landing strip cut through what had been the closest-in west pasture, a project that had taken a lot of effort and machinery. A runway, not wide but maybe a couple of thousand feet in length, threw every ripple of the adjoining mesa on either side into sharp relief, and tons of earth and rock had been bulldozed to the sides, with some of the debris pushed into raw hillocks fifteen and twenty feet high. It would take steady hands on the controls to set something even as small as a Piper Cub down in safety in this narrow slot.

He turned toward the stone wall. The Cadillac hadn't

seen its second year, but its big Fleetwood body was already
pitted by the first dust storms it had faced—another tiny
triumph for the basin.

He pulled in beside it and switched off his engine. A
heavy silence settled over the jeep. Odd that he could see no
people up and about. Was no one working around a place this
huge? *Siesta?* Spanish again. Well, there had been a time . . .

He left the Jeep and pushed through the wrought-iron
gate. The distance from the gate to the covered walkway was
greater than it had looked from across the arroyo, and sweat
had beaded on his forehead by the time he walked it.

In the shade of the walkway he felt cool again. He found
himself facing a wide double door—mahogany, he guessed,
with an intricate floral design carved into the grain. Amaranthus
leaves? The door was the color of the giant *vigas* soaked in
oxblood he had seen in mission churches south of the border
in the old days. There was a doorbell on the jamb a little
above a cast-metal latch and at eye level the outer plate of a
dead-bolt lock. There had never been a bell or a knocker
when this was the D Cross A, and no locks of any kind,
except the padlock he had hung on the door of the bunkhouse
when it became his studio.

His finger was on the doorbell, but for some reason he
found himself reluctant to break the silence.

It was broken for him. A call reached him from somewhere far along the shaded walkway.

"Hi! Down here!"

It was the voice of the woman, Sam Edwards, but clear
and steady now, without the staticky little halts he had heard
over the telephone. He could barely make her out in the
deep shade, but it appeared she was leaning out of another
doorway, fifty or sixty feet away from him. She called again.
"Come on down. I'm into something here I just can't leave."
She stepped out from the door into the walkway.

She looked tall, but close up he saw she was merely
trim. She wore jeans—not the designer frauds kids and
women were beginning to wear, but the faded, honest working pants he had once worn every day himself—and a man's
checked western shirt, open at the throat and for two snaps
down, with the sleeves rolled a couple of turns above her
wrists. One wrist carried a watch with a leather strap. There
were no bracelets or other jewelry. No makeup covered her
tan.

She had planted herself squarely in his path. Was she forty? Maybe. Certainly no older.

"So—you're my fence cutter," she said when he reached her.

"I'm Ian MacAndrews."

She put her hand out and he took it. If memory served him right, it was the first time he had touched a woman in more than a year. It felt good.

"You used to live here?" she asked.

"Yes."

"Maybe you'd like the grand tour—see how we've violated the old homestead."

He couldn't be sure, but he thought he was standing about even with where the kitchen used to be. "I don't think I'd like that." It sounded brutal. He wondered what had made him say it just that way. It didn't seem to bother her.

"This hand I'm holding doesn't look or feel like it's used to stringing wire."

He jerked his hand free and stared at it. He saw her eyebrows lift. "I don't suppose it does," he said, "but believe me, it's stretched _miles_ of wire in its time." He could still feel the touch of her hand.

"Sorry. Would you like a cup of coffee—or something colder and stronger?"

"No thanks. I'd better get under way. I wouldn't want to be up in the badlands if we get another storm like yesterday's." Why hadn't he answered her offer of a drink as he had B. J. Howland's?

"Makes sense," she said. "Maybe you could stop on your way out."

Yes, he could get things straight with her then.

She looked at her watch and gave a little gasp. "Come inside for just a second. I've got to monitor—right now!" She stepped through the door, and he followed but stopped on the threshold. Monitor?

It was indeed the old kitchen. The cast-iron sink was still under the window, and the small hand pump still bent over it, but was now just part of the decor. Potted plants filled the sink, and the pump, handle and all, had been painted a bright aquamarine. The room wasn't a kitchen anymore. Clay pots, seed flats, and small garden tools covered the hardwood drainboards on both sides of the sink, but that wasn't the biggest change. In contrast to the leafy greenness in the sink and the half dozen plants hanging in macrame holders, the far side of the room was filled with black-and-chrome radio equipment heated up and humming. It explained why she had used the word "monitor" and why her voice had sounded the way it had when he spoke with her from the Yucca; they had been talking on a radiophone. Now that he thought about it, he hadn't seen a pole or a foot of telephone wire on the drive across the rangeland.

Sam Edwards sat down at an armless swivel-chair, the kind typists use, and began flicking switches and twisting dials. She put one earphone of a headset to her right ear and brushed her hair out of the way in the same swift, easy motion. In the shade of the walkway he had thought her some kind of ash blonde. Now, under the hot light of a high-intensity lamp, her hair was light brown, tipped with gray. With her face turned away he couldn't tell the color of her eyes.

Intent on her equipment, she remained as still as a photograph for the better part of a minute. Then she put the headset down, hit a few more switches, and turned back to him. Blue—her eyes were blue.

"Sorry to ignore you like that," she said. "Hadley is flying in from San Antonio this afternoon. I listen for his transmission every hour on the hour when he's in the air." She glanced at her watch again. "I don't think I missed him."

"Hope I haven't messed things up, arriving when I did," Ian said.

"I wouldn't have let you."

Did she know she had just given away the fact that she was alone out here? Even without hired hands around the outbuildings, didn't she have household help at least? The place was too big for one woman to look after. Still, he could sense empty rooms beyond the inner door, and he felt more of an intruder than if the place had buzzed with life, as the radio had until she switched it off.

"Well—I'd better make tracks."

"Please stop on your way out. You might welcome a cold beer by then."

As he pulled away, he saw that she had stepped out from under the walkway and was watching him. It annoyed him that he hadn't told her straight out that he was an alcoholic. What had suddenly happened to that most important of his self-imposed rules? The truth hadn't cost him all that much with B.J., had it?

In a few moments, facing the task of teaching himself to drive a Jeep in broken country again, and working hard at getting up the rock slopes north of the house without wrecking Harry's, he had persuaded himself that he had forgotten her.

It took him fifteen minutes to get to the piñon line and another twenty to reach the fence.

When he considered that the new owners weren't working the ranch, the fence was in amazingly good repair. There wasn't a sag in any of the four strands of wire as far as he could see in either direction, and some of the wire looked new this season. It did seem a shame to cut it.

When he took the wire cutters Harry had found for him and snipped the top strand, he discovered he had forgotten that a tight fence could strike with the speed of a diamondback. The recoiling wire sliced the sleeve of his shirt from shoulder to wrist, and a barb streaked flame down his forearm. He rolled the sleeve above his elbow and looked at a thin, red welt. No blood came. Not that it would matter, but he rolled the other sleeve to match the torn one.

He took more care with the other strands, stepping clear as he cut, then grasping them and walking them out of the way to make an opening for the jeep. It was a few degrees cooler in these uplands than back at the house, and a small wind moved across his face.

Back in the jeep he looked óver his shoulder to where Cuchillo loomed against the skyline. High above the mountain a jet was painting a white streak in the sky—probably an airliner out of Dallas–Forth Worth on its way to Phoenix or L.A. A military aircraft bound for Holloman would have already begun its letdown and would no longer be at an altitude where it could leave such a vapor trail.

He drove through the break in the fence. For the first time in his life he was on land he owned. He wasn't entirely comfortable with the thought.

Almost at once the stands of piñon became fewer and farther between, and in five minutes he left any trees, and in fact, all growing things, behind him. Nothing but the smooth stones of the badlands lay ahead. This would have been the big-tree line had he been climbing the sides of the basin as he had yesterday on the Las Sombras road, but here the hard rock—and the winds that scoured it nine months of every year—had stopped off any growth but occasional, grimly persistent lichen. The rock itself was a bright bone-white, and he almost ran over the skull of a cow, nearly indistinguishable from the slab it rested on. No cow could have broken through a fence such as the one he had just opened up. The skull must have been bleaching here for a long, long time. Perhaps the old fence of the D Cross A hadn't always been as tight as Ignacio had thought it was.

He had climbed steadily since he left the fence, but now the slickrock began to fall away to the north and was opening into fissures, mere scratches at first, deepening then into genuine arroyos, sharp-edged canyons whose rims were difficult to see. Twice he had to back off and find another way. As the uneven ground rocked the Jeep back and forth and from side to side, he found he could no longer drive it with the confidence he had known back when he was carting his painting gear to every corner of this empty country so many years ago. He was a "city dude" now, with city hands—and city "smarts"—that didn't count for much out here.

That he didn't know quite where he was going didn't trouble him. All he had to do was follow the only path a horse could take and follow it as far as it might lead. It would have been smarter to borrow a horse from Sam, but it would have meant two horses, the second one to carry the gear, and none of the animals he had seen in her corral was exactly what he would consider a packhorse. Besides, there weren't good hitches for horses where he was going. The Jeep at least, ignorant of what a born-again tenderfoot he had become in twenty years, would stay where he parked it.

It was slow going. He had remembered the badlands as being slickrock, and although most of it was, great stretches were strewn with loose stones, and the Jeep's wheels spewed them out in back of him. There had once been a time when he could have recited the geology of these barrens pretty well. He had taken the subject in his first year at the university. He was painting mostly landscapes then, and it had seemed as important to know what was under the skin of the land as it was to know the bones and muscles that shaped the flesh he tried to capture on his life-class sketchpad. Lord, but he had been art-intoxicated then, as drunk as he had ever gotten on booze in later years.

Since he left the piñon line, there had been a wearying sameness to the slickrock—all of it remembered in general,

but not one square inch in particular—and he suddenly
wondered if he would recognize the place he was heading for
when he came to it. He had only been there once before,
when he wasn't more than eight years old.

Four of them had come out to this wasteland for a picnic.
Sarah, home from college, had brought along her New Yorker
roommate, Leila Balutan, a young painter whose brother Max
would one day become Sarah's lover. Ignacio had been their
guide. Ignacio hadn't even known what a picnic was then,
and this one was his first and last, if Ian didn't count
the sandwich lunches the rider and he had wolfed down in
the back country during that magnificent summer when the
paintings were stacking up like cards in a poker deck, filling
the bunkhouse-studio that was nothing but a cinder in his
memory now.

Young as he was on the day of that picnic, he had already
begun to draw. Blind to the others looking on, he sketched
the cairn over great-uncle Angus's grave. The young woman
from New York gushed over the drawing, and he had felt the
keenest pleasure of his life up to that point. It was nice, of
course, when his mother or the vaquero or his second-grade
teacher in town praised his first crude pictures, but it wasn't
the same as this. Leila Balutan was from outside the school
and family circle—and an artist herself. It mattered then; it
didn't now.

Many of the things that happened to him in the years
that followed he could recall no better than he could gather
wisps of smoke, but that day was still clear and sharp.

When he reached the tilted slope of scree leading to the
lip of the arroyo he was seeking, he wondered why he had
doubted he would know the place. Nothing seemed changed.
From the hard, grim look of it, nothing ever would.

The thought left his mind when he saw the two buzzards
circling above the arroyo's edge. For a wild moment, until he
realized how absurd the notion was, he was sure that one or
both of the graves had become uncovered, and that all he
would find of the vaquero and the old cowboy Angus would
be their bones.

He tramped down hard on the gas pedal and rammed
the Jeep up the steepening slope until the wheels began to
spin. Then he forced the gearshift into first, turned the
engine off, and set the hand brake. The Jeep slid back a foot
or two before settling into place.

He got out and started up the slope on foot. The buzzards had dropped beneath the edge and he didn't see them again until he reached it.

They had landed, not, he felt relieved to find, on either of the two graves, but on the carcass of a small animal, an old coyote. It had to be an old one, dead from natural causes; there was nothing out here to kill it, not even men.

If the slope leading to it had stayed the same as his memory of it over the years, the arroyo itself had changed. Forty rainy seasons and their torrents had worn a new, deeper, different channel in the bottom, and the cairns, which he had more or less expected to see at the lowest point of the arroyo, now sat on a shelf of caliche left behind when the water had carved its newer path.

He started down the steep side, and halfway to the cairns he wished he had brought the length of rope he had seen on the rear seat of Harry's Jeep. In one slick gully his feet shot out from under him, and only thrusting out his right hand kept him from tumbling thirty feet or more to the bottom. The palm of his hand was skinned red, blood barely oozing from it. He looked again at the long welt on his arm. It still hadn't bled. Had he lost the capacity to bleed?

At the cairns, he found they had fought time, and the rages of wind and water, to a standstill. Ignacio had built the one that covered Angus and built it to outlast the land itself. Whoever had erected the vaquero's had done as good a job. Sarah must have seen to it, maybe with Ian's mother's help. Like that of Angus, Ignacio's pile of rocks was an almost perfect, blunted cone, but when he circled it, he found one stone near its top jutting out as if it had been removed and not replaced quite right.

He tried to push the stone back in, but it wouldn't budge. He stepped back. What difference did it make? No one who knew whose bones were here would ever come this way again.

Still—perhaps it was due to some leftover sense of balance and proportion—the protruding stone troubled him.

He moved to the cairn again and wrested the chunk of sandstone from its place, thinking to find a smaller one. As it came free, he heard the clinking sound of metal. In the hole, its rowel wedged deep in a crack, he saw a hand-wrought iron spur. He slid the stone back in place. It still stuck out from the rest of the pile, but it no longer bothered him.

The buzzards had left the coyote's carcass during his noisy scramble down the arroyo's side, but they had settled back to their meal and were taking turns eating and watching him. Soon they stopped watching and were taking him for granted. It was pretty much as it should be. He didn't belong here and the arrogant scavengers knew it, knew he would soon be gone. He could pelt them with every stone in the two cairns now and they wouldn't stir. They had sized him up, all right.

He faced the vaquero's grave again.

"*¿Como estas, viejo . . . qué tal?*"

He hadn't put any force behind the words, but he thought he heard them echo, if only faintly. He shouldn't have heard a thing. The walls of the arroyo were too close together to permit an echo. It had to be his imagination. He had better leave before he began expecting an answer.

He turned from the graves to the wall of the arroyo. Getting out of here, like getting out of Chupadera County, would be less dangerous than coming in, but a lot more work, and he decided to scout farther down the small canyon for an easier way. The arroyo was narrow here. It made a sharp right-angle turn about a hundred and fifty yards east of the cairns, where floods brought by rains such as yesterday's, moving at express-train speeds, had gouged out a threatening overhang, but it spread out beyond that point.

He began walking toward this wider, flatter part of the arroyo. The heels of his new boots clicked on the caliche. There were no echoes as he had heard, or imagined he had heard, when he spoke to Ignacio at his grave.

Beyond the sharp bend he found a slope that would be easier to climb than the one he had come down, but with a lot more loose stone to be reckoned with. He started up, placing his feet as carefully as if the slope were mined. A turned ankle here could be more than a mere nuisance this far from the jeep.

Then a stone the size of a baseball skipped and bounded past him.

He jerked his head up toward the rim above him. Nothing. And yet—he got the impression that someone on horseback had just turned away from the rimrock.

He raced upward through the scattered stones. His chest was heaving when he reached the top.

If there had been a horseman up here, there was none

now. With the piñon line a mile away, it took fast riding to disappear by now, unless the rider had headed into one of the crevasses, a daring piece of horsemanship that would test the art of an Ignacio. He listened for a moment. The most sure-footed horse in the Ojos Negros couldn't cross this glass-hard surface soundlessly, shod or not—no matter whose hands were on the reins. No sounds other than those of the wind and his own still-labored breathing reached him. It was his imagination again, as with the false echoes at the cairns.

But when he reached the Jeep, he saw the horse droppings and rage mounted in his heaving chest. Why would anybody want to spy on him? For a moment he burned to give chase, to *do something*, but trying to find hoofprints on the slickrock would only waste what little time he had promised himself in this forsaken country, and the horse wouldn't leave more telltale droppings for a long time now.

Still, he looked hard for the sign of a man on a horse as he drove back through the piñon to the fence.

He pulled through the break in the fence and stopped. He walked every inch of the section he had opened. Yes, the ground here was soft, but no horse had come this way today.

It took half an hour to put the fence to rights. By the time he finished, his city hands were nicked and scratched in a dozen places. They wouldn't be city hands if he stayed as little as a week in Chupadera County, but they wouldn't be painter's hands by a long shot, either.

He looked at his watch. It had taken far longer to get to the graves than he had allowed himself. He would have to stay one more night in Black Springs, but, by God, only one.

As he rolled by the ranch house he remembered Sam's invitation to stop for coffee—or something. This time he would tell her he was an alcoholic. It would tidy matters up.

For some reason he wasn't sure of, he expected to see her outside her door beckoning to him, but there was no sign of her. He drove through the compound slowly, but he didn't stop, and at the bridge a wave of relief broke over him. All in all, it was a good thing he hadn't seen her.

It wasn't likely that ten minutes over a cup of coffee with a stranger would have brought him to the point he had almost always reached with women, but it could have. When he left Chicago for New York, he had vowed he would never use a woman again as he had used nearly every one he had known since Jo Martinez when he was just a kid.

For what it might be worth, he had passed one test on the way back to the Ojos Negros. When he crossed the Indiana-Illinois state line he had nearly turned north toward Chicago. Even if Laurie had found someone else—and by now she should have—she would have welcomed him back, and the whole sad, cruel story might easily have begun again. He had used Laurie for ten long years, soaking up her devotion with the same greed as he had soaked up that endless river of liquor, with never a pause to consider what was best for her—until the night he had beaten her twin brother Tom to a pulp when that decent, quiet man asked Ian to either sober up or leave Laurie alone. He had smashed Tom bloody, with fists driven as much by guilt as anger, while Laurie cringed in the corner of her living room sobbing—for Ian.

Even the marathon boozing of his war days had never made him sick—but something happened as he stood over poor Tom and looked down at the man's swollen, broken face. He had vomited in the hall the moment he slammed out of the apartment.

That was the "bottom" the regulars in Alcoholics Anonymous talked about when he went to his first meeting two days later, and the last time he saw Laurie . . . no, the next to last.

She had tried to see him, though. His phone rang night and day. He swore he could tell her ring from any other. Illinois Bell gave him an unlisted, unpublished number, but then she wrote him, sometimes twice a day. He read the first letter and nearly went to her. He tore all the others up, unopened, feeling as if he were shredding his own flesh. She began patrolling the street outside his building, and he moved to a suite in the Drake until he could find a new apartment. He couldn't trust himself to tell her to her face that it was over, and he knew she wouldn't listen, anyway.

Laurie came to the office. He caught a glimpse of her before she saw him, and he passed the word to Lisa Firelli, ignoring the question in the receptionist's black eyes, that he wasn't in to Laurie, wouldn't be in to her again, and that he didn't even want to hear about any of her calls or visits. He changed the lunch places Laurie knew of and often met him at. It became a nuisance for Gene Weaver, the senior partner

Ian was closest to, a three double-martini, noontime buddy, but he didn't take Gene into his confidence for several weeks.

Then Tom, whose left eye seemed to have something permanently wrong with it from the beating, turned his attorney loose on Ian.

Ian went to see the attorney. This escapade was going to cost him, as so many drunken brawls in the past had cost him, but some instinct told him that this time things would have to be reckoned up in more than cash alone.

He was right. Tom wanted him in jail.

"All right," Ian told the lawyer, "press charges. I won't fight it." Something like relief swept over him.

"It's not that easy. Tom *wants* you in jail. He doesn't feel he can afford to put you there."

There was a long silence before the lawyer went on, "It's his sister. She's threatened a complete break with him if he moves against you."

"I've already stopped seeing her. What else can I do? Tell me, and I'll do it."

"She'll never give you up if you remain in Chicago, Mr. MacAndrews."

In a week Ian was gone. Gene Weaver found him a job as art director—the position he held with Gene—at the New York shop of Wyndham & Keats, whose billings were the third largest of any agency in Manhattan. It was like going to the majors from Triple A ball, and Ian felt guilt at turning a profit, as he seemed to be doing, on the misery of two completely innocent people.

He shouldn't have worried. Whatever need he had for exculpation, it began to be filled after one short week in New York City.

His days on Madison Avenue posed no problem, but nights and weekends were empty. He haunted the Guggenheim, the Metropolitan, and the other museums, spent enough money on theater tickets before the first month was out to equal a week's pay back in Chicago, and ate in every one of Gotham's "little wonder" restaurants he could find, only to pick without interest or appetite at food that in other circumstances would have been ambrosia to him. He joined three different AA groups and was dutiful in attendance, but only that—dutiful. A marrow-deep torpor set in, and nothing in a year seemed capable of rousing him from it. It wasn't exactly boredom—he kept far too busy, or at least occupied, for

that—but rather that he found himself the victim of a clinging
malaise, like that of a sleepwalker treading an unseen and
barely felt, narrow ledge above a beckoning, black void.

It was no wonder that when Ernesto Gomez's call came
he didn't fight too hard the idea of returning to the Ojos
Negros. He was merely trading one vacant landscape for
another.

He had driven well past the butte now and had reached
the turn into the old south road, the overgrown trace that
once, before the paving of the highway even back in his time
here, had been the only way to get to Black Springs. He
nearly turned, but since the dismantling of the D Cross A,
probably three or four new fences he didn't know about had
been strung across the old road, fences he might have to cut
and mend with his burning hands as he had Sam Edward's
fence.

He shifted into a higher gear and sped toward the
highway.

Halfway there, he saw the plane. It was a twin-engined
job whose make he didn't recognize, but one of the executive
types he had seen parked on the fringes of big airports such
as O'Hare, JFK, and Heathrow. It seemed to be coming right
down at him, straight out of Cuchillo Peak, but it still had five
hundred feet of altitude when it flew over him. He stopped
the jeep and watched until it passed the butte and made its
two turns from the downwind leg to the final approach. For a
moment he lost it in the sun, found it again over the far end
of the runway, lost it for good after the gear came down and it
dropped into its landing run.

He got going again, smiling, but smiling with a little
nagging bitterness. He had looked at big cars and planes,
blooded saddle stock, and a king's ransom in radio gear, but
he still hadn't seen a cow on the D Cross A.

Nash Ortiz—Ignacio—wouldn't have liked that any more
than he did.

A note in what he guessed to be Jody's scrawl was on the
desk in his room. "Sam Edwards wants you to call her." She
couldn't yet have had time to get out and check his work on
the fence. Maybe the newly returned husband, Hadley, had
raised some questions.

Harry Kimbrough got the number for him. Sam Edwards answered with a curt, "Yes?"

"Mrs. Edwards?" he asked. Somehow, since he wouldn't be seeing her again, he didn't think calling her Sam would do any longer.

"Ian?" Her voice had turned light and warm.

"Yes. No problems about the fence, I hope."

A laugh came over the line. "I'll let you know. What I wanted is something else. But first, I'm sorry I didn't come out when you drove past the house on your way out. I meant the offer about the coffee, but I was on the radio, talking to the plane. You must have seen it. Tim—Hadley's pilot— always likes to check with me about any washouts in the runway before he touches down during the rainy season."

Hadley's pilot? It shouldn't have surprised him. It *had* looked to be a lot of airplane for a sport flyer, if that was all Hadley Edwards was.

"Here's what I wanted," she said. "Hadley and I are having a few people in for drinks and dinner tomorrow night, Saturday. Seven o'clock. Come in jeans, if you'd like."

"I'm sorry. I'm going back to New York tomorrow." He really was sorry.

"Can't you put off leaving for one more day?"

"Afraid not. Might not get under way then at all."

"Well, the latchkey is out when you're down this way again."

"If—not when," he said.

"Oh? But you've got that property."

"It looks after itself pretty well. I found that out today." Yes, it did—with ghosts on horseback guarding it.

"All right then, Ian. If I don't like the way you've fixed our fence, I'll send you a bill."

"Please do that—Sam." He could have bitten his tongue when he heard himself say "Sam." He had better finish now, once and for all. There wasn't even any need to tell her he was an alcoholic. He wouldn't be seeing her again. "Send a bill, if you feel one is necessary. I don't want to owe anyone in Chupadera County anything."

Chapter V

When he finished packing, Ian realized he hadn't eaten since breakfast. Now, the long drive in the unfamiliar Jeep, the struggle in and out of the arroyo, and the work on the fence had stirred an appetite he hadn't known in months—if he didn't count the cravings for sweets that had come in so many unexpected moments since his last drink. Would he ever get this hungry in New York?

It might be fun to eat at the Comida again tonight, but he knew he wouldn't.

Fun was the last thing, the very last thing, he wanted out of Black Springs, Chupadera County, or the Ojos Negros.

All he wanted out of the Ojos Negros was just that—out.

As a matter of fact there would never be a time for leaving it any better than the present. He was paid at the Yucca until morning. A fast-food sandwich on the road somewhere, even a snack at a Dairy Queen, would do for supper, and driving through the night held no terrors for him. He wasn't the kind to doze behind the wheel, and he'd see to it there were no more rash episodes like the one coming over Mescalero Gap.

He went to the bathroom and gathered up his shaving stuff and the shirt, socks, and shorts he had put out for the morning. He tossed the room key on the bed as he left the bathroom, and in four quick, hard strides, he reached the door.

Then, from the stoop in front of his room he saw Jody helping new arrivals carry their bags from a station wagon parked two units up from his.

It was a big night at the Kimbroughs' Yucca: two rooms occupied and it wasn't yet six in the evening. The station wagon showed Missouri license plates, and a rooftop rack carried a high load covered by a canvas tarp: migrant America; since dust-bowl days, Steinbeck's "westering" had never stopped.

A thin woman in a faded print dress was walking a big

dog, a Samoyed whose white fur showed the yellow tint of age; the leash between them stretched as tight as Ian had pulled the wires on Sam Edwards's fence. They were headed for the enclosure where Harry Kimbrough had tried growing grass. Ian wanted to call out to the woman, but they were deep into the tangle before he could make a sound. It was going to take a painful hour to pull the goathead weeds from the dog's coat and out of the woman's white cotton sweat socks.

At the front left fender of the station wagon, a bald man with the gray of utter exhaustion in his face was watching Jody and stuffing the tails of an aloha shirt into trousers that were too tight for him. The pocket of the shirt held enough pens and pencils to make it look like a clip of cartridges.

When Jody came out of the room he turned his eyes on Ian. There was something close to petulance in his look; it was a "so there, too" look, as if he wished he had the nerve to say, "See, Mr. Smart New Yorker? You're not the only guest we have." The look was there for only an instant. Doubtless Jody felt too old to cry, but he seemed close to tears all the same.

Ian turned on his heels, went back inside the room, and put his shaving gear and change of clothing back in the bathroom. If Jody was working the desk tonight, he probably wouldn't be on duty in the morning. Ian could stay the night and still get on the road early enough to avoid the boy. It would save them both from embarrassment.

But damn it all! He wouldn't make the added mistake of going back to the Comida de Anita and enjoying himself.

There were two pickups, neither of them blue nor a Ford, parked in front of the Buckhorn Bar & Grill across the highway from the Yucca. They were flanked by a Chevrolet coupe so old he had no idea of the year, and a new Olds 98 four-door that looked better than Sam Edwards's Cadillac.

He walked across the highway. The asphalt had softened during the afternoon, and his feet stuck with every step. Here went that first rule, the one that said he wasn't to go in a bar by himself. The hell with it. As hungry as he was and as derelict as the Buckhorn looked without its neon sign flashing as it had last night, the place should pose no threat to his recovery.

A screen door was hooked back against the stucco side of the building, its broken spring dangling. With the layer of dead moths plastered to it, it wouldn't be much of a screen, anyway. What would the Buckhorn do when fly-time rolled around?

Inside it was about as dark and dingy as he had expected.

Apart from the indirect sunlight throwing his shadow onto the cracked linoleum ahead of him, the only light in the place came from the electric Schlitz sign over the back bar, helped a little by another lighted sign, a grainy, garish north-woods scene the Hamms people expected would provoke a thirst for beer in general and theirs in particular.

The barroom and restaurant of the Buckhorn belied its squat exterior. Perhaps because of the gloom, it seemed cavernous, and an earth smell told him he was now inside a genuine adobe, built since his time here, but already old. It was funny that this dark, airless sewer should make him think of his bedroom at the old D Cross A.

Three drinkers, men, were at a bar that ran the length of the west wall, two standing together, with a loner seated nearer the one highway-side window. The barstools weren't fixed to the floor, and some had been pushed to the side to make a space directly across the bar from the bartender and his beer taps.

The bartender, T-shirted, with a good-sized paunch dragging his shoulders and chest muscles down, lifted his eyes to Ian, and it signaled his three customers to turn and see the newcomer for themselves.

The three men's faces, under broad-brimmed straw hats, were saved from total blankness by their deep tans, not the smooth, golden tans rich men and women get at the pool-and-racquet club, but the blotchy, brown-and-red complexions of men who work long hours in the sun and sweat streams of corrosive salt.

The three men turned back to their drinks. The bartender had stopped looking at him, too. They had seen all they wanted.

Tables and chairs were scattered around the barroom, and there was a row of four booths on the right-hand side. Ian headed for the one nearest the back, next to a pair of louvered swinging doors he guessed opened on the kitchen. The booth was the only one that had a tablecloth and a place setting. The Buckhorn must not expect any more tourist business than did the Yucca.

The bartender hadn't looked his way again, nor had the men at the bar, but as Ian seated himself a young woman wearing an apron came through the louvered doors. She did a double take as she started past the booth, stopped, and took a pad from the pocket of her apron.

"Howdy!" she said. Odd. Somehow it seemed more a challenge than a greeting. She flashed a quick on-off smile. "Ain't you the tourist from New York who's staying at the Yucca."

Tourist? Well, what could he call himself? Little in his two days here had made him feel a native anymore.

The waitress was short, husky and pretty in a haphazard way. She wore makeup far too heavy for her young skin, and she hadn't taken much care putting it on—or perhaps she had taken too much care; the result often was the same. She looked like a girl in a color layout where everything had been done right until the final printing. Off-register, they called it in the trade.

"Can I get you a drink?" the girl said.

"A plain club soda with a twist, and I'd like a menu, please."

"Sure." She started toward the bar, stopped, turned back to him. "Did you say *plain* soda?"

"Yes. Maybe I should have asked for a Shirley Temple."

That should make it as plain as the soda he had ordered. The Buckhorn probably didn't get many customers like him. As B.J. Howland had, the girl looked uncomfortable. He wished again he had told Sam Edwards. It would have been interesting to see *her* reaction.

"I'll put in the 'drink' order and then I'll find a menu for you," the waitress said. No, he wasn't imagining it. There had been an extra breath on the word "drink."

When she reached the bar, she leaned over it at the gap next to the two standing drinkers and spoke to the bartender. The bartender and the two men turned and looked at Ian. Then the bartender filled a glass with soda bubbling from a rubber hose. Soda had been splashed a lot less liberally on a lot of Scotch for Ian.

The girl was talking to one of the drinkers looking at him. He dug into his pocket and came up with a coin he dropped into her outstretched hand. She hadn't looked at the soda. She patted the drinker on the shoulder and moved quickly to a pay phone in the corner closest to where the loner sat, plugged the slot, and dialed a number. Ian took out a cigarette and discovered he didn't have an ashtray. He left the booth and got one from a nearby table and went back to his seat again. The girl must have reached her party. She nodded her head several times and spoke briefly before she hung up. She looked at Ian, but when she discovered he was looking at her, too, she turned and walked to the bar. Ian lit his cigarette.

A full minute passed before the girl returned to the booth with the soda and a menu in a cloudy plastic holder, put them in front of him without a word, and then pushed through the swinging doors behind him. He studied the Buckhorn's menu. It was a safe bet the bill of fare never changed. Another five minutes must have gone by before he looked up and found the girl fidgeting in front of him.

"What's good?" he asked.

"The steak—the steak's good." The girl sniffed.

"I'll have the sixteen-ounce T-bone. Medium rare."

"Salad?"

"Yes."

"I mean what kind of dressing." She turned her eyes toward the ceiling as if seeking support.

"Run them past me, please," Ian said.

She put her hands on her hips and closed her eyes as if picturing a list in her mind. "Thousand Island, Eye-talian, blue cheese, creamy—"

"Blue cheese," he cut in.

"—French, buttermilk ranch, vinegar and..." It registered on her then that he had already decided. "You want pinto beans?" She was tapping her pencil on her pad, the little clicks obviously meant to show annoyance.

"Sure. Beans." Maybe she just didn't like tourists, particularly New York tourists.

She jammed her order pad in the pocket of her apron and went through the louvered doors. There hadn't been any smiles since that first automatic one.

A man and a woman came through the front door of the Buckhorn, and Ian recognized the couple from Missouri.

The man didn't look quite as bushed as he had when Jody was unloading the station wagon. His face, not so gray now, carried the spaced-out, slightly bewildered look of the newly retired. The woman on the other hand looked as if she had indeed been through the ordeal of the goathead weeds with the Samoyed. They sank from sight in the booth nearest the door. The men at the bar took their ritual look at them and turned back to their drinks again.

The waitress came from the kitchen and went straight to

the booth near the door without turning her head toward Ian.
In another second she was on her way to the bar.

When the bartender filled the drink order, she returned
to the booth where the couple had seated themselves. The
tray she carried held a mixed drink, a bottle of beer, and a
double shot in an oversize glass. She looked at Ian as if to say,
"Well, at least *some* people . . ."

The girl and the Missouri people in the booth were
laughing, and the girl's laugh was still loud as she approached
Ian on her way back to the kitchen. She stopped at his
booth—and stopped laughing, too.

"The steak will be a while," she said. "Cook didn't have
the grill fired up."

"No hurry," he said. "Do you suppose you could find a
newspaper floating around anywhere?"

"I'll see." It didn't sound as if her heart was in it.

To his surprise, she was back with a copy of the *El Paso
Times* within fifteen seconds. It must have been lining a
garbage can. She dropped it on the table in front of him
without a word.

He was halfway through the lead story, something about
Nixon's planning a wage and price freeze, before he glanced
at the paper's date. It was three days old. It didn't matter. He
was completely out of touch with the world, anyway, had
been for nearly a week. A week? He wondered, as he had
wondered more than once since sobering up, how many big
stories he had missed in twenty years. His country had been
at war for more than a decade, and he couldn't have drawn
even a crude map of the troubled peninsula where American
boys were killing and dying.

He found one story in the second section of the *Times*
about something he *hadn't* missed over the years, although
he couldn't claim to have ever given it much deep thought. It
was a big story here in the high desert southwest and in
California, and he remembered it had gotten a good deal of
coverage in New York, too, where it was news in a slightly
altered ethnic form.

In this three-day-old issue the El Paso paper had splashed
a full-page feature with photos on the illegal aliens who
slogged across the damp putty bottom of the Rio Grande from
Juarez and the *frontera* every night, hundreds of them.

The feature quoted the chief of the El Paso district of the
border patrol. "We couldn't stop them with two full divisions.

We have three hundred fifty miles of border, most of it without a passable road near enough to do us any good, and I've got thirteen men to spread around the clock. If we catch illegals on a Monday, say, and if we can get them processed and sent back by Wednesday, we'll have the same poor fish in our net again on Friday—if we're lucky. We get to know some of them. Since they're not criminals, but family men or entire families just trying to escape slow starvation, it doesn't make the job a pleasant one." He sounded like a decent sort, and his picture made him look it, too. Even in New York not every cop had been a cossack.

Ian wondered now why he had paid even as little attention as he had to the Mexican and other illegals. Really big news such as the Bay of Pigs and the missile crisis had been only the faintest of blips on his personal radar screen. Maybe it was because Ignacio Ortiz had been a wetback, if Ian wanted to get strictly technical about it—gracious Ignacio, who had encompassed in his great soul more of this America than any of the jingoists Ian knew.

There were no illegals here in the Buckhorn, none in the barroom at any rate. This was white man's country in the narrowest sense of the term. If there were an undocumented worker anywhere on the premises, he would be the dishwasher, *maybe* the cook who was taking his own sweet time with Ian's steak. And when the Buckhorn closed for the night, the sweeper might be a wetback, fighting the fear of discovery as he pushed a broom through cigarette butts, bottle tops, and through his own shadowed memories of home.

He heard the louvered doors squeak open, and he turned to see the girl backing into the room with a loaded tray. Good. In spite of everything he was still as hungry as when he entered, hungrier. A glance at his watch told him it had been more than twenty minutes since the girl had waltzed into the kitchen with his order.

The tray wasn't for him. The girl unloaded the tray at the front booth and then walked back toward the kitchen, away from his booth and through the scattered tables.

He stepped out of the booth and in front of her.

"How about mine, young lady?" he said.

She tried to brush past him, but he backed against the doors.

"I told you the grill wasn't up!" she said. It was like the

cracking of a whip. "Them people up front had cold cuts. *I ain't the cook!*" This last was unguardedly snotty.

"Then let's forget the whole thing."

He stepped around her and started for the door.

"Wait!" it was a cry of panic.

He turned back to her—and looked into a face as white as the gypsum rocks he had picked his way through this afternoon. "Please—please stay," she said. Damned if she didn't sound frightened. Maybe that bartender turned mean if she actually *lost* a customer. "I'll bring your salad. And we got soup. It's vegetable today. It ain't bad. Honest."

He knew he should leave and forget about eating here. But there *was* this unmistakable plea in the girl's wide eyes, and the smeared lips were trembling. He slid back into the booth.

"Okay. Bring the soup and the salad."

The louvered doors hadn't finished their second swing before she was back, placing the soup and the salad in front of him. Her hand was shaking and a few drops spilled from the soup bowl, only a few, but enough to spread on the dingy tablecloth like blood oozing through a bandage. She didn't linger.

When he looked at the salad, he knew he had made another mistake by staying. The lettuce had begun life already too rusted and limp to hold up under the blue cheese dressing. He didn't have much hope for the greasy-looking soup, either, no matter what the girl had said. As he stared at the two straw-colored plastic bowls, he felt his hunger fade.

One thing, though: when she finally arrived with the steak, this girl was damned well going to sit down across from him and explain herself.

The bartender and his trio of drinkers were looking at him again. The exchange between the girl and him was high theater for these rednecks.

Then, the light in the barroom dimmed.

A big man had filled the outer doorway of the Buckhorn. He was wearing a hat like the men at the bar, and with his head and features backlit by the weak light coming through the open door, Ian couldn't make out anything about his face.

He didn't have to. The half-lit big frame, the stance, the outline alone: any of them was enough to tell him that this was the man who had left the handprints on the MG yesterday at Las Sombras.

The louvered doors opened again. The girl raced past. She didn't slow up until she reached the man and ran right against him. His thick body absorbed the shock of hers without a tremor. She wasn't a big woman, but she looked even tinier against his bulk, and Ian watched as she pressed herself against him. Her arms went about his neck and she strained upward to put her mouth to his. The big man didn't press back. He didn't put his arms around her. He didn't bend his head to hers. He just put two huge hands on her waist and put her aside, not with violence or even impatience, but the way a man might, with no consciousness of what he was doing, remove some inanimate object, a chair, say, from his path.

Then he began to limp toward Ian's booth.

It was an ugly limp, as painful to watch as it must have been to bear. The right leg shot out stiff and straight, and then sagged like a rope toward the sound left one as the limper's weight came down. And yet, bad leg or not, the man moved with a determined, awkward strength and grace.

The smell of him reached the booth before he did. He must have waded through a vat of whiskey.

As the man stood over him, Ian suddenly felt he had seen him somewhere—long before Las Sombras.

The girl had followed the man to Ian's booth but was now half hidden behind his shoulder.

"You see—" she said, "I kept him here just like you told me to when I called you." Her voice was thin, tinny.

"You did fine, M.L." the man said. He was carrying a nearly lethal load of alcohol, but his words weren't slurred and he didn't slobber. He didn't sway. Ian knew he was looking at the worst kind of drunk of all, the kind who can burn away incredible amounts of liquor with some awful, raging, inner fire.

Ian himself—when he had passed a mirror—had all too often seen a drunk exactly like the one in front of him.

"You're MacAndrews," the man said.

"And you're Jacky Begley."

There was something Sarah hadn't mentioned in her letter and that Ernie Gomez hadn't told him. Jacky Begley, although carrying ten or fifteen pounds too much in the way of boozy blubber, but with his blond hair curling over his ears and his deep blue eyes unblinking, was one of the handsomest young men Ian had ever seen.

"My name is *John* Begley—*not Jacky*. Get that straight."

"Fair enough. John, then. Why were you following me yesterday"—he decided on a shot in the dark—"and again today, out on the slickrock?"

"Never mind that right now." There was no denial on Begley's face. The chance shot had gone straight to the heart of the ten-ring.

"You once worked for Nash Ortiz at the D Cross A, didn't you?"

"Never mind that, either. Right now I'm going to buy you a drink." He turned to the girl. "Bring us a jug and a couple of glasses, M.L."

"No thanks," Ian said. "I don't drink."

The only change in Begley's face was that his eyes narrowed, but not quickly enough to hide the demons in them. John Begley was a sick man, a dangerous man. Ian had known fear before when faced with big, sick, dangerous men such as this, only fools didn't. It was a reasonable fear, the kind that could keep a man alive.

The girl broke in. "See, John, it's like I said. He only drinks the soft stuff."

"Shut up, M.L." Begley didn't look at her. "Move your ass."

The girl hurried toward the bar.

"Now," Begley said, "what's all this shit about how you don't drink?"

"There's no 'shit' about it. I don't drink." Ian listened to the sound of his own voice. He was grateful it didn't betray the fear he felt.

"So just *why*"—Begley was pressing him now—"don't you drink?" Begley's eyes were a little more open, and the demons were peering out again. It was hard to look at them. Telling this young brute the truth would be like putting a chip on his shoulder. This wasn't any B.J. Howland.

"I don't drink because I can't," Ian said. "I am an alcoholic."

"You're a *what*?" Begley stared, his eyes dead now.

"I am an alcoholic," Ian said once more. "I can't handle liquor."

"Bullshit! A man who can't handle liquor ain't a man."

M.L. had returned to the table with a bottle and two glasses. She put them on the table in front of Ian, she looked only at Begley.

"Good work, M.L.," Begley said. "Now get lost." The girl fled toward the bar. Begley looked down at Ian, and yes, the demons were back again. "All right, MacAndrews," he said, "I'm going to slide in across from you, and then you and me, we're going to tie one on together." Despite the leg, and the liquor in his system, he slipped into the booth almost gracefully. He propped his chin in his hands. "And after we tie one on, you're going to haul your ass out of Chupadera County as fast as that little trick car of yours will take it."

As suddenly as it had come, Ian's fear was gone. He knew now what had to happen. It wouldn't be his decision.

Begley had the cork out of the bottle and one of the glasses in his hand.

"Just pour one, Begley," Ian said.

Begley's thick arm shot across the table and his huge hand grasped Ian's throat. The glass rolled from the tabletop and hit the floor. The neck of the open bottle was at Ian's mouth. He wrenched himself free of Begley's grasp and left the booth with Begley lunging after him.

It couldn't have been the fight the bartender and his three customers might have been expecting, or hoping for. It was considerably *more* of a fight than the Missouri couple wanted. Out of the corner of his eye Ian saw them scurry through the outer door just as he avoided Begley's first blind rush.

He kept circling to the left, forcing Begley to plant his weight on the bad leg for every wild swing. He knew if he kept his head, kept digging hard to that belly full of booze, it would be an easy fight. He knew there was the one chance in a hundred that the younger man could land a big one, and that it might then be over, but he jabbed five or six times to Begley's eyes and soon enough the right one began to puff and close. From then on it was only a matter of surgery. Begley was strong, all right, frightening in two strength-draining clinches, but he was dumb. Hell, he had never had to be anything *but* dumb in a fight. It was clear he had never been up against anybody any good.

Begley tried. He kept trying even after he had been down two times, taking no more time to get up than it took him to wipe his bloody face.

Ian didn't finish it; the bartender did. Unnoticed by Ian, he had come from behind the bar. He laid a billy alongside

Begley's head with all the calm, unhurried skill Ian would have expected from a Rush Street bouncer.

"That's enough," the bartender said. "He's had it coming for a long time, neighbor, but that's enough."

"Thanks," Ian said.

He left the Buckhorn with M.L. lying stretched across Begley's chest, moaning. She didn't look up as Ian stepped around them and headed for the door.

When he reached the Yucca, he saw the couple from Missouri loading up their station wagon. The Samoyed barked from the backseat. The dog might mess the car, but the look on the woman's face said the animal wasn't getting in the goathead weeds again, no way. The couple moved to the far side of the station wagon as Ian mounted the steps of number 24.

Inside his room he went straight to the telephone. Jody answered from the office.

"Jody," he said, "could you ring the Edwards place for me?"

"Yes, sir." The hurt was still straining the boy's young voice. Maybe Ian should take care of that first.

"I've got to tell Mrs. Edwards that I won't be leaving Black Springs for a while."

There was nothing more from Jody in words.

As Ian hoped, it was Sam Edwards who came on the line after Jody placed the call.

"Sam, this is Ian MacAndrews. There's been a change of plan. Do you still want me for dinner tomorrow night?"

"Sure. But can I ask—"

"No, you can't. Not now. Seven o'clock tomorrow night?"

"Yes, seven. See you then." She hung up. Smart woman. She knew when to cut off questions.

He went to the bathroom and looked in the mirror. He couldn't remember Begley's getting in a real, solid punch, but sometimes you never felt them until long afterward. No, there were no marks. His knuckles were skinned, and his hands had actually bled a little. Or were those only the nicks and scratches from the fence? He had often felt a great deal more tired after finishing a painting.

There was a lot of thinking he had to do. Things between John H. Begley and Ian MacAndrews weren't over by a long shot, and Sarah, damn her contentious, meddling soul, had

known it, had known it all along. Begley and he would be
pulled together in some strange way from here on out.

No two ways about it, there was a *powerful* lot of
thinking he would have to do, but not right now... later, after
he got back from supper at the Comida de Anita.

Chapter VI

"Come in, Ian," Ernesto Gomez said. "Sam and Hadley
will be with us in a second."

Ernie answering Sam Edwards's door? Was he their
lawyer, too, or just a local friend? Well, Ernie had probably
gotten to know the new owners when they bought the place.
Gomez went on, "I was afraid I had seen the last of you. Glad
I was wrong. Changed your mind about staying in the basin?"

"Not really, Ernie. But something came up that's delayed
my leaving for a bit. By the way, can I have a few moments of
your time Monday morning?"

"Sure—" The attorney seemed to reconsider. "Wait a
second. I'm going to Santa Fe. Hell, I could put the trip off
until Tuesday if it's urgent."

"No. I'll wait until you get back."

"Thanks. I'll have Carrie—she runs our office—make
room for you on Wednesday if that's not too late. You'll still
be in Black Springs then?"

"I'm afraid so."

"I'll have her call you, or leave word for you at the
Yucca."

They were standing in a wide entrance hall beyond
whose far arch Ian could see an immense living room. The
outside of the Edwards house might have been mission style,
but the interior was Santa Fe New Mexican: pure white walls
hung with Navaho rugs and sand paintings, and in one corner
a beehive fireplace. There was the usual Mexican-colonial
furniture, but also some big, comfortable-looking leather
chairs and a couch of the Lake Shore Drive bachelor-pad

variety, a lot like things with which he had furnished his own cramped apartment in Manhattan, and the white walls also held some large oil canvases. The paintings were probably good. Good or bad he would have to ignore them.

People were moving around the living room. If he had expected the same air of somnolence he had found here yesterday, the scene would have disabused him of the notion in a hurry. The Edwards' rambling home was a busy place tonight.

"Sam didn't tell me you were coming," Ernie said, "but then, Sam Edwards doesn't give away much of anything." He began smiling and smiled almost to the point of laughter, looking quite unlawyerlike. Something had suddenly made an irresistible attack on Ernesto Gomez's notions of what was funny. "Let's join the others," he said. "We'll see if Consuelo can rustle you up a drink. Until Sam and Hadley moved in, the art of martini-making in Chupadera County was in its infancy." The smile left his face. "I'm terribly sorry, Ian. Forgive me. I forgot. You don't drink."

"No, I don't, Ernie," Ian said.

How did Gomez know? The subject hadn't come up between them, either on the phone from New York or in their meeting Thursday.

Gomez led the way into the living room. There were five people there, but Ian's eyes were drawn straight to the only one who didn't look to be a guest. A slender Hispanic woman of middle years was passing a tray of hors d'oeuvres. When the woman saw Gomez and Ian, she walked toward them and offered the tray. She was a striking woman, pure Spanish or close to it, he thought, with straight features of great delicacy, but with strength in them, too. Strange that he would see two faces of this same general type here in the Ojos Negros, and both of them here at Sam Edwards's ranch. When he had walked from the parking apron to the door just a moment ago, a tall, black-haired, graceful-looking man had been watering the lawn. He had gazed at Ian with utter frankness, with his head square to him, and his back arched almost like that of a torero. The man was perhaps a year or two older than the woman, had the same finely formed, high-bridged nose, and the same pale olive skin. Hispanic natives of Chupadera County usually had the healthy red-brown complexion of Ernie Gomez here. Brother and sister? No, with all the similarities in their looks, there were marked differences, too.

Ernesto took a triangle of toast mounded with caviar from the tray, saying, "*Gracias*, Consuelo." Ian shook his head and muttered, "No thanks." Another odd thing. The woman was looking at him with much the same forthright frankness the man watering the lawn had shown. Maybe things were indeed getting better for the Hispanics of the basin. While the looks hadn't been insolent, they were certainly the open ones of people who felt themselves equal to anyone, not the furtive glances of the few domestic servants he remembered in the wealthier homes of his boyhood. The woman placed her tray on a chest and left the room.

A young man with the bleached hair and cultivated tan of a Malibu beachboy pulled himself from the depths of a leather armchair, unfolding endlessly to something well over six feet. He pushed a hand out toward Ian.

"I'm Tim Springer, Hadley's pilot," he said. "You were the bloke mucking about in the Jeep when Had and I came in yesterday." Touch of a Midlands accent? Yes.

Ian nodded. He noticed the man wore his wristwatch with the face on the inside of his wrist as the British did. He had seen more than his share of this kind of English boy-man in New York in the wake of the Beatles invasion and the second wave from Carnaby Street, men quite unlike the RAF fliers he had known in Italy. Few had looked this healthy, though, and fewer—he discovered when he took the man's hand—had a grip like this.

The pilot sank back into the chair he had hauled himself from. He had been leafing through a magazine and now picked it up again.

Ernie spoke to a middle-aged couple sitting on a couch, "Jim, Cissy, I'd like you to meet Ian MacAndrews. Ian, this is Dr. Jim Pendleton and his wife, Cissy. They flew in with Hadley from San Antonio yesterday, but they're actually from Beverly Hills—slumming, I guess."

"Come on now, Ernie. You know we love this place," the man said as he got up, "Glad to meet you, Mr. MacAndrews."

If the pilot's handshake had been strong, the doctor's was a calculated crusher. Americans really make a test of casual introductions, Ian thought. The woman smiled sweetly. She looked likable, as did her husband, whose deep tan matched that of the pilot. Nice, comfortable people, but in appearance at least, the kind untouched by life. Both of them were dressed in the sort of clothes the country-club set wore so easily, the doctor in shantung slacks, a LaCoste shirt, and rope-soled sandals; Cissy, pink and pretty in slacks and blouse, and with a harness load of turquoise around her neck.

"Was it your family who used to own El Recobro?" Pendleton asked Ian.

El Recobro? Oh, sure, the Edwards' new name for the D Cross A. Ian said it was. Until he heard the name out loud just now he hadn't speculated on it. The Rescue? Perhaps sometime he would ask what had prompted them to call it that.

"And this," Ernie was saying now, "is my token *gringa,* Carrie Spletter. I'd ask her to make your appointment with me right now, but she gets sticky about working overtime."

"Don't listen to him, Mr. MacAndrews," Carrie Spletter said. "He's a great one to talk. He pays me in outdated writs, anyway. Token *gringa,* my foot." She looked at Ernie with eyes half-filled with good-natured reproach and wholly awash with adoration. Hard to tell if the adoration was for the boss—or the man. Stunning girl. Ian hadn't noticed in the office the other day.

"Carrie," Ian said, "was the Hattie Spletter who was librarian in Black Springs when I was a kid your mother—or rather your grandmother?"

The girl laughed. "Hardly, Mr. MacAndrews. Hattie was what she called a 'maiden lady,' and she never let the family forget it was by choice. My father was her younger brother."

The pilot, Tim, hadn't looked up from his magazine while Ian was being introduced to any of them except Carrie. He had the hungry eyes of the sexual shark, and he clearly found this shapely young woman with the honey-yellow hair appetizing.

But Ian sensed a kind of extra electric charge coming from him when Sam Edwards entered the room. The magazine dropped to the carpet and Tim Springer gazed at Sam as he had at Carrie, but with a difference. There was something more than sexual hunger in his look now.

"I'm sorry, everybody," Sam said, "I had to help Hadley with something. He'll be a few more minutes yet. Did you meet everyone, Ian?" She headed straight for him. The change in her from yesterday was remarkable, but he couldn't pin it down to anything. She was dressed every bit as simply:

a wheat-colored linen skirt down to her ankles, a white blouse—again styled like a man's shirt, but decidedly more the Brooks Brothers kind than the western check—sandals almost a match for the pair the doctor was wearing.

Maybe it was a heightened animation brought out for her guests, but it was more than just that. Maybe it was the attention she was getting from the pilot. Ian knew well enough what an effect this could have on a woman, even when she returned none of the interest shown in her, sometimes *particularly* when she returned none of it.

When she reached Ian, she stopped, planted her feet as she had in the walkway yesterday, and put her hands on her hips. She cocked her head to one side.

"Let's have a look at you, Ian. My God! It's true. Not a mark."

He heard Ernie Gomez chuckle. So they knew. It answered the question of how Ernie knew he didn't drink. Every word said at the Buckhorn last night, every move made, must have become common knowledge by noon today in Black Springs, and Ernie would have carried it straight to this gathering. Now he knew the reason for the stares he felt when he went to the pharmacy this morning to get toothpaste and cigarettes. At the time he had put it down to his being a stranger. All right, but if this was going to turn him into some kind of bush-league, overnight folk-hero in Chupadera County, his decision to stay a few days longer would be up for reconsideration. Another thing—he felt a small twinge of disappointment that Ernesto Gomez would carry tales. He hadn't expected that.

"Now that Ian's here," Sam said to the others, "let's finish our drinks out on the patio. We've got a treat coming—I hope. We froze a *cabrito* in March, and last night Hadley and Alejandro started roasting it. Hadley doesn't know roasting a young goat from his elbow, but I guess we can have faith in Alejandro."

They filed out, an eager Ernesto in the lead with Carrie, then the Pendletons. Tim Springer looked over his shoulder at Sam as he went through a set of glass double-doors to the tiled patio beyond them. Ian hung back. Sam turned to him.

"I embarrassed you, Ian. I'm sorry," she said. It pleased him that Sam Edwards hadn't missed it.

"Don't worry about it," he said. "Actually, I suppose I

should be embarrassed. Barroom brawls are for younger men."

"Still—" she said, "you didn't come off badly. I understand the man has terrorized half the county. Incidentally, I saw you look at Ernesto. *He* didn't tell me, if you're wondering. Herb Babcock—the bartender at the Buckhorn—was in the Piggy-Wiggly this morning when I was doing the shopping for tonight."

He hadn't misjudged Ernie, after all. "We're keeping your other guests waiting, Sam."

"No, we're not. We don't run much to guests and hosts here. That bunch on the patio is more or less family. At least I like to think so."

"And me? Surely *I'm* not family."

She smiled, but she didn't answer him.

"Sam," he said then, "as long as you feel we don't have to hurry to join the others, would you mind my taking a couple of minutes to look at your paintings?" Something twisted inside him as he heard himself. Too late.

Her smile grew wider and warmer. "I was hoping you would."

As they talked, he had noticed a bronze casting of a horse and rider on a stand by the doors to the patio. The horse was a raw bronco, as rank and ornery as reality itself, and the distinctive, twisting arch of its back under the clinging rider told him it had to be a genuine Russell. He hadn't even glanced at the oils yet, partly because of the slight sense of dread he felt just knowing they were there, and that when he turned to look at them he would find himself in danger. It would be, he knew, a familiar danger, one he had faced fearfully when in front of the Seurat in Chicago, the Monets at the Modern in Manhattan, and a hundred others at places such as the Louvre and the Uffizi—a danger he had sensibly stopped courting when he sobered up.

Actually, he should make some excuse and get out of here. The gossip had taken away his one real reason for coming here tonight: that he wanted to tell Sam Edwards himself that he was an alcoholic. Staying on would be adding risk to a mistake.

He turned and faced the paintings.

It was a peculiar way to hang fine art, mixed as it was with Indian weaving (there was a Germantown rug, a bit

tattered, as well as the expected Two Gray Hills, both next to
the flat, still designs of Navajo healers), but the apparently
careless look of the display didn't jar him as it might once
have. Beyond the Indian hangings a Modigliani nude reclined
in dark insolence. He had seen it once before, when it hung
in the Art Institute on Michigan Avenue on loan from A. J.
Klosterman's private collection back in 1963. It had taken
more than mere money to get this painting away from the
Klosterman estate when the old shipping magnate died.
Between two of the sand paintings he saw a small Corot, still
another "Grand Canal," and to the left of it a Klee wisely left
on its stretcher, unframed. In quick succession he walked by
a Pissarro, a Remington, a magnificent Wilson Hurley, and a
tiny, utterly priceless Degas sketch.

It wasn't a "collection." There was no discernible pattern
of planned acquisition. Nothing looked as if it need be, would
be, or could be added—or subtracted—by fiat or design.
Every piece had made it to this remote wall in the Ojos
Negros Basin on its own. Every new piece would have to
power its own way in.

"Hadley's choices," Sam said, as if he had asked out
loud. For a scary moment he wondered if he had. "Don't get
me wrong. I love them, too, and I know a little something
about art—but these are Hadley's."

He became aware of two more paintings on the walls on
either side of the hallway arch he and Ernie had come
through. A Turner, yes, he was going to see a Turner, and that
was fine—risky, but fine—because of all of them, Turner's
color had stirred him most. If he were in any position any
longer to say he owed any painter anything, it would be
Turner that he owed.

But he didn't look at the Turner. The other painting
caught him first.

In the foreground, a dark-haired, slender woman stood
in the crumbling stone foundation of a house that had never
gotten built. Big Cuchillo Peak, heavy with clouds and looking
as if it were ready to begin a march on the scene, blotted out
the sky. Around the stone foundation and against the hem of
the woman's skirt, thick, ugly, tentacled grass seemed to
grasp at everything. The woman, her head inclined a little,
was half-turned from the viewer, and her face was hidden,
but the sag of her shoulders carried a burden of anguish. The

painter had known that the human face could hide things the body couldn't.

"Hadley didn't choose this one, did he, Sam?" Ian said.

"No. This one isn't his. It's mine."

"How did you come by it?"

"Your mother gave it to me when we bought the D Cross A. She didn't want it to leave the place."

"It doesn't belong here with all these others."

"I think it does. So does Hadley. One of the reasons you're here tonight is that he wants to meet the painter, too."

"The painter of that picture left here a long time ago. I don't think he will ever come back again."

"Then who was the man who cut our fence yesterday?"

Laughter rang from the patio. Ernie Gomez was reciting a comic piece of doggerel in Spanish that awakened some remote memory in Ian he couldn't quite pull into place. The aroma of *cabrito* was suddenly overpowering.

"I have something else that goes with the painting," Sam said.

"Oh?"

She nodded toward the canvas. "The plans to that house. They weren't given to me. I found them at the back of a closet after we moved in and before we did the remodeling. Would you like to see them?"

No, he would not like to see them! If this painting held danger for him, those plans would carry far more risk. *But . . .*

"Yes, Sam, please."

She led the way down a narrow hall.

"This is Hadley's study," she said, "but I keep a few things here myself." She went to a tall chest whose top was covered with trophies: loving cups, a silver statuette of a polo player, a gilded horse's hoof, and a litter of ribbons, most of them blue. It was an old chest, and the top drawer creaked when she pulled it open. When she turned to him she handed him an ancient leather briefcase. In the lower left-hand corner, although most of the gold lettering had flaked away, he could read, "Douglas MacAndrews—D Cross A."

Sam said, "I suppose I should get out to the patio with the others. I can't imagine what's keeping Hadley. You take all the time you want or need. If you don't want to look at the plans now, take them with you. They're yours." She smiled. "The painting's mine, though." She leaned over the massive desk in the center of the room and switched on a long, green-shaded lamp. Then she was gone.

He placed the briefcase on the desk and stared at it. He held his hand out in front of him. No, it wasn't shaking. He opened the case and pulled out a thick sheaf of yellowing paper tied in cord. Across the top he read, "Plans for the Residence of Mr. & Mrs. James Hall MacAndrews—drawn by Ann Jennings MacAndrews, March 1916."

He decided not to look at them now. He put them back in the briefcase, snapped it shut, and reached for the switch on the shaded lamp, but he didn't turn it off.

The wall of the study opposite the desk was filled with framed photographs. Almost all of them were of horses or horse people, and he stepped around the desk and looked more closely. He remembered Hadley Edwards now: the Hadley Edwards of old Los Angeles money; the real estate tycoon who had been the darling of *Fortune* magazine seven years ago because of those tremendous shopping and residential developments in south Florida; the eight-goal polo player and Olympic silver medalist in the three-day trials; the sometime movie-producer Hadley Edwards in the picture there with Darryl Zanuck, and in the other photo that showed him handing a check, for some charity probably, to Governor Pat Brown. A big man, he dominated every photo, fine-featured, square-jawed, and with a smile bordering on arrogance.

Ian had been prepared to like the man who had chosen the oil paintings in the living room. He wasn't too sure about the man in the photographs.

He left the briefcase on the desk.

When he reached the patio, he found that Hadley Edwards had finally made his appearance.

He was holding court in the center of his guests, all of whom were standing and making an attentive circle around him. As in the photographs, he seemed overpoweringly vital. If he was handsome in the pictures, he was more so now, with the iron-gray that was beginning to touch his hair adding to the picture of wealth and power.

He was also in a wheelchair.

The thick, tough, strong legs of the photographs, which in jodhpurs and riding boots had looked as if they could "bestride this narrow world," were withered and flimsy under a pair of dove-gray flannel slacks.

As if he had sensed Ian's presence, he turned the wheelchair toward him.

"Mr. MacAndrews," Hadley Edwards said, "welcome to El Recobro. Forgive me. For old times' sake—welcome back to the D Cross A."

Chapter VII

He awoke to the sound of running water, and it took him a few seconds to decide it wasn't rain.

He got out of bed and went to the window. Jody, stripped to the waist, garden hose in one hand and sponge in the other, his jeans dripping and with a bucket of sudsy water at his feet, was washing the MG.

By the time Ian pulled on his slacks, jammed his bare feet into his loafers and opened the door, the wash job had reached the final rinse. Jody spun around when he heard Ian and the hose spun with him. The spray bounced off the stoop and a few droplets hit Ian's loafers and splashed on his ankles.

"Gee, I'm sorry, sir!" Flustered, Jody whipped the hose straight up in front of him, soaking himself even more. A fragment of a rainbow colored the spray.

"All right, kid," Ian said, bringing a mock growl from deep in his throat, "Wipe that car off good and then bring me my breakfast and the Sunday paper. And bear in mind I haven't got all day. Savvy?" Good Lord, how long had it been since he'd said "savvy" to anyone?

It was clear from the look on Jody's face that not all Ian's instincts were only hunches. Far from betraying hurt, the boy was smiling, apparently confident that his broken link with "Mr. Smart New Yorker" had been forged again.

"I savvy," Jody said.

Ian went back inside.

As he shaved, the face in the bathroom mirror looked better to him than it had as far back as he could remember. It shouldn't have. It might not for long. Begley would probably want more of him, particularly since word of the fight had gotten abroad in Black Springs, and there had been no mistaking the hatred in the man's eyes.

Ian would have to discover the cause of that hatred before he and Begley met again.

There was no reason—as yet—to think Begley knew what Ian was already sure *he* knew.

At dinner last night Ian asked Ernie if he knew why Begley should bear him so much demonstrably psychotic ill-will.

"Did he have a bad experience when he worked at the D Cross A?"

"None I know of, Ian."

Ian didn't want him to think he was making too big a thing of this, but he felt he had to ask one more risky question, "A set-to with my father, maybe? Something that might sour him on somebody named MacAndrews?"

"Not that I ever heard," Ernie said. Ian had been tempted to tell Ernie what he suspected, hell, knew, but Sam's party scarcely seemed the time and place.

Sam Edwards's dinner party had shed some light on the owners of El Recobro, but the light had produced more dazzle than revelation.

He liked Hadley Edwards. The coin he was prepared to toss in his mind in Hadley's study as to whether he would meet the "man on horseback" of the photographs or the man who had mounted the extraordinary display of art in Sam's living room never got tossed. The Hadley Edwards on the patio didn't seem to be either man.

The wheelchair and the shrunken, useless legs notwithstanding, it would be difficult to think of Hadley Edwards as "handicapped." As with other truly strong men Ian had known—physically unprepossessing Ignacio Ortiz came suddenly to mind—Hadley gave Ian the feeling that there was even greater strength held back.

His few words welcoming Ian had been measured, weighed, but spoken with no hesitancy, and with the confidence of a deep, feeling, thoroughly aware man, conscious of Ian and the other speakers, in touch at all times with every one of them.

The talk of the group on the patio stayed "small," almost a reductio ad absurdum, but it was enough for Ian to begin forming opinions—while withholding judgments. The pilot,

Tim, still couldn't take his eyes away from Sam even with her husband, his employer, on the scene. It was a bad case of something. Hadley Edwards saw it, too. His eyes panned from the pilot to his wife once when she was whispering something to Consuelo, and they stayed there until Sam returned his gaze. Then, as if she had received a "transmission" from Hadley, *she* looked at Springer, before turning back to Hadley. Then they both smiled.

Ian studied the others more carefully out on the patio. Shortly after he joined them he found out something that made him feel he had just won the Olympic gold in the running-conclusion jump.

Carrie Spletter was engaged in conversation with Dr. Pendleton.

"Will you *ever* return to the ministry, Dr. Pendleton?" Carrie said.

"In a sense, I don't feel I've ever left it."

Ian had jumped to *two* faulty conclusions about Pendleton: the first when he met the "doctor" inside, and then because of Hadley Edwards's infirmity. He had thought Pendleton might turn out to be Edwards's personal physician, one of those one-patient doctors. He wouldn't speculate on whether or not Pendleton might turn out to be Hadley's personal divine.

He had found a seat apart from the other guests, but he wasn't going to be left alone. Hadley Edwards had turned away from the group to talk with Alejandro, who had just carried the *cabrito* from the roasting pit to a long outdoor table. Now he wheeled himself toward Ian. Obviously Edwards didn't hold high court and wait for people to come to him.

"Don't tell me if you don't want to, Ian, but how old were you when you painted that canvas in the living room?"

"Seventeen—no, eighteen."

"Remarkable. You couldn't possibly have reached the extent of your powers then. Where is your later work?"

"There is none."

"None?"

"None at all."

Hadley Edwards shook his head.

"I find that difficult to believe, Ian. That canvas in there reveals an absolute *lust* to paint on the part of the artist. You couldn't have just stopped after that one picture. Please don't

tell me you didn't paint others. I don't think I would believe
that at all."

"Oh, I painted others, Mr. Edwards, in fact there were
perhaps fifty or sixty more at one time."

"Where are they?"

"Gone. They were all burned in a fire . . . here. The old
bunkhouse I used as a studio was—well, it burned down."

"What about the work done since then?" Edwards asked.

"There hasn't been any. I haven't painted since the fire."

Edwards's face didn't give a lot away. When he spoke
next, it was in a voice so low Ian had to lean forward to hear
him.

"Forgive me, Ian. I didn't mean to press you. I can see
how painful the subject must be for you. Excuse me, I think
Alejandro wants me to carve the *cabrito*. We'll talk some
more after dinner." He turned the wheelchair, then stopped.
"One thing more for now, Ian. I believe this might save you
from the embarrassment of having to ask—and the bother of
trying to decide whom to ask. I lost the use of my legs in a
riding accident. My fault. I tried to take a young hunter over
a water jump she wasn't ready for."

Ian looked toward the others and saw that Sam was
watching him.

The meal Alejandro and Consuelo served was superb,
and everything about the table was exactly right, and that
went double for the attention paid the diners by Alejandro
and Consuelo.

Yet there was something *too* efficient about the Hispanic
couple. They seemed to anticipate needs almost before they
arose, almost as if they had been seated there themselves and
knew exactly what was wanted. He wondered if that was the
answer. They would look more natural being served than
serving.

Jesus! Why did he always find himself thinking, analyzing?
The awareness that was such a virtue in Hadley Edwards was
a petty vice in him. Probably Alejandro and Consuelo were
just newly hired at El Recobro or put on temporarily for this
affair alone.

He was beginning to think Alejandro might be mute
until the man engaged Ernie Gomez in conversation in
Spanish. His voice stayed low, but Ian caught it, even though
his own Spanish had rusted over too many years ago for him
to catch many words. He did know that Alejandro's patois

was not that of the Rio Grande. It wasn't Mexican Spanish, either, and certainly not the lyric Castilian he had listened to in Spain.

He had heard this dialect before and he remembered where.

His first-semester roommate at military school, the tin-soldier son of some comic-opera general in Managua, had inflected his Spanish just this way.

Except for the trip to the study with her, he hadn't gotten a moment alone with Sam, not that he needed one any longer. The need to tell her he was an alcoholic had been taken care of by Black Springs's gossip about the fight. Not that it made more than the slightest difference how she came by the knowledge, but it took away his principal reason for being here at all.

Still, he was surprised to find that he felt faintly sorry when the evening ended and he drove toward the highway.

The red eyes of the taillights of Ernie's station wagon were half a mile ahead of him. The only other breaks in the pitch blackness were the cold lightpoints of the stars. Beside him on the seat of the MG the briefcase with the house plans bounced as if restless when the car hit a rare ripple in the roadway. He had forgotten the briefcase as he prepared to leave—or had he?

He had said good-night to Hadley and Sam, waved to them in the doorway from the parking apron. The door had closed, but when he backed the MG around the Cadillac, it opened again. Sam ran out light-footed through the shaft of light coming from the hall. She didn't say a word as she thrust the case through the open car window opposite him. He didn't talk, either. She ran back to the house as swiftly as she had left it.

When he got well past the butte he saw the outside lights of the house go out in his rearview mirror at the same moment a full moon ballooned over the top ridge of Cuchillo Peak. No glow had warned him of its coming. The sky was cloudless and the air must have been superdry to permit no reflection. One second there had been nothing in front of him but Ernie's distant car, no high black outlines of the mountains, nothing. Then, the moon was simply *there*, the whole round white disk of it.

Something inside him grabbed him hard. He knew exactly where he was on the old D Cross A.

He stopped the car but left it running, not even pulling off the road. To his left—in the tangled bunch grass—was the ruined foundation. How could he possibly have missed it on the drive out yesterday? Maybe because he hadn't *wanted* to see it.

He didn't leave the car, but he sat and stared at the old rocks while the moon cut a ten-degree arc in the night sky, washing away the stars in its path.

This was far and away more dangerous than looking at the painting, something he never would have expected.

As he finished shaving there was a knock on the door.

Jody had brought the rolls and coffee, and both Sunday papers. Somewhere, too, he had promoted a glass of what appeared to be real orange juice. The flustered look of earlier had gone, and the boy was a strangely sobered one.

"Can I talk to you for just a second, Mr. MacAndrews?" he said. His father must have told him about the names. Good.

"Sure, but make it fast. I'm hungry," Ian said.

"Well, it's this, sir. It has to do with what happened night before last across the road." Hell! Not that again. Jody blinked and swallowed, or rather, gulped. His voice had squeaked as if it were still changing. "It's John Begley. He says—he says he might have to *waste* you, Mr. MacAndrews!"

"Waste"? That ugly word from that ugly war that had played almost as much havoc with the language as it had with lives.

"People do a lot of talking, Jody. I wouldn't put too much stock in talk."

"I don't know, Mr. MacAndrews. John's a pretty fierce *hombre*, honest."

"Just where did you hear he was going to 'waste' me, anyway?"

"From my sister, M.L. She's the waitress across the road at the Buckhorn. She's John's—girlfriend—I reckon."

"Thanks, Jody. I'll be careful." That, apparently, was all the boy needed to hear. If his New York friend would just be careful, it would somehow make things right. Funny. Here was what well might be genuine danger, and yet it seemed as nothing compared to his dread at the foundation under last night's moon.

And M.L. was Jody's sister.

He ate his breakfast, chewing without tasting, as he contemplated the leather briefcase.

Chapter VIII

"All right, Jennings," Smith Wyndham, senior partner and general manager at Wyndham & Keats, said over the phone, "I'll give you a month. But if you're not back in town and on the job by then, we'll have to start looking for a new art director. These fall schedules can't wait."

"Thanks, Smitty." Ian smiled. Wyndham's heavy executive act never failed to amuse him. It usually *was* a country boy from Nebraska such as Smitty who came on tough when he made it in Manhattan, operating on the theory that if anyone in the trade discovered he was a nice guy they would knife him. Ian had asked for an extra ten days; the full month had been Wyndham's idea—not that Ian would need it. "Do me a favor, Smitty?" he asked. "There's an editor at Hampton House named Lee Berman. Find out something about her, would you?"

"Sure. I'll put Nancy on it. Where will she be able to reach you—at that Yuck Motel or whatever the hell it's called?"

"Yes. I'll be here as long as I'm in Black Springs. Oh, she'll have to ask for me under the name MacAndrews."

There was silence, but only for a second. Smith Wyndham was quick on the uptake and Ian knew, although he had never been told, that Gene Weaver had filled him in on the troubles in Chicago. Gene must have had to level all the way with Wyndham to get Ian the job with W & K. "What's the big interest in the Berman broad?" Wyndham said. He probably thought Lee Berman was another Laurie.

"She has something that belongs—that *might* belong to me."

"You want her to know you're asking about her?"

"Not for the moment."

"Okay. Nancy's pretty sneaky. She'll even get her bra size for you."

Ian chuckled. "It's not that kind of interest," he said, knowing it would disappoint Wyndham, a dedicated womanizer who assumed all other men were, too. "But if she looks interesting, *you* might want to know."

"I might at that."

"Thanks again, Smitty."

"Don't mention it. Just remember—one month."

Wyndham hung up. Ian looked at his watch. It was a quarter to twelve in New York. Smitty had probably been looking at his watch, too. Where would he be starting that three-hour lunch today... Sardi's?... the St. Moritz? Some agency people got jaded by New York and the high-voltage advertising game where big deals were cut over *boeuf bourguignon* and brandy; but not Smith Wyndham. He never tired of it, never flagged. Ian couldn't picture Smitty back in his hometown in the cornfields a hundred and fifty miles west of Omaha.

Quarter to twelve in Manhattan, quarter to ten in Black Springs—he was due in Ernie's office in fifteen minutes. He decided to walk. If Wyndham were going to Sardi's, he would be walking, too.

He glanced at the briefcase on the desk as he left the room. It wasn't the first look he had taken at it since Sunday morning, but he hadn't touched it.

M.L. was hurrying across the road to the Buckhorn. She must have been talking to Jody, who leaned against the outside wall under the canopy. The girl either didn't see Ian or didn't want to. The bartender was standing in the door of the Buckhorn and he tossed a careless wave in Ian's direction.

As Ian passed the office, he got a glimpse of Harry behind the desk. The poor devil looked like a man in a coma. Sunday afternoon Ian had stopped at the office and tried in vain to give Jody a couple of dollars for the car wash. They had talked a bit about Begley's link with M.L. The boy didn't come right out and say so, but it seemed certain that his sister was living with Begley—somewhere—and that it had Harry Kimbrough beside himself. He hadn't spoken to his daughter since she left home a month ago. All discourse had been through Jody. Ian guessed that M.L. had just now concluded one of the contacts she still made with her brother, and that

Harry had witnessed it. They looked to be a real brother and sister act.

Without really expecting any, Ian stepped inside the office and asked for mail. Harry looked at the pigeonholes behind him, shook his head, and bent again over the ledger he was writing in. He didn't say a word. Jody hadn't greeted Ian, either. All the Kimbroughs, apparently, were having a rotten day.

As he walked along the side of the north-south highway toward Frontera Street and the strip shopping-center where Ernie and his partners had their suite of offices, Ian picked up another wave, this time from the driver of a wrecker towing what was left of a late-model car. It took him a second to place the driver, the young man at the Texaco station. The car he was towing was crushed so badly it looked like a loser in a demolition derby, but the driver of the wrecker was beaming like a winner.

The shopping center that housed the law office sprawled across the street from Stafford's, and when he turned the corner on Frontera, Ian spotted the Edwards Cadillac parked in front of the old general store where the curb had been painted yellow for a loading zone. He almost crossed the street, but decided not to.

After he turned into the shopping center, with Stafford's now at his back, a shout reached him.

"MacAndrews—I say, old man!" It was Tim Springer, Hadley's pilot. Beside him stood Dr. Jim and Cissy Pendleton.

"Come and have a cup of coffee with us as soon as we stow all this," Pendleton called. He had a rich, ringing voice. Given any facility with language he must have been a real winner in the pulpit.

Cissy Pendleton piped up, "Please do, Ian."

"I have a date with Ernie Gomez," Ian called back. He checked his watch. "Right this minute, as a matter of fact."

"Another time then, Ian," Pendleton said. He looked disappointed.

Ian turned and headed across the center's parking lot to the offices of Gomez, Gomez, & Trujillo, wondering if Sam Edwards, too, was somewhere behind him.

The plate-glass door of the suite was propped open by one of the reception-room chairs he had seen on his visit here last week. Standing on a short stepladder and applying an oil-can spout to the cylinder door-closer, a diminutive, frail, old man was swaying a little as he worked. It was one of the old Spanish gentlemen he was beginning to call *los hermanos* in his mind and who had been his silent dinner companions at Anita's on Thursday night and again on Friday, when Ian had gone to the Comida after the fight with Begley. He was pretty sure it was the one called Juan, but not sure enough. He held himself to a *"¿Qué tal, viejo?"*

Juan, or Bautista, whichever one this was, tried to bow from his perch, and for a moment Ian thought he would have to put his hand up to keep him from pitching forward on his friendly brown face. He wobbled but righted himself, dignity intact.

"Buenos dias, señor," the old man said.

Ian entered the reception room.

"Ian!" Carrie Spletter said from behind her desk. "Nice to see you. Sit down for a moment, won't you? Tony got in from fishing just this morning and he's in with Ernie now. They shouldn't be much longer. It's a case Tony will take to court next week and Ernie's been going over his brief."

"No hurry," Ian said. He sat down on a settee at the side of the room and plucked a copy of *Time* from a pile on a low table in front of him.

The phone rang and Carrie answered it. He put the magazine down, but he tried not to listen. It wasn't hard.

He had been in Black Springs just a week tomorrow, and it seemed he couldn't take a breath or make a turn without seeing someone he knew, someone he had touched, brushed against, or collided with. How many faces had Smith Wyndham recognized in *his* fifteen-minute walk? Except for the people in the agency and a few clients, Ian hadn't met this many people in a year. . . .

"Ian, sorry to have kept you waiting." It was Ernie.

Tony Gomez had come from Ernie's office with him. He seemed a younger version of his brother, still in jeans and a fishing jacket, and with a couple of days' growth of dark beard. He looked as if he had driven through the night. Ernie introduced him. He had Ernie's warm smile.

"How was the fishing?" Ian asked as they shook hands.

"Not good. Caught a few little fellows before the rains turned the Chama into gumbo."

Ernie had moved to Carrie Spletter's desk and had been sorting through some letters while Ian and Tony chatted. He turned to Ian now.

"You mind if we get out of here for our talk, Ian? Once in a while I get cabin fever in that office."

"Where do you want to go?"

"I thought we might drive out to the country club. There won't be a soul in the lunch bar until noon, anyway. We can eat there when we're done."

"Sounds fine." He had completely forgotten the country club. It wasn't a surprising lapse of memory. Unless things had changed the two-room adobe clubhouse the ranchers and merchants had built right after the war was a highly forgettable place.

"Will I need to bring your file, Ian—or any part of it?"

"No. This is something new and different."

Ernie's forehead wrinkled. "I was hoping—" He didn't go on.

"What, Ernie?"

"It wasn't important." Ernie chewed at his lower lip.

"I *know* what you were hoping, Ernie. You were hoping I had changed my mind about meeting the terms of Sarah's will. Sorry."

Ernie turned to his secretary. "I don't know how long we'll be at the club, Carrie. Don't let anybody call us there, please... except Hadley."

"All right, Ernie," Carrie said.

Ernie turned back to Ian. Something seemed awkward, faintly strained, between Ernie and Carrie Spletter but it wasn't hard to figure out. There would have been some display of affection now if Ian hadn't been there.

"Let's go," Ernie said. "Sorry about exempting Hadley, but he'll be out of town tomorrow and I need to speak with him before he leaves."

"Perfectly all right," Ian said.

The Cadillac was gone from the front of Stafford's. Would Sam be going out of town with Hadley?

Ian and Gomez drove north on the highway and took a right at the crossroads. The east-west road Ian had taken down from Mescalero Gap bridged the railroad, and a block beyond the tracks a gravel road led away from the blacktop in a big, southwesterly, dusty sweep around the edge of Mex Town. Half a mile away, nestled among the adobe houses and trailers and corrugated metal shacks, Ian could see La Yglesia de San Jose, the little church he and Jo Martinez would have been married in. He didn't look away from it nearly as quickly as he had every time his eyes fell on it in the first few years after the war, but he didn't let his gaze linger, either. Jorge Martinez was buried in San Jose's graveyard. Another Chupadera grave to visit, the last of them, but it would have to wait a bit.

"Did you grow up here, Ernie?" Ian said.

"No. Tony and I are from Socorro. Our *barrio* looked just like Mex Town, though." Ernie made a faint, feral growl. "As a refiner of the virtues, Ian, poverty is greatly overrated."

"I suppose it is. Sorry I can't say I *know* it is. I guess I've never had any firsthand experience of it."

"For Pete's sake, don't apologize! I've never felt it a crime to be born with a silver spoon in your mouth. And I look with a certain amount of suspicion at people who want to spit one out."

Ian laughed. "Do you mean like me? Refusing to take Sarah's money?"

"No. Well, wait a second. Maybe I *do*." With the lawyer's dark complexion it was difficult to tell if he was blushing, but he did look honestly surprised at the thought. They didn't speak again until they reached the club.

"If you're wondering, Ian," Ernie said when he switched off the engine, "I am a member here, but I didn't integrate this dump. I understand they actually invited in the one *vato* mayor Black Springs has ever had, a popular guy named Espinosa. Word went out that he was decent enough 'to be an Anglo.' That was a dozen years ago, before my time here. I wouldn't have bothered the board for membership, but I actually like to play golf now and then. As a kid I had hopes of being the next Lee Trevino. I caddied for him at Socorro once—before he hit it big."

The Black Springs Country Club had seen some ups, but a lot more downs, in twenty years. There were only nine holes when the course was laid out, and that hadn't changed. There were bunkers now, but already clogged with weeds. The ninth green snuggled up to the clubhouse on its left. The first greens built here had been oiled sand. The present grass ones—ragged, unkempt—didn't seem much of an improvement. Hard work often went for nothing in this even-harder country.

Ian had never gotten interested in golf, but there had been a MacAndrews family membership once, and once the club had for three short months held on to a cook good enough to bring him here for drinks and dinner a few times. He had made many more trips just for drinks. They were sick drinks even then. Those excursions had stopped after a messy brawl with the captain who ran the North Oscuras tracking station on the missile range. Military officers stationed in Chupadera County were given guest memberships here. He had heard at the time that the captain never used his club privileges after the scrap, which neither of them, truth to tell, had won.

Ernie was right. The clubhouse was empty, its door locked, as a matter of fact. Ernie dug a key from his pocket, flipped a couple of switches once he opened the door, and set a swamp air-conditioner roaring. He led the way through the old dance floor section to the lunch-bar overlooking that sad ninth green. He motioned Ian to a table in the corner and went to a cooler at the end of the bar.

"Coke?" Ernie said. Ian nodded. Ernie picked up a pad hanging on a cord fastened to the cooler, wrote on it, and pulled two pop-top cans from the cooler.

"Dan Smith will be turning up in a while to tend bar and make sandwiches," he said as he came to the table and sat down across from Ian. "He lives over in Mex Town and he can see the club from his trailer. He doesn't bother to make the trip unless he sees a car in the parking lot. We haven't served dinner here since I've been a member."

Smith? Ian had to ask. "Please don't take this wrong, Ernie, but an Anglo in Mex Town?"

Laughter burst from Ernesto Gomez. "Shame on you, Ian! What do you think we are here in Black Springs? A *segregated* society?" He sobered. "Dan Smith—is as black as the ace of spades...no pun intended."

They opened the Cokes.

"All right," Ernie said when he had downed half of his, "you know you've got me as nosy as a young coyote. If it's not about Sarah's will or the estate, what is it you want to talk to me about?"

For the first time Ian felt doubt about what he was about to do. On Friday night he had well considered that it could be dangerous in some unknown way to press this scheme, had faced the possibility without a qualm. Up against it here and now it looked different.

Wasn't there an old axiom of physics that said something

to the effect that a system observed is a system disturbed? If that was so, how deep and violent would the disturbance be? And how many other people would it eventually affect?

How much did he owe to other people?

"Ernie," he said, "I don't know if you can do what I'm about to ask. Tell me if you can't do it, or won't. I'd do it for myself, except that for a whole bunch of reasons I want to stay outside the process." There must have been something powerfully arresting in his voice that he couldn't hear himself. Ernie had his Coke halfway to his mouth, but it stopped there.

"I want you to find out for me," Ian went on, "everything you possibly can about Jacky Begley's parents, particularly his mother. I want to know exactly where he was born and exactly when. If she was hospitalized for his birth, I want to know who paid the bill. I want to know her entire history— everything she did, the names of all her relatives and acquaintances and friends, if she worked and where, what people who knew her have to say about her. I want to know every move she made in the years right before and after Begley was born. I want to know especially if she's alive and where she can be found. And I want all this fast. Can you do it? *Will* you do it?"

Without the lag of a millisecond Ernesto Gomez agreed to do it.

"You're entitled to know what this is about," Ian said.

"That won't be necessary, Ian."

Chapter IX

The nineteenth-century road from Tularosa up to the Mescalero and Ruidoso had been widened and repaved since Ian left the basin, but it still ran about where the old one had—north of Little Round Mountain, right by the broken adobe wall that was all that remained of Blazer's Mill, and to the north of the stone cathedral the Apaches built forty-odd years before under the guidance of missionary Padre Albert Braun.

When he left New York, the last stretch of road he would have expected to find himself driving in the MG was this one. He hadn't thought of it in all the years since he left the basin. The usual way from Black Springs to the reservation and the resort town high in the White Mountain pines led up through the Arroyo Concho on the road he would take back down tonight, on the third leg of an isosceles triangle ninety miles along the sides. His map told him the county still hadn't paved long sections of that third leg, but the afternoon sun would slant sharply by the time he was ready to leave Ruidoso, and it would be late enough in the day for him to tell if a storm was likely to catch him. If a big one threatened, he could go back out by this good all-weather highway.

Pure whim had brought him up here and brought him in a roundabout way he couldn't possibly have foretold when he got up.

The only thing he had done in the three days between Sam's party and setting Ernie to work was to send Jody over to the Texaco station with the MG to get the carburetor reset for the mile-high air of the basin. He had started to tell the boy to take care of it at least a dozen times on Monday, but it wasn't until Tuesday afternoon when Harry came on duty at the desk that he gave him the word. It seemed a surrender of a sort. True, the little car had wheezed and gasped, but it could have managed well enough if he only stayed in Black Springs long enough to satisfy himself about Jacky Begley.

If he had still nursed any doubts about Jody's instincts, they were erased when young Kimbrough's eyes widened at the request and a smile rearranged the freckles on the bridge of his nose. The look was new, different, knowing. He looked almost sly. "I guess this means you're going to stay in Black Springs even a little longer, huh?"

"None of your business, kid," Ian said, playing once again the role he had cast himself in at the time of the car wash. "Look, Tommy Lee may be setting the carburetor, but you're the one I'll hold responsible. You'd better gas up while you're over there and then take a run up to some place high like Mescalero Gap, maybe, and see that the work's been done right. Savvy?"

"Yes, sir!"

It seemed Jody and the car might reach the Texaco

station before the words died away. He hadn't even reached for
the twenty-dollar bill Ian held out to him. One of these days
he would ask the youngster if he had a driver's license. It
might not matter, anyway. Perhaps in Albuquerque and Santa
Fe the authorities were tough about the legal driving age, but
in Chupadera County the cops probably didn't care one whit
more than they had when Ian was taking the LaSalle to town
at thirteen. Rural kids had it all over their city cousins when
it came to getting an early start on wheels.

Today, Thursday, marked a full week since he had checked
in at the Yucca. Since the dinner at El Recobro, time had
been playing tricks with him that by now should be familiar:
minutes and hours stretching out on the one hand, collapsing
on the other, so that it seemed at any one moment that he
had spent an eternity stranded in the Ojos Negros and in the
next that he had drifted over Mescalero Gap just this morning.

After breakfast he decided he ought to get hold of
something to read if he didn't want to find himself climbing
the walls as he had since Saturday, with the only break in the
monotony the trip to the country club with Ernie.

He drove to the Black Springs Public Library on Stanton
Street and found that a new sumpstone building housed the
books Hattie Spletter, Carrie's aunt, had guarded through his
boyhood. The librarian, a middle-aged woman in a bright
yellow shirtwaist dress, could have been Hattie Spletter's
twin, although plain, stern old Hattie would never have
decked herself out in the strands of turquoise and Indian
silver he saw on Elizabeth Maynes, if the woman at the
checkout desk was indeed the head librarian whose name was
burned like a cattle brand into the wooden plate in front of
the telephone.

She had her nose in a copy of *Harper's Bazaar* and didn't
look up as Ian passed her, but she probably looked him over
pretty well as he walked back toward the stacks.

Elizabeth Maynes had no other customers this morning,
and it didn't look as if a single browser had tracked caliche
dust across her carpeting in a month.

Two thirds of the books on the half-filled shelves were
probably gifts, and that thought brought another.

He went to the desk. "Miss Maynes," he said, "or is it
Mrs. Maynes?"

The woman looked up from her reading. "It's Mrs., but I

answer best to Liz." She peered at him as if she hadn't seen him enter, and maybe she hadn't. "Say, aren't you—"

"*—the tourist from New York who's staying at the Yucca*," he finished it for her. He heard the snap in his voice and regretted it, but for Christ's sake! Enough was enough.

She laughed. "I guess you've heard *that* about as much as you want. Black Springs is just as small as it looks, you know."

The laugh and her wide smile made him feel a little less put out.

"Perhaps you can help me," he said.

"Sure hope so."

"If you received a gift of books here from the estate of someone who died about three years ago, say, would you keep them all together as a sort of special collection or would they be scattered through the library?"

"I don't rightly know. I've just been librarian here a year and that kind of thing hasn't happened. Three years ago? They'd most likely be 'scattered,' as you say."

"Tell me then," he said, "where do you keep your Shakespeare?"

"What we have is in the classics section, that stack against the north wall, near the corner. Can I find something for you?"

"No thanks. I'll just nose around myself."

He found Shakespeare, the Doubleday Rockwell Kent edition his bombardier Peter Bergener had lugged overseas with him, cheek by jowl with *Valley of the Dolls* by Jacqueline Susann. Classics? The hefty Shakespeare looked as if it had done no more useful service than pressing napkins—if it had even once been taken out on loan.

He was about to give up on the book he was searching for and try to find something, anything, he could take back to the Yucca with him, when he saw it, next to *Gulliver's Travels*.

A small book—perhaps six inches by four, and an inch and a half thick—its once bright green leather cover had dulled to a muddy olive long ago, and the gold inlay in the filigreed tooling on the spine had filmed over to a flat, dead yellow. He had seen this book many times before. He stroked the spine with his fingertips before he pulled the tiny volume from the shelf. The old leather was rough and cracked in places.

When he opened it, he found a yellowed certificate pasted to the inside cover. It said the book had been awarded as an "additional prize for first place" to Miss Agnes Elizabeth Hall in the annual Elocution Contest at Edwardsville High School, Edwardsville, Illinois. The certificate carried the signature of the school principal, E. F. Barr, and the date, December 20, 1886. Whatever color ink the delicate, careful script might first have been written in it had faded to umber now. There were no endpapers—the title page faced the cover directly—endpapers must not have been the fashion when the book was published by Thomas Tegg, 73 Cheapside, London—MDCCCXLII, according to the lines of still clean, sharp-edged Bodoni at the bottom of the page.

1842! The little book had already seen forty-four years before Miss Hall won it. They made books to last for the ages then; some of those printed since he was born had already been digested by the acids in their own cheap paper.

What had made Miss Hall's speech in 1886 so memorable it deserved an "additional" prize? An old, hoarded, treasured book such as this one couldn't have been awarded as a casual afterthought.

He turned one more page, and there facing the beginning of *The Tempest*, in a hand far more firm than the principal's and nothing like as faded, he read: "To Nash Ortiz... Christmas 1905... Agnes Hall MacAndrews." He knew for a fact it hadn't been passed along casually on that occasion, either.

Drunk, sober, or in some stupefying limbo in between, Ian MacAndrews was aware that he had done a good many culpable things in his time—but he had never *stolen* anything, nor been tempted to, until now. To his shame, he actually sneaked a look at Elizabeth Maynes. The librarian was lost in her magazine again. No one else had entered the building. It was a small book. It would scarcely make a bulge if he slipped it inside his shirt. No one who prowled these stacks would ever miss it.

He closed the book, slid it back into its place on the shelf, turned, and began walking toward the door. He stopped near the desk. Elizabeth Maynes looked up with an absent, semiquestioning smile.

He stood there for a second. What if he checked Ignacio's book out, reported it lost or damaged, and paid for it? That wouldn't quite equate with outright theft, would it? Mrs.

Maynes would *have* to issue him a card. After all, he owned property in Chupadera County, and with all the taxes on it paid, even if it was Sarah Balutan who had paid them.

No! Taking out a library card would be even more of a surrender than sending Jody to take care of the MG's carburetor. In the Jonathan Swift he had found alongside the Doubleday Shakespeare, Gulliver had been bound fast to Lilliputian sands not by chains or cables, but by a net woven from flimsy threads—and Ian MacAndrews was as alien as a Gulliver here in the sands of Black Springs.

He nodded to Elizabeth Maynes and left.

Outside the library he checked his watch. It was 9:13. There wasn't a chance of finding anything fit to read in Black Springs now that Elizabeth Maynes had failed him. He hadn't looked very hard after he found Ignacio's book.

He could get down to Alamogordo and back by noon. In the larger town he could surely find some kind of store that sold books. He didn't remember one's being there twenty years ago, but the growth of Holloman and the White Sands Proving Grounds in the past two decades must have brought with it at least a handful of readers who wanted something besides the pulp the paperback racks at either base exchange offered them. And too, the drive would take him out of Chupadera County and the Ojos Negros for a few hours and into the even larger Tularosa Basin, not a dramatic change, but right now a welcome one as he killed some of that excess of time he had until Ernie got back to him.

Once past Three Rivers—a gas station, post office, and little more—the highway unrolled like Hadley Edwards's landing strip. A curving overpass led him past the Ruidoso road and then through sleepy Tularosa. On his left the twelve-thousand-foot-high twin peaks of Sierra Blanca, timbered to near the top even on this hot, dry side, kept pace with him for twenty miles. The malpais was running out on his right, and the Oscuras had hidden themselves well behind him. Even the jagged San Andres had long since rounded into the low, treeless lomas flanking Rhodes Pass, north of where the distant lift of the Organ Mountains came into view at two o'clock and level.

It was unprepossessing country, filled to the roadside with tangled mesquite and clumps of greasewood, flat as piss

on a platter, and not worth a glance—if he didn't look to the
hazy mountains. They made the difference.

Between him and the Organs, the great sand sea suddenly flashed into a solid bar of white. Twenty miles still
separated him and them. From here anyone who had never
been inside the White Sands park would never know what he
was looking at, would never dream of the mountainous dunes
the southerly winds had lifted through the ages as invisible,
powdery clouds from the old dry lake south of Holloman and
then piled up like improbable snowdrifts on the basin floor,
dunes awesome under the sun, spectral and haunting by
moonlight, as he had seen them so often during the picnic
suppers he and Jo Martinez had taken there.

Could he look anywhere in this land without some kind
of sand getting in his eyes?

He glued those eyes to the highway now, a new four-
lane, divided one, and kept them there the rest of the way
into Alamogordo, turning them from the lane he was in only
when they caught sight of a sign that read "Nike Cartage Co."
He slowed the MG.

B.J. Howland's truckyard consisted of a prefab office
building looking as empty as a dried cocoon from two springs
ago, a trailer home with a television antenna on a mast that
could carry most of the canvas of the *Cutty Sark,* and two
livestock trailers down on rims from which the tires had been
stripped. If he had spotted B.J.'s cab, or even a car or
pickup, anything that might tell him he was home, he might
have dropped in to rap with the old trucker, but the trailer
house looked as deserted as the office, and the yard was
empty except for a dumpy woman—wearing a bathrobe of the
same dreary maroon flannel U.S. Army hospitals issued in
World War II, and with her gray hair done up in curlers—
hanging clothes on a wire stretched between the trailer home
and the empty little office. He smiled. The flapping wash told
him that B.J. wore long johns every day of the week—even
in this week's searing weather. As he rolled by, the woman
jammed a clothespin in her mouth and waved to him. Sure, a
wife of B.J. Howland would offer a friendly wave to anyone.
He waved back and speeded up.

For the few more miles into town, the trailer homes,
singly, then in clusters, finally in full-fledged parks where
sprinklers tried to coax new green up through the caliche,
came thick and fast. The railroad he had crossed on the

overpass at the curve at Tularosa was on his right now, and as
he neared the center of town, long rows of Lombardy pop-
lars, not yet veiled in their August and September webworm
gauze, screened the tracks. In a long, skinny park, the shell
of a Nike rocket with blue-and-white Air Force markings
pointed its needle nose toward the sky. A sign for the
Alamogordo Chamber of Commerce, proclaiming the town
the rocket center of the known universe, came next, and then
he had to slow down again; he had joined a stream of traffic
heavy enough to dam up six or eight cars and trucks at every
stoplight.

He reached the heart of the business district at Tenth
Street and eased into the left turn lane, sure that if he was
going to find what he was looking for, this first block off White
Sands Boulevard was where he would find it, knowing, too,
that he would find something he *wasn't* looking for—the bar
where he had gotten into that awful, bloody dustup with
another missile-range officer, a colonel this time, whose blond,
globe-breasted, lute-bottomed wife had taken him to bed in
the married-officers quarters while her husband was on TDY
in Turkey. Damn it! Could he summon up no *pleasant*
memories? The wife, for all that she seemed willing to try
everything she had ever read or heard about, hadn't been
worth the fight. He still felt sorry for the colonel, more for
having that wife than because he had forced Ian to punch him
out when the woman's neighbors had spilled the beans. He
hoped the poor guy had retired with a couple of general's
stars at least.

He had guessed right about a place to buy books and
magazines. He swung into an angled parking space in front of
a store where the slanted plate-glass windows once common
in every American town framed a door whose transom was
plugged with a window air-conditioner.

Its sign read CHOLLA NEWSSTAND & VARIETIES—BOOKS -
PERIODICALS - NEWSPAPERS - TOBACCO - GUNS & AMMO.

Once inside, he found himself in an outback Marshall
Field's that sold everything—or stocked it, anyway.

Enough rifles, shotguns, and side arms to outfit a regi-
ment of Green Berets were racked against one wall, and
against the other the owners had installed a glass-walled,
walk-in humidor housing a selection of cigars and pipe tobacco that if lit at once would make a smoke screen big enough
to hide the *Forrestal*. Tiered tables held ceramic bric-a-brac—

some fairly expensive pieces, even a parade of Hummel
figurines. The complement of officers and men and their
dependents at the two military installations southwest of town
must have swelled enormously to bring to Alamogordo enough
of the kind of customers the Cholla would need to stay in
business.

One single display island that ran almost the entire
length of the store held the Cholla's books, arranged with as
little regard to subject matter as those in that woeful "classics"
section back in Black Springs. But to his surprise the books
seemed really there, stuffed and crammed into the shelves,
and piled so high on the top of the island they looked as
if they might avalanche. He discovered a paperback copy of
E. M. Forster's *Aspects of the Novel*, enough Teilhard de
Chardin to fill the wants of all the charismatic Catholics in
New Mexico, every single title of Hermann Hesse's he could
remember, found Camus, Sartre, Hemingway, Faulkner, and
all the "Big Boys" Dorothy Parker had recast in those wickedly
barbed rhymes. A *New York Times* best-seller list was
thumbtacked to a section of the display and penciled check
marks showed which of the new hot books the Cholla had in
stock. Only two titles of the twenty on the list were left
unchecked.

He started grabbing. A slim girl he hadn't noticed slipped
from behind a counter and handed him a shopping bag.

When his bag was almost full, he nearly tripped over a
stack of newspapers. Sunday's issue of *The New York Times*
looked up at him. Two more stacks revealed that he could
have had Sunday's *Washington Post* and the Chicago *Tribune*
as well. He took the *Times*.

After he paid the girl behind the counter he stepped out
into the sun and shoved his purchases into the passenger's
seat of his little car. He looked at the paper and the bulging
shopping bag. He could read for a solid month. Hell, he
wouldn't be here near that long.

He hadn't intended turning toward Ruidoso on his way
back to Black Springs, but when he reached the junction with
U.S. 70 on the northern edge of Tularosa, the thought of
holing up in his empty room at the Yucca—even with the
books, magazines, and newspapers—brought a return of the
brown mood of the morning. The billboard at the turn
announcing the quarter-horse races at the Downs turned the

trick. He would get to the track too late for today's first post time, but it would be good to see a race again. Betting the horses had never appealed to him, but he did like to see them run, and not from the clubhouse, but from the rail, where they thundered past him, charging to some brute glory he could only guess at.

The last horse race he had seen was the Stars and Stripes Handicap at Arlington Park three years ago when he still worked for Gene Weaver in Chicago. Gene, a heavy plunger at the tracks and in the bookie joints around the Loop, had hauled Ian with him to the northwest-suburban track. Ian hadn't spent a penny at the pari-mutuel windows, but he showed up at Laurie's that night five hundred dollars richer after winning a bet from the senior partner not *on* a horse race, but *about* one, the one run every Labor Day on the track at Ruidoso Downs he was heading toward this minute. Gene had scoffed when Ian told him that the richest horse race in the world, with a purse dwarfing those of the Preakness, the Kentucky Derby, or any of the races at other great tracks like Longchamp in Paris or Epsom Downs, was run each September in an obscure mountain town in south-central New Mexico. Gene had begun by jeering, "I got a C-note says you're as full of it as a Christmas goose, MacAndrews," and Ian had worked him up to half a thousand. After a call to the Chicago *Tribune* from the Jockey Club at Arlington (where the two of them had been knocking back double martinis before a lunch they didn't even order until three o'clock), Gene paid up.

The billboard that lured Ian into making the turn on the Mescalero-Ruidoso road hadn't promised anything that big today, just a run-of-the-season card, but with a couple of claiming races that could be interesting. He felt a little thrill of pleasure as the MG's tires whined along the new blacktop. He knew the tiny resort town well. He had fished the nearby streams countless times as a boy, and even as late as when he was painting so furiously in that last violent storm of work, and he had spent hours in the pines on Sierra Blanca with his sketchpad or his easel. Three of the oils that had burned with the bunkhouse had been done on the Mescalero, and one at least had truly pleased him, a portrait of an ancient, silent Apache, one of the last of the Mimbreños who had ridden with old Chief Nana after Victorio was killed at Tres Castillos, or so *el viejo* claimed.

As he entered the last curve before Padre Braun's cathedral something in his rearview mirror caught his eye. The mirror framed the Great White Sands and the Organ Mountains as if they were a painting on whose composition and texture a great deal of thought and feeling had been spent. The reflection was an unexpected, happy accident of discovered art. He pulled over on the shoulder of the highway and left the car.

Yes, indeed—the view would make one hell of a landscape oil.

From here the sands looked to be one long, wafer-thin, fog-bank streak. To the north the malpais made another lateral, as black as the first was white. Beyond the lava flow, the San Andres crouched like a pride of tawny lions, and far across the basin the granite flutes of the Organ Mountains piped to the heavens, their spiky peaks feathery and not quite perfectly defined in the faint summer haze. Any real artist would be humbled by the view. Nature held secret powers of abstraction even the most inventive modern painter knew nothing of, capturing the land in a way no artist could. A real artist, though, looking at this, would have to try.

He stretched his arms and hands straight out, palms flat against the distance, thumbs touching. He moved this half-frame about until he caught exactly what he had seen in the mirror. To have a chance of getting this on canvas would take a daring mixing of techniques, something he never shied from in the good days, not after he first saw the combined stone-and-metal Max Balutan had worked on up in Taos. An all-out attack with all his tools might work for this.

Yes. He could use the painting knife for the foreground, pile the color on as thick as frosting on a cake, almost sculpt it—the way Max might have done it had the old boy ever worked in oil. As he found his way then into the heart of the painting, dry-brush passages might bring it all together, but he could sense that better when he came to it. The whole thing would have to be done at the speed of light, maybe without even an underpainting, and as he worked he would have to feel his way into the incredible heat of not just today, but of all the billions of years since those sands drifted as wayward cosmic gas. If he was lucky enough and honest enough he could...

God in heaven. One brushstroke would be too many, a

million wouldn't be enough. And the rage was coming back. What had gone wrong with him?

He got back in the car and roared onto the blacktop. He was shaking, and the shaking didn't stop until he rolled through the Mescalero reservation and reached the village limits of Ruidoso. It had been a close, terrifying—a drunken— moment.

As he had expected, the town was crowded. What he hadn't expected, although by rights he should have, was how it had grown. New motel jostled even newer motel, and where a restaurant, a shop, or a bar had filled only the corner of a lot before, a dozen now beckoned. Men decked out in Stetsons and western suits, and women wearing everything from hotpants to squaw dresses to slacks and blouses, bustled in and out of doors or walked the sidewalks and parking aprons in front of the brightly painted buildings, enough of them to make him wonder if anybody was actually at the track today. Two out of three cars carried Texas plates, and three out of every four bore the emblem of Cadillac or Mercedes.

The old Nob Hill Restaurant that had commanded the empty acreage east of town in genteel solitude twenty years ago was now well within the village limits and surrounded by other buildings. On the heights, condos and hotel-sized A-frames bristled. Huge log cabins and even bigger stone dwellings, many with partly hidden stables and servants' quarters, peeped out from behind the pines.

If the races here were still a secret to most of the country, the resort complex itself was an even bigger one.

The parking lot at the racetrack was as crowded as the town. He had to tour six rows before he found a space, passing the rear bumpers of a lipstick-red Maserati, RVs as big as the *QE2*, horse trailers and farrier's vans, and pickups on tires big enough to land a 727 and girdled with chrome of dazzling insolence, with spotlights on bar mounts as lofty as any railroad signal bridge.

He was out of the MG and had it locked before he noticed the dented blue pickup he had pulled in next to.

It was Jacky Begley's old Ford pickup truck.

There seemed something a little different about it today. Sure! It was the rifle racked against the rear window of the cab. It hadn't been in the pickup on any of the other three occasions, he would swear to it.

His first impulse was to stay right here, wait for Begley, *have it out with him.*

But...damn it...beyond a couple of minor irritations, it had been a good day so far. There could be and probably was a quite innocent reason for Begley's keeping a rifle in his truck. Maybe some rancher had hired him to hunt coyotes. Begley didn't have it against his shoulder with Ian in his sights now, at any rate.

If he ran into him at the races, fine; if he didn't, fine, too. But there was no point in leaving the MG here and rubbing Begley's nose in it. He got back in the little car, backed out, and went looking for another place to park. He had to drive clear around the lot a couple of times before he found one.

Small world—and getting smaller.

Chapter X

He looked for Begley once, just once, as he went through the main gate, but when he joined the crowd at the rail, the general festival excitement of the race, the second of the day, caught him. He didn't want to see the man now, anyway, didn't really want to see him until Ernie Gomez delivered his report.

During the second race he found himself—to his amazement—cheering out loud for the ultimate winner, a long shot named Pecos Sal, a bay beauty he flattered himself he had picked right out of the gate. Good race. All in all, it could still be a damned good day.

These were strange horse races for anyone used to eastern tracks. He had forgotten the crapshoot (or maybe even Russian roulette) feel of them. Twenty or twenty-one seconds of pounding down a straightaway—no turns—and the run was done. A minor fault on the start could kill even the chances of an odds-on favorite, and there wasn't time in that lightning quarter-mile for much in the way of tactics, none at all for strategy. If the railbirds blinked, they could miss the finish, and if the purses here at Ruidoso were rich by usual racing standards, they were Croesus-like when you considered how much a winning horse and jockey earned by the second.

"Ian!"

In the hubbub around him he didn't even recognize the voice as that of a woman for a second, and it was another second before he remembered Begley wouldn't be calling him Ian.

He turned and saw Sam Edwards.

"Come on up to the box and say hello to Hadley," Sam said. He got the feeling that she had been standing there for several moments before she hailed him, and that the invitation wasn't an offhand one. She must have weighed the decision to ask him, weighed it carefully.

"I'd like that," he said, "if I won't be intruding." Yes, he would like that. It surprised him.

"You won't be intruding at all. No more than I was with you."

She was carrying a cardboard tray holding sandwiches and four plastic glasses of Coke, and he took it from her, one of his hands brushing hers. It was like that handshake the day he drove out to the slickrock. This brief contact carried the same light charge. They hadn't touched each other at all at the dinner party.

With so many people scurrying to the betting windows to collect from the last race or to place wagers on the next, and others rushing to the refreshment stand, it was impossible for the two of them to walk side by side when she stepped in front of him to lead the way. In the din around them talk was out of the question, too.

She threaded her way through the throng with her cotton skirt swinging from side to side, and with her hair, not exactly in a ponytail but gathered close in back, swinging, too. They walked in front of the section that held the boxes, and halfway past it she turned her head to the right, her face tilted upward and suddenly tight, eyes squinting. He turned and looked where she was looking.

Hadley was sitting in a box three tiers up, talking with Consuelo and Alejandro.

Couldn't the man even go to the men's room without servants?

Then he realized the three people in the box were in the middle of what looked to be a real give-and-take discussion, an animated talk among genuine equals, friends. The nagging feeling he had known when he sat at Hadley Edwards's dinner table came rushing back, but now it wasn't just a feeling.

There were no "servants" sitting in that box.

Then, as if a cue from an unseen prompter suddenly registered, Hadley looked down toward them—first at Sam.

There was just a nod to her, but in a quick shift of his eyes, unmistakably the result of whatever signal he received from her, he turned his head and looked at Ian. One big hand flew up and a smile broke across his face.

Consuelo and Alejandro, when they in turn looked to where Hadley's wave had been directed, seemed impassive.

A roar heralded the start of the fourth race, and the spectators in the boxes separating Ian and Sam from Hadley and the two Hispanics were on their feet screaming, and blocking Ian's view of the man in the wheelchair and his two companions. Sam and Ian had to go fifty feet past Hadley's box before Sam turned into a railed stairway to the aisle leading to the third tier, and from there back along another aisle to where her husband had beckoned to them. With the tray in his hands Ian had to keep his eyes on the narrow walkway, and by the time he and Sam reached the box and the waiting Hadley, he discovered that Alejandro and Consuelo had vanished. Something told him he had just been led a long, deliberate way around to give the pair time to disappear.

Once they were in the box Ian placed the tray on an empty seat and took the hand Hadley offered. Without a word Sam bent over the tray, picked up a Coke, handed it and a sandwich to Hadley, and then indicated that Ian should help himself. He shook his head and muttered his thanks. The refreshments were certainly intended for the four original occupants of the box. It struck him as odd that Sam hadn't commented on the couple's whereabouts, hadn't asked about them.

Hadley solved the puzzle for him—if only in part and only for the moment.

"The Vergaras will wait for us at the car, Sam," he said. "They seem to have had enough." Sam looked as if a weight had been lifted from her slim, square shoulders... but the weight came right back down when Hadley went on, "I guess they can't get excited about these short sprints, not after the hunter races Alejandro rode in back in Nicaragua."

He knew he wasn't meant to, but Ian picked up a quick, flickering warning, a slight shadow, in Sam's eyes as she looked at Hadley. If Hadley reacted to it, it was only with a half-smile of amusement, gone even as it came.

"Did you have any winners in the first four races, Ian?" Hadley said then.

"I never bet on horses, Hadley. I just like to watch them from time to time—and from trackside, where Sam found me."

"I must confess I like to put my money down, but like you, my personal preference is to watch them from the rail. In this damned rig, though, I can't see down there." He slapped the armrest of the wheelchair, not the electric one he had used at the party, but the kind that folded. He sounded mildly rueful, but there wasn't any self-pity in his voice. "I wouldn't be at all surprised to find that you and I have quite a lot of other things in common, Ian."

As he said this, he looked at Sam. Ian felt something twist inside him. Had he been this obvious, the other night and now? Hadley Edwards didn't miss much.

"Do you still ride?" Hadley asked next.

"No. I haven't been on a horse in twenty years," Ian said.

"Miss it?"

"Not particularly. I *worked* from horseback, Hadley. More often that not it was unpleasant work. Pretty hard to be sentimental about riding after a few years of working stock from the back of a cow horse. As I said, I like to watch them run, but—" He caught himself. Their attitudes on horses were definitely not one of the things they had in common. He remembered the trophies and photographs in Hadley's study.

Hadley Edwards laughed. "Don't spare me, Ian. I think I know what you were about to say. To you horses aren't playthings."

"That's close, Hadley. Sorry."

"Don't be. I'm not offended. This is why they make chocolate and vanilla." He fixed Ian then with a frank, curious look. "You were a *good* rider, though?"

"For our kind of riding—I think so." He thought that over. "That's not quite honest. I was a damned good rider. I should have been. I had the finest teacher in the Ojos Negros."

"Ignacio Ortiz."

Ian wasn't surprised that Hadley knew about the vaquero, but all the same, it would be interesting to know *how* he knew.

Through all this Sam sat in silence. She hadn't looked at Ian once. Perhaps Hadley hadn't missed that, either.

The bell rang for the fifth race, and the three of them turned to the track. When the field broke from the starting gate, Ian saw that Hadley hadn't really gained any great advantage by sitting in a box; the excited fans leaping to their feet in front of him didn't give him much more than a peek at the action. When the race was over and Ian turned again to his hosts, he realized that they hadn't followed it all the way to the finish line.

Still, Hadley signaled a runner collecting pari-mutuel tickets and tendered him one plucked from his shirt pocket. The runner's eyes opened wide. It must have been a sizable wager.

Then Hadley surprised him.

"We're having dinner here in Ruidoso. Would you join our friends the Vergaras and us?"

"Hadley!" Sam broke in. There was no mistaking the low-key alarm.

"Sam, Sam. I see no reason why we can't trust Ian."

"Of course we can trust *Ian*, Hadley. I'd never suggest for a moment that we couldn't. But damn it, I *do* think you're getting careless. It's Ian this time, and then it might be someone you *can't* trust next. I wouldn't care—except that you could be putting Alejandro and Consuelo at risk, too."

"You're right, Sam, of course, but the invitation stands. Now that Ian has probably guessed *something* about Alejandro and Consuelo, we couldn't very well go on with the masquerade of Saturday night, anyway. It served its purpose until Alex and I got our chance to look at Ian."

The exchange had gone on as if Ian weren't there.

Hadley turned to Ian again. "Well, Ian, *will* you dine with us?"

He saw another shadow in Sam's eyes and fought to crush his curiosity. He lost. The slight irritation he felt at the thought that he had been carefully watched at the dinner party gave way to the wish to know what his watchers thought about him, and why they felt it necessary.

"Yes," he said, "I'd like to—very much." He was sorry the moment he said it. By rights he should hit the road.

When the eighth race had been run, Hadley gave Ian a map he sketched on the back of his program, showing him how to get to the restaurant, a place called the Carousel.

"Don't rush, Ian," Hadley said. "Kill some time. Sam and I will stay in the box until the crowd thins out. They didn't build this grandstand with wheelchairs in mind, and it takes a while to get me in and out of the car, anyway."

At trackside, Ian looked back up to the box. Yes, she was looking at him, and Hadley was looking at her. Suddenly he was no longer sorry he had said yes to dinner.

To delay his arrival at the parking lot, he went around the grandstand toward the paddock and the horse barns. A particularly appealing spotted filly, marked like an Appaloosa, but a true quarter horse in size and configuration, had caught his eye when she finished a strong second in the seventh race. With luck he could find her stall. When he was a boy, he had ridden a cow pony that could have been foaled by a dam such as this one. Sweet-natured, showy Pavo, who had seemed to dance even when standing still, had been a favorite of Ignacio's, too, one of the many mounts the old vaquero had trained without compromise for the tough work of the D Cross A no matter how beautiful they were. Come to think of it, Ignacio hadn't yet been an *old* vaquero in Pavo's day.

As he neared the stables, he found that the sounds and smells of horses still held the power to stir something deep inside him—no matter what he had said to Hadley.

Grooms worked in the stalls and walked unsaddled horses in a training ring, and men in long white coats and carrying leather cases, racing commission examiners, he guessed, were comparing notes. A farrier was stripping shoes from a small gelding outside a trailer smithy under the eye of a man in an expensive western suit. Knotted groups of men in jeans and boots talked horses and cattle in ranch-country drawls.

He walked along the row of stalls looking for the sign above a door that would read something like "Miss Silver Slipper, T. T. Cannon, Hereford, Texas," according to the program Hadley had given him. Intent on what he was

looking for, he was almost run down by a tractor pulling a cart
with a load of feed, and he lurched out of its way, slipping on
the straw. The driver seared him with a hot glare and the
impatient snarl of the busy working man who didn't have
time to look out for fools, but rattled on by without a word.

It was a close thing—not the brush with the tractor,
though.

When the feed rig cleared the section of stalls he had
been exploring, Ian realized that if it hadn't put a halt to his
pilgrimage, he would have walked right into Jacky Begley.

The blond giant was leaning over the lower door of a
horse stall. If Ian had been intent in *his* search, Begley
seemed riveted. There was a rigid set to his broad back,
one held so fiercely it made him quiver. His outsize hands
gripped the sides of the opening above the lower door half
and were pressed hard enough against the whitewashed
frame they looked as pale and bloodless as the wood itself.

The sign above the door read MISS SILVER SLIPPER.

Only the side of Begley's face was visible, but it was
enough for Ian to see the man was crying.

Ian turned and started for the parking lot.

"I have no reason to doubt your faith in Mr. MacAndrews,
Hadley," Alejandro Vergara said.

The Nicaraguan's voice was hammered silver, entirely in
keeping with the finely wrought delicacy of his features, a
delicacy that belied the strength in them.

"I thought you'd feel that way, Alex," Hadley Edwards
said. "But Sam is right. It was indiscreet of me. May I tell
him the whole story, then?"

"I think I would prefer you to."

Ian, silent beyond the usual "glad to meet you both" to
Consuelo Vergara and her husband when he joined the four
of them at the table, noticed that Alejandro's English—he
hadn't used any at the dinner party—had no trace of a
Spanish accent of any kind, not Rio Grande, Mexican, Castilian—
nothing. Consuelo, on the other hand, had sounded just like
old roommate Eulalio Guzman-Lopez back in military school
in Roswell when *he* spoke English. If his guess was right,
Alejandro had gotten most of his education in this country,
while Consuelo had in all likelihood been turned out by some
Catholic girls' finishing school *inside* Nicaragua.

Hadley turned to Ian and began, "I knew Alex in prep

school, and again at USC. Our love for riding drew us together, but after graduation we lost touch. Then we bumped into each other, and I mean literally, in a polo match in Mexico City a dozen years ago. I wanted to meet him for drinks afterward, but he declined, damned curtly for someone I thought a friend. What I didn't know—and didn't learn for almost seven years—was that Somoza's National Guard was keeping pretty close tabs on him, even when he left the country to compete. He had tried to run for office on a reform ticket against one of Somoza's stooges. Well, on a horse-buying trip to Nicaragua five years ago, I ran into him again. This time I sought him out. I'm a stubborn guy. I wanted at that time only to find out why he had snubbed me. Strangely enough, he was under less surveillance in Managua than when he was abroad, and he met with me. He told me he had already been under house arrest a couple of times. The Guard would tighten the screws and then ease up, trying to bring him into line with the other members of his class. He said there were a lot of other Nicaraguans in an even worse fix than he was, that people were disappearing right and left. At first I offered sympathy, nothing more. I'm ashamed to admit now that Somoza didn't seem too bad to me at the time. I was still swallowing the standard gringo line that Somoza was a barrier against communism. I won't go into what brought on my change of heart, beyond saying that I began looking at a lot of things with new eyes after my accident.

"Alex and I eventually set up a sort of 'tourist bureau.' We've been bringing people out for five years now. Alex was there on the scene and providing the links. I had the means to set refugees up here in the States—and aircraft at my disposal. It worked like a charm until three weeks ago. We got a tip one of the 'victims' we were making arrangements for was an agent for the Guard's secret police. Alex and Consuelo got out just before they knocked on their door. That was two months ago." Hadley's voice had been light, almost effervescent through all of this. He could have been telling Ian about a movie he had seen.

Alejandro's face, in contrast, was as passive as it had looked in the box, but Consuelo was following Hadley's story with dark intensity. Sam was looking down at her hands.

"What brought you to the Ojos Negros, Hadley?" Ian said.

"I needed a remote place where I could build an airstrip I could use without the bother and risk of filing flight plans. I can't claim there's a lot of it going on, but Somoza has bribe money scattered all through the Immigration Service and the Customs offices. I'd already been dickering for a place near Tucson when a old lady from here in the basin who had worked for my family in L.A. told me that the D Cross A might be for sale. She knew your people when she lived in Black Springs as a girl. El Recobro—the D Cross A—was perfect. We can keep quite a few people there completely unnoticed until we can relocate them, get them new IDs and the like. And the move here pleased Sam for entirely different but equally compelling reasons."

Sam lifted her head, looked at her husband for an instant, returned to staring at her hands.

Ian could make a good guess about one thing, but not about Sam. A guess about her "compelling reasons" would have to wait—if it ever came. "Was the old lady in L.A. named Concepción Martinez by any chance?"

"Yes. I'm not too surprised you figured that out, Ian. Connie Martinez is a highly memorable human being."

"And that's how you knew about Ignacio Ortiz."

"Exactly."

In for a dime, in for a dollar, Ian thought. "Ernesto Gomez and Dr. Pendleton are in this with you, aren't they, Hadley?" He heard Sam Edwards draw in her breath, but he went on. "Tim Springer is, of course, but how about Carrie Spletter?"

"I won't answer about Carrie and Ernie, but I'll tell them you asked about them," Hadley said, smiling. "Tim? Yes. He'd already been with Amnesty International when I hired him. They do great work, but they move too slowly for Tim's taste. Jim Pendleton's and Cissy's church connections help me relocate the people who pass through El Recobro."

"And you've never been caught?"

Hadley roared with laughter. "The few authorities who've investigated me think I'm running drugs. It drives them up the wall when they can't catch me at it." In another man Hadley's glee might have come off as smugness. He was enjoying himself thoroughly. A glance at Sam told him that she wasn't. Consuelo wasn't, either. Women were more serious about things such as this, more mature. He turned to Hadley again.

"Why have you told me all this, Hadley? I know now you must have realized I had suspicions about the Vergaras Saturday night and this afternoon, but surely you must have known that any guesses I had would have gone back to New York with me. I'd have forgotten them in a week. I presented no problem to you."

"Of course you didn't. My reasons are entirely selfish." He leaned back in his chair. His face took on a new, different set. "I want to bring you in with us—in a way."

Ian laughed through his surprise. Shrewd as the man in the wheelchair might be, he was a dreamer. "No chance, Hadley. To begin with, it's not my kind of thing. And I'm leaving here as quickly as I can."

"That's final?"

"Absolutely."

"Pity. I was going to ask you to run cattle on El Recobro for me. Make it look more like the ranch it's supposed to be. A purely local tenant-rancher might see things that would hurt him and me if he talked about them. Think about it."

Ian started to say something, decided against it. There was no point in telling this man something he didn't want to hear. He was a man who was used to getting what he wanted. At any rate, Hadley was going on.

"And I also thought—forgive me, Ian—that if you were settled in something like the surroundings that prompted your first work—you might begin to paint again. . . ."

Sam had looked up from her hands now and was looking at Ian. Her face told him nothing.

After he turned onto the Black Springs road at Alto, Ian picked up lights in his rearview mirror. For three miles they didn't gain on him nor did they lose ground. Perhaps it was all the talk of the shadowy doings of Hadley and his people, perhaps the distorted look of the pines at the side of the road and the dark night itself, but he began to have thoughts of the rifle he had seen in Begley's pickup. Begley just might have spotted him. There had been killings on this road before.

At the far end of a sharp turn the MG's headlights picked up an open forest road gate. He couldn't see the lights following him, and in a quick decision he put on the brakes, went fifteen feet past the gate, stopped, and backed up through it.

When he switched his lights off, the world was darker than his thoughts, but in fifteen seconds his eyes adjusted to it. He wished his inner vision could adjust as well. He sure as hell couldn't get a clear picture yet of Hadley Edwards—nor of Sam. Was it necessary? He was leaving, and the two of them would soon be no more than faded snapshots in the album of memory. Wouldn't they?

When he left the restaurant, he had paused at the door and looked back at the four people at the table. Sam looked pensive, separate somehow from the other three, who were again deep in the kind of exchange he had seen when they were all in the box at the track as Sam led him to it. Something dug at him during the brief few seconds he watched them. Hadley, the Vergaras: they made an odd-looking trio. But why? During dinner there had been no mistaking the affection they had for one another, their shared rank in their two worlds, their breeding—and their clear commitment to their common involvement. These things should make them all alike.

Then it came to him. Consuelo was a very serious, fearful lady, but with her fear under tight control, and her husband was a dedicated, cool professional. Nothing odd about the two of them, considering they were involved in what in all likelihood was a fairly desperate endeavor. It was Hadley who was the odd man out, and who made the other two seem odd in his company. His recounting of his secret had been playful, boyish, gamelike. It was like the casual way he had collected on his bet after the fifth race.

None of it amounted to a row of beans to Ian MacAndrews, except . . .

Face it, none of it except Sam. Why did she seem to be apart from them?

He forced his thoughts back to the moment.

The headlights of the vehicle that had followed him from Alto appeared around the curve and in seconds had passed the forest gate. It wasn't a pickup. In the faint light from the stars he could see it was a big, four-door sedan—probably the Edwards Cadillac.

Not that the *Anatomy of Melancholy* he had picked up at the Cholla was as dreary as its title made it sound, but he knew he wouldn't make any headway in Burton tonight.

If there were such a thing as a thermometer to register

cabin fever, the mercury would streak to the very top were it to test the man in room 24 of the Yucca Motel.

His head reeled with too many thoughts, none of them lingering long enough for resolution, not that he had real hope they would.

Sam, Hadley, the enigmatic Alejandro and his wife, Concepción Martinez, and Begley slipped in and out of his head, as did Pavo, the beautiful spotted pony he had ridden to Kelly's Livery the day Ignacio Ortiz had given him his best lesson in honor and dignity, not that he could claim the lesson had been learned very well, or lasted nearly long enough. What had drawn Begley to Miss Silver Slipper as he, Ian, had been drawn?

When he got Ernie's report, what possible use could he make of it?

He had to clean up everything here—and leave, soon. He put the book down, switched off the bedside light, and stared up into the dark above him.

In this state he knew he wouldn't sleep.

He left the bed and struggled into his clothes again.

It would take a full hour to walk to the cemetery at San Jose and back. It was time he visited Jorge. The final chore. The only way to lay ghosts to rest was to face them squarely. Sleep would come soon enough then, even were it a troubled, haunted one.

When he closed the motel room door behind him, he found a new ghost waiting for him at the bottom of the stoop.

This ghost had a face as pale as death, for all that it was splashed with heavy makeup—still "off-register."

"I got to get back across the road to work in ten minutes, Mr. MacAndrews," M. L. Kimbrough said. "But I got to talk to you. Jody says I can trust you. He says I *got* to trust you. I want you to help me with John . . . John Begley."

He didn't need this, didn't want it. "Help? How could I help, Miss Kimbrough?"

"I can't claim I like you very much, but somebody's got to stop him from doing something crazy, and you're the only one who can do it."

"Something crazy?"

"You know. Jody told you. He says he'll kill you if you don't clear out. I don't want John to be no killer. Leave here . . . please!"

Chapter XI

He awoke before daybreak with a false hangover as sickening and throbbing as any real one he remembered.

His tongue, a thick cotton swab, filled his mouth, and the once-too-familiar burning shafts found the soft tissue at the base of his skull again. Far worse than the pain, though, was the feeling of naked exposure, the X-ray glare of lights too bright and unknown eyes too piercing that had always come with the hangovers, particularly after a night when he had once more treated Laurie badly and when she had made his suffering keener by not complaining.

It took him several moments to realize he had finally been victimized by the "'dry drunk" Father Francis Keegan— the deceptively irreverent priest who had befriended him at his second AA meeting in Chicago—had warned him might someday come.

Remembering, he knew it was just the leering ghost of a hangover, but he couldn't stop the aches or steady his shaking hands, couldn't hawk the taste of stale, sour liquor from his mouth (nor truly persuade himself that he hadn't actually been drinking) until long after he had brushed his teeth until his gums were sore and steamed himself in the shower until the Yucca's hot water turned to lukewarm drizzle. As he had always done when sullied with the imagined filth of legitimate hangovers, he scrubbed himself until his flesh was almost in tatters without feeling clean.

Funny, the actual dry drunk must have come in a dream, with parts of it surely a horror of a nightmare, but he couldn't remember any dream at all. "It generally happens," Father Frank had said, "when you climb high psychic peaks, or get mired in depression. Keep a steady state, Ian, a kind of stasis. Don't let yourself get too high or too low." The priest, always in mufti at meetings, had been off the sauce for seven years, faithfully serving Mass every one of his sober days and serving it by the book, never faking his sips of wine. "If I can make it—you can," he said more than once.

He could laugh about his misery now and he did, but he knew to a certainty he hadn't seen or felt the last of it. It would come again, and just this way—if he was lucky.

Father Frank was a huge, comic-strip-character Irishman, a younger, burlier, gutsier Jiggs, once a second-team all-American tackle at Notre Dame (it was this leftover notoriety that kept him from concealing his calling from fellow members, although Ian guessed he might not have tried to hide it, anyway), and a self-confessed violent brute when splashed, a man who had dismantled more saloons with his fists in his drinking days than Carry Nation had ever hacked to pieces with her hatchet. Those excursions into mayhem had been made in civvies, he had told Ian. "Bad-assed as I was, I never wanted Holy Mother Church to look like a breeding ground for dipso Gaels, not even to the limp-wristed Sasse-nachs I found when I stumbled into gay bars by mistake. Incidentally, the only one-on-one scrap I ever lost was against a fruitcake two-thirds my size, a goddamned *hairdresser* would you believe?"

The priest had one other dictum, usually uttered after a particularly self-castigating drunkalogue by a new member. "I don't tell no sumbitch nothin'! I just don't drink anymore."

Now, in the semidark of room 24 of the Yucca Motel, the shakes at last began a fluttering departure. Shaved, suddenly hungry, Ian dressed in the chinos and boots he had worn on the trip to the slickrock and stepped outside the door.

Big Cuchillo was a shapeless blue-gray mass in the east, a stone sponge that had wiped the stars from the lower sky, but even as he watched, the mountain began to find and fill its contours and take on character again, with its topmost ridge soon honed to sharpness by the rising sun rubbing against the rimrock.

With the Buckhorn closed, the only light he could see anywhere around him was the glow of the night-light in the Texaco station at the intersection. The station, like one in an Edward Hopper painting, looked more forlorn and deserted with its weak glimmer than if it had been completely dark. Somewhere toward the center of town a raven cracked the morning silence with a shivering cry.

When the screech died in the windless air, the silence

110   Norman Zollinger

seemed even deeper than before. It was the silence of a vacuum, the kind of silence he could imagine sliding along the curves of space; and as it held him in its cold, numbing grip, it would take little to persuade him he was the only living thing on the planet at this moment—if he *was* a living thing.

Pity it wasn't true. As the last man on earth he wouldn't have to consider any problems but his own.

"*I want you to help me with John* . . ." M.L. had said, her face as faint and pallid as the night-light in the Texaco place.

And Hadley Edwards: "*. . . you might begin to paint again.*"

This corroded, forsaken landscape, for all its emptiness, was a repository of demands he couldn't, wouldn't, and probably shouldn't meet.

Now he heard the sound of a semi still hidden by the long bulk of the Yucca, marching through the gears as it approached the corner now catching the first rays bending down from Cuchillo's ridge. He watched for the truck to show itself beyond Harry Kimbrough's sleeping office. Would it carry the crude logo of the Nike Cartage Company? If it *was* B.J. Howland behind the wheel, the web of coincidence would have suddenly become too sticky to tolerate a moment longer.

He sighed his relief when the tractor of the semi nosed beyond the Yucca's entrance and he read CONOCO on the stainless steel tanker-trailer.

Breakfast. Maybe Anita would have the Comida open by the time he walked to the plaza.

Los hermanos, he decided, must be three-meal-a-day regulars at La Comida de Anita; the two old men were seated together at the end of the little counter, their brown, corrugated faces deep in plates of *huevos rancheros* whose green-chili-and-corn-tortilla aroma filled the tiny restaurant. The two white-thatched heads turned and nodded to Ian in unison as he entered.

"*Buenos dias, señores,*" Ian said. The bell on the door behind him was still tinkling, and he couldn't quite hear the identical hummed replies of the two old brothers. Juan? Bautista? Maybe he would hear Anita address one of them by name . . . and where *was* she, by the way?

He took a stool at the other end of the counter from *los hermanos*.

"Señor MacAndrews," the nearer, younger Juan or Bautista said, his voice thick with eggs and salsa, low and musical in the diner's morning warmth, "Señora Anita will not mind if you help yourself to coffee." The old gentleman pointed to the Silex coffee maker on the back service counter.

"*Gracias, viejo,*" Ian said. He had to squeeze through the narrow opening between the end of the counter and the wall. "*¿Donde es la Señora?*"

"*En la cocina, señor,*" the old man said. He switched to English again for the rest of it. "She makes the tortillas fresh, every morning. Nothing remains from yesterday." Clearly he was aware that Ian's clumsy Spanish wasn't fit for more than the simplest phrases, but he was also too courteous to completely ignore the effort of an anglo to converse in the language of Cervantes. This was the old boy who had been washing the glass door of Ernie's office the other day. The other seemed shyer, not fearful, but with a wariness that didn't speak too well for the anglos of the Ojos Negros Basin he undoubtedly had grown to manhood and now quiet dotage with. Perhaps five years the elder, this one could possibly be of an age with Ignacio had Ignacio lived—and of an age with Jorge, too, don't forget. Jorge Martinez. Would he be able to summon up the will again to visit that final and perhaps most important grave at last, as he had summoned it up last night, before M.L. stopped him? That was a cop-out. She hadn't stopped him. He could still have gone to San Jose after the girl crossed the road, but he hadn't.

Maybe that was the abandonment of that "steady state" Father Frank had talked about. Maybe he wasn't truly sober yet, only dry.

He poured a mug of black coffee. When he sat down this time, he picked a stool just one away from the two old men, close enough, he hoped, to show friendliness, not so close as to crowd their space.

"Señor MacAndrews! *Buenos dias!*"

Anita filled the doorway to the kitchen. She had been wiping her strong, plump hands on an apron, but now she stopped with the apron twisted about her hands like a muff. It was an entrance that would have been the envy of any diva at the Met.

"Buenos dias, señora," Ian said. *"Huevos rancheros, por favor."*

"Si." The old flirt was actually rolling her eyes at him. As she disappeared into the kitchen, it came to him how *good* he felt, how good he felt in the absolute sense, not just relative to the counterfeit agony of his awakening.

It seemed she placed the plate of eggs in front of him before he could so much as blink. He dug into them without even looking up at her, knowing she would watch him eat again with those keen, black, assessing eyes.

He finished his eggs and mopped up the rest of the *salsa* with a torn half of a *sopaipilla.* A swallow of coffee heightened the pleasant fire in his mouth. It had been the kind of breakfast that would see a man through a long, hot, lunchless day in the branding pens.

"Señor MacAndrews," Anita said, "Bautista tells me you are a client of the lawyer Ernesto Gomez." Anita's remark had finally solved the names of the two old men for him.

He nodded. "Tell me about my lawyer, Anita," he said with as much innocence as he could manage. "Have I got a good one?"

She smiled as if her face had just been caught in a rosy spotlight.

She began with Ernie's boyhood in Socorro—Ernie had been a *bueno niño,* but mischievous—followed with his exploits as a running back at UNM in Albuquerque, where he was too *"pequeño,* but Dios, so fast, *señor!"* Next came the Gomez, Gomez, & Trujillo association with Jonathan Hardy, whom Anita obviously revered as much as did Ernesto, on through Ernie's being retained by Hadley Edwards. "He *must* be good to work for Señor Edwards." Clearly, though, something about the Gomez-Edwards connection defeated her. She didn't know what kind of legal work Ernie did for Hadley. She looked at Ian with luminous, sad eyes that seemed to say, "I have failed you on *this,* Señor MacAndrews," but almost immediately she brightened.

"And I know who broke Ernesto's jaw, *señor."*

Ian smiled. "So do I," he said, wondering then if he had made a tactical error by not waiting for her to tell him. It was never smart to cut a single line in a star's big scene. He needn't have worried.

She leaned over the counter with her arms crossed under her big, melon breasts.

"Ah, *sí, señor. I* know how and why it happened.", She paused, her head lifted now and her back arched as much as her excess of flesh would let it.

"It was a girl, of course, *señor,* but—not just any girl." Her smile turned brighter and became broader. "It was Ernesto's sister, the one in college in California now—Ynez. Ernesto warned the big *hombre* Begley away from her, but that *bruto* is not the kind to listen." There was a monumental shrug. "There was a terrible fight. Ernesto didn't have a chance against that animal, but, *señor,* that Begley did stop seeing Ynez, not that the *señorita* was very pleased with her lawyer brother for keeping him away from her."

Ian felt a little twist of guilt, hearing this from Anita. He would very much prefer that Ernesto had been the one to tell him. He looked to the two old men, partly to see if they had listened, but more to stop any further revelations on Anita's part. Juan and Bautista were smoking, lifting the cigarettes to their lips as if their delicate old hands were guided by only one shared nervous system, holding the smokes between thumbs and forefingers in that neat, special Latin way. No, they hadn't listened. They looked as if they had moved on to some equally shared dreamland.

He paid his bill and left to a farewell flourish from Anita. *Los hermanos* weren't too far sunk in reverie to turn their heads and nod good-bye.

When he returned to the Yucca, the sun had cleared the top of Cuchillo and the day was making another solemn promise to hit a hundred. Such a reading wouldn't begin to touch the inner heat that threatened him. The bad awakening, briefly forgotten during the early pleasantries with Juan and Bautista and the sly fencing with Anita, had come back again.

Something was still gnawing at him and he knew it wouldn't stop until he determined what it was and did something positive about it. Not for the first time he wondered if those years of hard drinking had left him with the "wet brain" that was the constant secret fear of many another alcoholic. The dry drunk might have been the first warning sign of it.

". . . I want you to help me with John . . ."
". . . you might begin to paint again . . ."
". . . I want you to help me with John . . ."
". . . you might begin to paint again . . ."

He lay down on the unmade bed, but in five minutes, in spite of the window air-conditioner, his back and legs were sticky, almost wet.

He took the Burton from the bedside table, riffled a few pages, and put it down again. Another walk? No. He needed something less aimless than sauntering through Black Springs yet again.

"... I want you to help me with John ..."

He left the bed and stood with his damp back to the draft from the rattling air-conditioner. The icy breeze chilled him to the skin. Across the room a stranger studied him from the mirror above the desk that held the phone, a tall man, thick black hair graying above the ears, eyes that looked at him without recognition and gave not the slightest hint of life.

When M.L. had asked for his help in the dark outside his door last night, what had he said or done? To the best of his recollection, beyond his one question he had simply stared at her, his eyes without doubt as dead as those of the stranger in the mirror—and that pale misprint of a girl had stared back at him, her eyes just as blank. After that quick plea and without another word she had raced across the highway to the Buckhorn. She had opened the door, letting the sound of the jukebox escape into the night, and had turned back to him.

Even at that distance he saw her smile before she turned and went inside.

He looked again at the stranger in the mirror. He knew he wouldn't get an answer there. "*Salud y pesetas, hombre,*" he said. The stranger mouthed the words.

M.L. had begged him to leave. But first he had to see Jody.

Every step he took as he walked to the Yucca office seemed heavy, plodding, as if he were laboring up a steep, rocky slope.

Jody looked up from the desk when the screen door squeaked.

"Morning, Mr. MacAndrews, sir. Win any money up at Ruidoso yesterday?"

God in heaven! Everybody knew everything about everybody in this grubby town. Was life here so devoid of interest that this was what remained?

"Jody—do you know where Jacky... John Begley lives?"

The look in Jody's eyes brought the false hangover back with a rush.

Chapter XII

"You're dead sure you can handle this, Jody?" Ian said as he and the boy sat in the Jeep on the shoulder of the highway, seven miles west of the Yucca.

"Yes, sir. Done it lots of times, honest."

They had parked where the rangeland ended at the lava flow. A gate broke the four strands of wire fence fifty feet this side of where the fence ended in an iron post anchored in the first slabs of the black rock. But if a road led from the other side of the gate, Ian couldn't make it out. The grass had run out a quarter of a mile behind them, and the hard, gray stone that edged the malpais wouldn't have held the dusty prints left by a half-track, much less have taken any from the rubber treads of the tires of the Jeep or those of Begley's pickup.

Jody showed none of the fright now that he had when Ian faced him in the office, but he still seemed uneasy. "Mr. MacAndrews," he said now, "I sure would appreciate it if my old man didn't find out about this, or that I been coming out here ever since M.L. moved in with John. It was bad enough in the family when she left us. It would like to kill Pa if he thought *I* was friends with John, too. Don't much care for lying to him, but I ain't about to break off with M.L., either." The youngster was suffering the generalized pangs of agony of a decent fourteen-year-old whom life hadn't yet equipped for making a choice such as this... if it ever would.

"Look, Jody, if you can't square this with yourself, draw me a map and I'll take it from here. I'm dropping you off when we get within a quarter of a mile, anyway."

"Gee, Mr. MacAndrews, I don't think you'd find the place even with a map. I kept getting lost myself the first three times, and M.L. was with me. Another thing. I sure don't want to sound disrespectful, but I think it would be better if I did the driving. There's a couple of them open lava tubes come up so fast you could be down in them before you saw them."

Jody was right. Cornering the MG, even on mountain gravel in a thunderstorm, was a lot easier than taking the Jeep over broken country he didn't know. The trip to the slickrock had been bad enough, and the nightmarish terrain beyond this fence could make the slickrock look like a billiard table.

"All right, Jody, you're the boss now. When we come in close to Begley's place, I'm going on alone, though. No heroics, no tricks, savvy?"

"Yes, sir. I ain't sure I want to be there when you talk to John."

The hairs on the back of Ian's neck tingled a little. "I'll get the gate," he said.

They weren't a hundred yards from the fence before Ian knew how wise he had been to let Jody do the driving. It was a different Jody behind the wheel now. The darting teenage eyes had narrowed to twin slits of concentration. He didn't so much as glance at Ian as he wrestled the Jeep through rockfall after rockfall, tipping it so far over at times that Ian was sure the angle had taken the center of gravity well past the point of no return. Not once did the driver show concern; clearly he knew his own and the machine's capabilities

They came to a section that for a few yards ran almost as smooth as silk.

Without turning his head Jody spoke. "John is an absolute dead shot with that rifle."

The road, if it was a road, turned rough again with a vengeance.

Jody was muttering to himself now. It sounded as if it was something he wanted to say aloud, but whose sound and sense he wanted to hear before he said it.

Sure enough, he braked the jeep to a stop and turned to Ian. His eyes were clouded.

"I said I was John's friend," he began. "Guess that must sound kind of funny considering how I acted when you beat him up. I thought it might make him a little less wild, more like he is when only M.L. and me are with him. He's real nice then, honest. People around here got no idea what he went through in Nam. I got to tell you I never would have brought you out if M.L. hadn't asked for your help. But now I got a bigger problem." Jody looked down to where his hands still gripped the wheel. His knuckles were whiter than they had been through the toughest of the driving. He looked at Ian again, his eyes clear now, and the ingenous, completely unselfconscious look Ian had come to expect was back on his young face. "I sure don't want you getting hurt. I meant that about him and the rifle." He paused. "What I'm trying to get at is . . . I'd like to turn around and take you back out of here. Please!"

With the jeep no longer moving they baked in the sun. They were parked in an arroyo with mesquite bushes to their right and the lava flow on the left. Ian would have sworn he had at one time or another ridden every inch of rock and caliche between the buildings of the old D Cross A and the malpais, but this particular stretch was new to him. That it was part of the ranch of his boyhood, though, he had no doubt, even if this stretch wasn't within the borders of the smaller El Recobro. The D Cross A had shrunk long before Hadley Edwards had breezed in from California with his money.

"Jody," Ian said, "have you any idea at all why John seems so intent on my leaving Chupadera County? I'm not talking about the fight. Maybe some crackpot idea he had even before he found me at the Buckhorn?"

"I don't know. Unless—"

"Unless?"

Jody shook his head. "Maybe it's because you're part of the old days for John—the ranch the way it used to be, and that old Mex he worked for. He's had a bad time and maybe you're all the things he wishes he could be. I think he figures you've had *everything*." His face had turned red enough to make the freckles disappear. "I'm only guessing. I don't know."

"Let's get moving, Jody."

"Okay, Mr. MacAndrews," it's your funeral." The color left Jody's cheeks. "Sorry I said that."

"Forget it, Jody. If it *is* my funeral, I won't very well be able to blame you if I want to, will I? How much farther?"

"About a mile and a half. We got to cross another fence line."

Jody slipped the Jeep into first and rolled forward. As they passed the mesquite three buzzards flapped away from it, not moving fast or flying far from the shade of the scrub. It was too hot even for those able-bodied scavengers to move about much.

Without advance notice the ground flattened some and then they were down in the bottom of another stony gully, but a wide, level one this time, more of an alluvial fan than one of the deep scars of raw rock that more often crosshatched this corner of the old MacAndrews holdings. He knew just about where he was now. When they crossed the high, bald rise ahead of them, they would see the peculiar, pretty little bosque where he and Ignacio had camped once when they had ridden out with bedrolls on a two-day search for strays.

The bosque, hidden in still another little cul-de-sac arroyo, was caused by a spring that leaped from a sandstone face, made a short oxbowed stream around a rock outcropping, then vanished into one of the open lava tubes Jody had talked about. Over the millenia, enough fine stuff to create silt had been leached from the sandstone ash and then dropped where the stream bent and slowed, enough soil created for a grove of cottonwoods to gain a foothold along with some tough wild grasses. The trees had been ancient when Ian had been a boy, had been ancient when Ignacio had first come to the little bosque with Ian's great-uncle Angus sixty-five or seventy years ago.

Suddenly he knew this bosque was where he would find Jacky Begley.

On the Jeep ride out it hadn't occurred to Ian to question just where Begley could manage to live in this desolation. The bosque was the answer; it was the only place.

"We'll find John and M.L. just over that rise, won't we, Jody?" The boy glanced at him, and Ian went on, "Thought you said we had to go through another fence."

Jody laughed. "We did. You just didn't see it. It's down more places than it's up."

"You can stop here. I'll go the rest of the way on foot." The boy paled to white again. "Wait here for me," Ian said. "I will be needing a ride back to town, you know. You can count on it!"

A few feet down the far slope of the rise, Ian stopped. In the hollow of the arroyo he saw the blue pickup and a dilapidated Airstream trailer whose once-bright silver had dulled to pewter. It must have been a man-size piece of work to get the trailer in here over the boulder-strewn hint of road he and Jody had just traveled.

He would wait here for a couple of minutes. He was sweating and breathing hard. The rise, as with so many other things about the Ojos Negros country, had cleverly disguised its capacity to fool him, and he didn't want to face Begley until he was sure of his reflexes and his strength, in case the younger man felt obliged to even things up for what had happened at the Buckhorn. There, Ian had held a couple of important advantages. Begley had taken him for a pushover, and when he found Ian wasn't one, he had already committed himself too deeply to change his tactics. Now he must have thought it over, not that he seemed the kind who learned much from mistakes, but you never knew.

The only thin edge Ian would have now was the fact that out of doors the quarters were even less confining than they had been in the bar. Again he would have to cut his opponent up quickly. Even with the damaged leg Begley's power and stamina would certainly tip things his way in any long struggle. There would be a strict limit on how many times Ian would be able to stab and dance and run.

Face it, walking down into the bosque would be as stupid as any of the stupid things he'd done when drunk. He should show some sense and turn and walk back to Jody and the Jeep.

Then, the only decision that was going to be made was made for him.

He saw Begley—and knew at once that Begley had seen him, too.

The man's blond head was framed in a crotch of one of the cottonwoods, a hundred, perhaps a hundred and fifty yards away. The barrel of the rifle rested on the rough, weathered bark of a foot-thick branch.

Ian saw the flash, felt through his pants and shirt the sting of shattered caliche as it kicked up dust and stone from a spot a yard to the left of his boots, and he blinked as the report from the rifle crashed and bounced from rock to rock. His bowels turned to acid that threatened to eat his belly and legs clear down to the soles of his boots. There was another flash, another spurt of stone and dust on the other side of him, another racket of echoes in his ears.

After the second shot his insides, if not his legs, somehow got back to normal. From the solid rest position in the crotch of the cottonwood and at this modest distance, no real rifleman, no "dead shot," could possibly have missed him twice . . . unless he intended to.

He started down the slope, walking with as much deliberation as his legs would grant him.

Begley remained behind the tree until Ian was within a dozen paces of him, then he stepped out and took a stance with his big legs apart and his boots rooted to the softer bosque earth Ian could now feel beneath his own. Begley looked anything but crippled now, with the rifle cradled across his chest. He held the weapon loosely and with seeming indifference, but with the thick right index finger still inside the trigger guard.

A movement at the trailer tugged at the corner of Ian's eye and he had to fight hard to keep his gaze straight ahead on Begley. He was fairly sure he knew what the movement was, anyway. M.L. had joined them.

"You dude son of a bitch," Begley spat. "Can't you get it through your head that you're not wanted here—or anywhere near here?

Now Ian did turn toward the trailer. M.L. was in the door, sure enough. She was wearing jeans and a shirt so large he guessed it must belong to the man in front of him. With the tails hanging out it looked like a maternity smock, and he realized something. She was pregnant. It hadn't shown in the waitress's uniform. He looked back at the blond giant.

"I'm going to talk to you, Begley, and you're damned well going to listen."

Begley glared at him. He lowered his big head and looked at Ian through eyes that showed the red from still another long night with booze. Ian felt a sudden impulse to burst out laughing; the man couldn't have looked more like an angered bull had he begun to snort and paw the ground.

Careful, he told himself, *there's nothing funny about to happen here*.

He heard the girl stirring at the trailer, and the impulse to laugh faded.

"Please, John . . ." It was a bleat, a half-strangled cry filled with fear, but with something else, too: tenderness, care, and Christ help her, love. How many shameful times had he heard that same tone in Laurie's voice?

"Please, John . . ." M.L. began again, "listen to him."

The angered bull's head swung toward her, but the big hands tightened on the rifle.

"Shut up, M.L. This ain't your affair." The words themselves were as brutally direct as the ones he had used with her in the Buckhorn, but there was a discernible difference. Begley looked back at Ian and then something pulled his eyes upward and over Ian's shoulder. "Yell at your kid brother to come on down, M.L.," Begley said. "His goddamned brains will turn to tapioca if he stands up there in the sun much longer."

Sure, Jody would have come running to the top of the rise when he heard the shots.

Again Ian struggled against the wish to turn and look, but he knew it was imperative that he keep right on offering this edgy, whiskey-sweated brute his full attention. If that óne tenuous link was broken, whatever doubtful little gain might yet be had from this ridiculous face-off could be lost forever.

"Come on down, Jody—hear?" M.L. called up the hill. "It's going to be all right, honey, honest!" Ian wished he could be as sure as M.L. sounded.

He heard Jody slipping and sliding through the loose stones on the rise, felt rather than saw the boy hurry past him to the trailer and wrap his arms around his sister. Begley, after that one quick flick of his eyes up the hill, hadn't looked at either of them.

"All right, MacAndrews," Begley said. "Talk quick—and don't talk much. I ain't interested in what you got to say to me, but for M.L.'s sake, I'll listen."

Now all the bets were down. There was only one pass remaining in this crapshoot. Hunches, guesses, unfounded, unwarranted speculation: none of it was much to go on as he faced this armed, wild-eyed, itchy-fingered, possibly psychotic man who so clearly hated him. Why—in his own sweet suffering ego, his own go-it-alone compulsion—hadn't he bothered to test this roll out first on Jody? Or M.L.? Or even Ernie?

Well, it was way too late for all that now. He might as well get on with it. As they used to say about parachute-jumping during the war: no sense in practicing something that had to be done to perfection the first time it was tried.

"Begley, people tell me you were a fair-to-middling cowboy—once."

The bloodshot eyes yellowed with suspicion, but Ian plunged ahead.

"Would you like to take a stab at running stock on the old D Cross A again?"

Chapter XIII

They pulled the horses up short about a quarter of a mile from Hadley Edwards's runway.

Begley must be suffering through the worst of his hangover by now. The sun had been drumming on their heads for nearly an hour, and at no point on the ride had they reached a place where they could let the horses out to as much as a slow lope and make a little breeze, but Begley, unlike Ian, at least wore a hat. Still, his sweat was probably scalding one-hundred-proof, and even if, like Ian, he wasn't the kind of drunk who sickened easily, he must have been close to puking.

Back in the bosque Begley had ducked into the Airstream to stow the rifle and had come out with a half-pint of whiskey. Ian hadn't said anything, but he watched the younger man as he stuffed it in his hip pocket. Begley met Ian's eyes, and with a sour look on his face he took the bottle out and handed it to M.L.

"Take it along if you feel you need it," Ian had said.

"Never mind. Let's get moving before I change my mind."

Everything had seemed wrong with this ride from the beginning.

Ignacio's old Mexican saddle with its upswept cantle wasn't right for either of them, but Ian wished now he had insisted Begley use it—even if he was fifty pounds too heavy for it. The small of Ian's back had daggers in it.

And twenty years away from horses seemed a lot more than just twice ten. It would have seemed an age had they been on the backs of sound animals, instead of the two old bags of dog meat carrying them. He had almost balked when Begley led them out of the tiny corral hidden in the bosque.

Begley obviously had problems of his own with riding, but he had apparently worked out ways of solving them. It was a wonder he could make his mount look so good; it took some doing, with the stirrups let out to different lengths to accommodate the bad leg. How had the man been able to do all that fancy riding the day he had spied on Ian on the slickrock?

The worst thing about the ride, though, was that neither of them should be crossing this land at all . . . not without permission. Hadley Edwards wasn't likely to trouble himself about it in the slightest—but that wasn't an excuse. They should have put the visit to Hadley off until tomorrow and driven out. But back at the trailer Ian had gotten the feeling that if he lost this slippery hold on Begley for even one day, he would never get it back and a quick, pleading look from M.L. had made him agree to ride.

Now he considered how he was going to tell Hadley Edwards about the more significant trespass: that Begley was secretly squatting on Edwards property.

Ian's first thought had been that Begley and he would take the truck and transfer to the MG at the Yucca. But when he figured it was an hour's hard drive to the highway (more, the Jeep had taken that long, and the pickup couldn't match its speed through the rocks by half) and seven miles from there to the motel and twenty-six more to El Recobro, Begley's insistence that they ride did make sense.

"Forty minutes across the range—no more," Begley said. They were making it in thirty.

"This is no promise, Begley," Ian had said, stopping for a moment the hope and enthusiasm bubbling in Jody and his sister. "It's up to Hadley Edwards. But I do know for a fact that he'll listen."

"Good enough for now," Begley said after a moment. "It ain't as if I got better things to do these days."

His tone had barely approached civility, and now as they rested the horses, Ian realized they were the only nearly civil words Begley had uttered to him since they had first faced each other in the shadow of the cottonwood. The ride from the bosque hadn't even been a truce, never mind any kind of lasting peace.

Ian dug his heels into the flanks of the dilapidated roan
pony Begley had provided and started it for the runway. He
didn't even look to see if Begley and his creaky, ancient gray
were following. They hadn't talked at all during the short
rest, and Ian knew they weren't going to until they reached
the compound whose outbuildings were just beginning to
show their tops over the bulldozed mounds of caliche and
rock lining the landing strip. The hangar's arched roof still
hid the Edwards ranch house.

When they rounded the corner of the hangar they saw
the twin-engined airplane parked on the apron in front of it.

A vehicle he hadn't seen before at El Recobro was
snuggled up to the aircraft. It was a full-size bus with curtains
at the windows. A sign on its sky-blue side read BETHANY
METHODIST SUNDAY SCHOOL—GREENLEY, IOWA. Two Hispanic
men were transferring luggage from the plane to a storage
compartment under the bus's windows, and a pair of thin
Latin women were watching them.

Framed in four of the windows where the curtains had
been tied back were six or seven small, brown, tired-looking
children.

He didn't realize he had reined his pony to a halt until
Begley stopped beside him.

"I have a feeling we're looking at something we're not
supposed to see," Ian said.

"Nothing new," Begley grunted. "Edwards and his people fly four or five loads a month in here. I seen buses from
Oregon and Connecticut and another one from Iowa, maybe
this same one, just in the past three weeks. They bed them
down in the house even if there's a crowd like this."

Ian looked Begley over hard. The ride must have at last
beaten most of the hangover out of him, and if there had
been any residual drunkenness, it was gone.

As they moved forward, the parking apron came in sight.
A group of people stood talking by the fieldstone wall.
Hadley was there, erect in his wheelchair, and Ian recognized
the Pendletons, but the couple facing them he hadn't seen
before: a boy and a girl, maybe just past college age. None of
them seem to have noticed the two riders. Sam wasn't in the
group.

"If we'd come out by the blacktopped road," Begley
said, "all of this would have been out of sight, the bus, too,

ng before we crossed the bridge. They keep a sharp eye on
e road."

"You know what's going on here?" Ian asked.

"Sure," Begley sneered. "I know *everything* that goes on
ere. They don't know I know, though."

"How many other people know?"

"Nobody hereabouts. Not that I've heard. They're fairly
areful."

"And you've never told?"

"No skin off my ass."

"But the buses. Don't they ever get spotted?"

"Naw. They take another road in and out if here, one
at leads off to the northwest and the Estancia Valley."

Ian remembered the old north road. It wound around
egrito Peak and had been a shortcut to Albuquerque, but
efore his time. The road had died when the town of Williston
ithered away sometime in the twenties, according to Ignacio,
nd was only the shadow of a trace when he had herded stock
cross it as a boy. It would make a useful secret exit from El
ecobro. Once past the ghost of Williston, seventy-five miles
f echoing emptiness stretched to the north before any traffic
as likely to be encountered. Chances were good that there
ouldn't be a soul to give a second look at a dusty bus, no
atter what its origin, until it reached the interstate and
lended with the stream of tourists in RVs and the other
uses, trucks, and cars headed to or from Los Angeles. Seen
at far north no one could connect the bus with the Ojos
egros Basin.

Ian was speculating that Hadley's "tourist bureau" was a
t bigger and busier than the owner of El Recobro had
inted at the Carousel in Ruidoso when a voice that wasn't
egley came from behind him.

"Do you chaps have business here?"

The first thing he saw when he turned wasn't the speak-
r, but the service automatic in the speaker's hand, the
uzzle opening a perfect black circle dead level with his
yes. The hand holding the gun belonged to Tim Springer.

The gun dropped. So did Springer's jaw. "I say... I'm
orry, MacAndrews! From the back I had no idea it was you."
he pilot broke into an easy grin, but in the fraction of a
econd before he did, Ian had glimpsed a different face from
at of the boy-man he had met at Sam's dinner party.

Springer was a hard-eyed pro, capable, confident, relaxed, but as alert and quick as a stalking cat.

"Now don't you two rush off before Hadley's had chance to say hello," Springer said. "Why don't I just put you gee-gees in the paddock? I'll unsaddle them if you like. Yo will be staying, won't you?"

The automatic was now tucked into the waistband Springer's jeans. Ian stared at it. In twenty years the on firearms he had seen up close had been in the holsters New York and Chicago cops—and now two of them had bee pointed at him in little more than a hour, and by two me who might have no compunction about using them.

Ian turned to Begley. "Do we want them unsaddle ...John?" He wondered how the "John" had come o instead of "Begley."

"Naw," Begley said. "These plugs would think they w done for the season. We'd never get them on the move agai Do we go on with this, MacAndrews, or just forget it?" Th S.O.B. was enjoying himself. It must have been the gu held on Ian that did it.

Ian slid from the saddle that had gripped him so cruell wondering if he could promote a lift to town when the finished. He'd had all he wanted of this nag and the crampin saddle for today.

Springer stepped forward and took the reins of Ian horse. "I'll take good care of them," he said when Begle too, dismounted. "Go on over to Hadley. He's seen you now.

The Englishman's voice sounded friendly enough, bu Ian knew an order when he heard one.

Sam met them at the front door Hadley had waved the to from his wheelchair. She stared at Begley. With the cu and abrasions from Ian's fists in the Buckhorn still cruste over and with whiskers growing through the scabs, the youn brute looked anything but a solid citizen. Sam's eyes widene when Ian introduced them. "Go on in to Hadley's stud Ian," she said, her eyes still on Begley. "I'll come along wit Hadley as soon as he finishes out here."

As smoothly as everything seemed to have gone, rig up to the departure of the bus with the unknown young ma driving, and the girl acting as some kind of stewardess (Ia and Begley hadn't been introduced to either of them), ther was no getting rid of the persistent thought that, with th exception of Springer, they were all a bunch of amateurs—even Hadley. They acted, especially the Pendletons, as if they were sending this busload of subdued, probably still frightened, deathly silent refugees off to summer camp. By rights Hadley should be incensed by the intrusion of the two unexpected riders, or at the very least disturbed; he looked as proud and pleased as a child showing off a birthday present. The Pendletons had larked around Ian as if he were a prodigal son once the bus had gone, and even Springer had shown mild pleasure.

There had seemed on Sam's face a little flicker of a smile at the sight of Ian, but one look at Begley and her smile was turned off with an almost audible click. She had hurried to where Hadley sat in his wheelchair on the walk inside the wrought-iron gate, hovering over him then as if she were guarding him from blows, but staying in back of him as if she didn't want him to see her there.

Begley seemed to make a determined effort not to look impressed with the house and its furnishings as he and Ian walked to the study. He had managed to be *anything* but deferential to Edwards's wife. The thing that seemed to hold his interest most had been the sight of Hadley's frail legs draped limply from the seat down to the footrest of the wheelchair. He had said he knew everything that went on at El Recobro, but Ian got the feeling this was his first close look at Hadley Edwards.

In moments the electric hum of the chair announced Hadley's arrival. Sam came through the study door behind him.

"Delighted to meet you, Mr. Begley," Hadley said after they had shaken hands. "May I offer you a drink?"

Ian, thinking of how quickly even a beer might bring back the Begley of the bosque, held his breath until the younger man said he *would* "hold still for a Coke or an iced tea, maybe, whatever MacAndrews is having." Ian could see it was costing him something.

Sam now seemed actually irritated by Begley's being there, probably because he had seen the transport being organized by the Pendletons and Tim Springer. She nodded at Hadley and left the room. It seemed impossible that she could return with the drinks before any of them uttered another word, but she did. She must have hurried. She handed Cokes to Ian and Begley in silence, gave Hadley the gin and tonic he had asked for, and took a seat on a hassock just behind Hadley's right elbow.

Suddenly the whole venture seemed ridiculous. The tension in the room, between Sam and Begley, between Begley and Ian, was palpable. Only Hadley seemed at ease. Well, he was the one who counted.

"With Ian to vouch for you, Mr. Begley," Hadley said after Ian told him why they were there, "I wouldn't even think of questioning your credentials as a working cowboy. You strike me as a man who might even be able to handle men, but are you qualified to run the business side of things? I'm no expert, but I gather there's more to a stock-ranch operation then merely roping and branding."

When Begley stiffened at Hadley's words, then turned as red as if he had been slapped, Ian wondered about him as much as Hadley clearly did.

"I can goddamned well *learn*," Begley growled. There wasn't as much confidence in his voice as Ian would have liked.

Was he wrong, or did Sam look pleased at this tiny failure on Begley's part?

Ian broke in, "Hadley, the main thing is that you're looking for a man whose discretion you can count on. John has already proven himself on that score, unknown to you. He's been aware of what you've been doing on El Recobro since you started—and he's kept your secret."

"So it would seem," Hadley said. "I'm grateful to him for that. But quite aside from his capabilities as a ranch manager, would my neighbors believe he was legitimate? Wouldn't they be apt to ask where he got the money to set himself up like this?"

Begley, the hotheaded, giant brawler, the man who had, in Sam's words, "terrorized half the county," suddenly looked beaten, far more beaten than he looked lying on the Buckhorn floor with M.L. cradling his bloody head.

"I could learn," he said again. But his words were quite beside the point now, as lame as the leg he was nervously massaging.

"I don't believe you heard my second objection, Mr. Begley. I'm not entirely sure your capacity to learn would be enough," Hadley said, "I still wonder if people would really believe that I would stake you. I think you can see that questions of *any* kind about what goes on out here must be avoided."

Begley didn't answer. The silence was awkward.

"Hadley," Ian said. "Let's get something straight from the outset. It never was my intention that you put up any money. I'll take care of that." When Ian heard himself he could have ripped his tongue out. It wasn't the truth. He *had* intended that Hadley would provide the cash. Inadvertent as the lie was, bursting out of him without his willing it, he felt himself a fraud. Even a small operation would stretch his resources beyond their most elastic limits. But now said, it was too late to take it back.

"I'll have to think this over," Hadley said.

"How much time do you want?"

"Ten minutes."

That was a surprise. Ten days, ten *weeks*, in fact, would have seemed reasonable enough. But Ian didn't have time to speculate on Hadley's methods before the man in the wheel-chair spoke again.

"Sam, please show these gentlemen into the living room. I'll join you there once I've thought this through."

The air of the living room was heavy. Ian wondered what he was going to say if Hadley asked him to put his money where his mouth was, not that it was likely to come to that. Hadley wouldn't go along with Begley. Making them wait was just the prelude to easing Begley out without too much damage to the young man's feelings.

Sam stood looking through the double doors that led to the patio. She hadn't spoken to Ian since they left the study, hadn't looked at him.

It was *her* opinion that worried Ian.

Begley sat frozen in his chair, looking as close to catatonic as a young, powerful man could look, and his condition wasn't helped a bit by the last twisting viciousness of the hangover that had seemed to have let go of him for a bit while they sat with Hadley in the study.

Ian stared at the painting of the abandoned house.

Then he heard Hadley's chair in the hall, and he knew—without checking the watch on his wrist—that when the man rolled through the door he and Begley had watched with such intensity, ten minutes precisely would have passed.

Hadley was smiling. It wasn't exactly the smile of the victor, but of a man who knew victory was imminent. The two-minute warning had been given, and Hadley's team had possession with an eight-point lead.

Sam left the window and went to stand behind her husband again. This time the protective look was even more pronounced than before. Protection, it seemed to Ian, was the last thing Hadley Edwards needed.

"I have a counterproposition for you and Mr. Begley," Hadley said to Ian. "And it won't cost you anything. I've decided I'd like very much to put *my* money in his cattle business. I want to finance the entire operation. It is, after all, on my behalf that you've come to me with this proposal. There's only one condition:

"I'll take Mr. Begley only if *you* come with the deal."

Ian, Hadley, and Sam watched Begley start back toward the malpais with his two sorry horses before Tim Springer drove Ian back to the Yucca in the Cadillac.

After Ian had agreed to Hadley's terms back in that art-filled living room, he had looked at Sam.

Unless he was imagining things, she was feeling every bit as trapped as he knew he was.

Chapter XIV

"It wasn't hard at all, finding what little there was to find, Ian," Ernie Gomez said. "My first guess was right. Begley was born in Grant County, and from then on it was a piece of stale cake. You could have found out everything I did with just a couple of phone calls."

"As I told you, Ernie, for reasons of my own I wanted to stay on the outside of this. Go on."

"All right. John H. Begley was born to Irma Tull Begley in Silver City on May twelfth, 1938, which will make him thirty-five on his next birthday. A midwife named Clara Simpson took care of Irma. Begley was delivered in the Simpson home as a matter of fact, and Irma stayed there until the baby was two weeks old. I imagine there was some kind of payment made, probably in cash. Clara died seven years ago and left no records. Who, if anybody, paid her—and how much—is one of several things in the trail that isn't clear or showing promise of getting that way."

"Who was Begley senior?"

"I was just coming to that. Travis Begley was a drifter from Oklahoma. He married Irma in Deming six months before she gave birth to Jacky. It was a big surprise to her friends. None of them even knew she was seeing Travis Begley. He'd been a jack-of-all-trades around Deming and Silver City for a few years before Irma apparently met him in a café where she was waitressing. After the marriage he didn't work at all. Neither did she. They aren't remembered as deadbeats, though. Travis joined the army in 1941, the day after Pearl Harbor as a matter of fact. He never came back to New Mexico after the war, but there's no local knowledge that he was killed or missing and Irma never acted like a war widow. I haven't had time to run that down, but I've got Pete Runnels's office in Washington checking for me."

"You're saying she *never* worked again?"

"She went back to waitressing when Jacky was five years old. Hung on at the same place, Murphy's Steak House in Silver City, until just before Jacky was due to graduate from high school in 1955, when she quit without notice and moved to Albuquerque. She's still living there, working a cash register in a Skaggs drugstore on Lomas Boulevard. If her old neighbors are correct, she's fifty-five now. And if they're right about something else, she and her son haven't seen each other since she moved there."

"A falling out?"

"Nobody knows. It hardly squares with the facts, but it well could be. In his senior year Jacky damned near killed one of his classmates in a fight. The other kid was hospitalized for a month, and it looked for a bit as if young Begley would wind up in reform school, if not jail. Irma stuck with him all the way. Must have cost her a bundle. At any rate she left soon after the court put him on probation. He started working on the ranches around Tularosa, she went to the city, and Jacky put in a year with a probation officer. That was apparently it for the two of them. Neither of them are remembered as being very talkative, particularly about private matters."

"Were there other men in her life before Travis Begley?"

"Lots of them. She had a reputation as a party girl from the time she was fourteen. Funny thing, though. After she married Begley, it all stopped. Started going to church. People who know her pretty well in Albuquerque character- ize her as straight arrow, a hard worker in her church, quiet—the 'nice widow Begley.' Same was true of her all the time Jacky was growing up, according to the old-timers at Murphy's. Never had another thing to do with men. Period." Ernie smiled. "I sensed a little regret about *that* on the part of some of my male informants. They remember her as a hell of a good-looking woman."

"And she hasn't seen her son in all those years?"

"Not that anyone who knows her can remember. Never talks about him, either. My sources in Albuquerque were amazed to hear she has a son."

"Ernie, among these 'lots' of men she knew before she married Begley, was there any *one* in particular?"

"Now that you mention it, yes. Some big wheeler-dealer who said he hailed from Texas, an older man, used to take her down to El Paso and Juarez for long weekends from time to time. Spent a good-sized chunk of change on her. Faded right out of sight when Begley came on the scene."

"Have you got a name?"

"No. I struck out completely there. I suspect he was married and covering his tracks pretty well."

"Any description?"

"Not a good one. Never had anything to do with her friends or the people at Murphy's. Big fellow, though. Cattle- man, probably. Drove an expensive car, a LaSalle, I under- stand, but one that carried New Mexico plates. Suppose that's a clue, since he claimed to be a Texan. Oh, they remember he limped some."

Ian nodded. He had nearly all he wanted now, not that he really wanted it. There was just one more question.

"What does the birth registry say the 'H' in John H. Begley stands for, Ernie?"

"Hall. John Hall Begley..." The lawyer's mouth dropped open. Yes, he was quick. "My God, Ian..." he whispered. "I'm sorry... I've no right to speculate like that."

Ernie knew. Perhaps in Jonathan Hardy's old records he had discovered that when James MacAndrews catted around the state, he called himself John Hall.

"I told you before, Ernie, that you're entitled to know
what this is all about. And your speculation is absolutely
right. If James Hall MacAndrews were still living and thirty-
five, he could be John Hall Begley's twin. Jacky Begley is my
half brother—and Sarah knew it."

Chapter XV

Not for one moment did he consider telling Begley—or
anyone. It was enough that Ernie Gomez knew, safe as Ernie
was. That the young man in question didn't know seemed
clear.

And that he would have to remain in the basin far longer
than planned seemed clear, too, thanks to the way Hadley
Edwards had so cheerfully suckered him. Even without the
hurts and haunts of twenty years earlier to tear at him, the
last thing he wanted to do was get back in the cattle business,
but he hadn't hesitated long enough to draw a breath before
he nodded to Hadley's insistence that he join the venture.
The way Hadley had *suckered* him? Blackmail was a far more
fitting description of what had taken place in the living room
of El Recobro, but the winning charm and sheer force of
Hadley had made it hard to feel anything but admiration for
him. As bland and uncommitted as Ian had tried to look
when he first proposed that Edwards have John Begley start
running stock on the pastures of the old D Cross A, some
extra sense on the part of the man Ian had assumed an
amateur led that amateur past Ian's guard and straight into
desires Ian himself hadn't guessed he had—not while it
seemed certain during the ten minutes they waited in the
living room that Hadley was going to turn them down. Ian
had wanted the offer badly then—but only for Begley.

He should have seen Hadley's punch coming and slipped
it, or at the very least rolled with it. He should have been
ready for it even when it landed; Sam's almost hostile silence
throughout the conversation should have signaled it was on

its way. She knew what her husband was going to say. And she wanted none of it.

The ten minutes Sam, Begley, and he had waited for Hadley to roll into the living room were ten of the most unsettling minutes of his life.

Enough. It was nut-and-bolt time now.

Smith Wyndham was silent at the New York end of the line when Ian called him and told him he was quitting his job at the agency.

"All right, Ian," he said finally. "God knows why a man of your talents wants to exile himself like this, but for Christ's sake don't send me any letter of resignation. You can come back to W and K next month, next year, anytime at all as long as *I* run this shop."

He might have expected Smitty's next question. Was there a woman? Except for the decency Wyndham had just shown, Ian might have joked it away.

"I honestly don't know, Smitty," he said. It wasn't enough if he was really laying it all on the line. "Yes, I guess there *is* a woman. But I think I'm leveling with you when I say that I don't think there's a woman in the way you mean."

Smitty, soberly for him, began the usual good-bye, good luck, and keep-in-touch stuff, but suddenly interrupted himself.

"Hey!" he said. "Do you want Nancy's report on your 'editor lady' at Hampton House?"

As serious as the conversation had been to this point, Ian couldn't check a quiet laugh. *Nancy's* report in a pig's eye. Smitty had done the snooping himself. And the faint note of disappointment in the words "editor lady" told Ian he hadn't found anything at Hampton House close to what he was always looking for.

"I got there about twenty years too late," Smitty said. There was an awkward cough from the New York end of the line as Smitty realized he had just let the cat out of the bag. "She's sixty-five if she's a day, but she must have been a knockout once. One of those intellectual Manhattan Jewish broads whose brains—five will get you ten—never got in the way of the important things in life. Tops in her field, from what people at Hampton's agency tell me. You wouldn't believe her office. Looks like an auction room at Christie's. Sculpture, paintings, old leather books, all of it genuine, and if I'm any judge, worth a king's ransom. Oh, yeah, Lee

Berman is her married name. She was born Leila Balutan. Her brother was the sculptor who did all that great stuff in Taos that MOMA and the galleries went ape over a few years back."

God *damn* Sarah. From the grave she was dipping a lot more confining net than the one Hadley used. This time the trout had better wriggle out and head for the deepest pool. And it was a net, make no mistake about it, not just that filmy web of coincidence he had found himself tangled in ever since he had driven so recklessly up the far side of Mescalero Gap.

If he failed Sarah—as he had every intention of failing her—Ian would have to take the full weight, not only of the destruction of Max's bust of Ignacio, but the added weight of having forced Max's own sister to do the dirty work: Max's sister, Leila, who had known the vaquero and who had been Ian's first disinterested critic, not that this "intellectual Manhattan Jewish broad" was at all likely to remember the critique or the artist. Not so fast. Why wouldn't Leila remember? That crusty old varmint who refused to lie decently quiet in her grave up at Taos would have damned well seen to it that Leila knew.

For the next three days he gave little thought to any of them: Hadley, Sam, Begley, Sarah, or Leila Balutan. He ran up a hundred and fifty dollars of long-distance bills on the Yucca's phone, hoping that Harry, in his innocent, pathetic cupidity, had figured out a way to keep a little piece of it for himself. The rent on his Manhattan apartment was paid through the first of the year, but he had to make sure the super checked it from time to time, not that it contained much he cared about, but he was, by God, going to be coming back to it.

He closed his account at Chase Manhattan and had his officer there send a letter of credit to First Commercial in Albuquerque, parent bank of the branch on Frontera Street that had once been independent and the pride of Black Springs, the drab town's one imposing building. James Hall MacAndrews had been one of the original stockholders in the old bank when it organized in the twenties. He had lost his stake when he failed to come up with his pledged subscription.

He made three long calls to Kenneth Turpin, his broker at Bache & Company, who had always treated Ian's modest portfolio as though it were J. P. Morgan's. Ian had never been much of a market-watcher, but he wanted Turpin to take over completely now. He had other things to do besides checking the financial pages every day.

A call to the New Mexico Livestock Board began the reregistration of the brand "D Cross A" in the names of John H. Begley and Ian J. MacAndrews.

In the past he had been a careless manager of his own affairs, but he found the three days of busywork relaxing, and something else—strangely rewarding. It troubled him that he felt good about it.

There was, however, some genuine comfort in discovering that in an emergency he could lay his hands on slightly over a hundred and fifty thousand dollars, not that it appeared that he would need it now. Hadley had talked to Ernie sometime in the three days, and a bank account had been established for the ranching operation. Ian didn't ask how much the stake amounted to. Hadley wouldn't skimp, and they weren't planning to create an empire of beef like the XIT or the King Ranch, anyway.

It was enough to know that with Hadley's money (and his own, in extremis) there was no chance he would be tempted to put himself at risk by going after Sarah's.

Late in the afternoon of that third day he drove out to the foundation of his mother's unfinished house with Douglas MacAndrews's cracked leather briefcase on the seat beside him.

Again big doughy clouds had threatened rain without its coming, and now they had partly uncovered the western sky, shrinking back in sullen surrender from the tops of the Oscuras, leaving the earth and sky ripped apart along a horizon-to-horizon seam of blue. The sun had not yet dropped below the gray when he turned from the highway, but by the time he pulled up at the building site it was halfway down to the mountain ridges, deepening from yellow to burning orange. As he walked to the old stones with the briefcase under his arm, the sun now lit the slopes toward Cuchillo Peak, seeming to set the tilted rangeland at its feet afire, and making the churning underbelly of the clouds look even darker.

He sat on the broken wall on the west end of the foundation and slipped his mother's plans from the case. This was the house he was to have been born in. With more than sixty years of aging the yellowed drafting sheets, not much heavier than tissue to begin with, had hardened to the slick brittleness of old waxed-paper, and he feared that when he opened them they would crack along the folds. But open them he must.

When he got to where working prints were needed, he could run the pieces to Albuquerque or El Paso and have them taped back together and photocopied, and then the different trades would be able to work from expendable copies. And by God, they *would* work from these drawings, as quaint and old-fashioned, even laughable, as some of the delicate lines and outdated terms might seem to modern plumbers and electricians. There would be no gussied-up, state-of-the-art, high-tech computer printouts used on this house—no shortcuts taken, either.

He hadn't even mentioned the building of the house to Begley, had only told him that here on this gentle rise of land was where the corrals and holding pens, the squeeze-chutes and what small shelters they had to have, would stand, and that over there was where they would sink their well, and that out in the south pasture was where they would bulldoze out the first new cattle tank to dimple this vast expanse of grass in fifty years.

He hadn't talked to Hadley about it, either, except in general terms, and of course Hadley had said yes and that he would foot the bill for whatever kind of complex Ian thought was necessary.

He had no qualms about using Hadley's money. Above all he had to keep his own intact; he would, he knew, find more than enough rat holes to pound his personal financial sand into later on, getting reestablished in Manhattan.

He opened the drawings as he might have gently pulled a dressing from a wound, and to his surprise they *didn't* crack or come apart.

It would be a solid house; the architect's firm resolve on that score underlay the almost dainty rendering of the front, southern, elevation on the first page that gleamed now like gold leaf in the rays of the dying sun. Something had been kept by Ann MacAndrews of every house she had lived in during the odyssey that had stranded her in the Ojos Negros Basin. There was a hint of the one on D Street in Georgetown, remembered from the snapshots in her photo album, the house where she had played hostess for her widowed father when he became one of the few Democrats hired into the administration of William Howard Taft; and there was some of the territorial bungalow on Palace Avenue in Santa Fe, when Standish Jennings's failing lungs brought him and his daughter to New Mexico. There was a good bit more of the old place that had lately become Sam and Hadley Edwards's El Recobro mansion. Blessedly missing was the gingerbread and ornamental frippery most of the country considered the latest thing back before World War I. With all these bits and pieces from everywhere, it was still a simple house. Probably Ann MacAndrews had never heard of the man, but Frank Lloyd Wright would have liked this house. It grew directly from the land, embraced the rise behind it and spread to the east and west in sweeping laterals as natural and secure as the stratified rock the old foundation rested on. Soaring, overhanging eaves to fend off the sun's wickedest August punishment issued from a roof slanted low to slip the fierce basin winds that came with timetable regularity every spring, and that blew again without warning at other seasons.

There would have been a time when he would have wanted to paint this house... and without the malice that guided his brush when he put the foundation into the canvas hanging in the Edwards living room.

The second page, the floor plan, revealed some of the designer's aims. There, facing the north pastures, was the office intended to make an accountable manager out of an irresponsible, wayward husband; the nursery that was to have held an Ian or someone like him was separated from the office by the master bedroom; and across a deceptively spacious living room (it was called a parlor here) another sleeping room, smaller, a guestroom he supposed, looked out toward the butte that shielded El Recobro. Strangely enough, it was precisely the house someone might have sketched for Begley, M.L., and Ian. He would sleep in the smaller bedroom. He would only be a guest when all was said and done, and he wouldn't outstay the unexpected, blackmail welcome that had come his way.

He put the drawings back in Douglas MacAndrews's briefcase and walked the four sides of the fieldstone foundation wall. When he brushed aside with his boot the chaparral that masked the stones in several places, he was gratified to find that the wall wasn't in as bad shape as the weeds had made it look. No more than fifteen or twenty slabs of rock would be needed to set the level for the superstructure, and chances were that a search of the nearby grasses would turn them up. If he could locate the roman brick the specifications called for, and if he could find men who knew how to lay it up, the house would take but weeks to build.

He started back to the MG, turning twice to look at the place the house would stand. He could almost see it now.

His hand was on the ignition key when he heard Hadley's twin-engined plane on its takeoff run. That's right, the chief of the "tourist bureau" had said that he and Tim would be flying out today, to San Diego. Ian watched as the aircraft cleared the butte seeking altitude. He watched it as it hurtled toward the sun that was almost caressing the farthest of the rounded tops of the Oscuras. He watched it out of sight.

Sam was alone at El Recobro now.

Chapter XVI

In December of the year before Ian Jennings MacAndrews returned to the cattle business in Chupadera County, an inspector for the New Mexico Livestock Board stumbled on a case of psoroptic cattle scab during a check of a feedlot in the southeastern corner of the state. Eleven small ranches went under quarantine. None of them were in the Ojos Negros Basin.

It had always been more or less that way with the Chupadera ranches. Disease had never been a problem. The oldest stockman in the basin couldn't have recollected the last time there had been an outbreak of scabies or blackleg, and hoof-and-mouth hadn't claimed a herd since well before statehood in 1912. If fewer beef animals grazed the high Ojos Negros pastures now, the reduction had come about for other reasons.

Oddly enough, the same ring of mountains that formed an almost impassable barrier to disease also limited the number of cows, calves, and steers the land could feed, and the number had grown smaller year by year. A war of attrition raged on the basin range with no prospect of an armistice. The spring runoffs gouged the older arroyos deeper and wider every year and chewed new raw ones into the pastures when the melting snows roared down the great "closed system" watersheds each spring to force their way into the big river slogging its way south toward Mexico along the county's western side. At every summer solstice the sun rose on hundreds of new miles of dry watercourses cut into the land, fresh wounds that would never heal, on what had been level grassland the year before.

Left to themselves, the grasses—mostly grama, but with swatches of galleta and buffalo grass whispering between the stands of juniper, piñon, and scrub oak on the lower slopes of the mountains—might have sponged up the annual floods, might even have held them back, but a century of heavy grazing had left them too sparse and weak to do more than barely persevere against their other enemies: saltbush, grease-wood, creosote bush, and cholla. Long before the Shorthorn and the Hereford (and later in lesser numbers the Charolais and the Santa Gertrudis and the Angus) had nibbled at them, the grasses *had* done more than persevere—they had flourished. The floor of the basin from the foot of Cuchillo to the malpais was thick with pale green wands that bent with the wind and then stood tall when the wind had passed.

The only marks on these rolling meadows—and these marks seldom lasted through the growing season—were the narrow creases left by pronghorn antelope as they made their way to water.

Even the Spaniards couldn't wear out that verdant carpet, but they only had themselves and their Indian peons to feed—not an entire nation whose hunger for beef grew more ravenous with every passing decade.

In the 1880s, pushed out by the filling up of Texas rangeland during and after the Civil War, the first longhorns—wild-eyed, gaunt, stringy but durable—nosed into the Ojos Negros from the east, driven through dusty, windblown passes such as Mescalero Gap by a different breed of men than the basin had known till then. Long years of lonely herding had hardened these new arrivals, as ready for a fight as for a friendship, against the civilizing uses of society. They seldom talked, even among themselves, and the people of the small

Spanish towns and the bosque farms watched as the *Tejanos* strung their fences across the grass and hollowed out cattle tanks in the rocky ground wherever there seemed a remote chance of capturing a few drops of precious water. The newcomers built homes of timbers dragged down the sides of the Jicarillas and the other mountains, fortress homes quite unlike the squat adobes that had been the almost universal dwellings in the basin since the days of the Entrada.

These newcomers didn't know it, nor did their more settled neighbors, but their coming had doomed the thick, long grass.

The longhorns, and then the more easily fattened and more profitable breeds and crossbreeds that took the longhorns' place, cropped the grama ever closer to the thin soil that hid its roots—and the weeds moved in.

A few ranchers, such as Douglas MacAndrews and his brother, Angus, of the D Cross A, sensed the damage being done and gave huge sections of their acreage a rest from time to time. Some others, heedless, went by the board.

Hard lessons learned, the surviving ranchers scratched their way toward the second half of the twentieth century. Seven famous brands died during the drought years of the 1930s, and the Great Depression made victims of a dozen more.

In the year that Ian MacAndrews and his partner John H. Begley resurrected the brand of the D Cross A at the New Mexico Livestock Board, Chupadera County shipped 32,107 cattle off to the markets of the east. Hundreds upon hundreds of uncounted miles of double-twist, two-barb Glidden wire still crisscrossed the stunted grass. Some ranges, like that of the old D Cross A, had rested long enough to become almost lush again.

In that year the county's 3,678 square miles was home to 6,450 people. The 1970 U.S. census was the first to register the fact that Hispanics no longer made up the majority of the population. No one could tell to the nearest twenty thousand how many other Hispanics, illegals—wetbacks, they were called—had traveled either of the two highways that quartered the Ojos Negros, or had drifted north on half-forgotten roads like the one to Williston. No one asked.

Chapter XVII

"You lied to me, Jennings, or MacAndrews, or whatever your moniker really is!" B.J. Howland said. He squirted his tobacco juice at a rock, hit it, and wiped the stubble on his chin.

Two of the immigrants who had come in on Hadley's last flight were helping Begley unload the lengths of pipe and the plumbing fixtures B.J. had trucked to the building site. Ian held up his hands. "Hold on, B.J. I didn't exactly lie. I do use both names. Have for years."

"It ain't the *names*. You let on you was a greenhorn, a dude from the big city. Just look at all that stuff." The trucker jabbed his finger at the new corral, where Begley's two old horses, as listless here as they had been in the bosque, were asleep standing up, and he jabbed it again at the unassembled squeeze-chute and tiltable branding-table whose parts were stacked against the week-old feed shed. "You're bossing this outfit, ain't you?"

Ian hoped Begley hadn't caught that. B.J. was almost yelling to make himself heard above the hammering of the carpenters working on the roof trusses of the new house.

"Found out all about you when I stopped in town," B.J. said. "Always eat with Big Anita when I'm in Black Springs. She broadcasts more news than Cronkite. Where'd you get them wetbacks? Looks to me like they're still dripping."

"Wetbacks? I don't know that they're illegals."

B.J. grinned. "Wouldn't ask, either. What a boss don't know ain't apt to hurt him."

Ian's nerves twitched at B.J.'s quick recognition of the undocumented status of the working crew. He had argued with Hadley about using Hadley's Central Americans. Hadley had laughed away his objections. "Don't sweat it, Ian. There's scarcely a business in the county that doesn't crawl with illegals from time to time. Who would blow the whistle? Just

142

so we keep anyone from knowing where ours come from or
where we send them."

Ian had to admit that it was a lot more than mere
convenience to have this steady supply of labor delivered to
his doorstep every morning, and if the workers kept their
mouths shut, they couldn't be told from the aliens that flowed
regularly across the Rio Grande at El Paso.

As if by magic Hadley had even found bricklayers for
him, and the walls of the house had gone up in little more
than a week. For a month the whole project had moved right
along, perhaps too smoothly.

The truck unloaded, Begley joined them just as B.J.
changed the subject.

"Still on the wagon, MacAndrews?" the trucker said.
"Don't see how you do it. Maybe *I* ought to quit. Talk to you
about it sometime."

Begley caught the remark and stared at B.J. There was
flame in his eyes when he turned to Ian.

"Unless you got some other plans for me right now,
MacAndrews, I'll take the pickup out to Johnson's place at
Stone Creek and pick up those two new roans you bought. If
I'm going to ride fence tomorrow, I'd as soon have something
better under me than either of my old critters."

"Go ahead, John."

Begley gave B.J. a hard look and without another word
walked to the blue pickup with the double horse-carrier
mounted in the bed. He didn't look at B.J. or Ian as he
drove away and didn't wave to M.L., who stood in the door of
the Airstream they had moved up from the bosque the day
after the talk with Hadley.

If the building had gone smoothly, it hadn't been a
bump-free road Ian and Begley had traveled for almost seven
weeks now. Begley's meager conversation consisted of short
questions. "Where do you want this stowed?" "You going to
run purebreds or crosses or both?" "Will M.L. and me live in
the trailer or in the house with you?" The last was about the
only time he used any pronoun but "you," and Ian had yet to
hear a "we."

But he worked. Even if his heart didn't seem in it, by
the Lord Harry, how he worked. It was Begley who rigged
the corral. The piñon posts for it were dropped off at eight on
a Tuesday morning, and he had them all staked into the
caliche by sundown the same day when Ian returned from

seeing about a pump in Alamogordo. The corral didn't look
much like Sam Edwards's whitewashed paddock, but it was
what Ian wanted. It didn't surprise him that the younger man
wasn't more enthusiastic. When Hadley forced Ian into taking
charge, it would have dented anybody's ego.

At no time did Ian suspect Begley of drinking on the job.
There must have been gallons stashed in the trailer, though;
in the mornings he smelled like a sump and his blue eyes
were streaked with red. And red, blue, clouded, or clear,
those eyes fixed themselves on Ian a thousand times a day. It
was an odd, unexpected switch. By rights, Ian felt *he* should
have been the watcher. Begley had never recanted the threats
he had made in either the barroom or the bosque.

M.L., still unwelcome at the Yucca, had taken a room in
town, but she moved back into the trailer the day after the
newly drilled well spit up its first cupful of rusty water.
Begley's small generator was now lying smashed on the rocks
of the malpais where it had fallen from the pickup in the
move from the bosque. Ian, mindful of the girl's condition,
rented a portable generator at Stafford's until regular electri-
cal connections could be made.

It had taken an effort on Ian's part to persuade M.L. to
quit her job at the Buckhorn, even after he told her she
would go on salary as Begley had.

"Don't want to be beholden any more than I already
am," she said.

"You'll earn your keep, M.L.," Ian said. "It's going to be
a fair-sized house to run, and you'll have to do the cooking.
Most important, I want someone here all the time. They
won't get us our phone for a couple of months at least, and
someone has to take messages, maybe run to town when John
and I are riding."

She still didn't seem satisfied. "What I'm doing now sure
ain't worth a plugged nickel. It don't begin to make it up to
you for what you're doing for John."

Ian wondered again why he hadn't noticed at the Buckhorn
that the girl was pregnant. It made him realize how few times
he had been around women who were carrying. Women such
as Laurie and her friends simply didn't get pregnant. In ten
years there hadn't even been a scare. A scare? Funny thing to
call it. How might things have turned out if Laurie and he
had made a baby? He would have married her of course, but

would it have put an earlier end to his drinking? He doubted
it.

He wondered, too, if Begley and M.L. had talked marriage. This was hardly the country for young women to have
babies out of wedlock. A marriage, even to Begley, should go a
long way toward closing the rift between Harry Kimbrough and
his daughter. If M.L. and Begley hadn't discussed marriage, it
was probably because Begley didn't want to. Little bits and
pieces of his fragmented talk—all there would ever be, it
seemed—revealed a determination to thumb his nose, the nose
that had bled itself empty on the Buckhorn floor, at the town,
the county and every last thing the town and county held to.

Ian stayed on at the Yucca while the house was going up.
It wasn't easy. Harry had turned sullen as soon as he discovered
what Ian was engaged in with the two young people. He
didn't speak when Ian spoke to him, just handed over mail or
whatever, and Ian finally began making all his trips to the
motel office only when he knew Jody was on the desk, not so
much to avoid Harry's accusing eyes as to avoid inflicting
further pain on him.

There were, it turned out, just the two children in the
Kimbrough family. He was surprised to learn that the girl
hadn't reached twenty yet, wouldn't for another month. Perhaps it was the heavy makeup that had caused him to think
her older, or perhaps the look of instant maturity some
otherwise juvenile women don with their maternity clothes.

If Ian still felt trapped, if M.L. still felt she wasn't paying
her way, and if Begley still raged inside, at least Jody felt that
the star of everybody at the reconstituted D Cross A was in
the ascendancy.

When he drove out in the jeep, which was almost every
day even though school had started, his grin was as much a
permanent feature of the landscape as Cuchillo's beetling
brow. Ian didn't ask him how he was managing it with his
father feeling as he did. The younger Kimbrough was worth
his weight in gold running all those time-consuming errands
that would have taken Ian or Begley or M.L. away from their
other tasks. The MG had lost none of its allure. Ian abandoned
the half-formed notion of trading it in on something heavier.

Finally he met the only Kimbrough he hadn't met. Elsie,
Harry's wife, paid a visit to her daughter. There was no
unbridgeable gulf between *them*. Elsie, who looked from a

hundred yards' distance more like M.L.'s older sister than her mother, ran from the jeep Jody parked at the trailer and wrapped her arms around the pregnant girl as if she would crush both lives. They both bawled like infants. Then, the pair walking as if they were roaming a cathedral, M.L. showed her mother the half-finished house. Through a rear window Ian saw them standing in front of the roughed-in door of the master bedroom like pilgrims before a shrine. Later, when M.L. brought her mother to where Ian was working in the squeeze-chute, he was terrified Elsie might kiss his hand when he held it out to her to shake.

"Bless you for what you're doing for my baby, Mr. MacAndrews," Elsie said. *Kiss* his hand? She might have licked it if he hadn't pulled it away.

He would have liked to have seen how the father-to-be reacted to M.L.'s mother, but Begley was riding fence.

M.L. stayed inside the trailer every morning, and in the house when the water and power were switched to it from the Airstream; Jody confided that she was having morning sickness "to a fare-thee-well." She made good recoveries; there wasn't a sign of nausea when she brought lunch to Ian and Begley outside, nor on the few occasions when they ate indoors on crates. The furniture they had ordered hadn't yet arrived. She tried to lighten the mood at these meals—and at the rare supper when she fed them both—but they were hushed, funereal affairs. Begley fed himself without looking at Ian for a change, stoking the food in like some throbbing piece of machinery, but one with clanking dissonances amid the throbs, as if the machine were wearing out. He never talked. After a few cheerfully inane remarks M.L. would stop talking, too, and just stare at the two of them.

They didn't lack visitors.

The Pendletons shuttled in and out of El Recobro on "business," and they never missed dropping by. They wore well with Ian. With both of them it was a case of what you see is what you get. Ian had always shied from "dedicated" people, but he could make allowances for the Pendletons. He still thought them amateurs suited up for a pro's game, though, and secretly hoped Hadley would bench them before they got roughed up.

It wasn't the same with the Vergaras, who also commuted to the Edwards place. Something fierce burned inside Alejandro and his wife. Unlike the other Central Americans

who rested at El Recobro before moving on to a safer if not a
better life, the Vergaras weren't refugees; they were exiles. It
made a difference, and Ian could see it in their eyes. When
they called at the building site they came on horseback,
riding two of the American Saddle Breds from the El Recobro
stable and showing superb show-ring seats, posting classical-
ly in their English saddles over broken ground that had once
only known the hoofprints of cow ponies.

He liked Alex, but the burning look in his eyes, even
more heated than that in Consuelo's, made him appear
. . . what? . . . messianic?

M.L. was taken with Consuelo. "She sure is a lady. I never
met a Spanish woman before who talks such keen English."

Between flights to God-knew-where Hadley put in frequent appearances, driven over by Tim Springer in the Cadillac
or the Land Cruiser. He always went to the trouble of getting
into the wheelchair and touring the entire site, nodding approval, offering more help or money, and asking questions. He
had never seen a squeeze-chute or a branding-table. Ian more
or less forced Begley to explain the way they worked, hoping to
involve the younger man and perhaps whip up some enthusiasm. Begley just went through the motions.

Springer, it turned out, had been born and reared on a
farm in Nottinghamshire and knew something about raising
cattle, but as milkers, not for beef. "How are you going to put
weight on grass-loving animals in this bloody dry desert,
MacAndrews? On our farm you couldn't take a step without
your Wellies filling up with water."

"It will consist mostly of just keeping them alive, Springer," Ian said, conscious of how the difference in context made
the use of surnames sound so much friendlier coming from
the Englishman and him than they did when the "MacAndrews"
came from Begley.

He had wondered if Hadley would show alarm at how
much money he was spending on the house. Hadley was
ecstatic.

"You know, Sam guessed you would use your mother's
plans. It couldn't look more right for this sweeping country.
Hers must have been the forerunner of your talent." Ian let
that pass.

He insisted on seeing the house even though it wasn't
ready. It was a chore to get the wheelchair inside, particularly
since the veranda and its stairs weren't finished. He was

silent throughout the tour, but he turned expansive when Ian introduced him to M.L. in the bare, unpainted kitchen. He treated the girl—who twisted her apron feverishly in an attack of nerves brought on by meeting this rich and powerful man—as if she were the dowager Duchess of Kent.

"When you're all settled and ready for entertaining, Miss Kimbrough, you simply must have Mrs. Edwards and me to dinner, or supper as you southwesterners prefer to call it. Forgive me for inviting us myself, but whatever it is you have there on the stove smells marvelous."

M.L. was terrified and tongue-tied, but smitten. Ian made a note to build a ramp at the side of the veranda while wondering if Sam's guess about the plans meant she thought he would be staying on indefinitely. He would have to set her straight on that.

She drove Hadley over herself just once and didn't leave the car. Ian talked with Hadley through the open window on the passenger's side, but he bent his head to get a view of her. Beyond an almost undetectable nod she didn't pay him any particular attention, nor did she say a word. She stared at the crew working on the house, her hands clenched on the steering wheel as if she feared the car might jump out from under her.

"Yes, Ian," Hadley said that day, "as I commented once before, it will be a lovely, gracious house, but—" He looked up at Ian, smiling. "I didn't see a place in it where you could set up a studio."

Before he could stop himself Ian snapped, "Put that right out of your mind! *There will be no studio!*"

Sam whipped her head toward Ian at his outburst. Her blue eyes went as wide as lakes. She reached down and turned the key in the ignition. Hadley nodded and the car moved off.

Ian felt a little ashamed of himself for barking at Hadley in front of Sam that way, but damn Hadley's eyes, anyway!

Until now he had been almost happy. The hard, muscle-burning, sweaty work readied him for a good night's sleep when he returned to the Yucca, and moving around the range, particularly when he was doing it alone, kept his mind away from things that bothered him. Suppers at Anita's, good talk with *los hermanos*, and his reading on those evenings when he wasn't too enjoyably exhausted for it, provided all the entertainment he had needed. It wasn't an exciting life,

but it was more than just endurable for the few more months
it would take before he felt he could leave the basin.

Best of all he found he was able to think about the things
Ernie had told him without too much soul-searing anguish.
Still, Begley was the one-and-only hitch. The cloud over the
two of them, while not as threatening as in the first days, had
spread into a dull, gray blanket.

Ian admired Hadley for never complaining about being a
chair-bound cripple, but he now realized that Hadley actually
had little to complain about. Of all of the amateurs at El
Recobro, Hadley was the biggest amateur of all. He had
played amateur games all his life. Horses, and what went
with horses, had once been the most important game, but
never the only one. The fall from the hunter had only been a
minor setback. Building shopping centers, creating towns
around exclusive golf clubs, investing in films, making corpo-
rate raids with the ease of an undetected card-counter at a
Las Vegas blackjack table: these were games, too. He was like
one of those grand masters who tour the remote provinces of
chess taking on all comers, playing a dozen boards at once
and never losing. The accident had been a mere draw, not a
loss. His rescuing of the anti-Somoza Nicaraguans was a
game, and the ranching was now a smaller game within the
smuggled-alien game.

Ian MacAndrews had probably become a game to Hadley,
too.

Ernie Gomez and Carrie Spletter came to call. While
Ernie and Ian toured the compound, M.L. and Carrie, whose
attitude toward the pregnant girl gave no hint of censure or
condescension, chatted in the kitchen. Begley and Gomez
acknowledged each other curtly, but the meeting didn't seem
to spoil Ernie's pleasure in what he saw. He and Ian sat on
the veranda steps when Begley went back to work, and the
lawyer spread his arms wide, as if he wanted to embrace the
world.

"You know, of course, that you look like you belong in
this setting, don't you?" Ernie said.

"Now don't *you* start!" Ian said. "This is temporary, and
don't forget it for a moment."

He hadn't snapped as he had at Hadley, but Ernie's
protests of "all right, all *right!*" made him aware of the
sharpness in his voice.

Ernie glanced to where Begley was nailing battings to the feed shed. "Have you tipped your hand to him about my report?"

"No."

"Going to?"

"Don't know yet. I doubt it. What worthwhile purpose would it serve at this late date?"

Ernie shrugged, tacitly acknowledging that he couldn't answer, then he looked at Ian with a different, fresh anxiety written in his face.

"Don't get sore, Ian, but as your lawyer, I'm obligated to remind you of something. The deadline for delivering that portrait of Max Balutan to Hampton House is March thirty-first."

"That's just another date on the calendar, Ernie," Ian said.

Begley, for once, sought Ian out on a day when he had come in from a late-afternoon sweep of the northern pastures.

"You had another visitor today, MacAndrews. Guy in a Jeep a mile west of where you went through the fence the day you drove out to the slickrock." Probably it was as close to admitting he had spied on Ian as Begley would ever get.

"Did he cut his way in?" Ian said.

"Don't think so. I didn't see any breaks. He must have come in on the Williston road. Least that's the way he drove away from me when I spotted him. He was giving you and the Edwards place a good look-see through binoculars from that high ground south of Negrito Peak. Lost, I guess."

"We'll keep an eye out for him if and when he gets lost again, John. You're sure he's gone?"

"Yeah." It didn't seem to matter. It probably didn't, but he could have shown some concern.

"Good," Ian said. "We won't be on the place tomorrow. We're driving M.L. to Albuquerque to do some shopping. While she's busy, you and I will head down south of the city and hit a cattle auction. It's time to stock our range, John."

"Sure," Begley said, his voice toneless, flat. "Why not?"

Chapter XVIII

The drive to Albuquerque, with all three of them cramped in the MG, began badly.

Begley, at M.L.'s urging, had offered the use of the pickup, but Ian pointed out that the old heap's tires were worn to the cords and it had no spare. A check of the Greyhound schedule told them the bus times wouldn't fit, so it was the MG or nothing. Begley looked sour.

Ian first planned going through Williston, but when he picked them up at the new house an hour before sunup, he saw how Begley's bad leg would suffer on the old road. M.L. was jammed in the jump seat, turned sideways, and there was no way Begley could slide his seat back with her body blocking the way. Ian turned the little car around and headed for the highway. The three-hour trip would still be murder on Begley.

It would be no picnic for Ian and M.L., either; the stink of last night's liquor blown his way from Begley almost made him gag, and the fumes could hardly be a tonic for M.L.'s morning sickness. It was too chilly for the first hour to do more than crack the window if he didn't want to freeze the girl to the marrow.

They were halfway between Corona and Estancia with the sun pouring through the hatchback window and the air in the car getting close when M.L., who had been shifting about behind him every thirty seconds for the last twenty miles, leaned forward and begged him to stop.

Begley, whose only sounds so far had been wet snores when he dozed off once, struggled from the car when Ian braked down on the shoulder and walked with M.L. toward the fence running along the right-of-way.

She wasn't sick; just had to go. Poor kid. The last of the piñon was five miles behind them. There wasn't even a sprig of sage for her to crouch behind as far as the eye could see across the bunch-grass *llano,* and as bad luck would have it, half a dozen cars were going to pass from each direction as she squatted in Begley's shadow. Ian couldn't see her face, but he knew she must have nearly died when one of the passing drivers blasted his horn at her. At any other time of the morning this road would be as empty as a noontime alley in a Mexican village. Begley hovered over the girl until she finished, his thick arms spread wide in a futile effort to hide her, the pose actually attracting more attention than if he had stood some distance off and gazed out over the *llano.*

M.L. was still blushing when she returned to the MG. Begley muttered, "Thanks, MacAndrews," as if it had been squeezed from him, and they got under way again.

Ian stopped at an Exxon station in Estancia under the pretext of using the restroom himself, but really to give M.L. another chance, and she took it, her eyes registering relief and gratitude. He did the same at the Stuckey's on the interstate before they rolled westward through Tijeras Canyon and into Albuquerque.

He had expected the city to have changed in twenty years, but not this much. In his days at the university and for some time afterward, Albuquerque had been twenty miles long and one street wide, Central Avenue, old Route 66 of Johnny Mercer's kicks. Now, elevated concrete ribbons arched them over surplus stores and drive-in restaurants on East Central Avenue, and down in the valley the city had the makings of a skyline. To the right and left raw, unlandscaped subdivisions spilled against each other like a child's building blocks knocked askew in a sandbox, with urban sprawl punctuating lines of new architectural oddities stretching right up the lower slopes of the Sandia Mountains.

He meant to swing off the interstate at Central and get his bearings, but he missed his turn and he didn't get another chance that looked right until he read the green-and-white sign that said, LOMAS BLVD—EXIT ¾ MI.

It was the street where Irma Begley worked.

He looked at Begley, wondering if he knew. From the undisturbed, still-hung-over, faintly insolent boredom he showed, he clearly didn't.

They hadn't passed any Skaggs drugstore by the time they reached Louisiana Boulevard and turned north to Winrock Center, where M.L. wanted to do her shopping. He could have stayed on the interstate right to Winrock's entrance and saved himself the better part of a mile, but then he would have missed checking out that stretch of Lomas.

The girl began to sparkle as they neared the big shopping center spreading over land that had been empty mesa in his days at UNM. Begley looked more bored than ever.

It was only 8:15 when they parked in back of J.C. Penney's, and a check of the stores just inside the mall revealed that almost none of them would open until ten o'clock. Ian spotted an exception, a baked-goods shop with tables where some early birds were eating in front of the display cases, and he suggested breakfast.

"I don't dare," M.L. said. "I'm okay now, but if I drank so much as a half a cup of coffee..."

"How about you, John?" Ian said.

"Suit yourself, MacAndrews."

"Sure," M.L. chimed in. "You two go ahead and eat. I'll just window-shop until Monkey Wards opens up."

Begley shrugged and Ian felt his blood begin to simmer. The surly son of a bitch—why had he signed on for this operation in the first place?

"Forget breakfast!" Ian barked. Begley looked at him with a suspect blandness that certainly hid something else. Ian turned to M.L.

"Don't know when we'll get back for you, M.L. We'll come to the front end of Penney's. If you won't be there, leave word at the first cashier's station inside that door. Sure you've got all the money you need?" The girl nodded but looked doubtful, glancing from Ian to Begley and back again. It wasn't money.

Ian turned and started for the car. "Come on! Let's hit the road and get to work." At this point he didn't care if Begley came along or not.

They had just climbed into the car when Ian suddenly rebelled. He was hungry enough to skin and eat a skunk. Screw Begley. "Wait here," he said. "Be right back."

He walked back to the bakery, bought a piece of prune Danish and got a cup of coffee at a self-service urn, and went back to the car. He took his own sweet time eating and drinking. He lit a cigarette. He didn't even look at Begley as he smoked and finished the coffee.

He stepped hard on the gas pedal as he wheeled the MG toward the shopping center exit, and a cop in a black-and-white that was cruising the parking lot tapped his siren, but

then waved him on. He slowed. In this mood the last thing
he needed was a ticket.

After he turned south on Louisiana, the ramp for the
interstate came up on his right almost at once. He nearly took
it, figuring to take the freeway to the interchange and catch
I-25 for the south side of the city, but at the last second he
decided to go straight back down to Lomas.

He turned right on Lomas and passed the north side of
the state fair grounds. When he stopped for the light at
Lomas and San Pedro, he saw the big yellow-and-black sign,
SKAGGS, in a small shopping center on the northwest corner of
the intersection.

He watched Begley out of the corner of his eye, but the
other man didn't so much as glance at the drugstore.

Cattle auctions hadn't changed much in the thirty-five
years since he had gone to the one in Roswell with Ignacio.
The prods were all electric now, but the chalkboard with the
lot numbers and the hundredweight price the seller wanted
could have been the one he had seen back then. The gate to
the barns through which the stock would parade must have
been whitewashed a thousand times, as had the pineboard
walls of the building. It was lumpy where it had been sloshed
right over the splatter of manure. The rapid-fire, manic
babble of the auctioneer hadn't changed, either, and the
silent, studied calm of the cowmen sitting in the three-
section bleachers—the outer two angled in to make a crude
amphitheater—was as he remembered it from his boyhood.

There was a feeling about the place of a more recent déjà
vu, too. Six years ago Gene Weaver had sent him to Britain to
oversee the making of a commercial for BOAC, and while in
the north he had wandered into an auction at the Yorkshire
Livestock Center. The countrymen in from the dales and the
moorland farms were interchangeable with the men seated
around Begley and him now, or would have been had they
been wearing Stetsons and Acme boots instead of flatcaps and
Wellingtons. Perhaps there were more pipes than cigars or
cigarettes in the hands of the Yorkshiremen, but the bidding
nods, the touches of the fingers to the brims of the caps, the
dour silence: they were all more the same than different.

That trip to England had been a good one, except that
he had found the damp little island entirely too good a place
for a serious drinker. Leeds and London bobbies were as

courteous as clerks at Harrods, but a damned sight sterner with Yanks who picked fights in pubs than any Fourteenth Precinct cop. He couldn't charge all the trouble he got himself in to his expense account.

"It's been a long time since I judged beef cattle, John," Ian said. "I want you to do the bidding."

Begley still hadn't talked. He yawned when the first lot of yearlings, seven Herefords on the small side, but clean and healthy looking, entered the auction ring, their hoofs striking the thin layer of fresh straw covering the mud and cowflop like muffled drumbeats. He and Begley had looked this bunch over when they toured the pens before the announcement that the auction was about to begin had come over the loudspeakers. Actually, only Ian had really looked at them. Begley had merely stared at the animals with a monumental lack of interest. With three or four other lots these seven wide-eyed, rust-and-brown young cows appeared to be the best stock to be had today, although a try for Begley's opinion only brought another noncommittal grunt.

There hadn't been any good Hereford bulls in any of the pens, and Ian didn't need Begley to tell him that, but they didn't have to buy bulls today, anyway. According to the July issue of *New Mexican Stockman* he bought at Stafford's three days earlier, there were plenty of registered Hereford sires to be had for a phone call or at most a visit to one of the smaller, purely private sales in the counties around Chupadera. But mother cows they had to have, and now. They didn't need many, just a small herd two men could manage through the late summer months and then the winter, before they invested in a larger breeding pool. Ian wanted these seven, or some just like them, to settle in on the high summer pastures in good weather before they moved them down to the lower grass, where the bulls they would buy could cover them.

"Make a bid, John, if you think these critters are right for us." Ian tried for a laugh. "Remember, we're using Hadley's money."

There was no answer, no sign of a response from Begley. Okay, maybe he didn't share Ian's opinion of the seven. Maybe he would bid on the second lot of eleven.

"What do you think?" he asked Begley as a handler prodded the yearlings and set them to pushing and shoving each other around the auction ring.

"It's your show," Begley said. "I'm along for the ride."

So they made no bid on the first lot, and in the end the seven Herefords went for twenty-seven cents above the minimum posted on the chalkboard.

They did not bid on the second lot of eleven, either.

By the time the third lot was chalked on the board, a lot Ian very definitely had set his heart on, he was seething. He wished he had the handler's electric prod in his own hands. Good thing he didn't. He would hold it on Begley until his blond hair sparked and sizzled.

Begley was yawning again, his head back and his big hat tipped forward. Jesus! Was he going to go to sleep?

"Look, John," Ian said, not even *trying* to hide his anger and disgust, "I *want* this next bunch, savvy? You jump in the minute the bidding falters. Go right up the ladder. Don't let them get away."

"Shit, MacAndrews, I can't even sign them checks you brought along. If there's any bidding to be done, *you* do it. Period!"

Ian had to rein himself in tight. Only the fact that Begley had a little justice on his side (the check-signing business had been an oversight on his and Hadley's part) kept him from throwing in his hand here and now and going back to Hadley and telling him the deal was off.

He had brought the checkbook in Douglas MacAndrews's old briefcase. He fished it out, spread it in his lap, took out his pen, and signed the three checks on the facing page. He closed the checkbook, still half an inch thick and heavy with unused checks, and slapped it against Begley's big chest— hard. The men around them looked to the source of the sound, looked away again. They could have been the drinkers at the Buckhorn bar that first time Ian entered it.

Begley turned a startled face toward him. He opened his mouth, but Ian didn't give him a chance to speak.

"I would have sworn," he rasped, "that I heard you tell Hadley Edwards that you could 'damn well *learn*' the business end of ranching. Well, you had better start learning now!" He stood up. "I'm leaving—going back up to Winrock to find M.L. We'll be here for you at four." He leaned over, pushing his face close to Begley's. "If we don't have the beginnings of a herd when I get back . . . you've lost a partner, *partner*." He straightened up and stepped down to the next row of seats, stopped, turned back. "One last thing. If you call me MacAndrews instead of Ian one more time, that will end it, too, you sulky, infantile son of a bitch! *Hasta la vista.*"

Since he was back hours earlier than M.L. could have expected, he feared he might have to prowl the entire shopping center to find the girl. She was probably in one of the fast-food places having lunch, if she felt she could hold things down, and they seemed the best places to begin the search.

To his surprise he found her just fifty feet inside the main section of the mall, slumped on a masonry bench, with the plastic bags piled on either side of her looking as if they were all that held her up.

Had he thought she looked older than her years? Or at the very least mature? He didn't now. Even with her thickened body she was a pale, fragile waif—and a scared one at that.

When she saw him, her face was lit as if by flame, but the flame was doused as quickly.

"*Where's John?*" Panic. Pure, headlong panic.

He smiled at her, hoping there was reassurance in the smile, even if it was a fraud.

"I expect he's buying us the makings of a herd, M.L. Left him to do the bidding by himself. He'll be fine." That said, he knew he had better leave the subject before his own doubts began to show. "Feel up to getting a bite to eat?"

"Sure." She had brightened. "And I bet," she went on, "that you're starved, not getting any breakfast."

He laughed his way into the restaurant, a dark, wood-paneled cavern barely lit by phony carriage lamps jutting from the walls. It was another predictable, dreary, pedestrian franchise outfit, but M.L. gazed around her in awe, eyes as wide and mouth as open as if he had steered her into Maxim's or Claridge's.

A waitress, in a miniskirt so short it made the fairly skimpy one M.L. had worn at the Buckhorn look Victorian, waved them to a table for four near the back.

He stacked her parcels in the chairs they wouldn't be using and pulled one out for her. She gave him a curious glance. Clearly, no man had ever held a chair for her before. The waitress, whose eyes had gone straight to M.L.'s telltale bulge, poured water and placed two menus the size of Rand McNally road atlases in front of them. M.L. waited until he opened his before she picked hers up. It was upside-down and she had to right it.

"Gee, was I ever glad to see you. I was all done shopping. Didn't know what to do with myself the rest of the afternoon," she said.

"Would you like a drink, M.L.?"

She peeked around the giant menu that hid her face. "Is it okay? Without *you* having one?"

"Absolutely," he said. "I basically don't like people who don't drink...if they don't drink for what I consider the wrong reasons." Now that he thought about it, he realized he had never seen liquor or even beer at any of the meals she fixed. Was that her decision...or Begley's?

"I sure would like a beer," she said. It was still a question. "It ain't that I'm much for drinking, but I been getting these cravings lately."

He ordered her a Coors, and a club soda with a twist for himself. The waitress, obviously making two-and-two equal five, asked him to repeat the order before she left.

M.L. laughed. "I guess you threw her just like you did me the first time I saw you...." The laugh stopped. Her face was an instant replay of the moment when Begley had told her to "get lost" that night.

"Let's change the subject," he said. "When exactly is your baby due?"

"I don't know—exactly." She knit her heavily penciled brows until they almost touched. "Right after the first of the year, I think. Maybe not till February."

"I know it's none of my business, really, but how does John feel about it?"

"He's been swell, Ian—honest!" Her eyes begged him to believe her. Her need for this belief was probably as strong as any need she had ever known. To his not very great surprise he found he did believe her. Perhaps his need was as strong as hers.

She went on. "He's been swell about you, too, Ian. He's come to think a heap of you."

Well, on that, the best he could muster for the moment was a suspension of *dis*belief.

"Getting back to when the baby is supposed to arrive. What does the doctor have to say?"

"Doctor?" She looked frankly puzzled. "I ain't seen a doctor. Lots of time for that."

The waitress came back with the beer and soda and took their order, and there was no more talk while they waited for the food, a BLT for her, and chopped sirloin with mushroom sauce for him. And neither of them talked as they ate. When they finished, M.L. excused herself with a sheepish grin. "I just got to go again. Sorry."

While she was gone, the waitress brought the check.

"Miss," he said, "could you bring me the Albuquerque phone directory, please?"

"I'm sorry, sir. The only one we have is locked in the manager's office and he doesn't come on till five."

"Maybe you can help me then. Where can I find a good baby doctor, an obstetrician-gynecologist?"

The girl's eyes narrowed. "The doctor I see is four blocks straight north of here, on Cutler. Dr. Eric Bjork." Ice had formed on the smile she wore. It took him a second to figure out that she knew she was looking directly at the author of M.L.'s problem. He laughed and leaned toward her.

"Tell me," he said, shaping his mouth into the nastiest leer he could manage, "does this Dr. What's-his-name do abortions?"

The waitress stiffened, grew inches taller. "You'll have to ask *him* that, sir! And his name is Bjork!"

She turned and marched toward the kitchen. No one could have called it a retreat.

He left the money for the check on the table, trebling the tip he had intended leaving.

M.L. came from the restroom wearing the sweetest smile he could remember seeing. The waitress, now back in the dining room, stared daggers at her. She didn't even look at Ian.

As they walked to the car from the office of Eric Bjork, M.L. showed Ian the pamphlets—most of them HEW government freebies—that the doctor's receptionist-nurse had given her. "It was embarrassing, Ian. I never had no doctor looking at me there or poking around like that. But I sure did like him. He ain't any bigger than a minute, but he acts like he really cares. Near as he could figure out from what I remember of when I missed my 'times,' I should pop about the twentieth of January, pretty close to what I thought."

"But everything's all right?"

"Sure is. He says I'm healthy as a horse. He was glad I

don't smoke. And he says I can have a beer now and then if I watch what I eat. He don't want me gaining too much weight." She turned her earnest face up to him as they walked. "Sure do thank you, Ian. I had no idea of all the things I got to look out for before it comes."

When they were in the car and on Louisiana Boulevard again, she said, "Hey! I almost forgot. He gave me a list of vitamins and some other stuff I'm supposed to get. Would it be too much trouble to look us up a drugstore? I ain't sure I could find everything in Black Springs."

He had to force himself to go inside the Lomas Boulevard Skaggs with her, and once inside he waited near the door pretending interest in the television sets behind the lobby counter.

There were three women on duty at the checkout registers, but only one of them anywhere near the fifty-five years old Ernie said Irma Begley had to be by now. That the woman who rang up M.L.'s purchases was John H. Begley's mother he had no doubt. What wasn't James MacAndrews in Begley's face had come from this pleasant-looking lady. He tried not to look at her too long, but he knew he could still pick her from a thousand other women ten years from now.

He watched them as they talked, knowing from the way Irma Begley glanced at M.L.'s waist exactly what the topic of their conversation was. He almost shouted. He wanted to tell this woman just whose grandchild that bulge would be. He was shaking. He left the store and waited in the car.

Begley was standing in the parking lot of the auction barn.

Ian tried to read his face, but gave it up. M.L. moved to the jump seat. She would be even more crowded going back with her packages stacked beside her and beneath her feet.

"Well?" Ian said to Begley when they got under way.

"I spent one hell of lot of Hadley's money," Begley said, looking straight ahead of him down the highway. "We'll be on the receiving end of two shipments totaling thirty-seven young Herefords in about a week . . . Ian."

Ian should have felt tired by the time they reached Black Springs. He didn't.

Chapter XIX

"I was beginning to wonder if you were ever coming to see me, Ian," Sam Edwards said.

He could almost see her words hang in the air so he could read them. That "me" hadn't slipped out in place of "us"; Sam didn't make that kind of slip.

He wanted to tell her he hadn't come to see her, should just ask again to use her phone, but he knew he wouldn't fool her. If the well-pump shaft hadn't broken, there would have been something else: a faulty generator; sick cows or horses; a Martian invasion; something. He hadn't known he had been looking for an excuse until the moment this ready-made one came. Then, chagrined, he had almost gone to town to make the call. He would have gone to town if M.L. or Begley wouldn't have been curious about why he had driven twenty-two miles to Black Springs to call Alamogordo instead of the five to the Edwards place.

"Use the phone in Hadley's study. It dials direct through the radio room," she said. "When you've finished, come out on the patio. I'll have coffee ready."

"Thanks, Sam. Just sitting and talking for a few minutes would do me good. I've been hitting it pretty hard lately."

Alamogordo Hydro-Engineering promised to come and fix the pump first thing in the morning.

On his two other visits to Hadley's study he hadn't looked to see if Sam was in any of the pictures, nor if there were separate ones of her. He did now and found none. Hadley, in his life before the accident and the move here to El Recobro, had lived in a purely man's world, one where women were consorts, not corulers. The few women who smiled from the framed black-and-white prints, mainly of horse shows and polo matches, seemed to be merely scenery.

They must have been Sam's competition once. They could be still; Hadley's being in a wheelchair would only have marginally diminished him as a "catch" to women such as these.

He had seen their like more damned often than he wished on Chicago's Gold Coast; acquaintances, not quite friends, of Laurie and her brother Tom. And he had met dozens more on the skiing trips he and Laurie had made to Europe. They had never shown much interest in Ian beyond a quick, casual trip to bed, something almost never sought again by either him or the women, despite their avowals that he was something different and exciting (like a hunchback or a gangster?); social predators, they had been on the track of more satisfying prey, several *seasons* of eating, not a bolted meal such as him, but something more perpetually nourishing—such as Hadley Edwards. He couldn't blame them.

Sam wasn't one of them. She lacked their high polish, the glassy, brittle confidence that probably hid legions of insecurities. Sam had her own deeper luster, of course, but you had to look for it; it wasn't on display. Even looking for it, not every man could have seen it. It was to Hadley's lasting credit that he had, but given the awareness he had shown in Ian's dealings with him, no surprise. The surprise was that Hadley had found Sam at all. It wasn't putting her down in the slightest to guess that they had come from entirely different worlds, one of games and wealth, and one of— what?

He left the study and walked through the living room to the patio. It took an effort not to look at the paintings as he passed them, particularly the Turner he had ultimately been too preoccupied to study that first night.

Sam waited with the coffee, the mugs and the glass decanter resting on a low, glass-topped table. There was nothing else on the table but an ashtray. She must have remembered from the dinner that he took his coffee black. He remembered *she* did. He had complete recall of every moment they had spent together.

Half-reclining on a wrought-iron chaise with thick foam cushions, she was looking east toward Cuchillo Peak, but not quite at it. He lowered himself into a chair across the table from her, dug a cigarette from his shirt pocket, and lit it, thinking that he had opened this pack sometime early yesterday. The hard work had cut his smoking.

She didn't appear to realize he had joined her, and it startled him when she spoke.

"Did you know I can see your house from here?" she said without turning.

Just a speck at five miles distance, the low contours of the house would have been lost in the dots of yucca and piñon and the broken patterns of the rangeland, except that the rise on which the house sat was outlined against the solid, nearly monochrome mass of Cuchillo Peak. The mountain was tawny and olive today, the different textures and colors blending together at this distance, washed out to a dullish sameness by the three o'clock sun. He knew he couldn't see El Recobro from the house. At night he could see its lights, but under any sun at all, three o'clock, noon, or nine, its distant shape merged with the butte, the rocks to the north, and the hillocks that lined the runway. He wouldn't tell her that. She would guess how many times he had tried to see it during the day and how many times he had gazed at its lights at night.

"Your house," she said, "looks as if it has always been there." Now she turned to him. "I suppose in a sense it always has been."

He looked for something in her eyes, resentment, perhaps, found nothing but tiny signs of worry, troubling doubt.

Maybe it was because she was all alone at El Recobro again, the same solitary chatelaine who had greeted him that first time, but now with infinitely less composure and a good deal less amusement than on the day he had cut her fence and driven Harry Kimbrough's jeep across the slickrock.

"I saw cattle trucks at your place last week. Is the new D Cross A in full swing again?"

To that moment he hadn't thought of what he and John were putting together as the D Cross A, not in the sense of "place" at any rate, but yes, that was what it was.

"Oh, we're swinging all right," he said. "We won't know until next summer whether it's a *full* swing or not." Next summer? Someone else would have to judge how full the swing was then.

"How are you and your partner getting along? I wasn't

sure the two of you would get even this far from what I saw the day you talked to Hadley."

"Passably well." He thought that over. "That's not right. Damned well. John isn't an easy man to know, but I'm working at it."

"Will he make it, Ian? When you leave?"

"Yes. Cowboying becomes him. He was a little mechanical, but he worked like a dog from the very start. Now his heart seems in it. I know I couldn't get along without him. I had no idea how much I'd forgotten in twenty years." He laughed. "In Manhattan I'm an expert on raising beef; in the Ojos Negros I don't know beans."

"And how's that girl? What's her name? I'm sorry."

"M. L. Kimbrough."

"M.L.? For Mary Lou?"

"Could be. You make me ashamed of myself. I've not only never asked, I've never even speculated."

"When is she due?"

"Late January, I've been told." He grinned. She was genuinely interested.

"Are they getting married?"

"I don't know, Sam. There's been no mention of it."

Things turned dark on the patio, but it wasn't a change of mood, even if it felt that way at first. The sun had gone into hiding behind a passing cloud. In ten seconds it blazed away again, bringing back into sharp relief the terrain the shadow of the cloud had flattened.

The doubt, worry, whatever he had seen on Sam's face, had left it. Her questions seemed to have been answered. And yet he had the feeling she hadn't asked the ones she really had wanted to ask.

"And you, Ian. Have you ever married? Wait. I'm asking the second question first. *Are* you married?"

"I'm not and never have been."

Would there be more questions after all?

"When is Hadley getting back?" he said, sure as he said it that it would steer them to higher, safer ground, safer for him at any rate. Then he wasn't sure of his safety at all when she told him she didn't know—tomorrow, the day after, the day after that. She wouldn't know till morning. Hadley was in Kansas City, she thought, at some church gathering with Jim and Cissy Pendleton.

"Jim married us," she said. "Eleven years ago." That

seemed to set her thinking. Whatever it was it went on for
the time it took another cloud to pass.

She looked him full in the face again. "I'm curious about
something," she said. "You have never seemed curious about
me."

He laughed. "Oh, I'm curious enough. It's just that
you're one of the things that are none of my damned
business."

"Tell me something if you can, Ian," she said. "Since I've
been in New Mexico I keep running across the word Cíbola.
Is it an actual place?"

"Not really. It's an old Spanish word for buffalo. In this
country it refers to the seven cities of gold Coronado came
looking for. He didn't find them, of course." Should he tell
her that Ignacio Ortiz had ridden this land in front of them
searching for his own personal, *spiritual* Cíbola all his life?
Should he tell her he had always been sure Ignacio had found
it somewhere along the line? No, he had better save that for
some other time.

"What about the word Quivira," she said next. "Anything
to do with those ruins north of here, Gran Quivira?"

"Maybe. I'm not sure. Quivira was another golden dream,
another land of riches. It took the place of Cíbola for Coronado
when he failed to discover Cíbola. Perhaps there is always
another dream, Sam."

She laughed. "Fits *me*," she said. "I gave up on *my*
Cíbola in Los Angeles. But I've a pretty good idea what my
Quivira is. Do you have one?"

"I don't let myself think about it."

Their eyes were now fixed on each other in a way they
had never been before, and he knew he should leave. In a
moment he had become far more than a neighbor using the
telephone.

Then suddenly, without warning, without really leading
into it, Sam Edwards began telling him the story of her life,
as if, despite what he had said, it *was* his business.

"My family moved to Anaheim from Iowa when World
War II broke out and I grew up there. Dad figured on getting
rich in the aircraft plants, and my mother became a defense
worker, too. That meant I was pretty much on my own by the
time I reached junior high, and all through high school.
Tough on kids growing up alone, but maybe it's even tougher
in California, at least it was during the war. My folks did

make lot of money compared to what they had been used to in Cedar Rapids, but it took them sixty and seventy hours a week to do it. They were generous with my spending money as much to keep me quiet as straight, I guess. I wasn't wild but I could do pretty much as I damned well pleased. Don't get the idea I was a tramp, Ian. I wasn't. Not then . . . that didn't come till later."

He didn't want her to go on, but he didn't want her to stop, either. She bit her lip and began again.

"Like thousands of other kids I was movie-struck. I was going to be a star if it killed me. I didn't talk about it much, not after the boy I was going steady with laughed at me, but the idea never left my mind.

"Well, to make a long story moderately bearable, the war ended, Dad and Mom were out of work for a long time after the plants closed, and when I graduated from high school I got a rude awakening. I had registered at UCLA to study film and acting, but there wasn't enough money left to pay tuition, never mind room and board. No chance of scholarship of any kind. I'd spent most of the afternoons should have been in class in movie theaters, and my grades were barely good enough to get me my diploma."

So far it had been a recital, not a confession, but he knew that when and if it changed to something more revealing she wouldn't be asking for absolution. He listened to her as he would have listened to one of those people you meet on airline flights, those compulsive, ready narrators of the naked truth who babble away to you about their kids, their dreams, even their love affairs, safe in the knowledge that they will soon find anonymity again in your forgetfulness once you have reached the terminal.

But Sam and he weren't even in the landing pattern yet. She was going on, speaking more deliberately, sometimes only in fragments, and watching Ian with a new intensity.

"Got a part-time job as a model in a boutique in Beverly Hills . . . I wasn't tall, but thin enough . . . small place . . . shared a room with another girl and enrolled at Pasadena Junior College. I became realistic with the speed of light and took typing and shorthand . . . never took my eye off the main chance, though. I wangled a job in the steno pool in the payroll department at MGM, and when an opening came in casting, I felt I was back on track again . . . on the way to the top."

She stopped. Something had caught her eye, and he in turn looked to where she looked.

On the flat grasslands northeast of the butte, well beyond the bend of the arroyo and the better part of a mile away, a small herd was grazing. At first he thought the animals were some of the younger stock Begley had bought at the auction, and he wondered how they had gotten this far south, but then he saw they weren't even cattle. Pronghorns. He had thought they had moved north a generation earlier. He hadn't seen antelope in the five or six years before he left the Ojos Negros. These—there were six of them—must have come back into the range after all the old D Cross A stock had been sold and trucked away.

As Sam and he watched, two more came out of the scrub and neared the little herd, approaching it with nervous, mincing steps. One in the first group broke away from the other five and in a frenzied, dust-shrouded run charged the new pair, lowering its head, feinting at one, lunging at the other. Of course. The late-summer rut must be getting near. He turned to look at Sam, then turned back just in time to see the first six hightailing it through the yucca. The two intruders, losers now, lifted their heads and gazed off in another direction, trying, he supposed, to pretend none of it had happened.

"As I was saying," Sam said, speaking a bit faster now, anxious, it seemed, to get on with it, "I began to see myself as on my way, and at first it went well. In casting, I had advance notice of calls for extras, and by cozying up to the directors I had met in the MGM canteen I got to be part of crowd scenes in a dozen pictures in the next six months. I even got a few lines to speak—once. It got me my Guild card. But I never got anything bigger, and I couldn't interest any of the agents I thought I could trust. Then it became clear to me that there was a hell of a lot of truth in the stories everybody hears about the 'casting couch' and sleeping your way to the top. Boy, did it *ever* become clear! One producer propositioned me straight out. Nothing subtle about it, either. I wish I could tell you I did a lot of soul-searching, Ian.

"It took just long enough for me to gulp once and nod my head. This producer was at least halfway personable and I certainly wasn't a virgin. I had discovered back in high school that the 'Fate Worse Than Death' wasn't. So we started. It didn't work like the stories. Oh, he tried to make a starlet of me and actually came through and got me a couple of small parts in what used to be called 'B' movies, but then he moved on to another eager kid with bigger boobs. The experience hadn't seemed to have done me any damage, and I still thought there was some merit in the idea, so I tried again. Another bit part—in an oater that never even got released— and that affair ended, too. It gradually dawned on me that there were a couple of things I hadn't taken into consideration: I couldn't act for sour apples; and the camera was less than kind to me. The last was the biggest shock. I'd been told all my life that I was a 'looker.' It appeared I could screw my way onto a movie set, but once there I was on my own—and my own wasn't good enough.

"Then I got interested in the writing end of the business. I doctored a couple of scripts with a writer I'd met at a screening, and it seemed as if I had some talent. I did research for a novelist who came out from Connecticut when his book hit the top of the *Times* best-seller list, but who was Alice In Wonderland when it came to making it in Hollywood, and I was finally asked to finish the script he'd been hired to do and that he'd messed up pretty badly. I probably would have slept with him, too—it was a reflex action now—but he really and truly was an Alice. Nice man. Taught me a thing or two about tolerance. Well, I wrote screenplays for the next few years, never once getting a solo credit and more often than not getting none at all. There's a real thing with moviemakers—producers, directors, and even some of the stars—about getting their names in those credits not one in a million moviegoers ever reads. They robbed me blind of what little glory I finally thought would come my way. But I was making real money for a change. I got my own apartment just off Wilshire, bought a flashy convertible, and for the first time in my life I could afford to dress the way I wanted to.

"That's when I met Hadley. He had invested in a limited partnership doing a film I'd been assigned to write all by myself, one of those cold war cloak-and-dagger epics. Hadley is never a *silent* partner. Well, you already know how he feels about creative people—or people he thinks creative. When he saw I was going to get finessed out of the credits again, he raised hell.

"A funny thing had already happened to my thinking.

For some reason I'd never considered myself a whore for going to bed with men who promised to advance my 'acting' career. It was part of the game and I accepted it, and if it's repugnant to you, Ian—well, I won't make excuses for myself. But strangely enough, from the very start screenwriting seemed a little like prostitution. What made it worse was that I was good at it, a real pro, and just as facile and unfeeling about it as a pro. Now came this white knight, slaying a dragon for me . . . and without making anything like a pass. Of course it made me want him to. I went after him fang-and-claw. We married." She began laughing. "It sure made a crack in L.A.'s upper crust. It was really funny. I didn't have a glimmer about what a darling of high society Hadley was, nor how filthy rich he was. A lot of patrician noses went out of joint."

She stopped, but he knew there would be more. He looked away from her, not knowing whether he had done it to silence her or keep her going.

The two defeated male pronghorns had deserted the rangeland now, and without them in sight nothing out there moved.

"That credit Hadley got me . . ." she was saying now, "was for the last screenplay I ever wrote. I know now that Hadley was disappointed that I didn't go on writing for the screen, but he never said a word. I packed my typewriter away, for keeps I thought, but he's kept my Writers Guild dues paid up all these years. I was content—hell, delirious is more like it—to be a pampered society wife. I discovered that my love for the screen was really due to the world it had shown me; now I was *living* in it. Maybe I didn't love Hadley the way women loved men in the movies, but by God I worked at it.

"Then he had the riding accident and I think something like love came then. In case you're interested, we still have a damned good sex life!" The last came with a harsh note of defiance—too much defiance.

She was lying, he knew it, and he blessed her for it. She wasn't going to let her husband down no matter how honest and frank she intended to be about every other thing.

"The accident meant that as attentive as he had been to me before he got hurt, now we had even more time together. There was no one else in our world at all until he began this business with Alejandro. Don't get me wrong. It was good for him. I got involved myself for a while, but it scared me. Still does. Hadley never complained when I took myself out of it. But being out of it, I found I needed something of my own.

"I began writing again—but not screenplays. Fiction. I'm serious about it, Ian. There's none of the 'committee' feel about doing fiction that there is in writing for the movies. It's solitary, satisfying, and honest. That's why I love it here at El Recobro. Nothing interferes, not even the things Hadley is up to with Alex and Tim and the others. I'm totally committed to what I'm doing. And for the first time since I took that wild swing at the movie business, I know I'm not a whore.

"There's only one thing wrong with my life now, and it has nothing to do with Hadley or his accident. I think you already know how well he's come to terms with that."

She fell silent, drew a breath, and began to shake her head as if she were trying to shake thoughts into place, not rid her mind of them.

"Neither of the novels I've written nor any of the two dozen short stories in my filing cabinet are worth the paper I typed them on. With Hadley's help I know I could get them published, but that isn't the way I'm going to play the game."

This, Ian knew, was the only real confession she had made today. Everything else she had told him had been a mere preamble to it.

"I'll keep trying," she said. "And I'll probably keep right on failing—but I'll never be a whore again."

Then she looked him squarely in the face, her own showing pain.

"I don't suppose that you, of all people, can understand the absolute agony of wanting to do something, something that will last, and not being able to bring it off."

It was said without bitterness. Her head was lifted high. How could a camera be "less than kind" to a face such as this?

"Sam, why have you told me this? I had no need to know, certainly no right."

She shrugged. "I've given you the right. And maybe the need was mine. I've told you things I haven't even told myself before."

He decided it wouldn't be the best idea he had ever had to come here too often when Hadley was away.

Chapter XX

Things went well for the next month, so well, in fact, that he began to feel gritty rubs of irritation. He didn't want his life in the basin to come anywhere near seducing him. He *would* leave, and to shore up his determination he fixed the date, although he didn't tell John or M.L. or the two people at El Recobro. He would work the D Cross A for Hadley until the thirty-first of March.

It didn't escape him that he had given himself the same deadline to the day that Sarah had given him for the delivery of Max's portrait to Leila Balutan. Nothing had changed his mind about not meeting Sarah's deadline; nothing would. And John Begley would take charge on April first, ready or not.

That John would be ready was becoming more and more certain now.

He had changed since the auction. The change wouldn't have been apparent if they weren't so welded together in common tasks that Ian could examine the joints. John worked hard at disguising the change, but out of pure instinctual stubbornness, not conviction. He was still as short and gruff in talk as before they began to stock the range, but less surly; he continued to pretend indifference about his work, but moved quicker by far even than Ian at fixing things; and if he was still a sphinx at mealtimes, his eyes began to turn blue earlier in the working day and he no longer waited for Ian to make every decision, give every order.

John's eyes were still red-rimmed and bleary at dawn. The nighttime boozing hadn't stopped. He never drank in front of Ian, but if M.L. didn't shut the door to the master bedroom when she and John left it in the morning, Ian would on occasion see a row of empties sitting on the dresser. Since they spent so much time together, either in the saddle or doing the chores that never seemed to end—it seemed John must be doing all his drinking in the dead of night, although Ian knew he could well be wrong about that.

Alcoholics became Blackbeards at burying their treasured bottle where even another lush couldn't find it, and Houdinis at escaping the clutches of people they feared might stop them from digging it up. Old Bob Thompson, an insurance company president in Ian's Thursday noon AA meeting in Chicago's Loop, spent seven years restoring a 1927 Packard in his garage in Western Springs, coming in each night at bedtime, he told Ian, stinking, slobbering, and gloriously sodden. "Sally used to go crazy," Bob said once. "She tore that garage apart. I stashed my vodka in the radiator. Who would look for booze in the antifreeze? That Packard turned out to be the most expensive restoration in the entire history of the West Suburban Classic Car Club."

Ian didn't even try to seek out any cache of John's. As for catching him in the act, that could prove more disastrous than the drinking.

M.L. was really beginning to bulge now, and for the most part kept herself as contented as any of the cows in the far north pastures. Her eyes no longer sparked with apprehension at mealtimes as they had in the first days, when she would glance from John to Ian to John, back and forth like a watcher at a tennis match who expects the ball to become a hand grenade. She kept a happy little river of talk running at meals now, too, instead of following John's lead and falling silent. Ian, lost in thoughts of his own, seldom heard what the girl was saying, but he felt her chatter was intended more for effect than information, and calculated to draw responses from John, not him.

January twentieth? When he looked at the way she was swelling by the day, he wondered if she and the doctor in Albuquerque were right about the date.

Well, Christmas or Groundhog Day, it made little difference. The baby would arrive early enough not to interfere with Ian's departure. M.L., ingenuously smug, asserted it would be a boy, admitting of no other possible result.

Dr. Bjork had given M.L. the name of an OB man in Alamogordo, and Ian assumed she would go down to the hospital there for the delivery. It would take some planning. He didn't want to intrude, but he felt he had a right, even an obligation, to find out how M.L. and John intended to handle things. John certainly was as ignorant as Ian about these matters, and if—as brief bits of overheard conversation seemed to indicate—the young father-to-be hadn't given thought to the logistics of the event, Ian knew he should start to ask some questions.

"You really should get settled in Alamogordo a week or so before you're due, M.L.," he said once, when John was out with the herd alone and the girl and he were sharing a noon meal together. "If you go into labor out here, John might not get you to the hospital on time."

She looked at him with eyes wide with wonder.

"Hospital?" she said. "I ain't going to no *hospital*. He's going to be born right here!"

The fright must have showed in his face; she hurried on, looking suddenly scared herself. "That is, if it's okay with you, Ian." It seemed her fear was not about having the baby, but of his, Ian's, not agreeing to her plan.

"Well, certainly it's okay, but—"

"Me and John been reading up on how to do it 'natural.' Don't seem like nothing we can't handle. Gee, we been talking about it at dinner for a week."

"But, M.L.," he began again, "you'll still want a doctor with you, won't you?"

"Midwives is just as good," she sniffed. "Mrs. Maynes at the library, where John got the book on natural birthing, knows a lady over in Mex Town who's delivered a couple dozen babies. Anyway, if we do it right, she won't even be needed—honest. And I expect my ma will come out from town for afterwards."

He dropped it. He would have to figure out how to get at this business with John, the man he was now calling to himself the "silent" partner. That made two silent partners he had; in spite of what Sam had said, it seemed Hadley planned to leave them strictly on their own.

And Ian was going to have to start monitoring M.L.'s table talk. How many other nifty little surprises had he missed in his overweening preoccupation with his own concerns?

M.L.'s mention of the possibility of her mother's coming out to the D Cross A to help with the baby when it finally arrived set him to thinking about the woman he had seen in Skaggs in Albuquerque.

Wouldn't it be something if . . . ? *Butt out, MacAndrews!* He was furious with himself.

The D Cross A was beginning to look, feel, and smell like a genuine Ojos Negros cattle ranch; small, but as modern and well-equipped as any of the operations he and John had visited in the past weeks in their search for reliable breeding stock, the good Hereford bulls that would sire a thriving herd.

He sent John to Alamogordo to buy a new pickup truck.

"You won't need me with you. I've plenty to keep me busy here. Sell your Ford and pocket the money," Ian said. "Damn thing uses as much oil as gas and you'll sure as hell *need* money when the baby comes." It was the first time he had said "baby" in front of John. He switched the subject back to the new truck. "Get something husky enough and with a power takeoff." He wrote out a list of books he wanted from the Cholla, hesitated before he handed it to John, but then asked him if he would look for them.

"You actually read this highbrow stuff?" John said when he looked at the list. Ian nodded. A month ago the question would have carried with it a heavy load of sneering criticism. It sounded like honest curiosity now, and unless Ian was kidding himself, there was also a grudging note of respect— make that a grudging growl of respect.

"What I store up with this 'stuff,' nobody can ever take away from me."

The same day, after John went to Alamogordo, a crew from the public service company came out and tied the house to the underground power cable that served El Recobro, and just in time; the generator they had rented from Stafford's was threatening to wheeze its last. When Ian turned on his reading lamp that night, it struck him that at least one thing connected him in a physical way with Sam. He laughed. *Man,* was *that ever a seven-league reach!* He laughed again, but kept his reading lamp on long after he closed his book; didn't even reach for the switch until minutes after the last light winked out at El Recobro.

John was taking over more and more of the riding. Ian still marveled at how well his partner handled a cow pony with his handicap—the damaged leg sticking straight down, the stirrup under the boot dangling loose to keep it from putting pressure on the leg, which looked painful even in repose and made it nearly impossible for John to exert any pressure with his thighs. Once, before Ian could stop himself, he remarked on John's skillful horsemanship. The reply, of course, was another grunt, but one with what could have been a small ring of pleasure in it. Ian was mildly surprised that John would even tolerate a compliment.

Then John surprised him again by saying, "Ortiz used to talk about you a lot, Ian. Said *you* were pretty damned good on a horse yourself."

"Maybe I was once, but not anymore. And I never could touch Ignacio on horseback—not on my best day."

"Hell!" Begley said. "Ain't nothing to moan about. Nobody could touch Ortiz on a cow pony. Even when I went 'down the road' and tried the rodeo, I never seen a pro as good as he was." He went on in a voice that had become suddenly distant, hollow, "Guess you don't know. I was with him once when he fell from a horse, a spotted pony named Calico. I'd bet my last buck it was the only time it happened in his life. And he wasn't throwed; he fell. Turned out it was his first heart attack."

Ian started to ask something, let it go. He would be trying to force an answer. It wouldn't do. Things had to come in their own time and at their own pace and from their own secret, shadowed corners.

If he spent a lot of his waking hours thinking about Begley, it came as something of a surprise to him that M.L. was filling a lot of hers with thoughts of Hadley. Edwards couldn't possibly have been the first millionaire M.L. had known; seedy as the Buckhorn was, rich oil and livestock men and big-spending honchos from the racing crowd at Ruidoso frequently slummed in Herb Babcock's bar on Saturday nights. Hadley was different. He looked and dressed like the millionaires she had seen in the movies and on TV. To her he was the real thing, not just another of the local men grown "too big for their britches" because their daddies left them seventy or eighty sections of rangeland or perhaps got rich in the oilfields on the other side of the Sacramentos or lucked out with a champion quarter horse.

She worshipped Hadley—adored him on the basis of just that one meeting, even though she had been too flustered to have gotten him in sharp focus through eyes fogged with awe.

In the days that followed Hadley's tour of the unfinished house, she pestered Ian about having Hadley and Sam come to supper—"or *dinner*," she said, "as Mr. Edwards likes to call it"—swinging wildly between happy anticipation of what surely would be the first party she had ever given, and dread at the actual giving of it.

No sooner would Ian say, "All right, all right, M.L.! I'll drive over and invite them for next Wednesday..." (or Thursday or Friday or whatever night the girl named for the absurdly gala feasts she planned aloud, affairs he knew were quite beyond her), than she would shrink from him like a wild creature faced with a flaming brand.

"Oh, God, Ian. I just can't! I'd make a mess of it. Let's forget it."

Her despair then seemed to banish the notion once and for all, but in a day or two it would come again, the proposed dinner a more modest one at first, but as succeeding days went by, again reaching the same mountainous proportion that would inevitably loom above her as twin pinnacles of ecstasy and fright, which, once scaled in her imagination would bring the same pathetic tumble. She didn't cry, but her eyes got damp, and the dampness smudged her mascara.

John never took part in these conversations, but he didn't miss them.

At these times Ian wished Ernie Gomez could be there to see him.

For all Ernie's decency, understanding, and even a certain amount of sympathy, it was clear he looked on John Begley as a clinical sociopath, a textbook case.

"Watch him, Ian," the lawyer had said earlier, when Ian went in to sign the ranch papers Ernie had drawn up for Hadley. "A leopard perhaps can't help being a leopard, but *your* wishes can't make him change his spots, either." He had rubbed his jaw, the jaw John had broken.

After he left Ernie's office Ian turned a bit shamefaced that he hadn't taken issue with him and defended the man he was now thinking of, without reservation, as a partner, but in fairness to himself he hadn't had much to go on then.

He did now.

For if John didn't fuss over M.L., he was gentle with her and as quick to be helpful in the house—doing dishes, even running the vacuum cleaner—as he was in working with Ian in the compound and on the range. The man who had told her to "get lost, M.L." that night in the Buckhorn seemed to have left the scene for good. Ian would have to bring Ernie up to date.

When John returned from Alamogordo, still driving the old blue pickup (the GMC he had dickered for wouldn't be

ready for a week), he handed Ian a shopping bag full of the
books he had picked up at the Cholla. It wasn't until after Ian
had gone to his room that night that he checked the contents
of the bag. To his astonishment he found a copy of the Sunday
New York Times. The paper hadn't been on the list he had
given John.

Buried deep inside the second section he found another
surprise lying in ambush for him. There was a half-page
feature with pictures on Alejandro Vergara. Hadley's friend
had just won a three-month battle to gain asylum in the
United States. The State Department, aided and abetted by
Somoza's agents in Washington, had fought tooth and nail
with the INS, trying to get Alejandro returned to Nicaragua to
face some vague corruption charges there, charges the *Times*
correspondent hinted were trumped-up, completely unfounded, and clearly designed only to put this particular political
foe of the regime out of circulation. The writer also let slip
that while Somoza's efforts were reprehensible, they were
also justified, from the dictator's point of view. Vergara,
according to the article, was a far more important figure than
Ian had judged him or Hadley had presented him. There
seemed little doubt he would be a major player if the
sub-rosa anti-Somoza game going on in Nicaragua ever became one of open revolution.

The thing that turned the trick for Alejandro had been
an appearance by the Mexican ambassador at Alejandro's
senate hearing. An attempt had been made on Alejandro's life
after he had chaired a conference of Nicaraguan émigrés held
at Puerto Vallarta. The failed assassin, not named, had been
caught by the Mexican Secret Service and deported, but not
before discovery that he was an active-duty colonel in the
Nicaraguan National Guard.

The story didn't discuss what Alejandro might be doing
in the States nor was there a hint of his involvement with
Hadley Edwards.

Elsie Kimbrough and Jody drove out in the jeep for
M.L.'s birthday.

Luckily for Ian, Jody had run his mail out for him two
days earlier and had tipped him off to the upcoming party. A
quick trip to Black Springs and some frantic rummaging
through Stafford's had turned up a pressure cooker M.L. had
admired in *Woman's Day*, and Ian supplemented the gift of

the appliance with a housecoat he felt she might welcome when she outgrew her jeans and could no longer button the shirts she had been borrowing from John. He had looked for a maternity dress she could wear in case the fantasized dinner for the Edwardses ever became a reality, but the only one he found in Stafford's meager stock was drab, shapeless even for what it was, and he finally passed it by.

As it turned out, he was lucky again, about the dress. Elsie showed up with not one but three roomy smocks, all of them homemade and all of them handsomer by far than the pitiful garment at Stafford's. Jody came through with a Max Factor makeup sampler and got a sisterly hug that would have done for a dozen brothers.

John surprised M.L.—surprised Ian even more—with a Hummel figurine, the "Girl With Umbrella." He must have spotted it at the Cholla in Alamogordo when Ian sent him there for books. They had gift wrapped it at the store, but when John took it from the sack it came in, the sales slip fluttered to the floor. No one saw Ian rescue it. He glanced at it before he stuffed it in his pocket. Another surprise. The date of the slip told him John had made a special trip to the Cholla, a week after he had gone there for Ian. The reason John picked this particular Hummel was no surprise to anyone. The face on the small porcelain figure was that of a smaller, younger, but no brighter nor more winsome M. L. Kimbrough.

John didn't drink at supper nor afterward nor did he disappear into the room he shared with M.L. at any time during the evening. He didn't seem to be suffering any pangs of withdrawal, either. It was a heartening sign, but Ian knew it to be an inconclusive one. Still, he permitted himself a little hope.

John Begley was never going to be an affable man, but he did smile from time to time during the party and even laughed once, when Elsie feigned horror at the thought of becoming a grandmother "when I ain't hardly old enough to be a *mother*."

It should have been a dull evening, filled as it was with some of the corniest, most mundane talk in Ian's memory, a lot of it local gossip. To Ian's recollection, when he thought about it after Jody and Elsie had gone back to town and M.L. and John headed for the bedroom, there hadn't been one witty, intelligent, perceptive remark made by any of the five

of them. No affair in Chicago or Manhattan, even the cocktail
gatherings he despised, could have been more outwardly
boring. It was a *great* party.

Jody came out to the D Cross A again the following day.
To Ian's amusement he oohed and aahed over the new GMC
pickup and fidgeted and scratched himself until Ian finally
took pity on him. There was a load of cottonseed cake in the
bed to be ferried out to one of the pastures near the new
tank, and Ian handed Jody the keys to the truck and climbed
in on the passenger's side.

"You can give me a hand with this chore, kid."

"Gotcha, sir!" Jody said, and away they roared.

Once the task was done they leaned against the hood of
the pickup and watched three cows saunter toward the feed.

"Bet John is happy to see real critters on this grass
instead of make-believe ones," Jody said, more to himself
than Ian.

"What do you mean make-believe ones, Jody?" Ian
asked. It was a reflex question and he could have bitten his
tongue right through when Jody looked at him. The clean-cut
young face was red to the hairline with mortification. He had
been talking to himself and only to himself.

"I was just shooting my mouth off." He sighed; a monumental sigh for one so slight. "Well, I guess I said it. You
might as well know. It came out once when John was so
drunk he didn't know what he was telling M.L. and me."

An insistent bell rang at the back of Ian's head.

"Jody," he said, "does this have something to do with
why John was so determined to get me out of Chupadera
County?"

"Yes, sir." He turned and looked Ian full in the face,
showing again that now-familiar trust, a trust so vast it
troubled Ian; a gift he didn't want, certainly hadn't earned.

"It's like this," Jody began. There was little point in
stopping him. The last thing this nice kid needed at the
moment was rejection. "When John got out of the VA hospital
and found out the D Cross A had gone broke, it liked to have
killed him. Even with that old foreman dead I guess he was
sure he could get his old riding job back. When he couldn't,
he bought the trailer and moved in by the malpais. Anyway,
this one time M.L. and I was out there he got drunk and got
to raving. For three years he's been imagining cattle roaming
all over the old range . . . and he's been herding them in his

mind. I mean actually riding around and acting like they was
real. He even reports to the old guy buried out in the
slickrock. Would you believe he kept tally sheets? John is the
one who kept the fence up, too; it wasn't the Edwards
people. I guess it's taken nearly every penny he put by while
he was in Nam and what he gets for being wounded." Jody
wiped his forehead, pretending it was sweat he was wiping
away, but with his hand sneaking down to rub his eyes.
"Look, Ian. I don't want you to get the idea John is nuts. He
knows he's making believe—when he's sober. Even laughs at
himself. But I guess when he's all screwed up with whiskey
it's real to him. He must have ridden a couple thousand miles
taking care of this land, chasing people away that don't belong
here, taking care of that grave . . . them *two* graves."

Now he was studying Ian's face hard. "Will this make a
difference to what the two of you are doing together, Ian?"

"None at all." He looked at the three cows at the
cottonseed cake. "Look, son. I don't want you getting some
crazy idea that you've got to tell John you've told me this.
Don't let any pangs of conscience bother you. This little talk
never happened, savvy?"

Jody couldn't rub away the cascade of tears that came
now, and it was a satisfying, small victory for both of them
that they neither embarrassed Ian nor shamed Jody.

Answers. They had taken their own sweet time in coming. When he thought of those first two days back in Chupadera
County, he realized that if he had never gone to visit Ignacio's
grave, he very likely never would have met John Begley.

The young giant, his world a scattered wreckage, had
appointed himself caretaker if not restorer of everything good
that had grown with the grass inside the long, once-tight
fence.

And he was going to do it by himself. He didn't want
anyone else, above all not the deserter Ian MacAndrews,
reporting to Ignacio.

But now John Begley had a partner—for a while.

"John," Ian said that night at dinner, "right after the year
turns over, you're going to have to start looking to hire a hand
or two."

The spoonful of pinto beans stopped halfway to John
Begley's mouth. "You planning on us getting that big that
quick? It don't figure, not with the bad weather coming on."

"No."

"Well then, why can't the two of us handle things without no extra help?"

"There's no rush," Ian said. "But after the first of April it won't be the two of us. I'm pulling up stakes and heading back to New York on the thirty-first of March."

The beans never got to John Begley's mouth, and M.L. seemed to be having a hard time swallowing hers.

"Have you told Hadley Edwards this?" John said.

"Not yet. I'll drive over when I see the plane fly in. Don't know when he's due."

The somber, thoughtful looks John gave him the rest of the evening didn't square with Ian's calculations.

Chapter XXI

"I know it wouldn't do to buy you a drink, MacAndrews," Tim Springer said when Ian met him in the lobby of the bank. "On the other hand, I'm not aware that Black Springs boasts a tearoom."

"Not likely," Ian said. "Although I've heard a nasty rumor that a fish-and-chips shop is opening, thoroughly franchised, sanitized, and Americanized. I could do with a cup of coffee. If we drop by at the Comida, I'm sure Anita could boil some red blotting paper into something remotely resembling tea. Want to chance it?"

"Absolutely. The sahib doesn't have anyone interesting at El Recobro now, and we shan't be going bye-bye in the big birdie for another week. I'm going dotty."

Ian's ear had cocked when the Englishman said "sahib," but he decided the pilot wasn't giving it any pejorative twist.

October had slipped in without Ian's noticing it until he asked the date of the bank teller who cashed his check. The cottonwoods on Stanton Street were showing the first traces of the yellow that would soon light them like candles. The showers of the basin's second rainy season were over with,

and the mornings of the last three days of September ha
nipped noses a little during the day's first chores. Th
afternoons, though, had been like this one, warm and dry, s
dry that even if the thermometer nudged ninety-five, as
was doing today, the hardest sweat evaporated before it coul
even bead. Hard to believe they would find ice on the surfac
of the tanks some morning soon.

When they reached the diner, Springer mentioned tha
he had never been in Anita's place before. The man was n
snob. He didn't seem put off by its plainness, the simpl
spotless counter and the two small tables.

The Comida was empty until Anita filled it moment
after Springer and Ian sat at the counter. It was a bit too earl
for *los hermanos,* but not too early for the roast corn smell c
fresh tortillas baking. Ian found himself wondering how h
had managed to get along without the aroma in his years awa
from here. In Chicago he had eaten for a while at Su Casa o
Ohio Street, had taken Ignacio there for dinner when the ol
vaquero had tracked him down on that painful visit, but h
had abandoned the restaurant for the same reason he no
hinted Springer should probably give the fish-and-chip
place a miss. Su Casa never smelled genuine in spite of a
the owner's efforts.

"Buenos dias, señores!" Anita said, her voice a rich soni
boom. Ian braced himself. His Hispanic Sarah Bernhardt wa
on stage again, front-center. From the way she looked
Springer the pilot was new to her close up. She certainly ha
seen him before. She had seen everyone in Chupade
County; but now she could study him and perform as she ha
with Ian three months earlier and ever since.

"Por favor, señores, take one of the tables. You will b
more comfortable," she said.

Ian suppressed a smile. He would have fun taking her t
task about this sometime. She had never offered *him* a seat
one of the tables, not in twelve long weeks. When h
followed the gaze of her black eyes, he saw how this situatio
differed. Poor Springer's knees were jammed against th
counter front, but his hips and buttocks hung well over th
back of the stool.

It was, he realized then, a sacrifice on Anita's part
offer them a table. One of them would have his back to he
and her audience would be cut in half. *Verdad,* courtesy an
art were unnatural siblings, not at all like the real ones ju

coming through the door, Juan and Bautista. Ian returned
their nods as Springer and he moved to the little table.

"A decided improvement," the pilot said. "We can chat
each other up a bit better here."

"Provided our hostess will let us," Ian said, hoping
against hope Anita wouldn't. For all Springer's insouciance he
knew the pilot for a shrewd observer. Perhaps Ian would
unwittingly let slip something of his feelings about Sam.

For the moment he was safe. He watched Anita sail
toward them in front of the counter, a full-rigged galleon of a
woman.

"Your pleasure, *señores?*" she said when she reached
them. Ian chuckled. He had lost her, temporarily at least.
The dark, liquid eyes were only on Springer now, liking what
they saw and not hiding it.

Springer gazed back at her with the frank assessing look
of the addicted womanizer, a nondiscriminating Don Giovanni
who found something irresistible about anything in skirts. You
would have thought Anita was Goya's *Naked Maja*.

"I should like tea, *señora,* if it's possible—with milk if it
doesn't offend your New World sensibilities," Springer said.
"And *señora*—has anyone ever commented on the uncanny
resemblance you bear to Delores Del Rio?"

For once the big woman was struck dumb, but it was the
dumbness of ecstasy. Ian had to hand it to Springer. The
Englishman was that very best kind of flatterer, the kind who
never handed out a compliment that didn't have some slight
touch of truth in it. It hadn't occurred to Ian before, but by
God, yes, there *was* something of the lovely old Mexican
screen star in Anita's face. Melt fifty pounds from that
massive but still superbly proportioned body and the owner
of the Comida could have trekked north with Little Wolf and
Dull Knife in *Cheyenne Autumn*.

Ian ordered coffee when Anita returned to something
approaching consciousness and then studied Springer. It was
hard for him to tell the pilot's age. He could look twenty or
fifty. Hair like wavy flax, cut longer than Ian generally liked
seeing on a man, but not offensive on Springer for some
reason, fair skin fortunately not the kind that burned or
blotched, eyes of that delicate faded blue seen on cornflowers
pressed in a family Bible: Tim Springer was probably a man
with instant, overwhelming appeal for women. Ian knew he

•would need a woman's opinion, but clearly Big Anita was giving it. And now she was floating back to her kitchen.

Ian wondered why he had worried about Springer's discovering his interest in Sam Edwards. Springer had made no attempt at all to hide *his*. He remembered too that Hadley had been aware of it and had reacted only with bemused detachment. Sam knew of it, too.

Strange situation. El Recobro was the home of a desirable woman, a husband almost certainly incapacitated sexually— and a sexual freebooter, Springer here. Sam. She was the unknown quantity of the three people at El Recobro in spite of her effort to explain herself to Ian, a man who required no explanation, not from her.

"How long have you worked for Hadley, Tim?" Ian said.

"Four years. Seems a fortnight, though. They've been absolutely splendid to me, both of them. I was doing a frustrating job of work with Amnesty in the Argentine, trying to help people locate missing relatives, and doing it badly I might add, when I met them at a black-tie gathering at the Israeli embassy there. I was bored silly and a bit miffed with myself, principally because I was queering the do for Amnesty, and Had pulled me out of a rather sticky spot...." He looked at Ian as if he weren't quite sure whether it was the better part of wisdom to continue. "You've guessed, I suppose, that I suffer, to a lesser degree perhaps, from *your* affliction. In my case I'm now convinced it's merely an infatuation. I watched you a bit at Sam's dinner party." Ian's spine turned rigid.

Springer was smiling at him now, but he had little time to decide what the smile meant; Anita was placing the mugs and the teapot in front of them. Springer reached for the pot, but he didn't stand a chance. Anita's plump hand beat his to the handle, but not so quickly the two hands didn't touch. It was nothing short of amazing that she could pour and look at the Englishman without a drop gone astray. With that graceful curtsy, she left.

As he added the milk to his tea, the pilot went on, "Yes, indeed, MacAndrews, the 'craychur,' as my Irish flight instructor used to call it, had me in its toils. I spent most of that stint in Buenos Aires smashed into oblivion. Hadley offered me the job as his personal pilot on the condition that I sober up. Never insisted I give the gargle up entirely, but took my word that I would watch it. And I have."

Ian felt relief. Booze—it was only booze the man was talking about. He wondered what had happened to his thinking. *Only* booze? Three short months ago he couldn't have conceived of a worse obsession.

Something of the hard-bitten, cynical professional who had held Ian in the sights of his automatic the day John and he had ridden to El Recobro to see Hadley had come back into the Englishman's ageless face as he talked. Perhaps the man *was* an alcoholic despite his own assessment. Ian had to remind himself of something Father Frank said at AA once. "I never make judgments, Ian. Nobody is an alcoholic as far as I'm concerned unless he says he is. I know I'm one. That's all that counts."

Springer was still talking. "Of course it's not all beer and skittles for me. I saw you watching me the night of the do at El Recobro. I knew in a moment that not much escaped you. Alex and Connie Vergara, for instance, didn't fool you for a minute. And I'm sure you saw how it was for me with Lady Sam. Let me disabuse you of any notion that any 'slarp-and-tickle' goes on between the two of us. Sam would never have it. Being the rum sort I am, I had a go at her. Stupid, wasn't it, trying it on with the sahib's wife? I don't think she ever told him, but she bowled my stumps as cleanly as any woman ever has. I rather imagine you can tell I'm a man who doesn't like to be turned away, but she almost made me like it. Enough of that. Just let me say there's scarcely a length I wouldn't go to to please Samantha Edwards. Never have given much credence to the romantic rot you Yanks live by when you're not chasing money, but . . ."

And that, it seemed, would be the finish of it. Anita returned with a refill of Ian's coffee, and Springer turned a look on her that would have corrupted the most avowed feminist on the planet, then he glanced at his wristwatch and turned back to Ian.

"Got to dash now, MacAndrews. Sam is having her hair done at that perm shop next to Ernie Gomez's office and she's due out now. Care to tag along and say hello?"

He couldn't think of an answer, but before he had to, Anita—it took a mighty effort for her to disengage her attention from the Englishman—turned to Ian and said, "Señor MacAndrews, could I have a private word with you before you leave?" He would have kissed her, except that she looked as if Tim Springer already had. He said good-bye to the

Englishman. At this moment he knew he didn't want Spring
er seeing Sam and him together no matter how innocent the
circumstances. So far he had been lucky—but those pale blue
eyes had an X-ray quality about them.

"Sure, Anita," he said. "Why don't you pack up about
two dozen tortillas for me to take back to M.L., and then we
can sit and talk as long as you like."

It was quite a different Anita who took the chair across
the table from him. The flirt was gone, and so was the
Hispanic *dama*.

"There was a strange *hombre* in the Comida yesterday,
Señor MacAndrews. He was asking some pretty funny questions—
about you."

She wasn't fooling around now. She looked worried as
she went on.

"He was Latino, but not from around here, maybe not
even from this country. He pretended he didn't speak Spanish,
but he gave himself away when Bautista there, from where
this man couldn't see him, said he looked crooked, speaking
in our Rio lingo. Snapped his head around before he could
stop himself."

"You said he asked questions. What kind of questions?"

"How long you had been in the basin... if your people
were still alive... if you had lots of visitors at the D Cross A."

"Nothing funny about those questions, Anita."

"I suppose not. It was more in the way he asked them,
señor, like a policeman. And he watched me like a snake
when I answered, like he was sure I was lying."

Ian smiled. "Anita... what kind of questions did you ask
him?" It was a safe bet she had asked. *Los hermanos* were
almost strangling in silent laughter, and Anita herself had
turned maroon.

"*Senor!*" she said. Then she calmed herself. "Of course I
asked. You are my friend, no? But he wouldn't answer. I do
know he drives a Jeep. He parked it across the plaza, but
Juan followed him when he left and took the license number."
She fished in the pocket of her apron and pulled out one of
the Comida's dinner checks. The number was on the back of
it.

"BEJ nine one four," Anita said. "Bernalillo County. It's
a rental."

"How do you know?"

"I called my cousin Andy Gabaldon. He works for the DMV in Albuquerque. The Jeep was rented to a Pedro Sanchez from Corpus Christi."

"Do you know where the man went from here?"

"Just that he went north on the highway toward Corona."

"I wouldn't worry about it, Anita. Did he ask about Hadley or Mrs. Edwards?" She shook her head, but her eyes narrowed. Did she know or guess what Hadley was up to? John had said no one in town knew about El Recobro, but . . . he went on. "What did this *turista* look like?"

"Small. Not as small as Bautista, though. Trying to look younger with that fancy shirt and silver hishi choker. Greasy black hair that looks like a toupee, and . . ." She hesitated. He had never seen her hesitate before. ". . . sneaky *yellow* eyes. I swear it."

Well, he now had a description of the man, although a subjective one. Ian laughed. He couldn't swear that Anita's prejudices had weakened her powers of observation, but if John Begley had gotten a better look at the "lost" traveler he saw on the Williston Road some time back, and if it were the same man, he would probably have turned out to be a six-footer in a three-piece suit and wearing horn-rimmed glasses.

"Bring your *amigo* again, señor," Anita said as he left.

He had intended telling John of his conversation with Anita after supper, but the subject never came up. Something strange seemed to be going on between M.L. and John.

M.L. giggled like a schoolgirl throughout the meal, and even John permitted himself a rare smile from time to time. When Ian finished the *natillas* the girl had fixed for dessert and after she poured his coffee, he pushed his chair from the table and looked from one to the other of them.

"Is one of you going to tell me what the hell is so damned funny?" he said.

M. L. looked at John and then at Ian.

Without makeup, Ian thought, she *is* an uncommonly pretty girl.

"Ian—" she began. The giggles erupted again, but she finally bottled them up.

"John and me . . . ," she said, ". . . have decided we want to get married before the baby comes. Could you help us make the arrangements, please?"

Chapter XXII

He should have known what Sam Edwards's reaction would be.

"Marvelous!" she exclaimed, as Hadley applauded from his wheelchair. Her pleasure didn't surprise him, but the degree and intensity of it did. She didn't know M.L. or John in any intimate way. Perhaps it was a reflection of his own satisfaction.

But although he was satisfied, something in him held back. Why couldn't he just turn his emotions loose? There had been a strange static lightness about things in recent weeks. He had tried to fight against the notion that he might be enjoying himself. Why? He certainly shouldn't dread the prospect of leaving the basin this time with feelings that were bittersweet, instead of the acid that seeped through his bowels twenty years ago.

"Do you suppose," Sam said after she caught her breath, "that they would agree to be married here at El Recobro, Ian?"

"They might like that. At least I think M.L. would. I'm not sure about John. I'm still not sure about John on a lot of things."

"Jim Pendleton could do the honors. Neither M.L. or John are Catholic, are they?"

"I don't think so."

"We could have the wedding when Consuelo and Alejandro are here. Make up a list of people you want." She was bubbling like a mountain freshet, showing perhaps more vibrance and enthusiasm than at any time since she looked him over for marks of his fight with John.

"Hold your horses, Sam! M.L. does have a family. I don't think she would want to shut them out of the planning if they want in on it. You haven't met Elsie, but she is a thoroughgoing mother, believe me."

And John, he thought, has a family, too, for whatever it might be worth.

"I'm sorry," Sam said then. She had become suddenly—and he realized, deceptively—calm. "I have no right to start playing Lady Bountiful—yet." There was sheepishness in her smile, but quiet determination, too. Sam was going to run this show, and the more Ian thought about it, the more he liked the idea. With Harry Kimbrough's feelings about John, and given her worship of Hadley, M.L. would probably like the idea, too.

"I'll get back to you on this, Sam," Ian said.

Hadley had just worn that air of detached but not indifferent amusement through all this, and now Ian spoke to him. "I have news for you, too, Hadley."

"Oh? Nothing wrong at the D Cross A, I trust."

"Quite the opposite. We've shaped up better and faster than I'd hoped. John is ready to take complete charge now. I plan to return to New York on the last day of March."

Hadley only nodded. It was clear he had expected something like this. Ian didn't dare look at Sam.

"End of March?" the man in the wheelchair said then. "That's almost six months from now. Yes, I believe that's all the time the three of us will need for everything we have to do." He turned from Ian to Sam, and Ian knew that the "three of us" didn't mean Hadley, John, and Ian.

It was time to tell his partner of his plans.

"By now it shouldn't be any secret that I'll be sorry to see you go next March, Ian," John Begley said.

John was right, it was no longer a secret, but Ian had hoped it would come straight out like this. Now that it had, he knew it wouldn't pay to inquire too closely into the younger man's complete change of heart.

All he said was, "Thanks, John."

They were riding together more often now. Some of Ian's skill on horseback had returned to him and he no longer felt he was the drag on John he had been in their first days as partners. About the only part of the old D Cross A they hadn't covered together was the sixty-section tract that strangely enough was the only part Ian MacAndrews actually held title to. He knew John had made intermittent solitary visits to Ignacio's grave since the house was finished. He had no doubt, either, that John knew Ian had gone there by himself as well.

Twice in his lifetime he had known the services of a guide through the vast loneliness of this particular stretch of desert rangeland. Ignacio Ortiz had shown him places on the D Cross A he hadn't dreamed existed, and now John began the process once again. It was a deceiving land; the brilliant blinding sun, in a mystifying reversal of what the keenest observer might expect, hid far more than it revealed. And what it did reveal quite often was ephemeral or illusory: broad, swift, whitewater rivers as real to the eye as the great Rio itself would fade from sight as riders neared their banks; low *cerros* quivering and heaving on the horizon would disappear like magic as he watched. There were spooky times when he imagined the whole basin to be but one giant mirage.

He wondered how many of the secrets of the country John showed him had first been shown to John by the old vaquero, but he didn't ask. The blond giant was sometimes like a child with a chest of toys when he showed Ian something new, as when he led the way into an arroyo completely hidden from the eye until it gaped suddenly before them like a monster canyon, or when he showed Ian the still barely visible trail left by Spanish travelers two centuries before, or the ancient Mimbres ruins in the northeastern shadow of Negrito Peak. Ian wouldn't have spoiled these revelations for anything.

They even began to talk. How far that might eventually lead was anybody's guess, a guess certainly not worth Ian's hazarding with his day of leaving here circled on the calendar and as fixed in his mind as flint.

Once they rested in the same bosque where John had parked his trailer and ate the lunch M.L. had crammed in their saddlebags. Afterward, with their backs against the trunk of the same cottonwood that had cradled the rifle, Ian lit his customary cigarette.

"Never have figured out why you still smoke, Ian," John said. "Seems to me that a man who could quit drinking the way you did ought to be able to quit smoking, too."

"It goes back to the war, John," Ian said. "I don't believe I'll ever quit. When we came off oxygen near the end of a long mission, and it seemed like we were sure to make it back to Italy and stay alive one more day, that first cigarette was like a reprieve. I would sink to the floor of the navigator's compartment with my back against the ammo can that fed the nose turret, light up, and suck the smoke right down to my toes. Heady stuff, made me forget the danger and the tension. When I'm tired enough or scared enough, I still get some of that same feeling from a cigarette."

John Begley laughed. He had laughed some before now, but nothing like this great, free roar.

"Funny about war," he said when the laughter stopped. "It kept you smoking and made *me* quit. I blew a lot of grass in Nam. I told myself it was what got me through the Tet. When I got back and realized what was happening to my head, I figured the only way to get off pot was to quit smoking altogether. Easy to do since I was in the hospital and stoned on painkillers most of the time."

Ian drew a breath and leaped in. "Quitting smoking would have been a lot tougher for me than quitting drinking."

John didn't bite.

Some day, Ian thought, they would talk about their wars, but not now. Some day, too, they might get around to more talk about liquor, but not now. They could perhaps talk about the wedding, but even about something such as that, talk wouldn't come easily for the two of them—not yet. Talk still had to be painstakingly circumscribed.

Talk came easily enough with M.L.

Ian was glad to find that the girl exhibited absolutely no self-consciousness about the fact that she would go to the temporary altar at El Recobro as a more than slightly swollen bride. Elsie was set to work on the wedding gown with its special requirements. M.L. was now wearing the smocks her mother had given her for her birthday, and although they perhaps made her look more pregnant than did the jeans and shirts, she looked considerably less misshapen.

As he had expected, the girl was pleased when he reported Sam's offer—or rather Sam's insistence—that the ceremony take place at the Edwardses' home, but she turned stubbornly shy when Ian urged her to drive over to the house behind the butte and make the necessary arrangements with Sam. Her lip trembled and her eyes went wide, much in the same way they had when she was concocting those elaborate, still-to-be-given dinners for Hadley. In the end John sur-

prised him by taking a firm line with the girl and hauling he
to El Recobro almost by main force late one afternoon.

They didn't return until well past dark, and Ian had to fi
his own supper. At first he was grateful for what amounted t
the only solitude he had known since he decamped from th
Yucca, but as the evening wore on he realized he missed th
young couple—and in the next second he chided himself
When he left for New York, he very likely wouldn't be seein
them for the rest of his life. He had better reacquaint himse
with his customary old solitary state soon.

He paced, and the sound of his footfalls on the bar
hardwood floors sounded almost as if someone were followin
him. He would have to get to a telephone tomorrow (Sam's?
and build a fire under that carpet company in Albuquerque
rattle their cages and get them down here before the col
weather arrived. M.L. walked the house barefoot a good bi
of the time and the chilly wooden floor couldn't be good fo
her or the baby.

Damn it! He should have driven to El Recobro with th
two of them. Obviously Sam had made them stay for suppe
There would be cocktails first, and wine with the meal. Risk
for John, with only M.L. along to monitor him. Yes, h
should have gone.

He went to the desk in the office that adjoined th
master bedroom, thinking to do a little work on next spring
grazing plan, the plan that John would have to implemen
without him, but before he started, he noticed that the doo
to John and M.L.'s room had been left ajar. He left the des
to close it, feeling that until he did he was somehow invadin
the personal space of his two young wards.

Watch it, MacAndrews. If you assume a proprietar
attitude toward M.L. and John, aren't you in effect grantin
them one toward you?

He didn't mean to pry, but when he reached the door, he
found that the weak light from the small lamp on the office
desk was enough to light the dresser.

No empty bottles cluttered it.

Not proof, of course, but evidence.

Buoyed suddenly, he turned from the door, but as he
did, his shadow, which had fallen across the headboard of the
bed M.L. shared with John, moved away from something he
had to forcibly stop himself from going to see close up. Nailed
to the wall above the headboard was a wrought-iron, hand

made Spanish spur, the twin of the one he had found in Ignacio's cairn.

He forgot the work in the office and instead went to his bedroom and sat on the side of the bed staring across the pitch-black rangeland to the lights of El Recobro.

"John hasn't taken a drink in almost two weeks. Not where I could see him, anyway. And he never was one to hide it," M.L. said two days later. He hadn't meant to ask, but it had slipped out when she recounted the events at El Recobro. "Gee, was it ever *elegant,* Ian. I never seen so many forks and spoons and glasses and stuff. I just couldn't believe Mrs. Edwards could do all that so quick, on the spur-of-the-moment like, without no help or nothing. They even had an imported beer for me. It was good, but I couldn't finish it. It's strong! Ain't a bit like Coors."

Now that he had asked he wasn't sorry—particularly as M.L. had at once recognized the wisdom of not telling John he had asked.

"I think John wants to tell you himself, Ian," she went on about the apparent abstinence. "But he don't quite know how."

"Telling me isn't all that important, M.L.," Ian said.

It didn't seem all that important to M.L., either. She was still too full of the dinner with Sam and Hadley and Tim Springer. "That English flyer sure is cute," she said. "But my God, Ian! The way he teased me. I swear he knows more about having babies than my mother does. He says he even delivered one in Africa once. They sure been around, them people. And Mr. Edwards! You wouldn't believe how nice he was to John. Kept asking him questions about the D Cross A. I never heard John talk so much in all the time I've known him."

Now Ian wished more fervently that he had gone along with his partner and his partner's wife-to-be. The solitude he had welcomed at the outset seemed abandonment of a sort.

He was pleased that Sam had put on the whole dog-and-pony show for these two uncomplicated country youngsters. He might have known she would. The only resulting drawback, even if the subject would probably never get through M.L.'s lips, was that the proposed dinner for Sam and Hadley that had brought such hopeful smiles and then despairing, scalding tears would now never come to pass. The girl was now smitten with Sam, too, but—we do, after all, compete with one another even when we *aren't* competing. To match Sam as a hostess was a quantum leap beyond the girl, and if she hadn't known it before, she knew it now.

A week after their talk M.L. called Ian and John to the living room when she had put away the supper dishes.

"You two are supposed to make yourselves scarce next Friday night. Mr. Edwards says you should come over to their place if you want. That Nicaraguan guy, what's-his-name?... well, Mr. Springer is going to fly someplace and pick up him and his wife. She and Mrs. Edwards are coming over here. I guess she called my mother and she's going to get some of the girls I graduated Black Springs High with— and they're going to throw me a shower!"

Ian faced the evening with Hadley, Springer, and Alex Vergara with some minor tremors. Jim Pendleton would be on hand, too. Cissy and Jim had been gathered up in the same flying roundup that had produced Alex and Consuelo, and Hadley, with his whole squad on the field, might make a try at keeping him here. Cissy was to attend the shower along with Sam and Connie, as he now was being urged to call Alex's wife.

When the MG neared the plank bridge, Ian discovered there would be an added starter in the gathering at El Recobro. In his rearview mirror he saw headlights. Ticking off possibilities, he knew it had to be Ernesto Gomez. Sure, Sam would have made certain Carrie would be at the shower, and Ernie must have dropped her off at the D Cross A and still caught up with them.

For a moment he became unnerved. It wasn't likely that Ernie and John might have it out again. Gomez was a self-controlled, intelligent young man, and this was the home of his most important client. For his part, John wasn't about to get violent now with what he had at stake. But—although no one had billed this all-male get-together as a "stag," it amounted to that and there would be booze. If John really was trying to quit, the mere presence of Ernie might trigger something.

When Ian and John were out of the MG and at the ornamental gate, Ernie's station wagon pulled in next to the Edwards Cadillac. The lawyer waved to Ian and looked at John. John stared back. Something in their looks and the nods that ended them seemed to promise there would be no trouble, not tonight.

The three of them walked to the house together, but in silence until they reached the door.

"Go right in, Ian," Ernie said. "Nobody's on the door tonight." He motioned John ahead of him. As Begley passed him, the lawyer spoke again. "Evening, Jacky. How's M.L.?"

Ian froze at the "Jacky," stayed frozen until the answer came.

"Just fine, Ernesto. Thanks. And Carrie?"

"Almost as excited about M.L.'s shower as if it were her own."

"Any chance of her having her own sometime soon?"

"*¿Quien sabe?* A greaser mouthpiece I know is getting ready to ask her to marry him. He's kind of uppity. Doesn't know his place."

They both laughed and Ian breathed easier. Of course he would have to straighten Ernie out on the "Jacky" thing before too much time went by.

Hadley had set things up in the game room of El Recobro, a room rich in old leather and polished wood Ian hadn't seen before. Springer and Jim Pendleton were playing pool at a massive table that must have dated from the nineties. The minister showed surprisingly good form with the cue, and a professional flair in the way he chalked it after all his shots, most of which left the object balls rattling into the pockets and dropping with emphatic finality into the nets beneath them to the accompaniment of Springer's groans. When Pendleton missed, which didn't seem to be a regular occurrence, Tim Springer revealed in *his* pitiful efforts that if he had lived a prodigal youth, the spending of it hadn't been done in billiard parlors; not surprising to Ian from what he remembered of Midlands villages, those sleepy hamlets such as the one the pilot came from. Probably not a good idea to tangle with Tim against that dart board on the far wall, though.

Ian, John, and Ernie stood in the room for a full thirty seconds before their host or any of the others noticed them. Hadley had parked his electric wheelchair alongside a long couch on the other side of the pool table. The elegant figure of Alejandro Vergara sprawled uncharacteristically on the couch, but the Nicaraguan, his relaxed posture notwithstanding, was intent on something the owner of El Recobro was saying.

Then Hadley spotted the new arrivals.

"Aha!" he said. "Mr. Begley. Welcome, John. *Como estas,* Ernesto, Ian."

A round of earnest but subdued greetings began. Some stag party. It was about as raucous and southwestern as a meeting of stockbrokers in the second-floor dining room of the Union League Club on Jackson Boulevard.

"Fix drinks for yourself and John and Ian would you please, Ernesto?" Hadley said. "There's a good Cordon Bleu in that ice bucket. I rather suppose a toast to the happy couple is the proper order of business now."

"Ian?" Ernie said, when he had moved to the mahogany-and-chrome wet-bar that angled across a corner of the room.

"Anything cold and wet—and soft," Ian said.

The lawyer looked at Begley.

"The same for me, Ernesto," John said. There wasn't a shadow of hesitation on Begley's face, nor any skepticism or curiosity on that of Gomez. *One swallow does not a summer make . . .* and all that stuff of course, but it did feel good.

"Health and happiness, John," Hadley said when everyone had a glass. "No need for us to wish for progeny. . . if you'll forgive my saying so."

Springer had racked the balls and moved to the bar to refill his champagne glass just before the toast.

"One of you other chaps take my place at the table," he said. "The padre here has cleaned me out. Ernie?"

"Not me! I don't care if Jim does give all his winnings to charity; I'm not the United Way. I had to run foreclosure proceedings on three widows with young children after the last time I shot pool with this shark in Christian clothing." Ernie smiled wickedly and turned to Begley. "I saw you handle a cue once down in Tularosa. Maybe you can give him a little competition—John." Good. The lawyer had tumbled to it.

"I'll try, Ernie," John said.

"Go ahead and break, Mr. Begley," Jim Pendleton said.

"Not so fast, Doctor," John said. "Let's lag for it."

"Ah, dear." Pendleton placed the cue ball on the balk-line. "There's so little trust in this sad world. How does a dollar a ball strike you, Mr. Begley?"

"Fine, sir."

Pendleton lost the lag by a millimeter. In mock despair he chalked his cue.

It was a good break. The seven ball rolled clear, but across the rack from the cue ball, which was railed as tight as a tick. In his turn John freed up two more, but not by much, and Jim failed to make the seven in the corner after two fairly accurate caroms made it close. It was all the opening John needed. Hardly pausing to sight them in, he ran the table in nine swift, sweet shots.

The second rack wasn't quite as devastating, but Begley won handily again to the great delight of Hadley.

"I think John has decided that charity does indeed begin at home, Jim." Hadley laughed, slapping one of his useless legs. He was a great-hearted watcher of games as well as a player in them, Ian concluded.

Ian took a seat on the couch beside Alex. As he looked at the Nicaraguan, something occurred to him.

"Alex," he said, "I read the article about you in *The New York Times*. Just how close *was* that affair in Puerto Vallarta?"

Alex held his hand in front of him, the thumb and index finger less than an inch apart.

"And they caught the man and deported him?" Ian said.

"Yes."

"Did you know him?"

Alex nodded. "But only by reputation, not by name. Assassins for the Guardia go by number. I believe this one was called Capitán Cuatro, although he actually held the rank of colonel. The Mexican *justicia* likes to close matters such as this with great rapidity. I only saw him when he shot at me."

"There was no trial?"

"No. Anastasio Somoza has no visible political power in Mexico, but his money does. It didn't even appear in the papers there."

"But you do remember the man?"

"Ah, *sí*. One does not forget."

Even while watching the third rack between John and Pendleton, Ian saw that Hadley hadn't missed a word. Now he turned the chair away from the table and gave Ian and Alex his full attention. Clearly theirs was a more absorbing game.

"Tell me what he looked like," Ian said.

Alex shrugged. "Very undistinguished, Ian. He was a small man, very thin, perhaps your age and mine, swarthy, with black hair. He could have been any of a hundred thousand Nicaraguans. I would know him again, yes, but to describe him, no. . . ." He spread his hands at the futility of it. Then his black brows lifted a little. "Please do not think me imagining things, although I suppose I could be. He had one distinguishing feature . . . an impossible one. I swear his eyes were yellow."

Yellow eyes! God bless Big Anita—and let her forgive me.

He told Hadley and Alex then about Anita's inquisitive visitor and of John's sighting weeks ago of the man who had looked at El Recobro and the D Cross A through binoculars, the "lost tourist" on the Williston road. When he finished, the other two looked at each other for a moment and then Hadley turned to Ian.

"Coincidence, I'm sure, Ian. Nothing to worry about."

Alex's face was blank.

They're shutting me out. Good. The last thing he wanted was *in.*

Hadley, his face pleasantly bland, turned to the others in the room. "Sam left snacks and the like in the kitchen, gentlemen. Would you lead the way and do the honors for me, Ernesto? *Gracias, amigo.*"

John and the minister placed their cues in the wall brackets and followed Ernie from the game room. Pendleton, a good sport, was thumping the younger man between the shoulder blades. Ian stood up and started for the door. When he reached it, he looked back. Springer, clearly having responded to some subtle signal from Hadley, had taken Ian's place by Alex on the couch. The three of them were giving each other mighty serious looks.

They talked for a couple of hours after eating. Jim Pendleton had apparently taken a genuine liking to Ian's partner and was asking the usual layman's questions about cowboy life. Springer talked golf with Ernie. The Englishman was a five-handicapper, although he claimed he wasn't playing anywhere near the figure nowadays. He made a great show of enthusiasm over the fact that Ernie as a youngster in Socorro had caddied for Lee Trevino. Alex and Hadley rode in memory a course in southern California on lightweight hunters—cleared again every jump with uncanny photographic recall. There was a certain amount of predictable teasing of the prospective bridegroom.

It was club talk, man talk—good, interesting talk. And to Ian MacAndrews it was totally unreal.

He was glad when Sam, Cissy, Consuelo, and Carrie Spletter, back from M.L.'s shower, appeared in the doorway.

According to Cissy and Carrie, the shower had been a roaring success. It had taken a while to thaw M.L.'s two high school friends, but Sam, they said, had managed it neatly before the night was out. Connie Vergara smiled agreement. She was even more beautiful than she had appeared at Sam's dinner. Brave, too. Even someone unacquainted with her history might have seen it.

Ernie poured champagne for everyone but John and Ian, and another toast to John brought these proceedings to a close as well. The Pendletons and the Vergaras said good-night, and Hadley and Sam showed Ernie and Carrie and John and Ian to the door. Hadley stopped his chair there, but Sam walked to the gate with the four of them. John and Ernie shook hands. Neither man was effusive, but there was warmth in the gesture. A big, nasty gap had been narrowed some tonight.

"I want to talk with John and you, Ian," Sam said. It was the first time hers and Ian's eyes had so much as met. Ernie backed the station wagon out and pulled away.

"You two ought to know something before you get back to the D Cross A," Sam said. "Things aren't all peaches and cream. They didn't spill it to the others, but for some damned reason Elsie and M.L. took *me* into their confidence. Harry Kimbrough hasn't softened one little bit about this wedding. He won't come, and he's told Elsie she can't either. And he says he'll leave her if she tries to help M.L. after the baby gets here. I'm sorry, John."

When they got in the car, Ian rolled the window down. His elbow was on the sill and Sam put out her hand and pressed on it for a fraction of a second. Hadley was silhouetted against the light from the hall as he had been the night of the dinner party. He waved good-bye.

"Don't get so heated up about it, John honey," M.L. said. "Ain't nothing we can do about it, so we might just as well forget it. If I know Jody, *he'll* figure out a way to get his ma to his sister's wedding. And nothing will keep my little brother away."

"But when the baby comes . . . how can you handle tha
alone?"

"Women have done it before. Hundred years ago in thi
country they did it alone all the time. We ain't gone too so
yet for me to do it again."

Tough little monkey, Ian thought. Both of them wer
tough. There were some things he wanted to say himself, bu
they would have to wait.

"I'm going to bed," M.L. said. "No, John. You sit ou
here with Ian for a while. I'm entitled to cry a little, I reckon
and if I do, I want to do it by myself." She kissed him the
and left the living room.

John sank into a chair by the fireplace in a way tha
indicated a stay of some duration. Ian knew he should b
weighed down now, depressed, but he wasn't. He had jus
made a discovery about his partner. If John Hall Begley wa
going to drink tonight, nothing would have kept him out o
that bedroom now, M.L.'s half-promised tears notwithstanding—
or he would have left the house for some other source o
alcohol. But if the man wasn't going to drink, there wa
something he had to hear from John himself.

"You've stopped drinking, John."

"Yes, I have!" He looked astonished.

"May I ask why?"

John looked him in the eye, but not before a panicky
moment where he seemed about to run.

"I'm an alcoholic, Ian."

Chapter XXIII

On Wednesday, three days before the wedding, freakish
winds swept the pastures of the D Cross A from the east
hooting their disdain for the barrier of Cuchillo Peak and the
windbreaks of the high Sombras and Capitans as they sho
through Mescalero Gap. That night at supper sleet or pelleted
snow bounded off the darkened windowpanes, sounding spookily

like flak had when it rattled on the aluminum skin of the
B-24. It seemed early for sheepskin time, but they decided
that when M.L. and John got back from their three-day
honeymoon in Juarez, the two men would move all the stock
in the high meadows and piñon groves just below the slickrock,
herd them into the lower pastures near the house, and then
set about the too-easy-to-postpone work of closing off the last
quarter-mile of fence that would keep them there.

"The Weather Bureau's forecast," John said, "is that
we're going to have a milder winter than usual. That crap
hitting the windows sure don't make me a believer."

M.L., to the surprise of neither man, with her mind
occupied solely by the wedding on the coming Saturday
afternoon, wasn't much interested. She ended the weather
talk by remarking, "This is just one storm we won't get in
February. It will be warm and dry again tomorrow. You wait
and see."

Thursday proved her right. In Chicagoland they would
have called the bright, blue, balmy day the beginning of
"Indian summer." Bolstered by the success of her prediction,
M.L. was more unshakable than ever in her certainty that the
child she was carrying would be a boy.

"Just let us in on how come you're so goddamned sure,
M.L.," John said. "Has that little blob been acting as mean as
his old man?"

"It just *feels* like a boy." She had no answers for their
questions about what a boy "feels" like, insisting blithely, "Us
women know these things."

"From the look of you it could be one of each."

"Good grief! You don't suppose—"

"Calm yourself, M.L." Laughter, honest-to-goodness open
laughter, was getting to be a somewhat regular thing for the
big cowboy now. "That doctor we saw last week would have
known if it was twins, wouldn't he, Ian?"

"One thing *I* know," Ian joined in, "if it *is* a boy—he'll
damned well be the 'best man' at the Edwards place on
Saturday."

He hadn't struggled against John's request that he stand
up for him in front of Jim Pendleton in Sam's living room. His
first, automatic resistance to the idea faded once he was
reminded that *his* suggestion for best man, Jody, might not be
able to make it to the wedding. Poor Harry Kimbrough was
still forbidding Jody and Elsie to come. And it *was* "poor"

Harry, even to the young people directly affected. The elder
Kimbrough's mean-minded obstinance in their view (an
unexpectedly charitable view Ian blessed them for) was as
elemental as last night's storm and as sure to pass. Demon-
strating a maturity Ian wished he could claim for himself,
they hadn't shown any bitterness.

It eased his mind that they had driven to Alamogordo to
see the doctor, but it would have pleased him more if they
abandoned the idea of a midwife and the "natural" birth
in favor of a conventional stay in a hospital. He didn't
press this, though. Something told him that choosing the
method they had chosen was a great deal more than whim.
He could imagine that M.L.'s determination to "do this our
own selves" was her way of making a satisfactory end to
something they had begun, even unintentionally, as a nose-
thumb at the small society that had snipped at them all their
lives.

The fact that Elsie wouldn't be able to come out for those
first couple of weeks after the delivery loomed as a potentially
far more serious worry. The midwife, a pleasant, competent-
sounding woman named Rosa Candelario, had visited the I
Cross A to conduct a training session for John and M.L., but
she flatly, if regretfully, said no to Ian's request that she move
in for a while after the child was born.

"I'm sorry, Mr. MacAndrews, but I've got three babies
due that same week. I just hope they don't all arrive at once.
I could look for someone for you, but it would be much nicer
if someone in the family could—" Something in her face and
voice told Ian that Black Springs on both sides of the tracks
already knew about Harry's edict.

Family? He wondered if he could summon up the nerve
to talk to John about that subject.

If Thursday and Friday were beautiful, the day of the
wedding was perfection. The veranda thermometer read
seventy-eight degrees when he and John left the house
at one o'clock for the short drive to El Recobro. Sam had
picked M.L. up at nine to help her get ready. Not a breath
of wind threatened to ruffle hairdos, and the incomparable
southwestern air was dry enough that the inevitable nervous
sweat of the groom and his best man would evaporate to
nothing.

Not a cloud marred the sky.

Chapter XXIV

"... I pronounce you husband and wife."

M.L. thrust her shining face up at John with such sudden eagerness their mouths almost failed to meet. Over their heads Sam Edwards smiled at Ian, but he had no time to respond before M.L. rushed to him and presented him her cheek. Cissy Pendleton, sweet lady that she was—and the only one in the gathering besides Elsie to have spilled tears—was doing something weird to the Lohengrin recessional on Sam's spinet.

There wasn't much chance for anyone but Carrie Spletter to catch the bouquet; M.L.'s two high school friends had backed about as far from the El Recobro people as they could get, eyes glistening but wary.

It had been a simple ceremony, one that left Ian even more impressed with Jim Pendleton, and yet M.L. (Martha Lucille, not Mary Lou, Ian had belatedly discovered) couldn't have asked for more. Jim's words had taken so little time that John was saved from going into complete paralysis.

Unlike her husband, M.L. was more alive than ever, beaming, as Hadley, who at Jim's question had "given" her in Harry's absence, said, "You're an absolutely beautiful bride, M.L."

"Kind of a fat one, Mr. Edwards," she said.

"No, no!" he protested. "No woman is as lovely as when she's pregnant. It's when she looks most loved—and *loving.*"

In spite of the earnestness of the words he sounded a little strange, distantly sad. It wasn't stretching Ian's speculations too far to imagine that Hadley Edwards, even if he didn't desperately want children, would be pleased to have

them. He looked to Sam to see if she had caught Hadley'
remarks. She had.

"Everyone out on the patio!" she said. There was
funny, almost strident, urgency in her voice.

When Ian had come in with John, she had told him tha
she had thought about holding the ceremony outside in th
full warmth of the sun, but had decided that moving the flora
decorations (Springer had taken the Toyota to Alamogord
and cleaned out the flower shop on Tenth Street) and the
delicate piano over the flagstones was more trouble than i
was worth, since the crowd would be out there in a few
moments for the wedding feast anyway.

And it was a crowd—to M.L., in any case.

"Look at all of them, would you? Three weeks ago I wa
thinking we'd be doing this in the town hall with maybe m
ma and Jody and you, period," she confided to Ian. "Bac
then the last thing John and I wanted was any fuss. This sure
is better. Makes me feel really married."

Perhaps more than the bride and groom it was Jody wh
claimed Ian's attention. The youngster's piggy bank ha
produced enough to outfit him in a brand-new western suit
one off the rack at Stafford's surely, but looking as if tailore
for him. A navy-blue string tie accented a gleaming whit
shirt, and with the old hat he had worn when he firs
showed Ian room 24 at the Yucca safely stowed on the table i
El Recobro's entrance hall, he looked like a million dollars i
newly minted hundreds. Other changes in him ran eve
deeper. Suddenly gone was the teen slouch, the ingenuous
bubbling eagerness. He had taken a sizable step towar
manhood.

Outside, with the cake cut—M.L., one small han
guiding the knife, the other on top of John's unstead
giant one—Hadley again demonstrated his unerring sens
of form. Ian had confidently expected the man in th
wheelchair to offer the toast, but he insisted that Jod
do it.

The toast wasn't any marvel of rhetoric, but the boy
voice after one understandable opening stammer was clea
and steady.

"Here's to my sis and her husband, John. I gues
they now got about everything in life a body could as
for, and I hope it gets even better for them." He took
suspicious sip of the champagne in his glass, swallowe

t., and finished, "And thanks to Ian and the Edwardses or helping them so much."

The two Black Springs girls who had blended with he wall of Sam's living room during the recital of the ·ows were under pleasant siege by Tim Springer. Ian had ittle fear for their "honor," whatever amount of that dubi-)us commodity they might still possess. He dared hope the ‡nglishman still lived by some vestigial Victorian sporting :ode where women were concerned; he shouldn't unsling a ›ig-game rifle to bring down a brace of rabbits. That the ›air didn't know that, though, was evident in their faces; :ach of them, so adroit were Tim's words and body lan-¿uage, seemed blissfully persuaded that he was offering hem a personal tour of the highroad of romantic and ›robably sexual adventure.

Consuelo and Alex Vergara were silent, as usual, but at east for the moment the zealous, sometimes fierce, black 'yes grew calm and gave way to a simple enjoyment of the ιappiness around them. Like a real trouper warmed by the ›ootlights of his latest successful performance, Jim Pendleton noved through the small crowd, glass in hand, now trying to ‹empt Ernie Gomez to the billiard table when the party ›roper finished, next squeezing the arm of Cissy as he passed ιer, then chatting with Hadley and conspiring with Carrie 5pletter, but not about matters dark and secret, obviously, ‹rom the way the two of them looked at Ernesto from time to ime. As regular as a metronome Elsie Kimbrough clicked ‹rom sobs to smiles, delighting equally in both.

Then Ian studied John Begley. He had been standing for ι long time and the bad leg must be giving him all kinds of its, but his face had thawed. In the first moments after Jody's ›oast he even managed a smile from time to time, watching ιis bride as she flitted from group to group. Ian kept looking ‹t him until he finally returned the look. Across the entire vidth of the patio Ian felt they were now closer than they had ·ver been. Brothers at last and indeed, even if the younger nan didn't know it.

Jody and Ernie disappeared to decorate Hadley Edwards's Cadillac with crepe streamers and the "Just Married" sign. It ιad taken a certain amount of argument, not successful until an added his voice to Hadley's, to get the stubborn Begley ‹o use the big car for the trip to Juarez. M.L., while ›bviously hoping her husband would give in, had insisted that the old blue pickup or the GMC would do just fine. Jody and Elsie in the Kimbrough Jeep, the two Black Springs girls in the Chevrolet Camino they had driven out to El Recobro and Springer in the Toyota would root and toot the couple the length of Black Springs before they let them go. Springer, it appeared, would meet the girls afterward at the Buckhorn.

The party would soon be over.

Ian left the patio and made his way into the empty living room. The aroma from the floral pieces was like a drug. He went straight for the paintings, stopping in front of the Turner he had twice missed looking at. It was a familiar scene of the Thames, but whether sunrise or sunset it was impossible to tell, and it didn't matter, anyway. The painter had emptied his palette of color. Sprays of yellows, mauves, pinks—ordinary pigments, but worked subtly against each other to produce still other colors that weren't even in the spectrum—hung like brilliant webbing across the sky, draping and obscuring the hinted masts and yardarms of ghostly sailing ships. Ian had tried to do this with the basin's more muted tones when he was painting. Damn it! There had been times when he had almost glimpsed success in his work. If he hadn't come so close, it never would have mattered . . .

"Some of it *is* there. In the painting alongside it."

He wasn't even surprised that Sam had come to stand beside him. And he wasn't even surprised that she knew exactly what his thoughts had been. He was surprised at the next voice, which came as he turned and his eyes met Sam's.

"Tempted, Ian?" It was Hadley. He had wheeled his chair just inside the door to the patio.

Ian looked at the man in the chair. "It's not a temptation I can't deal with, Hadley."

Chapter XXV

Shortly after daybreak on the Sunday morning following the wedding, the twin-engined airplane climbed from the

unway at El Recobro and made its downwind turn toward
ie Oscuras from directly above the D Cross A.

Hadley and Tim were ferrying Jim and Cissy back to
everly Hills. Then they would take Consuelo and Alejandro
n down to San Diego to testify before some ad hoc panel of
ie OAS, a highly irregular committee looking into abuses of
uman rights in several Latin American countries, a meeting
eing boycotted by Richard Nixon's American delegation. It
as a good day for flying; it was a good day for almost
nything, even work, perhaps especially for work. It was
efinitely not a good day for introspection.

When the plane became a dot, then finally disappeared
omewhere down toward the Black Range, it meant that some
iree to four hundred square miles of empty Ojos Negros
ingeland contained only Samantha Edwards and Ian Mac-
ndrews.

It was an unsettling thought.

Lord how he already missed the two young people now
n Juarez. Five months earlier he would have laughed if
mitty Wyndham or any of the people at W & K had hinted
iat he could harbor so much affection for a pair of semiliter-
es who between them couldn't name an opera, had never
een the inside of a museum or a real theater, seldom read
iything but the funny papers, and whose sense of history
ook absolutely no account of anything that happened more
ian fifty miles from Black Springs. Maimed as he was from
ietnam, John paid scant attention to the war and less than
iat to politics.

When the black, lonely moods took hold of Ian in
hicago and New York, there was always work to numb the
neliness until the moods had passed, even when booze still
arped him. Well, Times Square or the Ojos Negros, work
ould still provide the answer.

The trouble was—there wasn't exactly one hell of a lot of
ork to do.

In the ten days before the wedding John had labored like
strung-out dervish. There now wasn't an inch of wire that
ad to be stretched except on the fence needed to secure the
outhern pastures, a job that would take both of them; there
as no harness or other tack left untreated; not an ounce of
upplemental feed to be carted to the tanks nor a single salt
lock that needed dumping from the back of the GMC. The

moving of the herd from the high country would have to w
until the newlyweds returned. He couldn't possibly manage
alone or close that last quarter-mile of fence all by himsel

He could ride fence, though. There was always fence
be ridden on a stock ranch, no matter how small the oper
tion. Some of the owners of the larger spreads were no
bulldozing and grading perimeter roads just inside the wi
that enclosed their holdings, so they could "ride" their fenc
in air-conditioned trucks with automatic transmissions, pow
steering, and with thousand-dollar quadraphonic ster
tape-decks.

All right, MacAndrews—ride!

If he couldn't herd white-faced Herefords, he cou
perhaps herd this strangling mood across the last horizon.

He was in the corral with the saddle blanket already ov
the reluctant back of the larger roan pony when he saw t
Toyota Land Cruiser turn in at the gate.

He pulled the blanket from the pony's back, folded
and laid it across the top of the piñon fence, all the whi
trying to ready an excuse for turning away the woman wh
had left the Toyota and was now almost at the corral. H
determined strides had done little to make him forget h
mood. His neighbor lady hadn't driven five miles in th
stiff-springed monster just to borrow a cup of sugar. He wou
have to send her packing, fast, or he might never send h
away at all.

She reached the gate of the corral, placed her elbows
the top bar, and cradled her face in her two hands.

"Hello, Ian," Sam said. "I've come to kidnap you. There
a big picnic lunch in the Toyota. Let's get out of here."

No excuses came except the general, nonspecific, mur
bled one that he had work to do.

"I don't believe you!" she exploded. "I've done n
homework. I had a little chat with John yesterday just befo
he and M.L. left. There's not one thing needs doing he
before they get back from the honeymoon. And who kno
how long this good weather is going to hold."

"Sam," he said, "I'm not sure this is such a good idea

She shrugged. "Neither am I. But don't you think v
had better find out . . . once and for all?"

She was right. Not that she had chased, not until now
least, but he couldn't run forever.

"All right . . . you're on," he said. "Where to?"

"I've been told there's a jewel of a mountain lake some-here past Las Sombras. Do you know it?"

Oh, yes, he knew it. Perhaps it was the only safe place in he high country they could go. It was on the shore of the ny Lago de las Sombritas that he had asked Jo Martinez to arry him.

"Let me change these boots for something a little better r walking," he said. "Have you got something besides those afers with you? It's rocky country up beyond Las Sombras. here's a hike of another half a mile past where even a ur-wheel drive can get to."

"I've a pair of clodhoppers in the car." She laughed. "I'm eady for just about anything today."

The day's loveliness itself held a threat, as if it were the st brilliant flare of a faulty match, the flare whose sudden, nexpected, incandescent violence would extinguish the flame rever. Even the aspen stands on the hillsides seemed ready burn themselves away, their gold molten, combustible, mething that couldn't last.

At Sam's insistence, Ian drove. He hadn't wanted to; he anted the freedom to look at her when, if, and how he leased. She must have had the same idea. Even when e was busy on the switchbacks leading to Las Sombras, he uld feel her eyes fastened on him.

"Do we have time to stop at the graveyard in Las ombras for a moment?" she said.

"I can't imagine why you want to."

"I've never seen your mother's grave. And I should. I idn't know her long, but we got to know each other with mething like immediate intimacy when we were in the rocess of buying El Recobro. She had a better impression of e than I deserved. I'd like to stop and ask her if I've turned ut too badly in her eyes."

"I can answer for her."

"Of course I want your answer, too, Ian. But I must have ers."

"That grave in particular was mute when I was up here st, Sam."

"Perhaps it had nothing to say to you then. It might ow."

"And perhaps I won't want to hear it."

"That's not like you."

"You misunderstood me. I would listen. I just would n
do what it might ask of me."

They were silent then as they pulled to a stop by th
cemetery. When they left the Toyota, he led the way to th
MacAndrews plot. The grasses and weeds that had clung
the granite blocks in July were longer, more tangled, a
drier now, and their whispers in the slight breeze were th
only sounds he heard.

Back in the Land Cruiser they drove the main street
the silent, scattered town and found the ruts that led off
the northeast and Lago de las Sombritas.

The last time he had traveled this faint road he had be
nineteen, driven along by the cleanest passion of his lif
Nothing that night had sullied it, either. One chaste kiss a
he had become engaged. Or had it happened to someo
else? It simply couldn't have been the shopworn, case-har
ened, embittered ex-drunkard, free-lance fornicator a
former barroom brawler who had now spent eighty seasons
a sordid hell of his own creation. They say the boy is father
the man, but there could be no way on God's green ear
that the innocent dreamer who proposed to Josefina Martin
that soft May night, when the stars danced themselves diz
above the circling pines, could have parented the pitif
excuse for a man who drove this road this morning. Sa
wasn't Jo Martinez, either.

When they pulled up at the rockfall where the path
the lake began, he asked her, "Did the grave speak to you
He kept his voice light, and so did she when she answere
him.

"You bet!" She chuckled. "Said that I was a fine, unde
standing woman, a real gem—and that if her miserable s
didn't treat me right, I should come back and snitch on him

They started up the shaded path, Ian carrying the wick
basket Sam pulled from the rear of the Toyota, she drape
like a packhorse under ponchos and a checked wool blanke
Their breath came short on the steep, stony trail.

The age-old ponderosas parted like the great fire-curta
of some nineteenth-century opera house, and Lago de l
Sombritas, the lake of the little shadows, sparkled in front
them. Not more than five hundred yards across at any poin
it formed and almost perfect circle, ringed at three sides
the water's edge by the big pines that had escaped the bu

f 1905 that had scorched the high, wooded cirque above.
spen stands had replaced the conifers taken by the forest
re, and now they added their own touch of splendid fire.
Vith the wind aloft now shivering the bright yellow leaves of
ie aspens, it really did look as if the wooded ridge beyond
ie lake raged with flame.

At shore level, though, there wasn't a hint of wind.

They spread the blanket on the grassy bank.

The hamper held a meal that made him think of poor
4.L. If the dinner at El Recobro and the rich variety of the
uffet Sam had spread for the wedding had overwhelmed the
irl, she very likely would have wanted to take to the gas
ipe had she seen what Sam Edwards thought was right for a
mple, wilderness picnic.

It would take them an hour to put it all away, a leisurely
our that would keep them on high, safe ground. Food was a
aarvelous buffer, always had been, either against liquor or
nything else.

He laughed.

"What's so funny?" Sam said.

"You've enough food here to last a week."

"Have we got a week?" She looked out across the lake.
God, but it's beautiful up here, Ian. Wish we had a year."
'here was a dream tone to her voice. She shook her head
ien and began to unlace the mountain boots she had changed
ito on the ride up. "How can anybody be comfortable in
iese cast-iron clamps? I won't enjoy lunch unless I can
'iggle my toes. My feet hurt."

"They'd hurt more from a stone bruise," he said.

When the boots were off, she glanced at her wrist. She
'asn't wearing her watch. "Is it time to eat? I'm starved."

"Anytime, Sam. It's twelve-twenty."

She laid the meal out on the blanket. It wasn't what he
'ould have called hearty food, but there was so much in the
'ay of canapés, tiny trimmed sandwiches, two different pâtés,
nd even caviar and lemon wedges, that he knew the two of
iem couldn't eat it all. There were thin-stemmed glasses for
is iced tea and for the half bottle of Pouilly-Fuissé she had
rought along for herself.

They didn't talk as they ate, but he watched her closely,
illowed every mouthful of food she took. She wasn't a dainty
ater. He had noticed that before. Samantha Edwards was a
oman of highly developed senses in every way.

What an indifferent observer he was. He had been s
intent on her face and eyes since she found him in the corra
that for the first time he noticed that today she wasn't wearin
the man's western shirt or the faded jeans. The pale blu
blouse must surely be pure silk, he thought. Neutral-colore
slacks of Irish linen, not tight but snug enough around th
hips, clung lightly to her thighs as she sat with her legs an
now bare feet pulled up on the blanket.

When they finished, he helped her clear the mess an
put the plates and glasses back in the wicker basket. Twic
their hands touched, and twice they looked up from the
and into each other's eyes.

She brushed the blanket clean of crumbs and stretche
out on her stomach, propped herself on her elbows, facir
the lake. They had laid the blanket out in the shade of a sma
pine on a knoll a hundred feet from the water's edge, b
now the sun had cleared the tree's branches and the air wa
cradling them in warm, golden cotton.

"You leave here March thirty-first?" she said.

"Yes."

"Well, then, there are a few things we have to sett
before you leave."

He didn't ask what the few things were.

"Not to change the subject," she said, "but is that a *dee*
lake?"

"Deep enough. It's an ancient crater; drops straigl
down from the edge for thirty or forty feet I've been told."

She stood up.

Then, before he could say a word or lift a hand to sto
her, she was racing toward the water.

"No, Sam! *No!*" he yelled.

It was too late. Her light-footed run had already take
her to the shore, and then she was slicing into the shimmeri
water like a knife.

He ran to the lakeside himself, arrived just as her hea
broke the surface. In clean, swift strokes she reached th
bank and he held his hand down to help her from the wate

"This is a mountain lake, you idiot!" he said. "You dor
swim here."

"I . . . I know. . . *now!*" she stuttered. Her lips were a
ready blue. As they walked back to the blanket, she wa
shaking violently. "It seemed like a good idea at the time. M
God, I'm frozen." The wet silk blouse had become almo

transparent, a second skin. She was wearing nothing under it and her body was trembling so that her breasts danced wildly, her hard, stiffened nipples poking almost through the fabric. Water ran in rivulets down the linen slacks. He wanted to wrap himself around her, but he knew his own body heat wouldn't be enough to warm her now.

"Get out of those clothes!" he snapped. "Bundle yourself in the blanket."

He turned away from her. His heart was pounding, his own still-heated blood drumming in his ears, but he could hear every move she made as she stripped off the dripping blouse and slacks.

"I'm decent now," she said, and he turned to look at her. She was swaddled in the blanket to her chin, and the blouse and slacks were a soaking pile on the grass beside her with a pair of bikini panties on top.

He gathered up the wet garments, wrung them out, and draped them on the needled branches of the pine tree where the sun could reach them.

He unrolled the two ponchos and lifted her onto one of them and then sat beside her on the other.

"Did you know I was that impulsive, Ian?" she said. Her teeth were still chattering a little, but the worst of the shock seemed over.

"I guessed it the very first time we met."

"It's gotten me in much worse trouble than this a few times in my life."

Yes, he could bet it had. But it had won some battles for her, too. He'd bet on that as well.

She had been solid but not heavy when he lifted her, her legs and back yielding and soft, and even the sudden chill hadn't turned her rigid. God almighty, but he needed her.

And why not have her? Where was the harm even if it wasn't, in the long run, love with a capital L? They were consenting adults: two seasoned sexual campaigners. The world in its skewed vision on these things made entirely too much fuss about casual sex—or too little.

If, as he was certain, Sam was as deprived of sex as he had been for far too long, it verged on the psychotic not to rip that blanket from her and take her as she should be taken and must want to *be* taken, here on this scented mountain grass. That fine body he had seen so plainly in the wet, clinging

clothing was naked and ready beneath that blanket, warm
again.

The trouble was with that haunting four-letter wor⸱
... "love." It should have sent him to her in a gentle rage
Instead, it held him back.

"Ian," she said.

"Yes?"

"If just one of us said 'yes' at this moment, the othe⸱
would. Am I right?"

He nodded.

She went on. "But neither one of us will say it, will we?⸱

"No, Sam. We won't."

She was silent as death itself for another second. "Ca⸱
you tell me why?"

"I can guess—but saying it out loud it would sound to⸱
pompous, too ... precious, too goddamned—oh, hell—I don⸱
know."

"Say it anyway. I think I need to hear it."

He thought perhaps he blushed.

"I guess that in spite of everything we've known an⸱
done, we've suddenly come down with a terminal case ⸱
decency ... and God help us ... honor."

When they reached the D Cross A, he left the car an⸱
she slid behind the wheel. With the heavy door betwee⸱
them, it seemed safe to take her two hands in his. She lean⸱
toward him and offered him her cheek. His lips would bur⸱
for weeks.

"When does Hadley return?" he said.

"Hadley's at El Recobro. He didn't go with Tim thi⸱
trip."

"Did he know where you were today?"

"Yes. And he knew exactly what I intended to happen
too."

"It must have been a terrible day for him."

"I'm not so sure. I don't know if he's done it deliberatel⸱
or not, but Hadley's been putting us to the test since the da⸱
he met you."

He smiled, but the smile hurt his face.

"Well, then, I suppose we passed the test."

"Knowing Hadley, he might think we *failed*."

He watched her drive toward the butte and El Recobr⸱

Not once did she look back at him. He hadn't expected that she would.

Chapter XXVI

"No more fooling around," Ian told John the day after Thanksgiving. "I want you to get started on a bunkhouse, pronto—before we have a freeze. It's only a month to New Year's. And no stalling around while Hadley finds wetback labor. Get some men from town and get it up. *Now,* damn it!"

"All right," John said, "I heard you the first time."

"And while you're in town, start beating the bushes for hands to live in it. I want a couple of good men on this place before the baby comes. You'll be too busy to be of much use for a couple of weeks after that."

John turned without another word and walked toward the GMC. He was limping pretty badly today. The limp always seemed a little more pronounced if he was tired, of course, but it got worse, too, at those times (rarer and rarer now) when he was out of sorts.

That he was out of sorts this morning wasn't his fault, it was Ian's.

Ian, while trying to guard against it, had been more and more edgy and occasionally downright bad-tempered since the honeymooners returned from Juarez. He told himself it had nothing to do with Sam and perhaps it didn't. Certainly he had been calm enough, strangely at peace with himself, between the time he said good-bye to her that Sunday and the Wednesday night John wheeled the Cadillac into the gate of the D Cross A, put M.L. and the luggage in the house, and asked Ian if he would pick him up at El Recobro when he returned Hadley's car.

It seemed a simple enough chore. Ian kissed M.L., thanked her for the pair of mock-Mayan bookends she had bought for him in the Pronoff Center in Juarez that had eclipsed the gaudy, old Mercado Central, kidded her about putting on even more weight, and got in the MG to follow John to Sam and Hadley's.

By the time Ian reached the compound, John was already inside the big house. Ian intended waiting for him in the car, but minutes passed. He realized John couldn't simply drop Hadley's keys into the man's hands and run off without giving at least a sketchy report of the honeymoon, but enough was enough. He sat in the darkened MG feeling more alone than he had when he had first returned to the basin back when he really and truly *was* alone.

A huge, silver moon had risen over the top of Cuchillo Peak, a white disk not quite full and perfectly round, but one of those slightly squashed ones he once heard called a gibbous moon. Funny that anything less than complete fullness could so drastically reduce the amount of light that fell and shattered on the rangeland. Nothing around him stood out in sharp relief, shadows merging not with light but with other shadows, and for a bad moment he felt he could be back in the compound of the D Cross A of his boyhood, or much worse, the D Cross A of twenty years ago. In his rearview mirror, its outlines blurred and indistinct, the hangar looked hauntingly like the old bunkhouse where he had done so much painting. For a ridiculous, weirdly attenuated second he feared that it, too, might rip the night with flame.

The hell with this. I know I can't run anymore. Can't hide, either.

He left the car and walked the path to the door.

Sam answered his ring. "Come on in. Hadley and John are in the living room. Would you like a cup of coffee?"

He wouldn't, but he said he would. *No more running or hiding, remember, pal?*

"Go on in and I'll bring it. Tell John and Hadley I'm bringing cups for them, too." He expected that she would turn and hurry off, but she stood looking at him, a marvelously quizzical look, in light of what had happened to them at Lago de las Sombritas on that afternoon that seemed a century ago, knowing now there were still a few things they wanted to say to one another and couldn't, things that would forever remain unsaid. They had displaced themselves now, put themselves for all time on tracks that paralleled each other, but which—in this still Newtonian universe to whose fixed order they had retreated—would never intersect.

*   *   *

He had his coffee with Hadley and John. Sam sat with them, too. She kept her eyes on Ian.

"Sam tells me that the two of you went exploring the other day, Ian," Hadley said.

To Ian's surprise Sam didn't turn her gaze from him. But why was he surprised? This lady wouldn't run or hide, either.

"Yes, Hadley. We made a discovery or two."

No more was said, but Ian knew that had Hadley pressed, he would have told the man in the wheelchair exactly what the discoveries were.

It was on the trip back to the D Cross A that Ian began working on John in earnest about hiring men to help him. John merely nodded, his face in the faint light from the MG's dash noncommittal.

As they rounded the butte, Ian said, "I've even been thinking of leaving on the first of March. If it weren't for M.L. and the baby, I would."

He caught a glimpse of John's turning to look at him.

There was another reason, of course, one he couldn't tell John, for staying as long as he originally planned. Leaving earlier would have meant running again.

"About M.L. and the baby," John said. "She won't tell you, I reckon, but we stopped to see Harry on the way home tonight." He laughed. "I stayed in the car. Didn't have to wait long. He wouldn't even talk to her. We thought he might soften up a little now that we're married."

"There'll be no chance of Elsie coming out then?"

"Nope. Can't blame her. She has to live with Harry. And Jody needs her as much as M.L. does. Harry's been pretty tough on the kid since all this happened."

"Have you found a woman in town to come out and help?"

"Hell, Ian! I could get any one of half a dozen. It's M.L. I'm having trouble with."

"In what way?"

"She's surprised me since the wedding. I thought she didn't give a particular shit what people in Black Springs thought, but now, maybe because she's a married woman, she's fearful about what they might say about her."

"I guess I can understand that, John. But she will need help. Or we will, anyway."

*   *   *

Between the young couple's return from Juarez and Thanksgiving, Ian worked on both of them. M.L. at least argued with him.

"I just know anybody who came out here would be laughing behind my back."

"What about Rosa Candelario? You don't object to her, do you?"

"She's just like a doctor."

"How about getting some nice, older woman from Mex Town?" He really thought he was taking the right tack here; it had to be the Anglo women of Black Springs whose tongues she feared.

"No! They'd laugh even harder. And I wouldn't blame them. People like us been snickering at their three-month babies for years. No. I'll get along just dandy by my own self."

Respectability could make some pretty wicked sneak attacks.

So it was John he had to persuade about both matters. Perhaps help for M.L. was the more important of the two, but there was *some* time left to get a decision made on that score. The bunkhouse had to go up now while the weather held. Putting a hand or two in it could wait almost until Ian left, but the actual construction of the building he showed John in a copy of the stockman's magazine couldn't wait another week.

He got on the subject hard and stayed on it.

It took a scant week for the bunkhouse to take shape, and when it was done, Ian found little to comfort him in the sight of it. It blocked his view of El Recobro's lights at night, and in the daytime it reminded him all too much of that older bunkhouse.

He knew he couldn't put the other matter off much longer.

Part of John's tardiness with the bunkhouse had been due to the misleadingly splendid autumn weather, but the last nights of November and the first few of December saw the thermometer on the veranda plunge below freezing even though it rebounded with regularity by two o'clock each afternoon into the high sixties. M.L. laid a fire in the stone fireplace every evening, turning aside Ian's protests by saying, "Hey! I ain't sick or a cripple. I'm just having a *baby*!" An orange blaze lit the living room at night, the mixed piñon and oak popping and snapping while the girl sewed, Ian read, and John gazed into the flames, his face placid and genuinely content. Ian put off what was on his mind time and time again. It seemed almost criminal to risk a setback with a man who had come so far.

M.L. went to bed almost an hour before the two men did most nights; for all her assurances that her pregnancy was "no big deal," she did get tired now. Rosa Candelario had warned them that while there was nothing for any of them to worry about, from the look of M.L., she was carrying her burden "a little on the low side—puts a strain on her back. When the baby comes, it will come fast." But despite the efforts of both men to slow her down and relieve her of some of her heavier tasks, she insisted on a full plate of work for herself every day. "Makes the time pass quicker," she said. And indeed, she more than pulled her weight, only coddling herself to the extent of that early-evening retirement.

It was the fifth of December when he finally talked to John.

He waited until he was sure M.L. was asleep. The fire that had made the living room as bright as a ballroom earlier was just a heap of glowing coals.

"John," he said, "we've never talked about your family."

He got the one reaction he hadn't figured on: absolutely none. John went right on staring into the dying fire as if not a word had been said. His look of easy, somnolent contentment hadn't changed. He didn't look at Ian, didn't move a muscle, didn't stir. It was several seconds before Ian realized that the man was totally in shock, and that the look he had been wearing before Ian spoke had merely frozen there.

Then John turned to him, and as he turned, the easy look drained from his face, making it as blank and gray as an overcast basin sky. In moments it filled again, with anguish now. *What in God's name have you done, MacAndrews?* John's mouth was working. It was hard to tell whether he was trying to speak or gasping desperately for air. Finally words came.

"There's just my mother. I ain't seen or heard from her in a couple dozen years."

Ian felt like a man who had to set a broken bone without an anesthetic.

"Do you know where she is?"

"Someplace in Albuquerque last I knew. I kept tabs on her for a while."

"Has she heard from *you*?"

"No. I wouldn't think she would want to anymore."

"How come?"

John looked back into the fire. "I'm not sure I want to tell you, Ian."

"You don't have to. Just forget I asked." Maybe this ranked right up there with the worst ideas he had ever had.

The light from the fire had faded further, and it was harder to read John's face. No, not harder—impossible. It would have been impossible to read it in the full glare of a noonday sun.

"Maybe we'd better call it a day, John." Ian stood up.

"No! Sit down, Ian. I guess I do want to tell you after all."

Ian sat down. Something told him it would take some time before John began to talk again and that whatever he was going to say would take even longer. Five minutes must have passed before John spoke.

"We come a fair distance since that night in the Buckhorn, Ian. There are times when I almost think you're the brother I never had."

No, MacAndrews! Not yet. It isn't the time.

John went on.

"My mother raised me by herself. Never did know my old man. I was kind of a wild kid and it didn't mean much to me that I didn't have a father. I was in high school before I found out that I came along a lot sooner after Ma married than kid's are supposed to. It bothered me, of course. Kind of funny now, when M.L. and me are doing the same damned thing. Anyway, the way I found out about it was that a guy I knew in school started spreading the news around. Everybody in town but me already knew, but Ma was pretty well liked, and until this big mouth spouted off, I guess they figured it was just her business. I guess I could have laughed it off, but when he used the word 'bastard' I went nuts. There was a fight, and I damned near killed him. Would have if two other guys hadn't pulled me off him. As it was, he was in the hospital for a while.

"Up until this happened I had considered myself a real tough *hombre*, hard as nails. But the thought that I'd almost killed somebody took me right off my rocker. I actually

anted to go to jail to even things, but Ma stuck by me with
ie cops and the judge and the probation people. Then I
iade an even bigger mistake. I asked her if what this kid said
as true. When she said it was, I went even nuttier. Never
·t her explain how it had happened. God knows she tried to
xplain and tried to make it up to me. I just told her she'd
·most made a murderer of me—and that was it.

"I never told Ignacio Ortiz about any of this, but just
eing around him began to bring me out of it. I'd almost
iade up my mind to look her up and get things back to
here they was, when I got drafted.

"By the time I got back from Nam and out of the
ospital, I just figured too much else had happened. I didn't
·ant to bother her."

The fire was so low now Ian couldn't make out the
·unger man's features at all. "John," he said, "it isn't too
.te, you know."

"Jesus, Ian! What could I say to her after all these
ears?"

In the silence of the house, the sound of M.L.'s getting
·ut of bed and going to the bathroom was deafening. Ian
·aited until the toilet had flushed and the creaking of the
·edsprings told him she had her head on the pillow again. He
·aited a minute after that. Surely the girl was sound asleep
·nce more.

"For openers, John, you could tell her she's about to
·ecome a grandmother. And then you could ask her for the
·elp she tried to give you once."

Chapter XXVII

For the trip to Albuquerque two days later John wore
ie new suit he had bought for the wedding. His manner was
·cross between that of a man's getting ready to walk the last
·ile and that of a youngster's heading for his Sunday school
·ommencement. He had a tight grip on the shopping lists

both M.L. and Ian had written out for Christmas gifts. M.
had purposely not listed the things she wanted bought f
John himself. There was a separate list for those in a seal
envelope; he was to give it to his mother along with th
money she was sending so he might be surprised Christm
morning.

"Do you want me to go with you?" Ian had asked hi

"Sure I do. But you ain't going. I got to do this b
myself."

"How about M.L.?"

"Springing *me* on her will be enough for now."

"Makes sense. Don't wreck my car."

"Hell, man. It wouldn't be all that much of a loss."

"Love me, love my MG, you stupid cowpoke!"

Of course, it hadn't been all that easy, or had it?

They had sat together in front of the dead fire all throug
the long night, not even conscious of the chill invading th
house, nor giving any thought to turning on the furnac
Gradually it dawned on Ian that John wasn't actually argui
with him about reconnecting with his mother; he just need
one reassurance piled atop another. Who would have b
lieved it was that hard to persuade a man to do something b
had wanted to do for more than fifteen years?

He was only faintly surprised, after M.L. and he watch
the MG buzz toward the highway, to discover that the g
knew all about John's estrangement from Irma Begley, and
pleased him that she did. Some marriages could drift for yea
through a Sargasso sea of secrecy about matters that should
be secret at all, only to run aground on the shoals of qui
unnecessary frankness and brutal truth best kept hidde
These kids were talking to each other already about thin
that damned well *should* be talked about. He was not eve
surprised at all that M.L. had never pushed for this reunio
It took someone not quite that close, someone such as Ian,
run that risk. Wise child, Martha Lucille Kimbrough Begle

It looked good for Christmas. An old poem that A
Jennings MacAndrews had learned from her English mothe
and that she in turn had taught to Ian, kept running throug
his head:

> *Christmas is coming, and the goose is getting fat*
> *Please put a sixpence in the old man's hat*

*If you haven't got a sixpence, a tuppence will do
If you haven't got a tuppence; God bless you!*

John might be gone two, even three days. Making the
connection with Irma wasn't simply a matter of waltzing into
Skaggs, announcing that he was the long-lost son, securing a
promise, and coming home to the D Cross A with a
mother-grandmother-nursemaid.

All sorts of tangles and troubles could present them
selves. As John had agonized and softened over the years,
Irma might well have agonized and soured. Still, some inner
optimism he couldn't check kept telling Ian that if any
pathetic tale would have a happy ending, this one would.
Well, let John take a week if need be. The fall work, give or
take a minor chore, was done. There wasn't even a lot for Ian
himself to do.

Of course, this gave him too much time to think about
Irma. But what, after all, was there left to think? Everything
of consequence that could safely be said between them had
now been said. It was the end of something; the end of
something that never quite began. And if it wasn't a satisfactory end for either of them, it was the correct one. He had no
regrets.

Dead sure of Irma Begley's reaction to meeting John
again, he had one satisfaction. His timetable for leaving the
Rios Negros was at last intact. There would be nothing left
undone to hold him here.

That wasn't quite the unvarnished truth. For one thing,
he still hadn't visited Jorge Martinez's grave.

And pure devilishness set him to work on the one other
thing he still needed to do. When he started on it, he
realized that he was getting to be a thoroughgoing busybody
and enjoying it.

John didn't return that night, and Ian and M.L. had the
fire to themselves. Perhaps out of a sense of duty, the feeling
that he might be lonely and that she had better fill in for the
absent John, whatever, the girl sat with him long past her
usual bedtime, nursing the half glass of beer she had restricted
herself to after his remark about her girth when they returned
from Juarez.

"I told you at the time, M.L., how much I enjoyed the
Thanksgiving dinner you cooked us. Sure was great!"

"Glad you liked it," she said, "but there's nothing to

doing a turkey and dressing. Stick it in the oven and let
rip."

"There was a lot more to it than that. The sweet po
toes, that relish you made—everything."

"What are you buttering me up for? I've cooked
Thanksgiving dinner ever since I was sixteen."

"You won't have any trouble with Christmas, eith
then?"

"Don't see why I should. You'll be getting the sa
damned meal."

Was she getting suspicious? No, her face was as innoc
as ever. He couldn't swear to it, but he got the notion t
rubbing up against Sam Edwards had lightened the he
hand she had used with her cosmetics until the weddi
Sure, Sam had done her makeup for her then. M.L. lear
fast.

"Speaking of cooking. You're going to have a lot m
mouths to feed here someday. There will be the new ha
when John hires them, and in just a couple of more seas
there could be a real crowd of hungry cowboys to cook fo
branding time."

"Well," she said, "I reckon I signed on for that. I a
squawking."

"Didn't think you would. You could handle a bunch
hefty eaters then?"

"Sure. Hey! Why are you making such a federal case
this?"

Now she was looking at him with narrowed, inquir
eyes. He had better move in for the kill before she put up
guard.

"I want you to do something for me. It's kind o
Christmas present you could give me."

Yes, he had said the magic word, "Christmas." Her ey
glowed from more than just the reflected fire.

"Golly, Ian!" she blurted. "Name it." She waited, look
as if she were the one expecting a gift.

"Well, since this is the last holiday I'll be spending at
D Cross A, I'd like to pay off a debt or two, do so
entertaining." He paused. "I want to invite the Edwardses
Christmas dinner—"

Her mouth went as wide as a lava tube on the malpa
but he bored right in.

"—along with the Vergaras. They're coming in this weekend to stay until New Year's."

It was exactly the same as it had been with John two nights ago: talking someone into doing something they already wanted to do. To her everlasting credit, snared as she had been, M.L. took it just as well.

John returned the next afternoon. The way he took the gate in the MG in a four-wheel drift Jackie Stewart wouldn't have sniffed at, Ian knew the news was good. The little car roared full tilt almost up the veranda steps.

"Well?" Ian said when John uncoiled himself from the bucket seat and left the car. John made a circle of his right thumb and forefinger and winked. His smile was as wide as the horizon.

"Where is she?" M.L. screamed from the veranda behind Ian.

"Hold it, hold it!" John said. "It ain't all that simple. She'll move down here right after New Year's Day."

"What about Christmas?" M.L. was almost whimpering.

"That's just the point," John said. "She does volunteer work for this orphanage supported by her church. They have a big holiday program going that makes or breaks their whole year, I guess, and she's running it this time. Then she's going to have to quit her job, pack, and take care of some other stuff."

M.L.'s face fell . . . and rose.

"All right! We'll have *two* Christmases. I never got enough of them when I was a kid, anyway." She sniffed the air. "Oh, my God!" she yelled. "My supper's burning!"

With work at a virtual standstill in the outbuildings and on the range, the two men were at M.L.'s beck and call for help with the upcoming festivities, and she beckoned to and called them with increasingly steely tyranny that third week of December. When errands for anything required a run to Black Springs, they weren't allowed to accumulate; they had to be done one by one and at the very moment they occurred to her, not a second later. "Do it now" was her response to any objection either of them made, a universally quiet but fervent response that brooked not even passive mutiny.

Ian couldn't remember being this lighthearted since he

had romped with Ignacio as a child. Even thoughts of Sam failed to dampen his enthusiasm.

The carpet people finally came down from Albuquerque and when they had finished, M.L. had John put more miles on the Electrolux than he had until now run up on the GMC's odometer. She could find a fuzzball or a leftover tack where neither of the men could have seen it with a magnifying glass. Ian was put to work polishing the silverware Sam and Hadley had given the couple for their wedding. M.L. turned a deaf ear to his complaint that, "For Lord's sake, you little bully— this stuff's brand-new!"

John had no better luck when he resisted washing and wiping—and never satisfying his bride—the new crystal that Ernie and Carrie had given them. Ian roared with laughter as the huge man, apron-clad and suffering fits of fear that someone outside the household might happen in, wrapped his giant paws around the delicate stemware.

For her part, M.L. actually rehearsed some of her cooking, pulling her nose out of a cookbook or her eyes from the pages of one of her women's magazines to try something new each night at supper. The main course was still going to be the standard stuffed turkey, principally due to Ian's remark that the Vergaras might never have had a traditional American Christmas dinner. "Alex might have," he said, "but Consuelo hasn't been outside Nicaragua much. The cranberry sauce and the dressing will be new to her." On this M.L. agreed. For all her cheerful domineering, there were a few times when the enormity of what she was undertaking hit her, and she implored Ian with her eyes for support while saying nothing.

And of course they would have to decorate the house. Wisely, in Ian's view, M.L. wanted tinsel, holly, reindeers, wreaths, and gilded cherubim, rather than the *luminarias* Sam had told her they were going with at El Recobro. "*Luminarias* are nice," the girl admitted, "but they only last for a few hours. This way everything will still be up when John's mother gets here."

John was assigned to drive up toward Las Sombras and cut a tree. Ian's contribution was something that made M.L.'s blue eyes blaze. He had found enough outdoor lights at Stafford's not only to garland the veranda with blinking color, but to create another spectacle that M.L. thought an absolute stroke of genius.

"I can run wire and lights up the framework of the windmill," he told her. "We'll have the biggest outdoor Christmas tree in Chupadera County, at night, anyway. People will see it from the highway—and El Recobro."

M.L. went into transports of ecstasy.

By the twenty-second, everything but the tree and the windmill had been done and done again.

For the first time Ian felt almost sad that he would be leaving in just three months' time.

Chapter XXVIII

"Thought you were taking the truck," Ian said as John rode out of the corral trailing a packhorse on the morning of the twenty-third.

"Ain't going to Las Sombras," John said. "There's a small peak stand of Colorado blues up at the piñon line straight east of Negrito Peak. There's one seven- or eight-foot honey in it that will be a sight better than them scraggly jack pines up on Cuchillo."

"You going to *shoot* us a Christmas tree?" Ian said, pointing to the rifle in the saddle boot.

"Oh, that?" John laughed. "I seen a few mule deer up that way from time to time. Chance in a thousand they'll show today, particularly this early, but I seem to recollect Ma was partial to venison. Maybe I'll get lucky."

"Good hunting, then. And for Lord's sake, hurry back. M.L.'s got the ornaments and lights for the tree laid out on the couch already."

"*Hasta la vista*, Ian." He dug his spurs, or rather the one spur on the boot of his good leg, into his horse's flank. The lead tightened, and after an upward toss of the head the packhorse moved and the rider and the two animals trotted from the compound. John lifted his hand as his small cavalcade reached the first of the upland grass.

It was a wave of studied nonchalance, and Ian smiled.

With John's leaving this early, he knew the big man was going to pay a visit to Ignacio today.

The day was overcast, the first cloudy one since the brief, belting, short-lived storm before the wedding: the sky a dull, lackluster, dirty pewter. Far from depressing him, the dark day gave Ian hope that with forty-eight hours still to go before St. Nick arrived, there was an outside chance they might yet be able to offer Hadley and Sam and the Vergaras a white Christmas for M. L.'s dinner. When he looked more closely at the sky, though, he knew that even a light flurry was a no more likely occurrence than John's getting a buck in the sights of the Winchester. What he saw was just close-packed high cirrus, not the thick, moisture-heavy, drooping blanket of dark gray they would need for even a modest snow.

He had laid the cables and lights for the windmill on the floor of the empty bunkhouse. There seemed to be miles of the stuff, and he wondered what he had gotten himself into with his insufferable big mouth. He thought for a moment of calling the project off, but then he knew his discontent was due not to the task, but to the bunkhouse itself. It felt like a prison cell. The builders had erected the small building so that its only two windows faced northwest. He could look toward El Recobro from the inside, and the extra beat his heart made when he saw that the people at the big house must have started their fireplace burning already today wasn't a welcome one.

Another thing irritated him. The bunkhouse was almost a prefab; inexpensively but not cheaply or shoddily constructed, but there had been a certain amount of "make-do" in the fabrication of it. The builders had obviously used whatever they had on hand or in their supply yard. The two windows were grotesquely out of proportion to the wall they opened in; much, much too large.

With the way the bunkhouse faced it would be only in late afternoon on midsummer evenings that it wouldn't be an ideal painter's studio.

He dragged the wires and cables and the box of lights out of the bunkhouse and hauled everything to the foot of the windmill in one awkward, struggling trip so he wouldn't have to enter it again.

Back at work on his rigging and wiring he calmed some and within an hour his buoyant holiday mood had returned.

even though the lighting of the windmill was a far more
demanding job than he had imagined.

From time to time M.L. came from the house to shout
encouragement to him and to warn him to be careful. He
showed off like a teenager for her, chinning himself on one of
the crossbars, leaning far out from the frame of the mill and
thumbing his nose at her foreshortened figure thirty-five feet
below him, until she screamed at him to stop.

He broke for lunch at noon and subjected himself to
another of M.L.'s culinary experiments, a bowl of French
onion soup she was sure would begin her Christmas dinner
with a bang. He didn't have the heart to tell her it wouldn't
really go with her Yankee turkey. It didn't matter. The decent
people who would be her guests would tell her it was
marvelous.

He was back on the mill at twenty minutes after one.

There seemed to be a new crispness in the small wind
moving at him from the north, but he knew from its dryness
and its direction that there couldn't be snow behind it. Wet
or snowy weather almost always struck the Ojos Negros from
the east, the heavier-laden clouds condensing out over Cuchillo
and the Jicarillas, dropping their load as, and immediately
after, they collided with the mountains.

Visibility, too, was better today than when the weather
threatened moisture, and from this high above the compound
mile upon added mile of pastureland opened up. All of El
Recobro could be clearly seen from the windmill's top, and
the hogback ridge of rocks that ran across the range from a
few hundred yards north of Hadley's house to within two
miles of the D Cross A were in full view. He hadn't needed
John to instruct him on the nooks and crannies of those
particular rocks. When Ignacio was teaching Ian to ride, it
had been their favorite training ground.

There had been a time when he could guide a cow horse
through those sentinel rocks with blindfolds on both the
animal and him.

He still knew them pretty well, still knew one small
pinnacle about three miles off with an intimacy that even now
brought a shudder. He had killed a diamondback there when
he was twelve years old.

He looked for the crag now and found it.

But it didn't look quite the way he remembered it.
There was something different about its shape. The change

might be due to his looking at it from this unaccustomed angle, and it was, after all, a long way off. Still, it was different; much broader at the base than in the picture dredged from memory.

Something stirred inside him. Damn it! Whether he was leaving her or not, the shape of things in the Ojos Negros had no right to change on him.

He had halfway made up his mind to climb down, drive the GMC to within walking distance of the crag, and find out why his memory had turned so faulty, when he remembered seeing a pair of binoculars in John's few personal belongings when they moved things from the trailer to the house. John must have used them when he was monitoring the old D Cross A and herding phantom cattle.

"Sure, I know where they are," M.L. said when he had climbed down and gone inside. "They're in the bureau in our room. Just a sec and I'll get them for you."

This was a good deal better. The GMC's tank was on "empty." He would have to gas up at the pump they'd installed. It would take him five minutes to fill the truck by hand, twenty or so more to get to the rocks, and as much time getting back again. He'd never finish his lighting job if he went up there today. If the field glasses didn't produce the answer, he could make the trip tomorrow. He could make it his turn to visit Ignacio, too.

When M.L. brought him the binoculars, he saw they were a good pair, powerful. Sure—there was the engraved "U.S. Army."

Idly, he checked his watch again when he reached the top of the windmill: 1:57. There was plenty of time to perhaps satisfy his curiosity and finish stringing the colored lights.

He put the glasses to his eyes, but instead of focusing them directly on the ridge, he trained them first on El Recobro. Between him and the Edwards place two riders were headed toward the D Cross A. He didn't need binoculars to know it was the Vergaras out for their afternoon ride. They were traversing the long slope that led to the hogback ridge, and he followed them with the binoculars.

He didn't have to shift the glasses to see the pinnacle rock. The Vergaras' swift passage was taking them right toward it, and as the glasses tracked the riders, it would come in sight in another fifteen seconds.

When it did, he saw at once what had changed its shape and his throat tightened too much, too quickly, for him to make the warning shout that couldn't have been heard had he made it.

A Jeep was parked at the foot of the rock.

He saw the puff of smoke rise and drift above the jeep, saw one of the two horses pitch forward on its nose and crumple like a sack in the bunch grass just as the first report of the rifle reached him, saw its rider running, saw more puffs from the Jeep, saw the spurts of dust at the runner's feet. The other rider, Connie surely, veered her mount toward the rocks and the runner clutched at something on the far side of the horse, clinging to it as a thrown bronc man does in the rodeo arena.

They couldn't make it. The Jeep began to move. Its driver could get in range again almost at his leisure. Alejandro Vergara and Consuelo with him were as good as dead.

Then, unaccountably, the Jeep stopped and Ian saw something else.

Two horses with only one rider had come through a break in the rocks and were heading toward the Jeep. One of the horses, the second one, had a spruce tree lashed to its back. The rider, on the horse out in front, was reaching toward his saddle boot.

Ian could shout now and did. He screamed, "No, John. No!"

There was yet another puff of smoke from the Jeep. This horse didn't fall or stumble. It kept on toward the Jeep—but without the rider. The bullet had cleaned him from the saddle.

The Vergaras had by now covered most of the distance between the rocks and the butte and the El Recobro road. The few seconds John Begley had bought them had taken them well out of range of their assailant.

The Jeep made a turn, went toward the same break in the hogback John had come through, passing within ten feet of where he lay on the ground. It stopped there for a count of ten, moved on through the break, then toward the road to Williston. Smoky dust billowed behind it.

When Ian began his climb down the frame of the windmill, he saw M.L. standing at the foot of it.

"I heard you hollering at John," she said, her pretty,

happy face turned up to him. "What were you yelling about
Didn't he get our tree? I'll kill him if he didn't."

"He got the tree, M.L."

Chapter XXIX

The first genuine storm of the winter broke over the
Ojos Negros basin on the second day of January, leaving three
and in some places four inches of clean, pure snow in the
high country above the upper rangeland, but only a dusting
of it in the pastures, and none in town nor at the D Cross A.

In the arroyo in the slickrock—where three cairns now
stood on their shelf of caliche—it wouldn't have made any
difference if the fallen snow had measured three or four *fee*
in depth, or if there had been none at all. Everything in tha
wind-blasted country was white winter or summer, spring or
fall . . . bone white.

The weather, bright and unseasonably warm until the
storm, had done a favor for the two Mex Town men who dug
the shallow grave, and who stayed on after the burial to buil
the cairn. Without the rock-hard freeze so usual in these high
badlands as the year turns over, the caliche, not the most
manageable of the earth's natural materials at any season, at
least wasn't frozen.

Almost one hundred twenty-five years had gone by
between the birth of the man who rested beneath the
westernmost of the cairns and the death of the man whose
monument was farthest to the east. During that century and a
quarter one of these three men, all working cowhands, had
ridden the rangeland to the south of the slickrock continuously,
save for a two-year period between the death of the second
man and the return from a foreign war of the third. There
had been times when the first and second man had ridden
and herded together, and other times when the third man
was the fellow rider of the second. And there had been scores

of other riders over the years. One of those was still on the
and; he had no intention of dying on it as these three had.

All three of the riders now beneath the spikes of stone
had been born in different countries, but the Ojos Negros
and they rode so well and hard, and which in the end had
received their bodies, was the only country any of them truly
claimed.

The fourth man claimed and wanted no part of the Ojos
Negros, even though sixty sections of it, the slickrock and its
cairns, actually belonged to him.

He was sick to death of graves.

He had been sick of them even before the week that had
begun with the third rider's death.

Chapter XXX

"You can't describe the man in the Jeep, Mr. Vergara?"
Chupadera County Sheriff Woody Morgan asked at the meeting in Hadley's study the night of the killing.

"I didn't really see him," Alex said.

"And you, Mr. MacAndrews? Have you any idea at all
who the man you saw from the windmill might be?"

"No. He was a long way off." It was the same answer Ian
had given one of the sheriff's deputies two hours earlier.

Hadley's face showed surprise, then approval and relief.
The man in the wheelchair hadn't been exactly nervous to
that point, but he had been tight and wary. He was clearly
still intent on keeping secret what he, Springer, Alex, and the
others were up to, and Ian knew he could have blown the
whole thing by talking about the man "with the yellow eyes"
and his two earlier visits to the Ojos Negros.

Suddenly there was no doubt in Ian's mind that Hadley
thought he was holding his tongue because he was another
loyalist like Alex and Tim Springer. There was no point now
in disabusing him of the idea, and he probably wouldn't

understand Ian's reasons anyway, no matter how aware and
conscious he might be.

Filled with sick anger as he and M.L. had bumped
across the upper pastures to where he had seen John fall, Ian
had wanted to take the rifle from where it lay in the chaparral, get back in the GMC, and start across the range for the
Williston road. He wanted to track the killer down now, but
then he realized he sure as hell couldn't leave a pregnant
M.L. out there in the cold, lonely wind with her husband's
body.

His second thought was to get John's body into the truck
and take it back to the house, but he knew Alex and Connie,
once they reached El Recobro, would get the authorities out
here as soon as they could, and M.L. had sunk to the grass
beside her husband without a sound. Something told Ian it
would be impossible to move her for a while.

He had rounded up the horse John had ridden and the
packhorse with the Christmas tree roped across it, tethered
them to the pickup, and sat down with M.L. to wait. Once he
had gone to the truck and pulled out a tarp to cover the body,
but M.L. had stopped him as he started to drape it over the
dead man's face.

"Don't, Ian. I can stand to look at him. I want to."

She sat close against the body, and once every twenty
minutes or so she put out her hand and stroked a face from
which, it seemed to Ian, all trouble and doubt had taken
flight. He had put his arm around her once, and she curled
into him for a few moments, then shrugged his arm away.

"Thanks, Ian," she said. "That was nice, but I don't
really need it."

They were the last words either of them spoke as they
waited on the darkening range. It was almost as if M.L. knew
exactly why this ugly thing had happened. She hadn't broken,
hadn't sobbed once.

Buzzards circled in the dusk. They would settle on the
carcass of Alejandro Vergara's horse once it was ripe enough.
Nothing went to waste in the Ojos Negros—except its people.

It was dark when two young deputies showed up in a
Jeep and began asking questions.

Ian hadn't had to dig at his psyche too hard to determine
why he hadn't at least described the assassin for the lawmen
as Anita and *los hermanos* had described him. In the first
place he had indeed been too far away, and the deputies

would have smelled a rat. And what good would it do now to finger some unknown Nicaraguan as the murderer? During the long wait he had already begun to think of this "Capitán Cuatro," as Alex had called him, not as a culpable killer, not even as an impersonal pro, but almost as a blind, random force of nature, something like the lightning bolt that had killed old Angus so many years ago. In the face of this he felt helpless and defeated. He didn't want vengeance and persuaded himself that John wouldn't have wanted it, either. And—yes, there was a twinge of guilt at this—he didn't want anything to thwart his plans for leaving a country that had cost him so dearly, twice. It was all academic anyway. The man in the Jeep had probably reached Albuquerque and safe haven aboard an outbound plane even before the deputies arrived.

After that initial questioning, and after some baffled headshaking on the part of the lawmen, the two sheriff's deputies escorted them back to El Recobro when Ian told them there wasn't a phone at the D Cross A.

At the meeting that night with Morgan, who had been out on some other sheriff's business when Alex called, the sheriff asked to talk to M.L. and Consuelo. Connie, remarkably, showed none of the terror she must still be feeling, and she only stated flatly that she hadn't gotten any better look at their assailant than Alex had. Morgan looked sad-eyed and resigned that neither of them could help. M.L., silent at first at his question to her, had then denied that John had any enemies in the basin, but Ian knew from the look on Morgan's face that the lawman was remembering all the locals John had savaged back when he had been the champion bad dude of Chupadera County. A number of patrons of the basin's bars could expect heavy questioning.

All in all, it had seemed easiest to let Hadley call the shots. Morgan and his department would soon close the case as just another unsolved killing. It was just as well. And yet . . . Ian had hoped that Hadley would lay it all out for the sheriff, clean it up, even if the killer was never brought to justice.

He forgot about that when M.L., without asking, picked up the phone on Hadley's desk and dialed a number.

"Albuquerque," she said. "An Irma Begley—on Cardenas Street."

*   *   *

Irma Begley arrived the next morning. Ian and M.L.
met her at the bus stop in Black Springs. The two women
embraced without even taking a good look at each other.

Without Ernie's report on her, Ian would never have
been able to see the "party girl" Irma Begley once had been,
if the report was true. A big woman (John hadn't gotten *all*
his size from James MacAndrews), she looked comfortable
and comforting—now—but it took no trick of imagination to
decide that, yes, men must have flocked to her in eager
droves when she was young.

She was keen, too, alert. Ian soon realized that she had
assessed him continuously since her arrival, but somehow he
was sure there was nothing judgmental in her examination—
yet. He had caught her once looking from Sam to him and
back just before the funeral service this morning, held in the
living room of the D Cross A. Irma had scrutinized them with
an intensity he could still feel long after she looked aside.

But although she hadn't been out of his sight in the two
days she had been here, he didn't get a moment alone with
her until he drove her to Black Springs and the bus that
would take her home.

"M.L. tells me you intend to leave New Mexico, Ian,"
she said as they drove through the gate.

"Yes. I won't leave, of course, until after the baby comes,
and I know they'll both be all right."

"I'll come down to help, if you think I'll be needed."

He hadn't dared ask. "You'll be needed. By me at least."

There was something else he wanted to talk with her
about, but it wouldn't come. The rest of the trip to town was
made in silence.

He almost broke the silence twice, but when the bus
arrived, he decided he couldn't burden her with any more
emotional freight until he saw her in circumstances a bit less
trying.

"I'll be back on the fourteenth or fifteenth," Irma Begley
said as she stood by the open door of the bus while the driver
stowed the small bag that was the only luggage she had
brought with her to the funeral.

"Please don't come unless you really want to, Irma.
Disrupting your life while John was still alive was one thing,
this is quite—"

"Oh, I want to." She smiled. "I'm getting too old to do
anything I don't want to."

The driver brushed past them and climbed into his seat behind the wheel, where he made a big deal out of looking at his watch. The bus was already a half hour late.

"Good," Ian said. He almost felt good about everything. "Now, remember, call Mrs. Edwards at El Recobro when you're ready and I'll drive up and get you."

"No," she said. "I don't want you to leave that child! I'll come down on the bus again. I wouldn't go back now at all, but I've simply got to take care of my obligations." She reddened a little. "And I do need my clothes. I don't think you'll want me in black all the time."

The bus driver bumped his horn and then gazed off to the far side as if it had been an accident, tapping his impatience in some personal Morse code on the steering wheel.

She put her foot on the lowest step of the entrance, turned back to Ian.

"There's something I want to thank you for, Ian, and all the others. It's a small thing. Except for me, you're the only people in his life who called him John. He despised 'Jacky,' even when he was a little boy. Did M.L. call him John?"

"Yes."

"Oh, I'm glad! I didn't hear her mention him by name at all—but I was hoping."

With that she mounted the steps. The door closed with a hiss that seemed deliberate on the driver's part. Ian walked back along the side of the bus, staying even with her as she moved down the aisle. No sooner was she in her seat than the bus pulled away.

He was angry with himself. He should have opened up with her, as he certainly would have to sometime before he left the basin. He would talk to her when she came back again. Ten or twelve days was nothing in the way of time.

But face it, it would seem an age.

And beyond his need to tell her what he had to tell her, he would indeed need her help with M.L. He flat out felt himself incapable of dealing with the grief M.L. was holding inside her as tightly as she held her baby, and Irma Begley had almost from her arrival known exactly what to say to the girl. Irma had shed no tears, but no one else had, either. Tear ducts couldn't work in the freeze of shock he saw on every face.

* * *

Alex and Consuelo were lying low for a couple of days before Tim was to fly them out to a safer place, and Hadley, at the service for John this morning, had asked Ian to return to El Recobro for another talk after he had seen Irma off. He really wanted to go straight back to the D Cross A to be with M.L., but there were a couple of things he did want to settle with Hadley, and M.L. was being looked after by Sam, who had stayed at the ranch house after the funeral without being asked.

The Cadillac was parked in front of the house when he passed it on his way to the meeting at El Recobro.

He wondered if M.L. had cried yet. It occurred to him again that no one had.

Hadley was in an unaccountably ebullient mood. It became accountable in an instant. "Thanks for not tipping our hand to the sheriff, Ian. Of course, I knew from the start you weren't the sort of man who needed pictures drawn for him. Naturally I'm shutting down our operation here at El Recobro. The word has probably been out to the wrong people much longer than we knew."

"If you're leaving the basin, Hadley," Ian said, "what do you want to do about the D Cross A?"

"More to the point, Ian, what do *you* want to do about it?"

"I'd like to hire a manger for it and leave it in trust for M.L. and the baby, but I couldn't buy it from you. I don't have the money."

"We can work something out."

"But if you sell El Recobro, where can the D Cross A run its stock?"

"Oh, I'm not going to sell the place. It's just useless to me as a base now. I've got to find somewhere else to fly in and out of. Tim and I will begin looking once he gets the Vergaras under cover—and does one other little chore."

"You mean you're going on with this ... business, after what's happened?" He had almost said, "insanity."

"I couldn't let a little thing like this stop me."

The rifle shot that had killed John Begley, and which Ian hadn't heard at the time, now echoed through the canyons of his mind like a thunderclap. The echo still hadn't died away when Hadley spoke again.

"My God, I'm sorry, Ian. I didn't mean that the way it

ounded. Hell, man—Tim's going to track that killer down.
He'll pay."

The disclaimer came too late—way too late.

Ian left without saying another world.

Halfway back to the D Cross A he pulled the car over to
the shoulder of the road, stopped, and put his head down on
the steering wheel.

"I couldn't let a little thing like this stop me."

A *little* thing? John Begley was dead. Was this only
another goal for the other team, a score Hadley would get
back the next time he swung his mallet?

Anger rose in Ian like some mixture in an alchemist's
retort, spilling over in waves of evil, burning acid. The feel of
it was all too damned familiar, but perhaps this time he
wouldn't know the deep-dyed guilt that had accompanied it
in the past.

Hadley Edwards, for all his seeming decency, his awareness,
his genuine (but maybe shallow) regard for the refugees he
was saving and the agents he employed to bring about the
saving of them, badly needed a lesson in humility—a loss, a
undeniable defeat. There was one way Ian could hand him
one. He should have done it that day at the lake. He should
do it now. He should make a real fourteen-carat loser of
Hadley Edwards by taking his wife to bed.

"I'm staying to fix dinner for you," Sam said when he
entered the living room at the D Cross A.

As he looked at her, he felt shame as deeply as he ever
had, as deeply as he had felt it in the hall outside Laurie's
apartment, back in that otherwise forgotten life. What had he
reduced Sam to with those rotten roadside thoughts? It was
going to be hard to talk to her and feel himself a decent
human being now, but he had better try or lose himself
completely. "How's M.L.?" he said.

"She's sleeping," Sam said. "Out like a light. And when
she's awake she's too...calm. I wonder when she's going to
break."

"So do I."

"Has she cried at all?"

Someone else was concerned about whether anyone
cried or not. Of course it would be Sam. "Not once," he said.
She's had that same dead-calm look ever since I told her

what we were going to find when we drove out to John in the truck."

"I guess some women can gut it out forever. I'd be basket case if... if anybody close to me died." She mean him. He didn't deserve it.

"No you wouldn't," he said.

She thought that over. "Maybe you're right. Maybe I'm tough, too. But I sure as hell would cry. I cried for days afte my father died. It got it out of me, though."

Her father? Funny, even after the story of her life tha afternoon on the patio, he still thought of her as without an antecendents. She was just Sam, had always—despite th things she had said had shaped her—been the Sam Edward of the day he came out to cut the fence. He had learned a their first meeting everything he would ever need to know about her. He had needed and wanted her, not history. H needed her now, desperately, but not in the twisted way h had thought he had needed her to hurt her husband.

"Don't you want to get back to El Recobro?" he said. *Sa no, Sam, say no. Lord, how he needed her.*

"I said I was fixing supper for you and M.L., and I full intend doing just—"

"No, you're not, Sam. I am." It was M.L., sleepy-eye but with the eyes still dry, coming out of the bedroom. "I ain't going to be the turkey, but I got loads of stuff in th freezer." Her face didn't look quite as dead calm now. Sh actually fixed her mouth in a tiny smile of triumph. He kne the reason for the smile. At least—and at last—one Edward was going to tuck her feet beneath Martha Lucille Begley' table. "You can help me if you want." Her voice didn't offe much sincere encouragement.

Suddenly he was relieved that he wouldn't be alone wit Sam any longer. Those promises made at the lake still held

He got a grip on himself again when the three of ther sat down to the *chili rellenos* and rice M.L. had on the tabl in fifteen minutes. Sam hadn't lifted a finger to help. He instincts were unerring.

It was a silent supper. As concerned as he was for M.L. Ian kept his eyes on Sam. When they finished, M.L. shooe the two of them to the living room and brought out the pot o coffee Sam had fixed.

"I'm going to do up these dishes," M.L. said, "and the I want to go to my room again."

When M.L. shut the door to the master bedroom, Sam
said, "She'll be fine, Ian. She's a fighter. But I am concerned
about the baby. Is she still going to try that 'natural birth'
business?"

"It hasn't come up. I'll try to talk her out of it."

"Be sure you do. It could be awkward. I don't see
anything wrong with a midwife ordinarily, but now..."

"If I need you for anything, I'll let you know. Maybe I
won't be able to leave her, though. In that case I'll turn on
the lights I put up on the windmill. Even in the daylight you
should be able to see them. How long will you still be at El
Recobro?"

"What do you mean? I'm not going anywhere."

"Hadley said you're moving."

"Only Hadley and the 'tourist bureau.' He'll fly back to
see me every month or so. I'm staying. This is where I have
to be. I owe myself something."

Shame came back in a rush.

But this time the shame wasn't only because of what had
happened between here and El Recobro.

He had been all too willing to blame Hadley for John
Begley's death. Had he only given lip service to all that stuff
about the man with the yellow eyes being a force of nature?

How many times had he said he wanted to leave the
basin only when all his debts were paid? There were even
some he owed himself, as Sam had said. He was running up
new accounts as fast as he was settling old ones. It had to
stop. He couldn't be sure, but there might be one way to put
a stop to it tonight.

"Sam," he said. "Could you stay here a couple of hours
more? I should run in to Black Springs. I'd feel a lot easier if
M.L. wasn't left alone for a second before the baby comes."

"Of course I can stay. I'll be close by whenever you need
me, Ian—either one of you."

Crushed and colorless paper flowers littered Jorge
Martinez's mound in the graveyard of La Yglesia de San Jose.

"Jorge," he whispered. "*¿Qué tal?*"

Ian MacAndrews looked up at the stars in the cloudless
night sky and found his old friends Sirius, Castor, and Aldebaran,
the reliable pinpoints of light he had used so often to fix his
position during the war. They couldn't help him fix it now. He
looked down at Jorge's grave again.

"Maybe I've killed another man in the Ojos Negro Jorge."

There was no answer, but something happened that h had known all along would happen, if and when he final came to San Jose.

> He is twenty-two again, dancing with Jo Martinez at their engagement party in her father's Cantina Florida. It is the happiest moment of his life. Nothing can ever touch this again if he lives to be a hundred. Even painting, with its surges of ecstasy, has never brought him this kind of joy.
>
> Ignacio watches him from where he leans against the bar, and from behind the bar Jorge Martinez beams, all traces of his doubts about Ian MacAndrews as a son-in-law faded away. Jorge's sister Concepción looks as pleased and satisfied as Ian has ever seen her. The mariachi band hired for the evening plays "Aquellos ojos verdes," and the Latin ballad, transcending the dissonances of the sounding brass, is sweet and swelling.
>
> Now a late arrival comes through the cantina's swinging doors. It is Ian's father—James Hall MacAndrews.
>
> This is a surprise—and a welcome one. His father has sworn until this morning that he wouldn't come, that he would never watch his only son marry a Mexican. James MacAndrews's changing his mind means that the last laceration ever has been inflicted on a Martinez by a MacAndrews—or the other way around. Ian MacAndrews's mother should come through the door in just a second, too, with as much joy shining in her eyes as he knew his own must have.
>
> But she doesn't ... and won't.
>
> What he hears next is not the music, but the heavy thump of James MacAndrews's cane as the big man clumps toward the bar—and then his voice.
>
> "Martinez! It goes without saying that there just ain't going to be no wedding." Then James Hall MacAndrews is throwing money at the stupefied cantina-owner. "There's a little something for your trouble. I've got a hunch the girl has earned it."

Now twenty-two-year-old Ian is outside the cantina, sitting at the wheel of the MacAndrews touring car while his father flails at him with that cane that will flash forever. Ian can't even see him through his blinding rage.

As the blows fall, his foot slips from the brake, the car jumps forward—and caught like a moth in the glare of the headlights, his hands full of the money he is trying to return, is Jorge Martinez. The big car grinds him into the dust of the Mex Town street.

A light wind rustled through the cottonwoods of the graveyard of San Jose, lifting the faded paper flowers and dropping them again on Jorge Martinez's grave.

"I've watched it a thousand times, Jorge," Ian MacAndrews said. "Will I have to watch it another thousand? I'm leaving the basin for the last time, old friend. Before I kill something or someone else."

Chapter XXXI

The next morning he began trying to persuade M.L. to let him drive her to the hospital in Alamogordo for the birth or, failing that, to agree to move in with Rosa Candelario in Mex Town where the midwife ran a small birthing clinic.

M.L. wouldn't even listen. He might as well have opened his bedroom window and shouted at the bunkhouse for all the response he could get from her. Finally he gave up and drove into town and found Rosa.

"I would have no worries at all if the husband was still alive," Rosa said. "I trained him good. He could have done it without me if he had to. But you let me know *fast* if she starts. I'll come as quick as I can." Ian looked doubtfully at her rusty old Plymouth.

While in town he gave the Comida a wide berth. He

trusted Anita; he didn't trust himself. If he let slip one wor
about what had actually happened near those lonely rock
particularly that the killer used a Jeep, the big woman woul
put two and two together and come up with a perfect fou
He could persuade her to hold her tongue, but she coul
slip. The sheriff was still questioning some of the youn
toughs who hung out at the Buckhorn, the Outpost, and th
other bars John had frequented until a few months ago, b
that the investigation was petering out he had no doubt. A
he had previously decided, in the long run this seemed bes
Even if Anita never said a word, it wouldn't be fair to her t
give her even one hint that the man with the yellow eyes wa
the killer. Her keen brain might get too busy for everyone
comfort.

He did see Ernie Gomez.

"I've already told Hadley I want the D Cross A put i
trust for M.L. and the baby," he told the attorney. "Th
money I have might cover the purchase of the cattle compa
ny, but we'll need to rent the pastures from El Recobro.
want you to have my power of attorney to act for me if w
can't shape things up before I leave. You might just as we
have Carrie get the papers ready now. When I move out, I'
be moving fast. I brought you my passbook for the local bank
and that envelope has a rundown of my portfolio at Bache &
Company as well as the name and telephone number of m
broker. Try and save me enough to live on for a couple o
months when I get back to Manhattan, but use every penny i
you must. I think Hadley's going to be generous; he alway
has been. See if you can plant the idea that I'd like M.L. t
have the house. I'd buy the rangeland, too, but there's n
way I could raise anything like that kind of money."

He waited. Would Ernie remind him that there was
way he could get all the money he needed, or enough of i
that any bank in the state would go the rest of the distance fo
him? No. Ernie must feel that whatever ammunition he ha
wouldn't have enough sting left to bring him down. He ha
readied a surly answer in case Ernie mentioned Sarah'
money. He was glad he didn't need it. But he wasn't ready fo
the hip shot Ernie *did* take.

"Did you ever tell John Begley he was your half brother?"

"No, I didn't."

He realized then that until this moment, he hadn'
mourned John Begley.

Like poor M.L., he had been bound too tightly in the
ııtjacket grip of shock to be prepared for the grief that
ke in waves across him now. He laid his head on Ernie's
k and wept himself sightless.

When he finished, when perhaps the last tears he would
·r shed had dried, he lifted his head and said, "Thanks,
friend."

Ernie shook his head in embarrassed refusal of the
nks. 'Will you eventually tell Irma Begley?" he asked.

"Eventually, I suppose. But only when I know her a little
ter. When I'm sure it will bring no new pain."

Ernie was looking at him as if they had just that moment
t.

"I know you're leaving us, Ian. Easy now. I appreciate
ur reasons. I won't make any effort to keep you where you
n't want to be. But this place will miss you. You're the best
nned thing that's—oh, shit. If I say any more I'll get
ppy."

Before he left Ernie's office he used the phone on
rrie's desk to put in a call to the cattle growers association
Albuquerque and two more to the livestock board and the
ction barn where John had bought the makings of a herd,
ing three pleasant-sounding young women to put out the
rd that he was looking for a manager who was willing to
ıble as a cowhand for a while. There was hardly time
advertise in any of the stockmen's publications.

As he turned from the highway to the El Recobro road,
saw Hadley's plane heading north. Soon . . . soon he wouldn't
getting that desolate feeling every time he knew Sam was
alone.

M.L. had the fire laid and ready for lighting again. They
·re now burning fairly heavy logs, and he would have taken
·r to task about straining herself, but he recognized that she
·arly intended life at the D Cross A to go on as usual. He
uld have sold his soul to get her to loosen a flood of tears
ch as the one that had drenched Ernie Gomez's desk,
uld have happily done the crying for her if he could. He
s beginning to understand some of the healing usefulness
grief. But he understood, too, that it was something she
uld have to discover for herself, as he had.

She wanted to get on with her cooking. He managed to
ıke her sit with him by the fire, but only after she insisted

on bringing coffee for him and her own half-glass of beer. S
lowered herself carefully into the chair John always sat in

"I suppose you've noticed," she said, "that I've taken
sitting in his chair at the table, too. And I moved to his s
of the bed. I figure it'll keep me from looking for him,
reaching for him—part of the time, at least."

She still hadn't used John's name.

"M.L., I talked to Rosa today. She says you should eit|
check in at the hospital in Alamogordo or move to her clir
She'll come out here if you insist, but she agrees with me t|
having the baby here would be taking an entirely unnec
sary risk. She gave me a whole damned laundry list of thi|
that might have to be done, things even she would wan
doctor for. She says she'll come down to the hospital if t
would make you feel better, and that the doctors there will
you have your own way with the delivery. Out here, with
telephone, if the baby came too fast, I would have to do i|

She didn't even look scared. Perhaps there were a
number of things M.L. Begley feared. Having a baby w
only him to help was not among them.

"No." She said it quietly. He would have felt better |
it come as an angry shout or with the eerie thinness
hysteria.

"Please, M.L." He was begging now, unashamed.

"No," she said again. She had been looking into the f|
but now she turned her eyes on him. They didn't waver.

"My baby's going to be born right here just like
planned."

She wasn't through.

"I suppose you could haul me out of here. It *is* y|
house."

"Yes, I guess I could," he said. It was a thought.

"But you'd have to haul me kicking and screaming, I|
I'm a whole lot stronger than I look."

He had no doubt she would fight him. So much fo
thought that wasn't much of a thought, anyway. How mu
damage might he do if he tried?

"Hey!" she said, her eyes wide, and a peculiar smile
satisfaction curving her lips. "Come to think of it, you got
right to kick me out of here. This is Mr. Edwards's house, |
yours. Tell you what, Ian, if Mr. Edwards tells me to go
town, I will. We'll leave it up to him."

The little minx! She, too, had seen the departing plane,

ard it. And she knew damned well that Hadley wouldn't be
ck at El Recobro for at least two weeks and would be out of
e reach of even Sam.

He knew when he was whipped.

After supper he drove to El Recobro to report to Sam.
ll of the problem of M.L.'s stubbornness, he didn't feel
kward talking to her, even if she was alone.

"You'll just have to do it her way then, won't you?" Sam
id.

"I guess so. Now look, Sam, in another week or so you
ay have to miss some sleep. I realize what an imposition it
but if she goes into labor, I'll be too damned scared—hell,
rrified—to leave her alone while I drive to Mex Town for
sa Candelario, so I've told Rosa we'll call her. You're going
have to start watching for me to turn on the windmill
hts. When you see them, get her out here fast."

"Count on it, Ian. I'll head over to your place, too, after
n sure Rosa's on her way." She laughed. "I know Irma
gley should be back by then to give Rosa help, but—
meone's got to look after the expectant stand-in father."

It seemed no one but him felt even faint alarm about it.

On some days even the most snake-bit man gets lucky.
Three days after his last talk with Sam, a blue Ford
ckup that looked painfully like the old one John had finally
wned off on the International Harvester dealer in Black
rings pulled into the compound of the D Cross A.

A wiry, curly-haired man in his late forties got out of the
uck, stuck a good strong hand out at Ian, and said, "My
me's Nate Burroughs. I understand someone named
acAndrews is looking for a man to run his place."

In ten minutes Ian knew he had his manager. He would
ve to get to town and call the three helpful ladies and tell
em the barely begun search was over.

Burroughs didn't balk at all at the bunkhouse as living
arters. "I've tossed my bedroll in lots worse places," he
id. They played "20 Questions" on the cattle business for a
hile, and Ian liked everything he heard. Burroughs in turn
ked what he heard about the money and the freedom he
ould have to make decisions. They saddled up and took a
ort ride to the new tank. While he wasn't as skilled on a
ny as John, nor by a wide margin, Ignacio, Burroughs

handled a cow horse well. He nodded approval at the Cross A's embryonic herd and they shook hands.

Ian would have hired Nate Burroughs anyway, but seal matters, the man showed him a note from, of all peopl B. J. Howland. Ian was even more impressed with Burroug that he showed him the letter after he'd been hired.

> Dear Jennings MacCity Slicker—
> Word gets around. Hire Nate Burroughs. He's what you're looking for. I knew his old man over in Catron County. Good cowman, an honest as a June day is long.
>
> B. J. Howland
>
> P.S. Be up to see you someday soon. I've decided you got to help me lick the booze.
>
> B.J.

Burroughs, who said he could report for the new job on t] fifth of March, was hardly out of the gate when Sam, on a tr to town, stopped just long enough to tell Ian that Irm Begley had called to say she would leave Albuquerque a d: earlier than expected. He could pick her up at the bus stop 2:35 on the twelfth of January.

On the night of the tenth, the outrunners of the secor big storm of the winter nosed into the Ojos Negros Basin.

It began with a wind directly out of the north, col bitter, but with nothing out of the ordinary to worry hir In the late afternoon of the eleventh the wind veered a: began whistling down on them from the east.

The snow didn't actually begin to fall until after Ian ar M.L. were fast asleep.

Chapter XXXII

"John . . ."
It was such a faint cry Ian wasn't sure he heard it.

He looked at the luminous dial of the clock on his
edside table: 11:14. John must have showed up in M.L.'s
reams. Poor kid. He listened, but there wasn't another
ound. He closed his eyes and went back to sleep. Perhaps he
ad been dreaming, too.

When M.L.'s voice came again, stronger, more urgent,
vaking him completely this time, it seemed as if it had come
n only three or four minutes, but another check of the clock
old him more than an hour had passed. It was nearly half
vast twelve. She hadn't called John this time.

"Ian! I think I'm starting." It was echoing in his head as
e swung himself out of bed.

He was still struggling into his bathrobe when he reached
he door of the master bedroom. He pushed it open. She had
he lamp on her bedside table lit and she had propped both
villows behind her back and was sitting up. Her mouth was
ound and she was gulping air like a swimmer breaking the
urface after a long time underwater. She looked too fiercely
ntent on what she was doing to be as scared as he was.

At the sight of him she smiled and slowed her breathing.
Between breaths she said, "I've had two contractions already.
Ie sure ain't kidding me."

"Will you be all right if I run out and turn the lights on
o Sam can put through a call to Rosa?"

"Golly, yes, Ian! There was twenty-two minutes between
he first and second. We got lots of time." He saw her
vristwatch on the bed beside her.

He had to make one more try. "M.L., are you sure you
lon't want me to drive you to Rosa's?"

"Now don't start that stuff again, Ian!" She really did look
ingry for a second and then her eyes went wide. "Wow! That
vas a real humdinger!" She looked down at the watch.
'Eighteen minutes," she said. "No . . . *seventeen*. You'd best
;o and get them lights."

At the kitchen door he stuffed his feet in his boots and
tepped outside.

Four inches of snow covered the ground of the com-
)ound and more was falling, the stiff wind driving thick wet
lakes forty-five degrees to the vertical in the beam of his
lashlight. He started to wonder if the windmill lights would
)e visible from El Recobro, then realized he wouldn't have to
vonder long. He would know when he passed the bunkhouse
ind could look toward the other house. What was he dreaming

of? Sam might have turned all *her* lights out, probably would
have if she had gone to bed. "Be awake, Sam," he pleaded
almost shouting it. "Be awake . . . please!"

El Recobro's lights were burning if only faintly, dimmed
to mere glows by the thickening snow. He moved faster.

In preparation he had run the wire from the windmill
into the bunkhouse. He plugged the line into the socket just
inside the door and the multicolored lights came on.

Looking up at the bright display, he couldn't help but
think that stringing the lights on the windmill had been a
truly good idea. With the snow swirling now, falling straight
from time to time between gusts and then sweeping almost
level with the ground again, picking up every one of the
colors and scattering them crazily through the night, not ever
the old D Cross A had ever looked this much like Christmas

He started back toward the house, but took one more
look at El Recobro as he did

A light was flashing from this side of it, brighter than the
ones he had seen a moment earlier. It must have been one of
the big floodlights on the patio. She was signaling to him
that, yes, she knew.

"Sam, God bless you!" He said it aloud. She mustn't
have been sleeping much at night, or she had somehow
known. Either way, he would never again second-guess a
woman's intuition.

Back in the house he ducked into his room and put on
his wristwatch. As he hurried toward M. L.'s room, he checked
the time. As near as he could figure, it had only taken six or
seven minutes to turn on the lights. She shouldn't have had
another contraction yet, but he wanted to start estimating
when Rosa would arrive. The snow would probably slow the
Plymouth some, but they should see the midwife here by
quarter to two at the latest. Still, it was going to be an agony
of a wait for M. L., and misery for him, not that he mattered
at the moment.

When he reached the bedroom, things had changed.
M. L. was sobbing.

"Any more?" he said.

"Not yet." She somehow managed to regain control of
her breathing even through the sobs. "I think I called for
John, Ian."

"You did, M. L. That was a while ago."

The sobbing stopped.

"He's been coming back to me at night when I called him. It was kind of like he was still alive. I knew he wouldn't answer if I called him in the daytime. I guess I can stop that stuff now. I've got other things to do."

Another spasm took her. "Fourteen minutes," she said. "Now don't get yourself all excited. It don't hurt near as much as you would think. And until the times are under five minutes, I won't be near ready."

She was calm now. He knew she was beginning to mourn her dead husband in earnest now. What effect might this have on the birth? Maybe it was something Sam and Rosa with their confidence hadn't taken into consideration. He could only hope nature had.

Two more contractions made her gasp. They both checked their watches. Only nine minutes had elapsed between them. She had disclaimed pain, but the distortions of her face tortured him.

He had little time to think about it, though. A car pulled up in front of the house, unheard in the howl of the wind but announcing its arrival by the sweep of its headlight beams across the living room and through the open bedroom door. Rosa. Thank God.

He was halfway to the front door to let her in before he realized it couldn't be Rosa. On clear roads she couldn't have made it by this time. Sam, it had to be Sam. Bless her again! He felt as if he could jump the windmill and its lights.

When he opened his door, he saw a face as white as the snow behind it.

"We've got problems, Ian," Sam said. "Rosa can't get out here. This storm came in through Mescalero Gap, and Black Springs has two feet already and more coming. Nothing's moving an inch tonight. Rosa's stuck in her driveway, but even if she could get out, the highway between here and town has four-foot drifts and it's getting worse."

In the half hour since he had come back inside, the snow in the compound had doubled its depth. The wind was picking up speed. It couldn't have been easy for Sam to get here even in the Toyota.

"How's she doing?" Sam said, letting Ian help her out of her snow-covered coat.

"Great so far. One or two bad moments. About John. Did Rosa give you any advice?"

"Mostly to do what M.L. tells us."

Us? He hadn't allowed himself that kind of thought yet
but yes, it had to be "us."

A call from M.L. took them both on the dead run to the
bedroom.

"Howdy, Mrs. Edwards." The girl was lying on her side
"I sat up as long as I could. Rosa said I'm to stay off my back
until right at the end. Which ain't going to be very long, I
think. He's getting might anxious to be born. Did Rosa say
when she'd get here?"

Sam looked at Ian, and back at M.L. Ian readied the bad
news, but before he could get it out, Sam told her. M.L. bit
her lip, but there were no hysterics.

Jody Ian Begley was born sometime between five forty-
five and six A.M. None of the three people involved thought
to check the exact time. As births go, it was a fairly easy one,
but you couldn't tell that to any of the three of them, unless it
was the mother. Without Rosa Candelario and her scales and
tape, no one would ever know exactly what Jody Ian weighed
at birth nor how long he was.

The new mother, with the infant wrapped in a blanket
that had rested in the bureau for this occasion, was sound
asleep half an hour after Jody Ian made his first ringing cry.
She had gone to sleep smiling, after gloating at how right she
had been all along. "I thought a little about calling him John,
but I kind of thought it might hurt too much to be saying
'John' all my life, 'specially when I have to scold him."

Ian made coffee and built up the fire that had been
banked for the night. Sam and he sank into the chairs flanking
the fireplace, smiling fake brave smiles at each other. They
knew, if the sleeping mother didn't, that they weren't out of
the woods with this delivery yet, not by a long shot. A look
outside the front door at first gray light showed them the
Toyota, the GMC, and the MG as white pyramids in a frozen
Valley of the Kings. The veranda thermometer had plummeted
to four below and was apparently still falling hard and fast.
They were marooned until someone plowed the El Recobro
road. If something they didn't know about went wrong with
M.L. or the baby, help might be a long time in coming.

But for now they could both be really brave and relax
into a happy exhaustion, one that for a while would produce a
quiet high that precluded sleep.

"You were a marvel, Sam," Ian said.

"So were you."

"Nonsense. You did it all."

She laughed. "Well, I'm certainly enjoying being a member of this mutual admiration society, but to tell the truth the genuine marvel was M.L. She guided us every step of the way."

True. It had indeed been something, watching and listening to both of them. He had seen a number of men die during the war, but the sight of this went a long way toward canceling those memories out: He hadn't wanted to watch, but M.L. insisted.

"You got to take John's place this one time, Ian."

Then Sam's hands gently easing the small head with the wet, matted hair through the pelvic opening, M.L. begging Sam to check the baby's puckered little mouth for "gunk." "You might have to use that rubber bulb thing that's with the stuff Rosa left here just in case." Sam's cutting the cord and M.L. barking orders through the pain while Sam yelled right back at her to "push... breathe deep... push!"

Finally, as they sat by the fire, Sam's eyelids began to droop.

"I guess I need forty winks," she said. "Where do I bed down?"

"Use my room," Ian said. "If you want clean sheets and stuff, I'll get them for you."

"Can't wait." She left her chair and more or less drifted toward the hall that led to his room. She turned back. "That's the most frightening thing that's ever happened to me, Ian. And easily the most wonderful." She was staring at him.

"You know," she said, "if the conventional wisdom didn't say I'm a little old to begin a family, I'd start tearing down that ridiculous wall of so-called 'honor' we built between us up at the lake that day. I'd tear it apart brick by brick—and I'd start in on you this minute."

He stared right back at her. "No, you wouldn't, Sam."

She sighed and made a face. "I suppose you're right. You're a son of a bitch, Ian MacAndrews. Somehow you've managed to make me as miserably decent as you are. Call me if M.L. needs anything."

He fixed himself eggs and made more coffee. After he ate, he went to the front door. The wind had veered again and was now coming from the north. One ragged cloud was chasing another toward the Oscuras and the San Andres.

There could be full sun in an hour. It wouldn't warm up for
while, though, perhaps for days.

He went out on the veranda and checked the thermome
ter. It had fallen another five degrees

The herd could take snow, and it could take cold. I
couldn't take both. He was going to lose John's cattle and h
knew it. But right now he could only allow himself to worr
about things he might be able to do something about.

When he came back inside, he could hear M.L.'s callin;
in her sleep: "John . . . John . . . John."

Chapter XXXIII

The cold front clamped the range for only half a day
before the second wave of the storm hit them, dropping
another foot of snow and sending the thermometer plunging
to twenty-two below that night, the coldest reading in the
Ojos Negros in more than half a century.

A few ranchers, those with money, telephones, and
important political connections, managed to save their herds,
or most of their animals, by dropping feed from aircraft.

Ian MacAndrews was only able to keep his horses alive.
They had huddled in the feed shed at the north end of the
corral, and he finally shoveled his way out to them cursing
Mountain Bell for taking so long to get him the phone he had
ordered on the twentieth of September. Watering the riding
stock wasn't easy. He carried boiling water out by the bucket
and watched the miserable creatures nose into it while it
was still warm. Scarcely one of them could slake its thirst
before the water he poured steaming into the trough froze
again.

He dreaded the day the thaw would come, and he would
have to get into the GMC and go out to the nearest tank and
view the carnage.

Sam was stuck at the D Cross A until the thirteenth. She
put a good face on it, borrowing a mix of clothing from M.L.

nd Ian, and she kept herself busy looking after the young
nother and baby. "It's like camping out," she said.

Ian thanked all their stars that there were no complica-
ions for either M.L. or Jody Ian. The infant coaxed nourish-
nent from his mother on the first try, ("Ain't real milk yet,"
M.L. said, "but he's sure latched onto the idea.") and the
wrinkles in his angry-looking little face actually seemed to
lisappear as they watched.

M.L. had Ian move the cradle John had built from the
nursery into the master bedroom. It brought a few tears, but
no real amount of fuss. She now talked about John from time
o time.

Late in the afternoon of the thirteenth the county plow's
ights flashed on the road leading from the highway, and Ian
et to work cleaning off Sam's Toyota so she could get back to
El Recobro, check things in her own home, and see if she
ould raise Hadley somewhere on the radio.

She hadn't been gone five minutes when Rosa Candelario
howed up in the Plymouth, but with Jody Kimbrough
lriving, and Elsie in the backseat with still another woman.
The buses from Albuquerque were running again, and the
midwife had discovered that Irma Begley had just checked in
t the Yucca to wait for Ian.

There seemed to be good news all around. Harry
Kimbrough had promised a visit to his daughter and grandson
'as soon as things settle down."

"Ain't too surprised," M.L. told Ian out of earshot of her
mother. "John's dead. He won't stick in Pa's craw no more." It
was a flat, matter-of-fact statement with no rancor. Ian's
admiration for her took another leap.

Good feelings piled on top of one another like the
snowdrifts that still billowed on the rangeland. Elsie Kimbrough
and Irma Begley, far from showing even any slight jealousy of
each other, got along like long-lost sisters. They complemented
each other. Where Elsie gushed and perhaps was a bit too
lighty, Irma was calm and settled.

If Jody Ian cried and M.L. didn't rush to him, Elsie
seemed to think disaster was looming over the crib. "Elsie,"
Irma said on one such occasion, "you've raised two of your
own. Relax."

"But M.L.'s a child herself!"

"Seems to me she was grown-up enough the night she

had that young man." When Elsie looked a little doubtful Irma added, "Gets it from her mother."

Of course Ian wondered how long Irma might want to stay, now that John was dead. He knew he would have to bring it up with her, but he had to talk with Hadley first.

There were a few hitches. His plan to leave the ranching business in trust for M.L. and the baby now had slipped completely down the drain. There was no ranching business. Nothing was left but the house. Well, he would see M.L. got that, but he wasn't yet sure he could make arrangements with Hadley about an income for John Begley's widow and son. Whether Hadley helped or not, he was going to have to get back to New York and make a lot of money. But he couldn't leave until he felt right about M.L.'s future.

On his first trip to Black Springs after the roads were cleared, he went to the Comida and raised Nate Burrough by phone in Alamogordo to tell him their deal was off. The man took the bad news every bit as well as Ian had been sure he would. Ian had more regrets when he made another call to B. J. Howland and told him how things stood.

"Sure sorry you can't use Nate," B.J. said. "He need the job pretty bad."

"You make *me* even sorrier, B.J. He didn't even whimper."

"Nate wouldn't. No chance of you starting up again with new stock later on?"

"I won't be staying in the basin even as long as I had planned."

There was silence on the other end of the line.

"Means you won't be around to help me with my problem, huh?" B.J. said when he came on again.

"I guess not, B.J. I'd give AA a try if I were you. It worked for me."

"Suppose I'll have to. Sure would have been nice if you could have put me on a lead and dragged me in, though."

"You'll make it, B.J. Good luck."

He had a bad moment about that.

He had another bad moment saying good-bye to Anita Juan, and Bautista.

The sun began to soak the Ojos Negros, and on the twenty-first of January, since he couldn't yet trust the GMC in the wet caliche, he saddled up and rode out looking for the herd.

The ice in the tank had melted, but it was too late for

ny of the cattle. Buzzards had already been at most of the
arcasses, and his plan to have them hauled off by some small
acker was shot, too. There wouldn't be much left of the
ides, either, by the time trucks could make it out here. In
ne hollow where the snow was still deep, he found three
oung cows had frozen to death standing up.

If he had been glad that Ignacio hadn't been alive to see
hese pastures empty last July, he was doubly glad the
aquero wasn't on hand to see the dead stock rotting on them
now.

Sam paid Tommy Lee at the Texaco station a small
ortune to rent a plow and put the runway back in shape, and
n the twenty-fifth Hadley and Tim touched down in the
win-engined plane. The first thing the man in the wheelchair
ad done when he landed, Sam told Ian when he drove over
fter supper, was to check on his horses. Warm enough, fed,
nd stabled, they had made it through the storm just fine.

Hadley made no fuss about providing for M.L. and Jody
an, even though there would be no ranching being done.

"Of course I feel responsible, Ian. I give you my word
hey won't have any money problems as long as I have two
limes to rub together."

"Thanks, Hadley. I can leave here with a clear con-
cience now."

"You *are* going, then?"

"In about a week."

"Pity," Hadley said. He didn't argue. Nor did Sam.

Hadley wasn't at El Recobro but three days before he
lew out again.

Ian decided he could put off his talk with Irma Begley no
onger.

Before he did, he checked almost all of what he was
going to say to her mother-in-law with M.L. She indicated
er agreement, eyes shining.

He waited until M.L. had gone to sleep, glad that Irma
vasn't an early-to-bed type.

"You're not only welcome to stay on here, Irma, I would
ike you to, and so would M.L. I'd vouch for her wanting you
xcept that she's anxious to tell you so herself."

"I can't tell you how happy that makes me, Ian. I don't

know what made me so sure I'd be staying on, but I mus
confess that I burned all my Albuquerque bridges."

"I'm glad it's settled, then," Ian said. "But there's some
thing else I want to tell you." Here came the part he hadn'
checked with M.L. "Perhaps I've no right to bring this up. I
might even hurt, and I'm sorry about that, but I feel I have t
tell you—I'm John Hall's other son."

"I know," she said. "I knew it the moment you picke
me up at the bus for the funeral."

That took care of just about everything.

The upper pastures had dried beneath a hot sun, and h
threw a saddle on the soundest-looking pony and rode t
Ignacio's grave.

"I think I've done all I can, *viejo*," he said to th
vaquero's cairn. "May I leave here now?" There was n
answer. Had he really expected one? Could he take th
silence for permission? He would have to.

All that remained was to say good-bye to Sam.

He waited until the night before he left and drove th
MG, already loaded, to El Recobro.

"When?" Sam said.

"First light."

The silence was as deep as it had been in the arroyo. H
knew then that had Ignacio's cairn had eyes, and had the
been filled with what he saw in hers, he could never leave

Ian Jennings MacAndrews left the Ojos Negros Basin o
the third day of March.

Chapter XXXIV

The morning of his departure forced a decision when h
was but ten minutes from the house at the D Cross A.

His intention had been to leave the basin the same wa
he had come into it last July, by driving south to Blac
Springs, and then east over Mescalero Gap. But when h

eached the highway at the point where he had said good-bye
o Ignacio twenty years before—in a blackness broken only
y the faint glow cast by the last flames licking the timbers of
he bunkhouse—he found the southbound lane clogged by an
ir Force convoy heading down to Holloman, and he had to
:op on the cattle guard at the ranch road gate. Most of the
ehicles in the convoy carried equipment, but there was a
ong string of six-by-sixes, maybe twenty units in all, loaded
ith sleepy, uniformed youngsters. The sun was just nosing
bove Cuchillo, pushing into some high cirrus behind the
nountain. As the last of the trucks passed, the convoy ground
o a halt, and he got a good look at the fatigue-clad airmen
itting in it. They looked bored, sullen. It was understand-
ble. They had probably come down from good duty at some
lace such as Lowry in Denver. Being assigned to the desert
vastes southwest of Alamogordo must seem like a burial to
hese kids, as the last nine months here had been kind of a
urial alive for him.

A jeep came up the northbound lane, spun behind the
ruck in front of him, and pulled its nose up to that of the
MG. A helmeted lieutenant stood up on the passenger's side,
laced his hands on top of the windshield frame, and when
an leaned out of the MG's window, said, "I'm sorry, sir. If
ou're headed south, you'll have to wait. One of my big-rig
rivers tangled with a semi coming out of Black Springs and
ve're all jammed up."

"Anyone hurt?" Ian asked.

"No, sir. Not a scratch. But it'll take half an hour to pull
hem apart." The young officer saluted, sat down, and the
eep backed across the road and headed south.

For a moment Ian breathed easier. B.J. had come to
nind. Then he gritted his teeth. Damn it! Not that he was in
 particular hurry to get anywhere—but he was in a hurry to
eave.

All right. He would turn north and leave Chupadera
County by way of Corona and Tucumcari. Actually, he could
et out of the basin even faster that way.

In five minutes big Cuchillo was behind him and out of
ight over his right shoulder, and the Jicarillas were the only
nountains keeping him company. Then, after he passed the
as Sombras road, the highway began a soaring sweep up-
vard, and perhaps it was this giddy sense of gaining altitude,
erhaps the sparkling, late-winter morning with its sunrise

shot with silver, but something brought him a sudden an
overpowering feeling of well-being, a feeling nine parts reli
and one part pure, reckless joy. That land on the left was sti
part of the upper range of the old D Cross A, but the piñor
were getting bigger, thicker, and denser as he climbed, an
in a few miles nothing but a few tan patches of the winter
burned rangeland could be seen.

He began to sing, to the melody of "It's a Long, Lon
Road to Tipperary'"

> *Farewell, Chupadera*
> *Good-bye, D Cross A.*

With the MG's little engine humming a counterpart,
didn't sound half bad. In three days, even loafing his wa
across the country, he would be back in Gotham and rebuildin
a life he could deal with. There would be no dead stock, n
dead brother, no other people to concern himself with—an
no claims upon him, just an easy drift through not unpleasan
work, and—with any kind of luck—a little rewarding pla
now and then. And there wouldn't be any memories, either
He would strangle memories at birth.

Had he forgotten anything? Probably. Whatever it migh
be, he could take care of it from New York. The two thousan
miles between the city and this retributive, wickedly de
manding country he was at long last leaving should keep hir
safe from the haunts and hurts of the dim, distant past, a
well as from the wrenching violence and heartbreak of th
last two terrible months.

But yes, he had forgotten something. He hadn't said
proper good-bye to Jody, and he knew it would trouble him
until he did. Then an idea came to mind, and he laughed ou
loud at how right, how good, it was. When he got settled i
New York, he would find some reliable kid heading west an
pay him to drive the MG to Black Springs and the Yucca. Jod
would be getting his driver's license in a few more months
and the little car couldn't be put in better hands. With Ian i
far-off New York, there wouldn't be an easy way for Jody t
refuse the gift.

Of course, there was another thing, but he hadn't forgot
ten *it*—and wouldn't, no matter how he tried. He hadn'
known how empty he would feel at saying good-bye to M.L.

d the baby. He had tried to say good-bye last night, but the
ung mother wasn't having any of it.

"It ain't like you was going for good and all," she said.

He didn't have the heart to press upon her how irrevocably
al this farewell was. She had been in the living room this
orning nursing the baby as he drank his last cup of coffee at
e D Cross A, and neither of them brought up the subject of
s leaving, not even as he went through the door. It was as
he were only going to town to get the mail. If it wasn't an
eal good-bye, it beat all hollow the tears and trembling he
ew now he had dreaded for weeks.

There was no denying that this was a sad, lonely road he
as traveling, for all that he felt so satisfied about it. The
ñons on the left had given way to stands of skeletal, dead
nes that even the powerful sun rising above the Jicarillas
uld never force back to life. No matter. In two more miles
e last pastures ever stocked by any MacAndrews in history
ould be behind him, and he would know a freedom that had
uded him since he was a boy.

He had been little more than a boy the last time he had
ent any time at all in this far corner of the ranch. He had
vouacked once with Ignacio in the grove of dead trees up
ead. They had been green with life then. His father had
een on that ridiculous rampage about suspected rustlers on
e range, and Ian and the vaquero had patrolled this section
f the highway fence-line together. They hadn't found evi-
nce of rustlers; there were none, save in James MacAndrews's
nagination, but he and Ignacio had smelled a mountain lion
the night, a lion that had no more business down in the
astures than he had now. That was the night, too, that he
ad told Ignacio he was going to ask Josefina Martinez to
arry him. He and the great, good rider had never been
oser.

Except . . . now?

He had better put that thought away from him. He
amped down hard on the accelerator and didn't turn his
ead as he passed the last northeast corner fence post of the
Cross A.

All debts were behind him now, stamped "paid in full,"
l debts he was willing to acknowledge. Oh, maybe he could
ave lingered in the basin long enough to help B.J. Howland
ith his problem, if the old trucker really and truly had a
roblem; Ian had a hunch he tended to exaggerate. Now

what he supposed could stand him in good stead would l
some secular version of the old AA admonishment "Let ̣
and let God." Someone else would have to look after B.J.,
he needed looking after.

The needle on the MG's fuel gauge was dropping towaɪ
the E. He hadn't had a chance in the last two days to get
town and fill up at the Texaco station, and he hadn't wante
to run any gas out of the ranch tank, in case Irma or M.Ʀ
needed it for the GMC. He would have to stop in Corona.
he bothered getting out of the car, it would probably be tl
last time his feet ever touched the ground in New Mexico

When he stopped, he did leave the car. The station w
just a hundred feet short of the junction with the road
he, M.L., and John had taken the day they drove to Alb
querque for the cattle auction, and while a silent old m̲
filled the MG's tank, he strolled to the edge of the highwa
He remembered a lot of other times he had turned th
corner—drunk. He remembered, too, the first time he hạ
turned here, with his mother and Ignacio. They had been
their way to Taos to pay that first visit to Max and Sarah.

The drive north to Taos from Santa Fe had taken the
through the gorge of the Rio Grande. The startling gash in tl
rocky hills north of the capital became the subject of one
his best early oils, the first of the semiabstracts Max Baluta
approved so heartily—even as he teasingly called them fing
paintings. In that last summer he had done four other pain
ings of the gorge.

While the old man who had filled the MG's tank ran
tattered rag across the windshield, Ian stared again at tl
signs that pointed west to Estancia and Moriarty on the roa
to Albuquerque.

Why not turn here and go through Taos instead of goiɪ
straight on toward Santa Rosa and Tucumcari? Whatev
irritation Sarah's will had caused him, it had faded mont̲
ago, and paying a call at hers and Max's graves—the last
ten—would set a final seal on any other possible obligation
the past. True, it would cost him half a day, but he didn't ha
to get to New York to punch a time clock.

Under way again, he made the turn and headed west. ʌ
he did, something jolted him as if he had taken a massive fɪ
in the middle of his stomach, and he could feel the relief aɪ
joy that had lifted him as he passed the Las Sombras roa
forty minutes earlier begin to leave him. He would haʋ

rned back right then, but some willful stubbornness took
old of him. Turning back would be like running.

Out on the *llano* the Gallinas Mountains loomed on the
south between him and the D Cross A, and the road sliced
the grass sea straight ahead of him to where the rising sun
was catching the timbered eastern sides of the Manzanos and
the Sandias, ninety miles away.

He reflected that for most travelers this would be dull
country, and in fact even he now felt a curious lack of the
sense of free flight he had known when crossing the *llano* at
high speed as a boy. The mountains to the left and ahead of
him were featureless and colorless under the morning sun,
mere suggestions of themselves at this distance. He coaxed
everything out of the MG it had to offer.

At Moriarty he decided not to take I-40 into Albuquerque, even though it meant postponing lunch until he reached
Santa Fe. State highway 41 through Galisteo would put him
in the capital at about one-thirty, and from there it was only
another hour and a half to Taos, a span of time that would pass
in an instant when he raced through the gorge. He could visit
the graves and still make it well into Colorado by nightfall.

For the next two hours he turned his mind off completely,
and it didn't even click on again through a hurried lunch at
Buckey's just this side of the road to Los Alamos, nor on the
divided highway that fed him into Espanola.

Then, just north of Velarde, he sped between the high
walls that clasped the sand and whitewater rush of the Rio
Grande—a slim, twisting, muscular body of water here. The
place where he had set up his easel for that first gorge
painting was only a mile ahead of him.

The walls seemed to close above him, almost touching,
and as they did, something inside him opened without warning, and he suddenly knew rage as he hadn't known it even
with Laurie's brother Tom, or with Hadley. He knew rage as
he hadn't known since he had crushed Jorge Martinez beneath his wheels outside the Cantina Florida.

If he had to clamp his eyes shut and drive blindly and
insanely through a red veil of rage, he wouldn't, couldn't,
look at the place where he had painted these rocks and that
rushing stream. He had clear recall of that painting. He had
known, even as he painted it, that save for the canvas Sam
now owned, it had been the real beginning for him. By God,
he had brought these gray rocks to life.

And even though he hadn't been inside the bunkhou
when it burned, he had seen those rocks die again a thousa
times as the fire set by James MacAndrews turned the
molten and sent them bubbling into oblivion. He had watche
them writhe and die with a secret inner eye that to this da
had no other vision.

If the MG had quit cold on him here and now, his ra
alone would have rammed it up to the high mesa south
Taos. He wouldn't stop, wouldn't look.

When he wound upward through the big curves that le
to the mesa top, he realized he was in no shape to maneuv
through even Taos's modest winter traffic, and he pulled in
an overlook that could have been the twin of the one o
Mescalero Gap. He sat with his hands gripping the steerin
wheel while a half dozen cars piled with skis passed th
overlook heading south.

To the northeast he could see the dark, zigzag crevice
the upper gorge, a thousand-foot-deep wound in the land th
he knew would heal a whole lot sooner than the one he fe
inside him.

*Come on, MacAndrews. This is even worse than ru
ning. This is absolute surrender.*

He got the MG on the road again, and by the time I
drove past the old mission church at Ranchos de Taos, fi
miles south of Taos proper, his grip on himself was approachin
steadiness. He even managed a smile. Ian MacAndrews mu
be the only painter to pass this church in seventy years wl
had never painted it.

But if he was steady, he wasn't stable..

Going on tonight would be suicidal. He decided to sta
the night at La Fonda on the plaza and visit Max's and Sarah
graves first thing in the morning.

When he checked in at the hotel, skiers, flushed, and
an almost ridiculously happy frenzy, filled the lobby. He ha
never skied here. Laurie in their time together had nev
nagged him except on this one small thing. "Let's ski Ta
this year, instead of Vail or Klosters, Ian." He hadn't told h
why he didn't want to come to the slopes above the Arroy
Hondo.

He hadn't wanted to see Sarah then. He didn't want
now. But he had crossed his personal Rubicon, and I
would—tomorrow.

In a room whose decor made too much of a pretense

gaiety for his mood, he sat on the side of his bed for a while, trying not to think. He was wrung out, felt gamy. He stripped down, shaved, showered, and dressed again

There was a lot of time to kill. He toyed with the idea of going downstairs and asking the clerk to let him into the room behind the check-in desk. Somehow this funny old inn had managed to come into possession of the erotic paintings of D. H. Lawrence. He had seen them first with Max. "Sure the technique is bad, Ian," Max said. "But look at the heart he put in them. There's a lesson there for any painter."

There wouldn't be any danger in looking at Lawrence's stuff. But then he remembered the on-target sexuality of it, and he thought of Sam. Bad idea.

He watched television on the balcony-lounge that hung above La Fonda's lobby until the inaneness of it, even the network evening news, made something scream inside him. He left the lounge without even going back to his room to get a jacket, went downstairs and out the door. Skiers were lifting skis from cartop racks. Some, down from the mountain earlier, were window-shopping the stores on both sides of the hotel entrance.

He was surprised to find that it had gotten dark. He must have spent more time in his room and in the lounge than he realized. Shock maybe; it could be a sneaky, unnoticed thing.

Stars shone between a few low clouds, and a round, indented moon was rising over the adobe shopping center that closed off the eastern end of the plaza. He must have missed a magnificent sunset somewhere along the line. Maybe he wouldn't have seen it, anyway. The fire of that rage that had chased him up the gorge would have burned it away to nothing.

He wasn't hungry, but he suspected he was weak. It would be a long, tough day tomorrow after he left the cemetery. There was a sign for a restaurant across the plaza. "Cocina de Taos," it read. He wondered if the *chili rellenos* were even a patch on Big Anita's.

The restaurant was only half full of diners, and a pretty Spanish girl showed him to a table in a corner and sat him down with a menu. As he studied the menu, two more tables near him filled, and he heard a male voice from the one next to him ordering a martini.

He was indeed weak. The print in the menu seemed

blurred, and he had the vague feeling that more time was passing him unmarked.

He closed his eyes for a moment, and when he opened them again, a waitress was placing a double martini on the rocks in front of him.

"I'll have your salad in just a second, sir," she said.

Before he could tell her she had made a mistake, she was gone.

He stared at the drink. The twist of lemon was rocking on a surface that hadn't yet had time to settle down. He could feel the muscles in his forearm tighten as his hand moved toward the glass.

Chapter XXXV

Back in his room he lit a cigarette after dropping his lighter twice, threw himself on the bed, and let the shakes wear themselves out. The only thing that had saved him had been to keep repeating that oldest of AA adages, *"One drink is one too many...and a thousand aren't enough."* It had been the narrowest escape he had ever had.

He almost told himself it wasn't an accident, but a signal, something meant to be, and that he couldn't hurt anyone but himself now. All the ties were cut. Laurie was gone and out of harm's way; John was dead; M.L. and Jody Ian were taken care of; B. J. Howland could find his own route out of his personal alcoholic slough; he wouldn't be seeing Jody ever again most likely; Sam was an unhurt, untouched part of a past that had never really been; and above all, he had done what duty he could by all the graves of Chupadera County.

Coming north to Taos had been a disastrous decision. For God's sake why hadn't he left Chupadera County the way he planned—straight east and over Mescalero Gap, out through the hungry mouth of that savage, barren country with it cruel appetites?

But *had* the decision been made just this morning?

Iadn't it in truth been made eight months ago, at the grave
f Ignacio Ortiz? Visiting that first grave had made it inevita-
le that he would come here to Taos to see the last of them.
nd he would see them. That would be, at last, that "paid in
ill" he had thought already stamped on everything.

But . . . *graves*.

He had already told himself he was sick of them. Time to
orget that sickness. Sick of them or not, there was a grave
vaiting for him somewhere, too. He would be gathered to
hat compacted earth and held in place by a crude, uncompromising stone soon enough. He would be silent. Graves
lidn't speak, as Sam had claimed the one in Las Sombras had.
And for all that he had done it a foolish time or two himself,
ou didn't talk to graves, either, and you sure as hell didn't
'report" to them as John Begley had at the vaquero's. You
ooked at graves, bowed your head, and went your way.

There was nothing in a grave but the detritus of the
iltimate indecency in this indecent world anyway: dust,
,shes, a bleached skull with a false, inhuman grin, a few
:coured bones with the flesh and fiber wormed away—the
nert matter of death itself. *"Imperious Caesar, dead and
urned to clay, might stop a hole to keep the wind away."* Fair
:nough. Death's junior partner, life, had never promised any
»ther end but earth and silence.

He pulled himself from the bed, undressed, and rum-
naged in his duffel bag until he found his Burton. When he
ettled his head against the pillow, he reached for another
moke and found the pack empty. The ashtray on his night
able was heaped full. He must have had a cigarette going
:onstantly every moment he had been in the room, before
ind after dinner. At the D Cross A he had cut his smoking to
ess than half a pack a day.

He decided to forgo the cigarette, picked up the book
ind tried to read, but it was hard going. There was no
·eading lamp either on the night table or the headboard, and
he ceiling fixture lit more of the book's back than it did its
pages.

He slammed the book shut.

The irritation triggered the same rage that had blinded
him as he had driven through the gorge. His painting burned
»nce more in his mind's eye.

It would, he realized, get him nowhere.

He had been willing to see John's killer as a natural

force, something impersonal and elemental. Why couldn't h
look at James MacAndrews in the selfsame way? Had th
world lost anything when the paintings burned? It was, afte
all, not a grasp of truth, but a reach for it. The reach made
results didn't matter.

He went to his bag, dug out a pack of smokes, and lit th
cigarette he had denied himself before.

In the final analysis, even the *reach* for truth had bee
ridiculous and self-defeating, not only for him, but for all th
other reachers he had known. Few things in life were mor
foolish than seeing people with their arms outstretched
trying with pathetic desperation to close their hands abou
something that wasn't there—and never would be. Yes, the
were fools. Did he have to go on being one?

Fools. There was John, the herder of phantom cattle
Ernesto trying to find a pearl in an oyster that still resiste
giving up its treasure to anyone not an Anglo; M.L., probabl
at this moment still planning impossible feasts for Hadley tha
she could never give, and seeking a gentility she could neve
win; Jody Kimbrough perhaps dreaming of becoming the nex
Bobby Unser; Hadley playing games in which he could b
the winner only because he alone kept the score; Sam beatin
her old Smith-Corona to a pulp with fingers and fists fuele
only by frustration; and in some lost life, Ann Jenning
MacAndrews still trying to come to some other kind of trutl
with her husband James.

Yes, again—they, no, *we*, were all fools, cosmic fools
And paradoxically, perhaps the biggest fool of all was tha
wise, kind, gentle rider who had the greatest reach of all o
them—and the only thing remotely resembling a grasp. H
had tried, for an unrewarding lifetime, to keep tight a fenc
that parted in a dozen new places every time he wired shut
break. His long ride had been a futile try for a Cíbola that hi
no gold.

But now he had to sleep. There was something mor
than a sleeve of care to be raveled up.

He heaved himself from the bed, found the wall switch
and plunged the room in darkness.

Then, even though he felt an exhaustion as bone deep a
any he had ever known, he realized that sleep would neve
come. His nerves hummed like a stretch of Glidden wire i
the wind.

There was only one thing to do. Hit the road. Until h

ft this country there wasn't a chance in hell that the puffed
roudflesh of his psyche would form a crust, that he could
turn to anything like the feeling of relief that had winged
im toward Corona just this morning. If he had to tape his
yes wide open, he would get out of here, stand before those
st two graves, and drive north and out of it.

He packed and hauled his duffel bag and carryall to the
bby. There was no one on the desk. He scribbled out a
neck for fifty dollars and put his room key on top of it.

In the parking lot of the cemetery he sat for a minute
hile the ticks and clicks of the engine and the gurgles of the
adiator died away, as the little car cooled after the six-block
rive from the plaza.

Cottonwoods, old giants, ringed the parking lot, and
eir trunks and naked winter branches looked like wrought
lver in the moonlight.

How did those other remembered lines begin?

'Tis now the very witching time of night,
When churchyards yawn, and Hell breathes forth
Contagion on this earth . . .

Why on earth should that come to mind? There was
othing gothic about this visit—certainly nothing contagious.
erhaps it only demonstrated once more that there was still a
irus of diseased, but certainly not lethal, romanticism in his
ystem—still infecting him as it had during his painting
ays—and to which he hadn't ever made himself immune.

And yet, contagion or no contagion, he couldn't escape
e feeling that some genuine peril awaited him beyond the
ottonwoods.

As he started walking, he looked up into the night sky.
lis old friends Aldebaran, Sirius, and Castor still winked in
e firmament, but they weren't winking reassurance. As in
e graveyard at San Jose, he would have to pinpoint his
osition by fixing on some cluster of *internal* stars.

It didn't take long to find Max's and Sarah's graves.

He saw them, or rather saw the marker that bulked
bove them, from fifty feet away.

Crosshatched by the shadows of the trees that arched
bove it, a monolithic sculpted figure dwarfed everything
round it.

As his eyes took it in, the earth seemed to break apar
under feet that somehow kept him moving toward it.

For a headstone Sarah had chosen one of Max's marbles
Even though it was in a different style from anything in th
entire body of Max's work, Ian would have known who th
sculptor was had he stumbled on it in Timbuktu or on th
dark side of the moon.

There was no other word for this moonlit marvel b
masterpiece.

He had seen the Rodins in Paris and the Henry Moores i
Leeds, but the only works of the sculptor's art he could relate t
the magnificence in front of him were Michelangelo's "prisoners
the rough-hewn, seemingly unfinished pieces that had stunne
him in Florence's Academia. Until now, here, at this otherwis
nondescript Taos gravesite, his time in the Academia had bee
the most intense moment of Ian MacAndrews's artistic lif
When he had looked at them, the "Atlas" in particular, i
tortured figure not quite set free from the confining stone, it wa
almost as if he could see the artist cast his mallet and chisel t
the floor of his atelier, could almost hear him cry, "Enough . . .
man and artist I can do no more!"

He could almost hear Max's soft rumble repeating th
imagined words when he had finished this one.

Yes—the marble looming above these silent graves wa
something like the work of the great Italian. But only *somethin*
like it. Nothing *exactly* like this had ever been done befor
by anyone—and never would be. Humble, self-deprecatin
Max, like any truthful worker in clay, stone, or metal, woul
have been the first to recognize how much a sculptor borrow
from the giants who have gone before him, but this was Max
work, and Max's only.

And Ian knew now why that cold warning of danger ha
come to him in the parking lot.

The selection of this piece by Sarah had been her la
shot at him.

The figure Max Balutan had hacked from the living ston
was that of Ignacio Ortiz.

The vaquero was mounted, and his pony was gathering i
self, as it would gather itself forever, to start up a steep slop
of rock. Coils of wire were strapped to the pony's flanks.

Ignacio was going out to mend his fence.

The rider's face carried that same look of quiet commi
ment Ian had seen a thousand times, the same look

urage, the same unselfish willingness to do the work set
fore him, the work meant for him to do, whether, at the
d, it could ever really be done or not. There was, in the
e face, the same avowal to make the reach—and the grasp.

Max, too had reached, and if he hadn't quite grasped the
eam in those powerful creative hands, the thick, tough
gers burned by the welding torch, scarred by the splinters
his medium, and bruised and battered by the hammer, he
d touched it . . . and left a print of glory.

This wasn't inert matter or silent stone. This was living,
eathing art . . . platinum in the moonlight . . . and deathless
yond any threat.

But far above and beyond the reach and grasp that Max
d made, had been the reach and grasp Max had seen in the
al artist in this graveyard—Ignacio.

And despite his, Ian MacAndrews's, boiling thoughts
hile driving through the gorge, what reach had *he* made at
e end? What grasp had he attempted? None. His efforts
d only been feeble waves. And now it was too late.

He raged, but it wasn't the rage of drunkenness or
tterness this time . . . and he wept. Enough. There might be
ntagion in this dark, lonely graveyard after all.

He turned and started for the car.

The highway at the cemetery gate stretched north to
uesta and beyond. One quick right turn and an hour's drive
ould put him in Colorado.

Three days would see him in New York.

All he had to do was make that turn.

Chapter XXXVI

"Señor MacAndrews!"

He awoke to find Bautista tapping on the window of the
G in the shopping center parking lot in front of Ernie
omez's office.

"I can open up for you, *señor*," the old *hermano* sa
when Ian rolled the window down. "You will be much mo
comfortable on the couch inside. *Verdad!*"

He had driven hard through the night and finall
exhausted, had fallen asleep with his head on his duffel ba
He hadn't dreamed. He had awakened once, rememberi
the look on Jody Kimbrough's face when the boy had spotte
him as he rolled by the Yucca, and he had gone back to sle
thinking of how he would have to argue with the kid when
handed him the MG's keys.

Two minutes after Bautista opened the glass door th
read GOMEZ, GOMEZ, & TRUJILLO, he was sound asleep again
the couch in Carrie Spletter's reception room. He did
awake until Carrie nudged him gently on the shoulder.

"Sorry, Ian," she said. "But you were thrashing arou
so, I was afraid you'd roll off and hurt yourself. Why do
you wait in Ernie's office? He should be here in fifte
minutes."

Perhaps he *had* been dreaming and didn't remember
Just as well. It couldn't have been a good dream, anyway.

"Thanks, Carrie," he said.

He entered Ernie's office and closed the door behi
him. Well, *he* was certainly being moved right along,
nothing else was. He sank into the deep chair in front
Ernie's, as always, uncluttered desk.

He was still staring at the wood carving of Don Quixo
and Sancho Panza, wondering if the skinny, metal windmil
of the Ojos Negros would have challenged Cervantes's picarequ
old knight the same way the bulky monsters of Andalus
had, when Ernie spoke from behind him.

"*Hola.*" Ernie's voice was low.

Ian turned in his chair. "You might act just a litt
surprised, Ernesto."

"Not my stock-in-trade." Ernie sat down in the swiv
chair behind his desk.

"I won't waste time," Ian said. "We've got a lot of wo
to do."

"Didn't think you came back here to dance. What's c
your mind, *amigo?*"

Here was where it had all begun.

"For starters, I want you to get Hadley Edwards to se
me the D Cross A—every section, every inch of fence, eve
tank and windmill. I want the house, of course, the one Job

l I built, not El Recobro. He can keep that. There's
hing of mine at El Recobro." No, there wasn't anything of
there, no matter how much he wished it could be
erwise. "And while you're buying the place, I want you to
l Nate Burroughs in Alamogordo and tell him we're still in
cattle business at the D Cross A. His number is here on
back of this envelope. Tell him he'll be manager, foreman,
vhand—everything—for a while. He'll have to start a herd
in from scratch, just as John and I did, and he'll be doing
y himself. I'll be there, but I'll be busy."

Ernesto was leaning forward in his chair. "Is your attor-
y permitted to ask just where you're going to get all the
ney you'll need for this?"

If the lawyer knew how to weight a subject, as Ian had
lected once, he also knew how to lighten a moment when
needed lightening.

"You know as well as I do where I'm going to get it, you
ous, smirking *cholo*. Call Lee Berman at Hampton House
l tell her the portrait of Max Balutan will be in her hands
time—and then get your brother Tony started administrat-
." He paused. "I'm going back to my house on the D
oss A and get some more sleep." He started for the door.

With his hands on the knob he turned back to Ernie.

"Before I leave, I'd like to use Carrie's phone. I've got to
ler some art supplies shipped down from Albuquerque. It
't wait. If the stuff isn't here before the week is out, I may
ve to do what I hinted at the first time we met. Open
artery to do my painting.

"I think that's exactly what that meddling old broad
ried up in Taos wanted from me—

"My goddamned blood."

Chapter XXXVII

He stood in front of his easel in the bunkhouse as he had
od in front of another easel in another bunkhouse long ago.

Wasn't it Gauguin who, in answer to a friend who
asked him why a man of his age and habits should sudde
want to paint, had replied, "You don't understand. I do
want to paint—I have to."

This wasn't going to be as easy as he had made it sou
to Ernesto Gomez five days ago. Painting the portrait it
wouldn't be all that hard, of course. It would be what ca
after it was done.

Until the drive back from Taos that night, he had
realized he had planned the painting of Max months ago, h
unconsciously dreamed and discarded a dozen different w
to do it, had somehow even gone further than just "rough
it out" in some seldom-checked corner of his mind.

The portrait wouldn't be quite representational, but
wouldn't be an abstract either. Who but a truly great god
art could hope to abstract Max? Ian MacAndrews wasn't ev
one of the lesser gods.

But the plan was there, and even if it didn't result in a
much less a masterpiece, it would be a *good* painting, a me
than acceptable frontispiece for Sarah's book. Nothing a
painter working today could do would ever be able to sta
against the sculpture of Max Balutan, anyway, not as seen
the plates Sarah had worked like a demon to fill the ma
moth volume with, not as seen in the marble work in the T
graveyard.

Most of it, perhaps all—he would have to feel this in
heart and guts as he went along—would be done with
painting knife, great gouts of pigment laid on with a spe
thrift energy in thick, carved bursts of color. If he was lu
as well as good, he might be able to bring Max's genius, t
integrity as strong and durable as the finest block of Carr
stone, to something approaching life again.

Sarah, of course, was dead, but Leila Balutan wo
want to find her brother in this painting. She would, by C
she would! One good painting was not beyond him. The
was still one good painting left somewhere within what g
he had that hadn't completely withered.

He would have to take it to New York himself. He kn
of no drying agents powerful enough to stiffen the hea
strokes of oil that would become Max Balutan, not by
thirty-first of March. Shipping it to Leila might bring disast
though even a smeared, worthless canvas would still meet
the terms of Sarah's will. But he wanted that bust of Igna

his hands, he wanted that fine face—the same face as the
e he had wept at in the cemetery—near him always now, to
ep his mind forever on why all this was necessary. He
uld never trust anyone with it for a second once Leila gave
to him.

Yes, he still had one good painting left.

It was all the others he would have to do before he died.
hat of them? Once he put the knife, or even a loaded
ight or sable, to the canvas, there could be no turning
ck. He wouldn't have a choice. One stroke—as he had once
d himself—would be one too many...a million wouldn't
enough. He would be a painter once again.

And if all his skill had left him...if whatever talent he
d had was gone? It wouldn't matter. He would go on...like
m. He would know the agony she claimed about her
lures, the reach without the grasp, the fistful of thin,
pty air alone.

Sam. Could he live a life with her so near and yet so far
yond his reach? He would have to. He had put her there,
de her, for whatever reason, untouchable. As for the
er...perhaps the rage he knew would come again could
e the place of talent.

He stepped to the easel. The knife was heavy with paint.
made that first deceptively easy passage.

It was as if he had just stepped on a steep slope of
settled shale.

He couldn't tell whether the slope tilted up or down.

Norman Zollinger's *Passage to Quivira* continues the story begun in his 1979 novel, *Riders to Cibola,* which is considered by critics and fans to be a classic tale of the Southwest.

Bantam Books is proud to announce the republication of *Riders to Cibola* in a new edition. For the many readers who already know this story of the courageous vaquero Ignacio Ortiz, and for readers of *Passage to Quivira* who have now visited the Ojos Negros Basin—here is a brief excerpt from the novel that won the Spur Award a decade ago. . . .

Origenes

Ramos, Chihuahua—1900

Ten-year-old Ignacio Ortiz looked across the carved desk
to where the troubled face of Padre Julian was bathed in the
flickering yellow light of the oil lamp. The deep furrows
which scored the old priest's face were beginning to soften,
and the stern passionless mask which had greeted the boy
when Brother Ramirez hauled him bodily into the study was
sagging into sorrow and confusion. Ignacio had squirmed and
twisted with all his might while in the grasp of the brother;
once released he stood quietly and respectfully in front of the
desk. As much as he hated everything else about the mission
orphanage, his affection for the good padre was so great he
could do nothing else.

It will be like the other times I ran away, Ignacio
thought. There will be the talk—which will solve nothing—
and then the whipping. He glanced to the corner where the
long cane leaned, wondering how many times its length had
flashed across his thin back. Well, it would hurt much less
this time. The frail old cleric's arm had weakened pitifully in
the three years Ignacio remembered, and he suspected the
heart and will to punish were almost gone as well. The good
man now suffered more than he did in these sessions. The
next time he ran he must plan more carefully and spare Padre
Julian this pain.

The padre laced his fingers across his chest and stared up
into the shadows while Ignacio waited. For five minutes there
wasn't a sound except for an occasional sigh from behind the
desk.

"I am sorry, padre," Ignacio said, finally.

The priest nodded. "I know, Ignacio." He stood up and

walked around the desk and placed his hands on the boy's shoulders. "Did you remember anything this time, Ignacio?"

"No, padre. Nothing. It was the same," Ignacio said. He drew a breath, and then asked again, as he always did, "Padre, will *you* tell me—now?"

The priest looked stricken. *Verdad*, the boy thought, nothing has changed, but I *must* try—once more.

"*Por favor*, padre." He knew his tone was flat and without fervor, compared to the pleas he had made so many times before. "Who am I, padre? Where did I come from? Why am I here?"

The aged priest slowly shook his head. "I cannot tell you, my son. Even if I did, you wouldn't really *know*. It would be like telling you about a stranger."

"But, padre"—he certainly could plead on this point—"it would still be better than the way I am!"

"No, Ignacio." The gentle voice did little to ease the agony of being defeated yet again, and as the expected words came once more, the boy made a vow that this time would be the last.

"No, my son. You must pull the past out of its dark corner by yourself—but with God's help. Pray, Ignacio, pray. Pray hard!"

Dios! Didn't Padre Julian know how many prayers he had offered up these past three years? Hadn't he seen him often enough on his knees in front of the Blessed Virgin? Didn't he know he had never passed a *camposanto* on the rocky hills around the mission without bending his back?

None of the prayers had worked, none had brought the faintest glimmer. The past, his past, remained as securely locked away as it was the day the old woman walked him up the hill to the mission. That was so long ago, he could scarcely remember her now, though it was the old woman he looked for when he ran away. He never told the padre or the brothers about her, nor had he told them of the only other clue he had—the dream.

It always took the same form, and he had dreamed it so often now he could see it clearly in the middle of the brightest day: the dim familiar figures in front of the wall; himself running toward them with his arms outstretched; the moment of recognition almost there—and then the wall growing whiter, becoming incandescent, blinding him, the wall alone, higher, thicker, more impenetrable by far than the massive adobe one around the mission.

"I *have* prayed, padre," was all he said.

"*Bueno*, Ignacio." The priest took his hands from Ignacio's shoulders and walked to where the cane leaned in the corner. "And now, my son, your punishment."

Ignacio was right. He hardly felt the blows. As they fell, one after another, each one softer than the one before, he made his final plan.

He had gone east to the great sea once in his searching flights, twice to the south, and once west into the Sierra Madres. Each time they had found him and brought him back. This time—and it must be soon—he would go in the last untried direction.

There was a river in the north, a great one, so he had heard. It was unlikely the brothers would follow him beyond its banks. He would cross that river and see if something was hidden there to help him.

1

Chupadera County, New Mexico Territory—1905

"Fifteen dollars a month, with room and board, of course," the big man said to the slim Mexican boy riding beside him. "Your own place, too, Ignacio—just a shack, but your own."

They rode on for ten more yards before the boy answered. He didn't look at his companion, but kept his eyes fixed on the three riders ahead of them.

"You know, *señor*," he said at last, only the earnestness of his voice making it rise above the sound of hoofs striking hard earth, "I have never worked cows on a ranch. Horses I know a little, *sí*—and I have gone with the trail herds like we did this week—but ranching, *quién sabe?*"

"How old are you laddie?"

Ignacio drew in his breath sharply, hoping the man hadn't noticed. *Por qué?* Why did even simple questions about him always bring this tight feeling to his chest?

"I—I am not certain, *señor*," he said, adding quickly "Fifteen—*sí*, I think fifteen."

"No matter." The big man's chuckle was the same warm rumble he remembered from the ride up, before they delivered the cows at the railhead. "You're dead sure young enough to learn. By the time you're twenty you'll be a top hand—a real vaquero."

Ignacio was silent again. He hoped this *señor* he already liked so much would not think him rude that he didn't reply to everything at once. If the rancher on the big horse felt that way, his face gave no sign of it. Instead, the older man hurried into more words of his own. It almost seemed as if he wanted to save the boy the embarrassment of speaking before he was ready—as if he understood the confusion and uncertainty the offer of the job had brought.

"Both my brother Angus and Mr. Terry up there"—the man raised a huge arm and pointed at the group ahead of them—"sure admired your work in the stock pens yesterday and on the way up with the herd. You move that old bag of bones you're on like she was a filly. Now, I sure don't want to press you, Ignacio. Think it over. We've a fair ride yet."

There shouldn't be much to think over, Ignacio Ortiz told himself. There should be no doubt at all. A place of his own to live in—and good work to do! No more jobbing himself out from valley to distant valley as he had done ever since he had run away from the mission at Ramos four years before, four years of drifting work and frightening, half starved idleness, with more nights spent under the cold stars than he wanted to remember, and not even a saddle of his own to bring along when he sought work as a wrangler's helper or apprentice drover. No, there shouldn't be the smallest doubt. Why not say yes—and quickly? He shook his head, hoping again the big man wasn't looking.

Usually, if he wasn't working from the saddle and a pony nodded along in the sunlight like this creaky mare, he could sleep on the move, but not today. He hadn't really seen this trail five days ago when they drove north to Corona; he had been posted behind the herd, and the frenzied dust and noise blotted everything but the cows from sight and mind. At that it had been no more heartpounding than this easy ride was turning out to be. Perhaps if he looked about him, he could calm his mind and give an answer.

They rode south, dropping deeper into the Ojos Negros Basin with every mile, but still high enough on its sloping im that the young rider could see sixty miles or more through the afternoon haze to where the double-domed head of Sierra Blanca lorded it over the Sacramentos. Just ahead of him the three horsemen in the lead were beginning to make their way past the ragged line where the piñon opened out on a long sweep of bunch grass. He watched the riders' shoulders bouncing as they let their mounts pick their own route through the first of the ocotillo, the trail boss Terry on the left and next to him the tall white-haired brother of the rancher Angus, was it?) looking far too big for the small gray he rode.

In the lead, riding the handsome young paint that Ignacio had looked at longingly for nearly a week now, was another boy. The young Mexican stared at the back of the other youngster, whose red checked shirt danced in front of the small procession like a pennant.

"You'd have company in young Jamie yonder." Ignacio started as if someone had come up behind him and taken him unaware. "True, he's a year shy of you," the rancher went on, "but he'd be good company all the same."

Well, that was where the problem lay. It was the boy who was the key. Something troubled the young Mexican about this Jamie, but he couldn't put his finger on it.

Certainly the boy had been decent enough from the very first, when Ignacio and Terry and the two other hands from the Staked Plains—since paid off at Corona and on their way back home—arrived at the fence of Douglas MacAndrew's D Cross A to join their two small herds together for the drive. They hadn't had much to do with each other during the two days of punishing riding which brought them to the railhead, but in camp at the stock pens after the cattle were loaded on the cars, and last night, when they bedded down in the piñons, their similar ages seemed to draw them together.

Jamie had shared a bag of gum drops with Ignacio after supper, almost demanding that the Mexican take more of them than he really wanted, and when the sun plummeted down behind the far Magdalenas and the evening warned of a night of bitter cold, he went to his pony and returned with a heavy saddle blanket to augment the worn serape the Mexican had been wrapping himself in for the past two years. They had joined the older men around a tiny fire, and Ignacio discovered that Jamie had a pleasant singing voice, although it tended to crack at times.

No, there was nothing Ignacio could name to account for his wary feeling about Jamie, nothing in the way the rancher's son had treated him or spoken to him. The boy had the warmest smile the young Mexican could remember ever having seen. It had flashed brightly in the firelight every time their eyes met. Why, then, did he hold back? He would have to determine that before they all rode too many more miles. As kindly as he was, and as patient as he seemed, Señor Douglas MacAndrews would want his answer.

Now the five riders reached the great stands of yucca they had been moving toward for an hour, and Ignacio realized that Jamie, Angus, and the trail boss were moving their horses at a faster pace than they had during the middle of the day. Suddenly, he realized also that not once during the journey had Jamie dropped back beside him. Indeed, he couldn't remember that young MacAndrews had talked with him since they saddled up at dawn—it was as if he had outlived whatever usefulness he might have had for the rancher's son.

Perhaps the wisest course was to return with the trail boss to Las Cruces. Terry would help him look for work. But what excuse could he give the man riding beside him?

Well, he was calm now, and the answer would come out of the calmness. He was sad, too, but the sadness, although deeper, was no different from his feelings at the end of any of the hundred jobs he had taken in the last four years. No, be honest *amigo*, he told himself. It is different. Even if he had known him for just one week, he would miss the big *señor*.

At this, the sadness became sharper, seemed driven into his chest like a pointed stick. How foolish! He really hadn't been thrown with the rancher much more than he had with Jamie; there was no reason to feel this way. Except—except that this enormous soft-spoken man seemed to know he was there.

The three mounted figures ahead of him urged their ponies up a barren rise, and when he and the rancher crested it in turn, the fence of the D Cross A stretched out in front of them, the posts and the wire strands marching out of sight to right and left as far as he could see.

Jamie, down from his horse, was opening a gate, and Ignacio knew that when he reached the boy he would give his answer. Almost without realizing it, he reined the mare a little, and the rancher moved on past him. A small wind had come up, and the rattle it made passing through the spikes of the yuccas was the loneliest sound he had heard in a long, long time.

Near the gate, not so much guiding the old mare as
mply letting her carry him, he saw Jamie watching him with
look of such intensity that it seemed it would bore right
rough him. Ignacio wondered what thoughts had inspired
is searching gaze. He would never know, most likely.

Then Jamie, still holding the gate in one hand and his
ny's reins in the other, gave Ignacio a smile which explod-
in warmth and brilliance. The young rider's heart lurched
ward, swelling until he couldn't breathe.

"*Señor*," he said, hearing his voice as if from a great
stance, "*sí*, I will work for you. I will try very hard to please
u." While he spoke, his eyes never left Jamie MacAndrews's
iling face.

"Good, Ignacio. It's settled then." The big man spurred
s horse gently through the open gate as his son swung
nself into the saddle. "High tail it for the house, son. Tell
ur mother there'll be two extra mouths at table tonight."

Almost before the words had died away, Jamie was gone,
king his smile with him, driving his pony past Angus and
e trail boss and through the yuccas, dust rising in sunlit
afts behind him.

"Welcome to the D Cross A, Ignacio", Douglas MacAn-
ews said, "and close the gate, *por favor*. When our fence
e's all closed up, everything inside is safe and sound."

2

Tired as he was when he pulled the rough horse blanket
 to his chin, Ignacio was unable to sleep. Remembering
erything that had happened since he said yes to the *señor*
ok half the night.

When they were riding down the last slope toward the
ildings and Douglas MacAndrews said, "There it is, Ignacio.
me," something hard to swallow came into his throat. He
uldn't recall ever using the word "home" himself.

Except that it was bigger than most, it looked a very

ordinary house, part adobe, with what seemed to be a new section made of timber. Outcroppings of tawny rock protect it from the full force of the north wind. Down the ranch roa past a piñon post corral and a shack nestled in the shadow o windmill, a plank bridge crossed an arroyo which skirted small butte.

Ignacio could see Jamie's paint nodding against a hit rail, but the rancher's son was nowhere to be found, and fo brief moment he felt strangely deserted. When he and t three other riders reined up he gave up looking for the oth boy, remembering that he was now a hand of the D Cross He swung from the saddle before the weary mare h stopped, and reached for the bridle of the *señor*'s big hors When the rancher had eased down to the caliche, Ignacio l the two animals to the wooden trough where Angus and t trail boss were watering their horses.

"Douglas! Welcome home!" It was the light voice of woman somewhere behind him.

"Hullo, Aggie. Good to be home," he heard the ranch say, his voice warm and strong. There was that word agai

"Jamie says we're to have company for supper, Dougla Who are our guests?" Beyond the question itself there w curiosity in the voice to equal his.

"Ransom Terry from Cruces," the *señor* said, "and a ne man I've put on. Ransom—Ignacio—this is Mrs. MacAndrew The last name is Ortiz, isn't it, laddie?"

"Ma'am," he heard the trail boss say. He turned, a blushed when he found that with both hands occupied couldn't remove his hat. He couldn't speak, either. All could manage was a clumsy little bow—and this before he even really seen the woman of the D Cross A.

She was small, particularly so standing next to her hu band, and at a glance he saw where Jamie had inherit his blue-eyed blond good looks. From that moment tho eyes searched him out relentlessly. Well, it was her right.

"*Cómo está*, Ignacio?" she said. There was somethi commanding in the way she held her head—not tilted back haughtiness, but certainly lifted high with pride. Her ey held him for another moment and when she turned to h husband it was as if they had been torn away.

"Supper in half an hour sharp, Douglas," she sai moving toward the house. Ignacio stared after her until t *señor*'s horse tossed its head and jerked him back attentiveness.

*   *   *

Dios! Even on feast days at the mission he had never
en a table hold so many different kinds of food. Hungry as
: was, he scarcely touched a thing. He tried not to look at the
hers, but he saw the *señora* eat as sparingly as he did,
rrying the food to her straight, careful mouth in tiny
rkfuls. Watching him constantly from beneath a cool brow,
e made no attempt to hide the looks she gave him. What
» you expect, *niño bobo*, he asked himself. Must you be
minded yet again it is her right?

The meal was eaten in silence, with every head but his
d the *señora*'s bent to the plates. When they had finished,
d the napkins were rolled and pushed back into the silver
1gs at every place (a rite he watched and imitated with care)
lk flooded the room. In a way, this left him feeling more
one than had the quiet. The meager English he possessed,
on painfully on the trail or at the dusty edges of towns where
: had bunked, wasn't good enough to follow the exchanges
hich flew across the table with the smoke and laughter.

Angus, he discovered, though mute while on the drive,
as a steady, easy talker once his long body was stuffed with
od.

"—and if the county don't shore up that bridge over
rroyo Blanco, the next good rain'll wash it clear to Ojo
aliente. I had a word with the county agent last time I—"

"Douglas," the *señora* broke into the pleasant drone of
1gus's words, "I'm sure the boys aren't the least bit interest-
l in all of this." Ignacio looked at Jamie, hoping for another
those dazzling smiles. None came.

"You're right, Aggie," the big man said, "I think they
ay be excused, provided they're back inside to help you with
e dishes."

Jamie made a face and shot from the table like a rabbit,
inging a laugh from Angus and the trail boss. At the door
: braked suddenly to a stop, beckoned to Ignacio to follow,
d was gone again.

Ignacio looked at the *señora*, and when she nodded, got
his feet and tried that same little bow he had managed so
dly in the yard.

He found Jamie on the low stone wall which surrounded
e house, facing westward to where the sky reddened as the
n dropped steadily toward the mountain rim. He had a
ndful of pebbles and was tossing them one by one into the
liche. The air was so still the puffs of dust they kicked up
ng there for long seconds.

Ignacio stood behind him, looking at the sunset.

"Well, come on. Sit down. You want to, don't you
Jamie didn't turn around as he spoke. Ignacio stepped ov
the wall and found a flat spot ten feet from Jamie.

There must have been five minutes more of silen
before the MacAndrews boy spoke again.

"You Spanish or Indian, Ignacio?"

"I—I do not know, señor. Maybe both." He felt chill
by something more than the evening air. Dios, he must n
let such questions upset him so. "In Ramos it didn't see
important," he added softly.

"Well, I'll tell you one thing sure. It's important as
get out in these parts. Where's Ramos?"

"In Chihuahua, señor."

"Mexico—then you're Mexican." Jamie said it as if sor
petty annoyance were now out of the way.

Ignacio said nothing. The implication of Jamie's remar
unwitting as it likely was, didn't bother him as it might ha
in those first days north of the river. It was like a slight sm
in the air. You got used to it—even if occasionally it became
little stronger. Far worse were those probes which might
some way turn on the hidden past.

He looked hard at Jamie. Sí, they were different. I
didn't envy the gold hair or the straight nose, the smoot
light skin, or the three extra inches of height, a gap whi
promised to increase; nor even the fine, soft bed in the b
house where Jamie would sleep this night. There were sor
things, though, things it was useless to hope for—and bett
not to think aout.

"Ignacio," Jamie still hadn't looked in his direction. "O
Hell! I ain't going to call you Ignacio. It don't sound right
a man's name. From now on you'll be—let's see—I got
Nash. Shorter and better. Yeah, Nash—savvy?" The wor
came spitting out and Ignacio winced.

He should not permit this. His name was about the on
thing he really owned. He should make some objection
now! But before he could utter a word, Jamie turned his he
and smiled, and Ignacio knew he had lost.

The MacAndrews boy was still smiling when the do
behind them opened, and Ignacio turned to see Doug
MacAndrews coming out with Ransom Terry.

"Ride safe then, Ransom," the rancher was saying, "b
you know you're welcome to stay the night."

"Thanks, Mr. MacAndrews, but I ain't seen my wife

ear three weeks. Besides, I thought I'd stop in Black
prings and have a vet look at that pony of mine. He ain't
een acting right. I'll put him on a lead and ride the mare
oung Ignacio was on. Thanks again."

"All right, Ransom, if your mind's made up. Ignacio,
ddle up for Mr. Terry, *por favor*. And Jamie, I think your
other's ready for some kitchen help."

Ignacio raced for the corral, grateful to the *señor* for
ving him man's work this first night at the ranch. Not that
e would shirk any chore, but he feared that his hands, sure
ough on leather, would find the fragile china more than he
uld handle.

In minutes Terry was gone, the horses and the lone rider
ounding their way across the bridge which sagged over the
royo, then fading into the twilight gloom of the desert
eyond the butte.

"Smart work, Ignacio," Douglas MacAndrews said. "One
ing, though. Never rush *quite* so much to saddle a guest's
orse." He chuckled, the sound warm and deep in his throat.
Ie might think we really didn't mean it when we asked him
stay."

"*Sí, señor.*"

"And now, Ignacio, I think we'd best get back inside and
e to the rest of those kitchen chores."

The dishes were almost done. A scowling Jamie was
acing glassware in a cupboard above the sink. Señora
acAndrews looked up from the table she was wiping.

"We're almost done," she said. "Go on in and make
urself comfortable in the sitting room. When I'm finished
ere, I'll fix you up with bedding and some other things for
e shack, Nash." There it was. Jamie had told the *señora*
out the name he had invented; doubtless the *señor* himself
ould be the next.

At first he thought the sitting room deserted, but a
und from the long sofa revealed the lanky figure of Angus
retched out in sleep. The sofa faced a fireplace flanked by
enormous easy chair and a wooden rocker tilting in
aceful balance. He stood stock still in the center of the
om, peering into shadows not quite dispelled by the lamplight,
ondering what he would do or say if Angus stirred. His eyes
ntinued their march around the room.

There was a sampler on the wall whose message
couldn't read, a shelf holding a slender vase stuffed wi
nothing more than common weeds. He shuddered, som
thing twisting deep inside him, when he saw the rifles a
shotguns racked in the corner, and his eye hurried on. T
fireplace, cavernous in its unlit state, stood against an ado
wall; he could see outlines of sun-baked brick bleedi
through a coating white as bone. Another white wall; fe
touched him, but lightly, and perplexity followed. He w
glad then to have Angus in the room with him. The ma
heavy breathing, regular and even as the gait of a good hors
kept the room to ordinary size. Comforted by this thougl
he found his own breathing easier, and his eye swept on
the south wall.

He almost gasped aloud. Here was something Ignac
Ortiz had never seen before in all his life. From right to le
across the room, from the floor to the ceiling with its gre
wooden beams, the wall was filled with books. Books of eve
size and shape, bound in a hundred different ways, stood
soldiered ranks, leaned against each other carelessly, or rest
on their sides in staggered piles. In the padre's study the
had been some books, but surely not a dozen. This marvelo
wall must hold every book the world had ever known. Ignac
was dizzied by the sight.

He found himself within touching distance of the wa
Leather spines gleamed, gold lettering sparkled, and on o
shelf an open volume spread its pages. Heart drumming,
put out his hand and—

"Do you read, Nash?"

Numb, he turned to see the *señora* standing in t
entrance to the sitting room. Wishing he could shrink
nothing, he forced himself to look straight into the blue-gr
eyes, certain he would find them narrowed in outrage a
accusation.

But there was no sign of this, nothing of indignatic
suspicion, or reproach. Instead, he saw an excitement
strong it might have been his own.

"Do you read, Nash?" Agnes MacAndrews said again

"Just a little, *señora*—and only Spanish."

"Pity." In a movement so definite and swift it left h
blinking, she was gone.

Behind him a sigh came over the sofa where Angus slep

Bedding piled to his chin, an unlit lantern swinging fr

crook of his arm, Ignacio stumbled down the stony
thway. The ponies in the corral moved a little but paid him
real attention. In the east, an orange moon was rising over
e brute black shape of Cuchillo Peak, and a few small
uds coursed across the sky. There was some wind at
ound level, too; even though the windmill lock was on, he
uld hear the blades groaning, straining to break free.

He took one more look up the moonlit slope toward the
house before he kicked open the door of the shack.

For what seemed like hours, sleep stayed just out of
ach, while his mind whirled so he wished he could lock it
place like the windmill still complaining in its captivity
ove him. His last waking thought had been of that astonishing
ll of books, but sometime during the fitful sleep which did
me, the other wall rose again, solid and menacing, as it
vays did whenever his life began to show a touch of
omise.

Awake now, and feeling keen and strong despite the lack
real mind- and body-mending sleep, Ignacio hurried into
clothes and out the door of the shack to find the sun
dging the last of the dark away from the top of big
chillo, its bright disc just a little lower in the sky than
ere he had left the moon last night.

He wasn't surprised to see Douglas MacAndrews stand-
g in the ranch house doorway waving to him.

"Come on, son." The rancher didn't shout, but the
ong voice carried well in the crisp morning air. "I've got
e coffee going. We'll have a cup together, and then get a
al breakfast after the first chores are behind us."

The Mexican boy started up the pathway. As he turned
cross the yard, the big man spoke again.

"We've got a day's work ahead of us, Ignacio."

Ignacio!

The new hand of the D Cross A broke into a run.

ABOUT THE AUTHOR

NORMAN ZOLLINGER is one of the best-loved contemporary authors in the American Southwest. He was born in Chicago and raised in Downers Grove, Illinois, and in his youth was active in dramatics, the school newspaper, and athletics. After an abortive attempt to join the Royal Canadian Air Force in 1940, he attended Cornell College in Mt. Vernon, Iowa, until the U.S. entered World War II. Zollinger enlisted in the Army Air Corps, though he was not yet of draft age, and flew fifty-one combat missions in Italy as a bombardier. Mustered out of the service as a captain, he married, had three children, and became a successful business executive before, nearing fifty years of age, he moved with his wife to Albuquerque, New Mexico, to fulfill a lifelong ambition to become a novelist.

Zollinger won the Golden Spur Award in 1979 for his first novel *Riders to Cíbola*, which introduced the MacAndrews clan and the vaquero Ignacio Ortiz to a wide audience of enthusiastic readers. *Riders* remained on the *Albuquerque Journal* bestseller list for 99 weeks (17 weeks at the No. 1 position). In 1981 Zollinger published a second western epic, *Corey Lane*, a fictional account of the Victorio War in New Mexico. *Corey Lane* spent 19 weeks at No. 1 on the *Journal* list. *Passage to Quivira* is the eagerly anticipated sequel to *Riders to Cíbola*. Zollinger owns and operates a bookstore in Albuquerque, is a frequent traveler and avid skiier, and he is at work on another book.

THE LEGENDS WEST TRILOGY

BY OAKLEY HALL

All the beauty and danger of the Old West come alive in these highly acclaimed novels by one of America's most respected authors, Oakley Hall.

☐ **WARLOCK**   27114-8/$4.50

Clay Blaisedell is a gunman first, a lawman second, who comes to Warlock to end the violence that has scarred the town. With a host of colorful characters drawn from history, the novel erupts with treachery, vengeance, and murder before justice is established.

☐ **THE BAD LANDS**   27265-9/$4.50

A young Easterner comes to the Dakota Bad Lands to escape a family tragedy, and is immediately drawn into the hard life of a cattle rancher—and learns a tough lesson in the politics of the prairie as vigilantes roam the land exacting a blood price from their enemies.

☐ **APACHES**   27541-0/$4.95

Based on the infamous Lincoln County War in New Mexico, this bold, brassy, bloody novel of human conflict is played out on a spectacular landscape of desert and mountain. This powerful narrative takes you into the heart and minds of the men and women of the frontier.

Look for these great novels wherever Bantam books are sold, or use this handy page to order.

DON'T MISS
THESE CURRENT
Bantam Bestsellers

☐ 26807	**THE BEET QUEEN** Louise Edrich		$4.5
☐ 26808	**LOVE MEDICINE** Louise Edrich		$4.5
☐ 25800	**THE CIDER HOUSE RULES** John Irving		$4.9
☐ 26554	**HOLD THE DREAM**		$4.9
	Barbara Taylor Bradford		
☐ 26253	**VOICE OF THE HEART**		$4.9
	Barbara Taylor Bradford		
☐ 26322	**THE BOURNE SUPREMACY**		$4.9
	Robert Ludlum		
☐ 26888	**THE PRINCE OF TIDES** Pat Conroy		$4.9
☐ 26892	**THE GREAT SANTINI** Pat Conroy		$4.9
☐ 26574	**SACRED SINS** Nora Roberts		$3.9
☐ 26798	**THE SCREAM**		$3.9
	Jonathan Skipp and Craig Spector		
☐ 27018	**DESTINY** Sally Beauman		$4.9
☐ 27032	**FIRST BORN** Doris Mortman		$4.9
☐ 27458	**NEW MEXICO—WAGONS WEST #22**		$4.5
	Dana Fuller Ross		
☐ 27300	**OMAMORI** Richard McGill		$4.9
☐ 27248	**'TIL THE REAL THING COMES ALONG**		$4.5
	Iris Rainer Dart		
☐ 27261	**THE UNLOVED** John Saul		$4.5

Prices and availability subject to change without notice.

Buy them at your local bookstore or use this page to order.

- -

Bantam Books, Dept. FB, 414 East Golf Road, Des Plaines, IL 60016

Please send me the books I have checked above. I am enclosing $_____
(please add $2.00 to cover postage and handling). Send check or money order
—no cash or C.O.D.s please.

Mr/Ms _____

Address _____

City/State _____ Zip _____

FB—2/89

Please allow four to six weeks for delivery. This offer expires 8/89.

★ WAGONS WEST ★

A series of unforgettable books that trace the lives of a dauntless band of pioneering men, women, and children as they brave the hazards of an untamed land in their trek across America. This legendary caravan of people forge a new link in the wilderness. They are Americans from the North and the South, alongside immigrants, Blacks, and Indians, who wage fierce daily battles for survival on this uncompromising journey—each to their private destinies as they fulfill their greatest dreams.

☐ 26822	INDEPENDENCE! #1	$4.50
☐ 26162	NEBRASKA! #2	$4.50
☐ 26242	WYOMING! #3	$4.50
☐ 26072	OREGON! #4	$4.50
☐ 26070	TEXAS! #5	$4.50
☐ 26377	CALIFORNIA! #6	$4.50
☐ 26546	COLORADO! #7	$4.50
☐ 26069	NEVADA! #8	$4.50
☐ 26163	WASHINGTON! #9	$4.50
☐ 26073	MONTANA! #10	$4.50
☐ 26184	DAKOTA! #11	$4.50
☐ 26521	UTAH! #12	$4.50
☐ 26071	IDAHO! #13	$4.50
☐ 26367	MISSOURI! #14	$4.50
☐ 27141	MISSISSIPPI! #15	$4.50
☐ 25247	LOUISIANA! #16	$4.50
☐ 25622	TENNESSEE! #17	$4.50
☐ 26022	ILLINOIS! #18	$4.50
☐ 26533	WISCONSIN! #19	$4.50
☐ 26849	KENTUCKY! #20	$4.50
☐ 27065	ARIZONA! #21	$4.50
☐ 27458	NEW MEXICO! #22	$4.50

Prices and availability subject to change without notice.

- -

Special Offer
Buy a Bantam Book
for only 50¢.

Now you can have Bantam's catalog filled with hundreds of titles plus take advantage of our unique and exciting bonus book offer. A special offer which gives you the opportunity to purchase a Bantam book for only 50¢. Here's how!

By ordering any five books at the regular price per order, you can also choose any other single book listed (up to a $5.95 value) for just 50¢. Some restrictions do apply, but for further details why not send for Bantam's catalog of titles today!

Just send us your name and address and we will send you a catalog!